PRAISE FOR 1998
HOLT MEDALLION WINNER
EUGENIA RILEY!

"Witty, over-the-top characters, sparkling dialogue, and scintillating sensuality combine to make this novel one of Ms. Riley's very best. An absolute must read."
—*Rendezvous* on *Lovers and Other Lunatics*

"Ms. Riley's . . . characters are delightful, as are the various subplots that make this a wonderful romance."
—*Romantic Times* on *Bushwhacked Bride*

"Ms. Riley has crafted an amazing tale that leaps right off the pages."
—*Rendezvous* on *Bushwhacked Bride*

"Eugenia Riley will sweep you away!"
—*The Literary Times*

"Eugenia Riley spins a brilliantly woven web, ensnaring readers with her ingenious plot twists, endearing characters and an unforgettable love story."
—*Romantic Times* on *Tempest in Time*

"A unique time-travel novel interlaced with mysterious secrets and intense emotions. Ms. Riley focuses on the magical potency of love, as it transcends the web of time to meld bleeding hearts together."
—*Romantic Times* on *A Tryst in Time*

SOULS IN NEED

"How do you bear it, Vickie?" he asked at last. "How do you live from day to day?"

"I don't. I just endure somehow."

She lifted her face to his and again their gazes locked in a moment of poignant communication. Adrian leaned over and claimed Vickie's lips with unbearable tenderness. With a soft whimper she kissed him back.

Such passion, such bliss he stirred in her! The sense of connecting with another soul in need was so intense that it filled her with a keenly physical aching. Adrian's kiss was like a touch of heaven, a ray of warm, beautiful sunshine penetrating the clouds of her grief, a merciful respite for them both. She realized she had needed this desperately, had needed to feel right and sane and loved and wanted—if only for a moment.

Their lips parted on a sigh, a smile.

"This is so sweet," she murmured achingly. "I had forgotten what it's like to be held. . . ."

EUGENIA RILEY

Embers of Time

LOVE SPELL 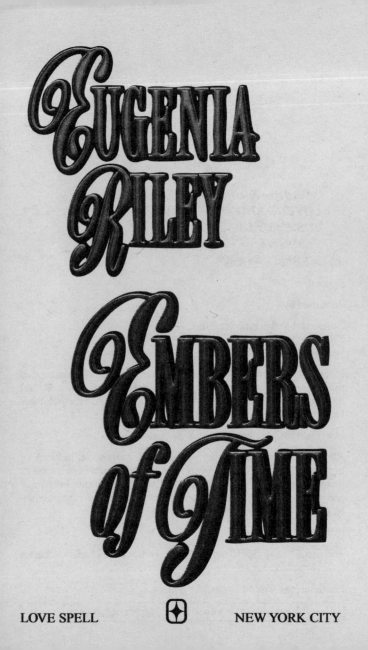 NEW YORK CITY

A LOVE SPELL BOOK®

December 2000

Published by

Dorchester Publishing Co., Inc.
276 Fifth Avenue
New York, NY 10001

ISBN 0-505-52408-2

Printed in the United States of America.

Visit us on the web at www.dorchesterpub.com.

This book is dedicated, with much love,
to Aunt Sister,
in honor of her ninetieth birthday,
and with deep gratitude for all
the joy and happiness she has
brought to everyone in our family,
and for her selfless devotion to others.
Thanks, too, for her
support on this project.

****

Special thanks to Susan Krinard for
her keen eye and excellent insights;
to Ed Hoeppner for sharing his
reminiscences of World War II;
and to Virginia Farmer and Brenda Rollins
for their gracious assistance
while I was in Charleston.

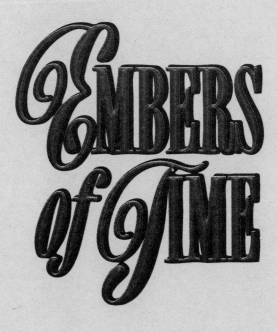

Prologue

Charleston, South Carolina
May 8, 1945

Tears and cheers filled the Charleston Battery. The cruel war that had demanded so much from so many was almost at an end.

The sun shone brightly on the crowd gathered beneath the ancient, gnarled oak trees in White Point Gardens at the southernmost tip of the Neck; from the bay beyond, a brisk breeze swept in, lacing the nectar-laden air with the scent of the sea, then wending on past the park to fan the porticoes and iron-lace balconies of the majestic old colonial mansions lining the street beyond.

In the gazebo, a hastily summoned navy brass band played "The Stars and Stripes Forever" to a throng of

13

enthralled citizens: children waving tiny U.S. flags; hunched elderly couples choked with emotion; young women dressed in widow's black and carrying babies too young to know the meaning of sorrow; veterans with missing arms, legs, or eyes, in military dress costume, with medals brightly gleaming and faces aglow with pride.

At the back of the crowd, two children clutched hands and craned their necks to get a better view of the bandstand. At twelve, Nate Bennett was tall and slender, blue-eyed and black-haired; he bore the aristocratic features of his English father, his handsome, angular face distinguished by deep-set eyes, high cheekbones, a cleanly etched nose, thin-lipped mouth, and strong chin. Wearing a plaid shirt and tweed pants, he stood head and shoulders above his companion, nine-year-old Cathy Cheney.

Cathy was a lovely child whose light blond hair was styled in "pineapple" curls with bangs; her large, lively cornflower blue eyes peered out of a wide, cherubic face with pink cheeks, upturned nose, and dainty mouth. In keeping with the festive occasion, she wore a jaunty green-and-white seersucker dress with puffed sleeves and fitted waist, her outfit complemented by a straw hat with flower-bedecked ribbon streamers; in one delicate hand she gripped a small U.S. flag that she waved in time to the rousing music.

The march ended to applause and cheers. Cathy turned to Nate, bouncing up and down in her glee. "Oh, Nate, I'm so glad that mean old war is almost over," she declared in her bright young voice. "Soon

Vickie and your dad will come back to get us, won't they?"

With the rousing strains of "God Bless America" spilling out from the bandstand, Nate blanched. He'd been expecting this question from Cathy all afternoon, ever since news of the surrender had swept the city in a tidal wave of euphoria, along with the sounds of car horns blaring, fireworks erupting, and citizens pouring into the streets accompanied by cheers and confetti. Mr. Graves, the jeweler for whom Nate worked as an apprentice silversmith, had closed his shop early for the day and told Nate to go home.

He could not believe how much his life had changed during those brief hours! With heart pounding in mingled excitement and trepidation, he'd run several blocks to St. Christopher's Orphanage, where he and Cathy lived, to share the news with her; but Mother Agatha had told him Cathy and several other children had already left for the celebration in town. After searching the thronged streets, Nate had found Cathy here listening to the concert.

"Nate?" Cathy pressed anxiously. "How soon will they come for us?"

I hope never! he thought to himself fiercely. To Cathy, he reluctantly smiled, reaching out and playfully tugging on a ribbon streamer. "The war in Europe only ended today, goose. We still have the Japs to defeat. It could be months before the soldiers come home. Your sister is in Italy, my dad somewhere in France."

Cathy's features filled with disappointment. "I hope they come soon. I can't wait to see Vickie."

"Well, I can wait to see my father," Nate muttered bitterly.

Cathy gasped in dismay. "Nate!"

"It's true," he retorted. "You know my dad abandoned me after my poor mum died. He couldn't abide the sight of me."

Cathy patted his hand. "But, Nate, he had to fight for his country. He didn't have a choice."

"He had a choice," Nate responded, clenching his jaw. "Maybe if I'm lucky, he'll be killed before he can come claim me."

Cathy sucked in a horrified breath. "Nate Bennett, what an awful thing to say!" Wide-eyed, she crossed herself. "Sister Eustace would have a stroke if she heard you say that. We must say a prayer at once for your dad's safe passage."

Nate scowled.

She tugged at his sleeve and spoke plaintively. "We must, Nate, or you'll be doomed to hell for your evil thoughts."

"Okay," he conceded at last. "But I'm only doing it for you, Cathy—not for him."

Slanting him a chiding glance, Cathy tugged him toward a nearby magnolia tree. Both children knelt and fixed their hands in an attitude of prayer. Nate dutifully closed his eyes as Cathy implored the Holy Virgin to bless and safeguard their loved ones still at war.

"There—don't you feel much better?" she asked afterward.

"No, I don't." His hurt-filled eyes reproved her. "Are you so eager to leave me, Cathy?"

She touched his arm. "Nate, we'll see each other again."

"Not when you're back in Georgetown with Vickie and my dad takes me home to England."

"We can write," she put in hopefully.

Nate shook his head sadly and struggled to swallow the emotion burning in his throat. Suddenly he felt old way beyond his twelve years. "It's not the same, Cathy. It'll never be the same again and you know it."

She sighed. "But there's nothing more we can do."

He gazed at her earnestly. "Yes, there is, goose. You can run away with me."

Cathy chortled. "And get married?"

"No, not now, goose," Nate answered, feeling his face redden. "I mean later, when we're old enough." He drew himself up proudly. "You know I love you, Cathy. You know we've promised we'll be together one day."

"I know, Nate," she replied solemnly. "I love you, too."

He smiled wistfully. "Do you remember that afternoon in the attic, the day it rained? When we crossed our hearts, swore to be best friends forever, and hoped to die if we were ever parted?"

"Of course I remember. How could I forget?"

"Then how can you go away with Vickie and leave me forever?" he demanded, his voice thick with the anguish of a child forsaken.

Biting her underlip, Cathy stared helplessly at her feet. "Nate, we're only children. We can't take care of ourselves yet."

"I can provide for you," declared Nate. "I'm doing

17

well in school, and Mr. Graves says I'm the most talented apprentice he's ever trained."

"I know you have a trade, but—"

"Here, I'll prove it." Nate dug in his pocket and pulled out a silver ring. "For you."

"Oh, Nate!"

Eyes aglow, Cathy took the shiny ring, turning its glittering facets toward the light. The wide band was intricately carved, with a smiling sun engraved on its face.

"Do you like it?" he asked, his heart in his voice.

She gazed up at him in awe. "Nate, it's beautiful."

His spontaneous grin betraying his pride, Nate took the ring and slipped it on the third finger of her left hand. "It's for you, Cathy, because you love sunshine. You brought the sun into my life when I had only dark clouds left."

"Oh, Nate." Cathy blinked away a tear. "That's the nicest thing anyone has ever said to me. I think you're a poet."

He clutched her hand. "It's a promise ring, Cathy, a promise that one day we'll be together always. Say it's true, Cathy. Just like before. Cross your heart and hope to die if it isn't true."

Cathy dutifully crossed her heart. "I'll treasure the ring always. I'll never take it off." She expelled a heavy breath. "And we'll be together one day, Nate, I promise. But we can't run away now. We have to wait till we're grown. Besides, I miss Vickie and I need her."

Nate was frowning, about to reply, when the music stopped. A man wearing a double-breasted, black and white striped cotton suit and a felt fedora stepped up to the bandstand. Grinning, he held up a hand to silence the cheering crowd.

Nate leaned toward Cathy and whispered, "Hey, that's Mayor Wehman. Come on, let's skedaddle, before he makes a boring speech."

Stifling giggles, Cathy left the park with Nate. Pushed along by crisp bay breezes, the children strolled up historic Meeting Street, past majestic pillared buildings and soaring church steeples; the thoroughfare was clogged with automobiles, buses, and old horse-drawn drays bearing laundry, produce, and kegs of beer.

Spotting the Negro iceman rattling past in his mule-drawn wagon, Nate grinned at Cathy, then ran ahead, grabbing two large slivers of ice from the wagon gate. He raced back to Cathy, wiped the sawdust from one of the chunks, and handed it to her.

Sucking on the ice, the children continued along the sidewalk, passing a stylishly dressed lady wheeling a baby carriage, three midgets in overalls bound for their shift at the shipyard, and an elderly gentleman in cap and dungarees, wearing an armband emblem proclaiming him an air raid warden in the Civilian Defense.

Nate glanced at Cathy; so young and carefree skipping along beside him, and remembered what he had almost told her in the park a moment earlier. She had argued that they were still children, but Nate felt already grown, a child no longer; the events of the past six years had stripped him of his youth. Back in England, at the tender age of six, he had lost his mother to diphtheria; at seven, he had watched his father desert him to go fly with the Royal Air Force. He'd been shipped off to America to ride out the war with his grandmother. Months later, she'd suffered a stroke and had been sent to a rest home, leaving him an orphan under the care of the Sisters of Mercy. At St. Christopher's Nate had become a loner, a shy, embittered lad who shunned the overtures of the other children and resisted the kindness of the nuns.

Then three years ago Nate had met Cathy, an event that had radically changed his life. He would never forget the moment when six-year-old Cathy danced across the orphanage parlor with a box of checkers, her yellow curls bouncing, her laughter drawing him out of his shell as she insisted he play the game with her.

She, too, had been a victim of tragedy, losing her mother at a very early age. When her widowed father died, she had been forced to come live at the orphanage until her sister, a nurse serving in the army, could return to claim her.

Yet, unlike Nate, Cathy had never allowed the tragedies of her life to touch her spirit, and her sunny outlook had attracted Nate from the outset. She had become his best friend, his reason for living. He loved her and wanted one day to marry her. . . .

Only now he was about to lose her. A heavy sigh escaped him. Perhaps she was still too young to fully understand what forever meant, but Nate knew. Oh, he knew. A forever had passed since he had lost his dear mum, another eternity since his dad had deserted him. How could he make Cathy understand that when his dad and her sister returned, they would likely be parted for the rest of their lives?

Well, he would not abide it! Somehow he must

keep them together, for Cathy had become Nate's entire world.

He smiled, watching her hop along the street, jumping over the cracks in the sidewalk that might break her mother's back, despite the fact that her mother had long dwelled in a heavenly place where cracks could no longer harm her. He listened to the chant she sang:

> St. Michaels is up
> The Battery down,
> Ghosts haunt the waterfront
> In old Charles Town.

Nate chuckled. "It's Charleston, goose, not Charles Town."

Skipping over a crack, Cathy shot him a saucy look. "It was Charles Town back before independence."

"Where did you learn that silly nursery rhyme, anyway?" he teased.

Cathy panted her indignant reply between leaps. "It's not silly! Brown Bessie taught me last night. Her mama taught her way back in the year 1810."

Nate snorted a laugh. "Not that crazy old Brown Bessie again. Sister Marie says she's dangerous, that Bessie's ghost has been setting fires 'round Charleston for over a hundred years."

"Oh!" cried Cathy, shooting Nate a look of hurt and indignation. "That's not so! How dare you say such bad things about Bessie! She's my friend! You take back what you said!"

Seeing the hurt in Cathy's bright eyes, Nate swallowed his angry retort. Brown Bessie was a ghost, the spirit of a slave who had been executed in Charleston a hundred and twenty years ago—and a very sore subject between him and Cathy. Although Nate doubted the phantom Bessie even existed, Cathy had believed in the ghost for some time now. He felt intensely jealous of the many hours Cathy spent in the orphanage attic, talking with her imaginary friend or "playing marbles" with Bessie. Nate was convinced that Cathy had invented Bessie out of loneliness, and could not understand why his friendship was not enough.

"So what else did Bessie tell you?" he asked grudgingly.

"Will you take back the mean things you just said?" Cathy said stubbornly.

Nate threw up his hands. "Okay, Bessie's not bad. There, are you happy? Now tell me what she said."

Cathy shrugged. "Bessie didn't say much. Mostly we played marbles with Rufus."

Nate ground his jaw. Rufus was a kitten Cathy had recently rescued from a garbage can, a kitten she claimed Bessie had named. Resentment surging in him, he demanded, "Why don't you just admit Bessie doesn't exist?"

"That's not true!" Cathy cried.

"It is so. If you didn't make her up, then why does Bessie disappear every time I go up in the attic?"

Cathy stopped to regard him proudly. " 'Cause you won't believe in her. Bessie'll come to you too if you'll just believe in her. She told me so."

Nate was mulling this over when he spotted their friend, Officer Paddy McIntire, emerging on a corner ahead of them. Dressed in the blue uniform and cap of the Charleston Police, armed with his Smith and Wesson revolver and a billy club, the pot-bellied man was ambling across Meeting Street.

Feeling grateful for the diversion, Nate pointed ahead. "Hey, look, there's Officer Paddy! Let's go see what he's doing. Maybe he'll give us nickels for candy."

But Cathy dug in her heels, her expression uncharacteristically wary. "No. Brown Bessie warned me we should stay away from Officer Paddy today."

"Bah!" Nate waved her off. "I'm not believing that silly old ghost again."

Cathy glowered.

" 'Sides, Officer Paddy wouldn't hurt a fly. What has he ever done but give us gum and nickels and tell us funny stories about the drunkards rolling around in Roper's Alley?"

Cathy set her arms akimbo. "I think we should stay away from him."

Nate grabbed her hand: "Come on, goose. He's crossing the street and we'll lose him!"

Cathy reluctantly fell into step beside Nate, and the two rushed for the intersection of Meeting and Broad streets, known as the Four Corners of Law. On opposite corners ahead of them loomed Charleston City Hall and the post office; across the street to their west stood the county courthouse, while beside them rose majestic old St. Michael's Church with its pillars, clock tower, and steeple.

Following McIntire, the children raced around the corner onto Broad Street, skidding past a hunched old flower lady with her cart; beyond at the harbor end of the street stood the Old Exchange and Provost Dungeon. The pair trailed McIntire onto Church Street, passing the old tenement known as Cabbage Row, where a jovial black woman stood framed in her kitchen window, singing "God Bless the Child" as she laid out squashes, potatoes, carrots, and onions for sale on her windowsill. They followed the policeman into a seamy alleyway filled with garbage cans, trash, and old dogs dozing on the steps of sagging back stoops.

Cathy sniffed at the unpleasant odors of rubbish. "What is he doing here?" she asked in an urgent whisper.

Nate shrugged. "Who knows? Maybe Officer Paddy is playing dominoes again."

"Then he won't want us around."

"He won't care." Nate paused, gripping Cathy's hand as, ahead of them, Paddy trooped up the back steps of a tenement. "There—he's stopping."

Cathy tugged at Nate's sleeve. "Let's go home."

"Naw, I want to see what Paddy's up to."

He towed her on, until the two stopped before a derelict brownstone building that towered four stories above them. Ahead in some garbage cans he could hear the high-pitched wailing of battling cats. Then a screeching gray mongrel sailed out of a pile of trash and vaulted past them down the alleyway, jumping over the legs of a drunkard who lay unconscious near the back door of a row house. The man didn't even twitch.

"Come on, Nate, we can't find Officer Paddy now," Cathy implored.

Nate spotted the old iron fire escape. "Sure we can. We'll climb up the fire steps!"

"Nate, I don't want candy that much."

"Oh, hush."

Nate jumped up and down until he caught the bottom rung of the fire escape ladder, then pulled down the creaky, rickety contraption. He and Cathy climbed up to the first floor landing, pausing at the sounds of men's loud voices.

"Stay low!" Nate cautioned Cathy. "I think that's Officer Paddy I hear."

Cathy crouched on the landing. Nate peered over the windowsill to see Officer Paddy sitting at a table with another policeman, a man Nate recognized as Paddy's boss, the one he called Keegan. The scarred tabletop was stacked with greenbacks and cluttered with beer bottles and ashtrays. The men were counting out the cash and arguing loudly.

"My God, look at all that money!" Nate whispered. "I'll bet he'll give us enough to buy the whole store!"

Wide-eyed, Cathy poked her dainty nose over the windowsill, and both children watched and listened. . . .

At the table sat two men in policeman's blues. Paddy McIntire sported a jovial face and a twinkle in his gray eyes; a smoking cigar dangled between his thick lips. Lieutenant Carmichael Keegan was older and thinner, with a pug-nosed face, shifty hazel eyes, and orange hair liberally streaked with gray.

Keegan was in a rage, chomping down furiously on the wad of tobacco stuffed between his teeth and his cheek. He'd been a member of the Charleston police force for almost two decades now. During most of those years, he'd been lord of his own little kingdom of corruption, "protecting" the brothels and juke joints in the harbor district—for the right price. His problems had begun early in the war, when the commander of Charleston Naval Base had declared the "sinful" city off-limits to military personnel. Now the mayor and the police chief had been forced to launch a major crackdown on vice in the area. . . .

Which was Keegan's sacred domain. Taverns and whorehouses were biting the dust left and right, and Keegan's remaining customers were balking, claiming he could no longer shield them from the authorities. Keegan's supply of easy money was drying up, and his chief foot soldier, that idiot Paddy McIntire, wasn't helping much.

"I can't believe Lottie told you she ain't gotta pay up this time," Mic Keegan snarled, spitting tobacco juice on the floor.

"She said Captain O'Moody come around last week, askin' if any cops was trying to fleece her," Paddy replied. "Now Lottie says she ain't paying up, and she and her gals is moving on to Walterboro, anyhow. Says O'Moody give her thirty days to clear out of town. Says if we pester her again, she'll squeal on us to O'Moody."

"That witch!" roared Keegan, waving a fist. "I'll teach that hussy to threaten me—and make her cough up double."

"It ain't just her, Keegan, all our customers is stiffing us. They're all feeling the squeeze." Paddy gestured disparagingly at the cash strewn on the table. "This ain't half what we used to collect."

"Yeah, and I think O'Moody is gettin' wise to us, to boot," groused Keegan. "He sure was askin' a lot of questions 'round police headquarters yesterday, like who might be on the take. Kept looking my way, funnylike."

"So what'll we do?"

Keegan drummed his fingertips on the table. "I think maybe we oughta get rid of him."

Paddy's mouth fell open, his lit cigar tumbling onto the table. "You don't mean bump him off, Mic?"

"I sure as hell do."

"No!" protested Paddy, grabbing the smoldering cigar and snuffing it out in an ashtray.

Mic gestured his frustration. "Yeah, it'll be easy. I'll just have me a little chat with Lottie, have 'er make a call and tell O'Moody she's ready to snitch. When he arrives at Marsh Alley to meet with her, you'll be lying in wait with your billy club."

"Me!" gasped Paddy, falling back in his chair.

"Heck, it'll be easy pickin's. Just make it look like a robbery and we'll be in the clear. I'll likely get O'Moody's job and then we can continue on like before."

Paddy had gone pale. "You ain't saying *I* should rub 'im out?"

"Yeah, it's him or us," snarled Keegan.

Paddy violently shook his head. "No, I ain't doin' it."

Keegan's face turned purple. "After all I done for you, stuffing your pockets with greenbacks for ten years, you're telling me no?"

"Mic, please. This ain't like stealing from whores and tavern masters. This is murder."

"Bah!" Keegan waved him off. "Do it right, and ain't no one'll ever know the difference."

"I can't," said Paddy, shuddering.

Mic made a sound of contempt. "Hell, then I'll do it for you, you miserable coward."

"No, Keegan," said Paddy, drawing himself up with dignity. "There I gotta draw the line. If you do in O'Moody for no good reason, I gotta turn you in."

Keegan shouted an expletive and pounded a fist. "*What* did you just say, you good-for-nothing pissant?"

Although Paddy gulped, he held his ground. "You're the Judas, Mic, if you up and kill Captain O'Moody. If you do it, I'm gonna 'fess up everything."

"You bastard!" Features livid, Keegan shot to his feet and whipped out his revolver.

Paddy's jolly face went ashen, his eyes widening in terror as he held up trembling hands. "Keegan, for the love of Saint Mary, don't go off your rocker now! No, Mic, please, don't—"

His terrified plea ended in the blast of a bullet that ripped through his heart. Wide-eyed, Paddy McIntire fell forward, dead, across the table.

Keegan smiled and blew at the smoke clouding the air.

A child screamed.

Keegan whirled about to see two young, terrified faces watching him from the windowsill. Mary, Joseph, and Jesus! It was them damn kids from St. Christopher's Orphanage, the ones always begging candy money off McIntire. And the whelps had seen it all!

"Brats!" Keegan screamed. "I'll teach you to spy on me!"

Lunging toward the window, Keegan recocked and aimed his revolver, but by then the two sheet-white faces had vanished.

"Run, Cathy!" Nate yelled. "Run for your life!"

The two children raced down the seamy alleyway, a hiccuping and sobbing Cathy tugged along by Nate.

"Nate, stop!" she cried, her wide, terrified eyes beseeching him. "We must go back and help Officer Paddy. He's hurt bad—I saw blood splashing all over his shirt when the mean man shot him."

"Cathy, we can't help him anymore," said Nate miserably.

"But we can!" she wailed. "When he fell across the table, his eyes were still open."

Nate groaned, hating himself for having put Cathy through this ordeal. "Cathy, you must believe we can't help him! Now run, or Keegan'll get us. We must hurry back to the orphanage and hide!"

Cathy was about to sob out another protest when an enraged voice bellowed from behind them, "Come back, you little sneaks!"

Nate frantically glanced over his shoulder to see Keegan in the street a block behind them, running after them and waving his billy club. Panic engulfed him.

"Come on, Cathy, hurry!"

The two tore onto Church Street and raced the final blocks to St. Christopher's Orphanage, a large three-story frame residence hall that faced sideways to the street, with a small chapel in the yard beyond. The children vaulted through the yard, up the side steps, and down the pillared piazza into the house, slamming the door behind them.

Pressed against the panel, both children stood trembling, gulping in huge breaths of air. Glancing about, Nate noted with relief that the corridor was deserted.

"You okay?" he asked Cathy.

She nodded bravely, blinking at tears. "Why did the mean man shoot Officer Paddy?"

"I'm not sure. I think they had a fight over bumpin' someone off." He squeezed her hand. "But we can't worry about that now. Let's get upstairs to the attic before that crazy cop finds us."

As Nate pulled her away, Cathy spoke in quivering tones. "Bessie is there. Bessie will help us."

Nate shot her a heated look. *"I'll* protect you, Cathy. Don't you worry."

The children rushed up several flights of winding stairs and finally creaked open the door to the attic, stepping inside a huge expanse cluttered with boxes, furniture, old school desks, and ratty clothing. Dust moats danced in the spikes of light streaming in through the front dormer windows.

Cathy sneezed, and in the shadows a kitten mewled.

"Rufus?" Cathy called, her anxieties momentarily forgotten.

A furry head peeked out of an open hatbox, then a fluffy orange, black, and white calico kitten leaped out, meowing plaintively as it danced across the dusty planks to rub itself against Cathy's ankle.

Leaning over, Cathy scooped up the furball. As she straightened and held the purring kitten against her cheek, her troubled expression melted into one of relief. "Rufus, I'm so glad to see you!"

Rufus purred even louder and licked Cathy's nose. She giggled.

Nate touched her shoulder. "Cathy, will you be okay for a minute?"

"Why?" she asked in sudden fear.

"I have to go downstairs and watch when Keegan arrives."

Cathy's eyes grew huge. "No! The bad man'll take you away and shoot you, Nate, just like he shot Officer Paddy."

Nate drew himself up with bravado. "No, he won't. I'll hide. 'Sides, no one knows we're back. Mother Agatha thinks we're still in town. I just have to make sure we'll be safe."

"What about Officer Paddy?"

He regarded her starkly. "Cathy, he's in heaven now."

She shuddered, clutching her kitten.

"We have to think of ourselves," he added quietly.

"Okay," she conceded. "But promise me you'll come right back."

"Promise." Crossing his heart and kissing her cheek, Nate was off.

Cathy carried Rufus over to an old Windsor rocker and sat down. Sniffling, she rocked and petted the kitten. Poor Officer Paddy! Now he was in heaven with her mama and her papa, making sure heaven was safe.

But Cathy knew when folks went to heaven, she didn't get to see them again—ever. Not unless they were guardian spirits like Bessie; and Cathy knew guardian spirits were rare. Cathy didn't want Nate to leave her and go to heaven, too. She prayed he was safe, that he wasn't being hurt by the mean policeman who had killed their friend. Cathy still didn't understand why Paddy and Keegan had argued; she only knew Keegan had been real mad at Officer Paddy. He had shot poor Officer Paddy to death, and now he wanted to shoot Nate and Cathy to death, too.

She shivered at the thought. Then she heard the low sound of bracelets jangling and gasped in wonder and relief. Bessie must be near! She would help them, even if Nate didn't believe.

"Bessie?" she called.

"Miss Cathy?" answered a soft, eerie voice.

The tiny hairs on Cathy's nape prickled as the air around her began to shift subtly, causing dust moats to swirl about. Then she watched Brown Bessie's spirit slowly float out from behind a scarred old armoire, the ghostly presence glimmering softly on the air, gradually becoming more defined and vibrant. At last fully formed and radiant, Brown Bessie glided forward, a young black woman dressed in blue slave cottonades and a matching turban, with two gold bangles on her right hand and a small burlap sack tied to the piece of rope that bound her waist. Appearing as real as any human, the ghost radiated an inner glow that had long ago convinced Cathy that her friend's spirit was genuine and kind.

"Hey, Bessie," Cathy cooed softly.

Bessie knelt in front of Cathy's rocker. Her skirts formed a soft pool on the floor. "Hey, Miss Cathy," she greeted in her low, soothing voice. "How you be? I hear you cryin', chile."

32

Cathy stared into her friend's brown, compassionate face—the wise, cocoa-colored eyes, the broad, blunt nose, the wide, generous mouth and white teeth. "Bessie, Nate and me, we're in trouble bad," she confessed, shuddering.

Bessie nodded solemnly. "I know, honey. You don't listen to Bessie."

"I listened, but Nate wouldn't!" Cathy burst out miserably. "He wanted us to follow Officer Paddy for candy money, and I told him you said stay away, but then he made me and . . . Oh, Bessie, it was awful! We saw some mean man murder Officer Paddy!"

Bessie's gold bracelets softly jangled as she reached upward to pat the child's heaving shoulders. "I know, Miss Cathy. But you be all right. Bessie protect you from the Evil One."

Cathy stared aghast at Bessie. "But he followed us back! I'm so scared. Nate went downstairs to see what he's doing. I'm afraid the mean man will shoot Nate, then murder me!"

"No, honey, you ain't gonna die, and Nate neither," Bessie softly reassured her. "You jes' stay put. You know Brown Bessie'll take care o' you both. You listen to Bessie and you be all right."

A smile quivered on Cathy's lips. "I know you'll protect us. You're our guardian angel." She sighed. "But Nate . . . he thinks you're bad, that you set fires and hurt folks—"

"He don't believe in me," put in Bessie solemnly.

Regarding her friend with utter devotion, Cathy crossed her heart. "But I do. I know you're here to protect all children."

"You believe in Bessie."

"I know you're good," Cathy continued earnestly. "And I promise I'll obey you from now on—and make Nate listen, too."

Bessie nodded and untied the small burlap sack at her waist. "You a fine chile, honey. Don't you fret about Nate. You play marbles with Bessie now? You, me, and Rufus?"

"Of course!" Cathy cried, her troubles momentarily forgotten in a child's delight at simple pleasures.

Setting down Rufus, Cathy slid to her knees. Bessie upended her sack, sending her brown and yellow crystalline stones spilling across the old scarred floor. Rufus leaped about, chasing after the bright pebbles that spun in all directions.

"Bessie, tell me the story of your marbles," Cathy implored.

Bessie smiled. "Oh, Miss Cathy. You knows my story by heart."

"Please," she pleaded. "I love your story."

Bessie reached down, covering several pebbles with her palm, then setting the stones whirling, to the delight of the cavorting kitten. "I find my marbles on the banks of the River Limpopo in Africa—way back when I be a baby, back before the slavers come."

"Back in the year 1806," Cathy finished solemnly.

Bessie nodded. "Back then. Before I come to America . . ."

"Cursed hooligans!" growled Carmichael Keegan.

By the time he had hauled himself up the orphanage steps, the police lieutenant was huffing and puffing. His angry knocks were finally answered by a nun he recognized as Mother Agatha, a sharp-featured woman of middle years.

"Why, goodday, Officer Keegan, may I help you?" she inquired.

Keegan ground his jaw. He didn't like this nun. She used to come calling on his drunkard wife—back before Gladys had kicked the bucket—used to scold him for knocking around the old hag.

No, he didn't like this sanctimonious biddy one bit.

"It's *Lieutenant* Keegan," he half-snarled.

"My, my, time does pass," the nun murmured. "What may I do for you, *Lieutenant?*"

Keegan hitched up his trousers and shot the nun his most formidable glare. "I'm after two of your charges I seen robbin' a citizen on Meeting Street."

The nun sucked in a horrified breath. "Sir, I'll have you know this is a Catholic institution run by the strictest standards. Our children are not thieves."

"Well, these two are!"

"Which two?"

"Hell, I don't know their names, but I seen 'em with Paddy McIntire times enough. A boy about yea tall"—he paused, gesturing—"with dark hair, and a shorter girl with them blond pineapple curls."

"Ah, you must mean Nate Bennett and Cathy Cheney," said the nun. "Those two are inseparable."

"Yeah. Well, we'll see how *inseparable* they are down at the jail," Keegan drawled sarcastically.

The nun went wide-eyed. "Why, I never! You propose to take two young children to such a disreputable establishment? That is totally out of the question!"

Keegan leaned toward her menacingly. "Are you

interfering with an officer of the law in the performance of his duties?"

A look of caution flitted over the nun's face. "Sir, the children you seek are not pickpockets. Furthermore, they aren't even here right now—they're in town celebrating the victory."

"Bloody hell they're not here!" blazed Keegan. "I just seen 'em return to this here orphanage."

The nun drew herself up with dignity. "Lieutenant, I am not about to tolerate profanity on these premises."

"Just hand over the little hooligans and I'll be gone!"

"And where is this man you claim they robbed?" demanded the mother superior.

Keegan avoided her eye. "He's at police headquarters."

"Indeed? And what do you allege the children stole from him?"

"His wallet."

"Well, I seriously doubt this so-called theft even occurred. In any event, I shall investigate the matter myself."

"You trying to do my job?" bellowed Keegan.

The nun faced him down unflinchingly. "Lieutenant, I seriously doubt your superior, Captain O'Moody, will approve of your taking two of our charges to jail. As you're aware, your captain is a faithful member of our parish and plays gin rummy with Father Timothy every Thursday night."

Keegan's face was reddening. "What of it? I want them little sneaks now!"

"Then let's go inside and telephone your captain,"

replied the nun with cool disdain. "If he agrees that the children should be apprehended, I'll accompany them down to the precinct house—where you had best produce this citizen you claim my children robbed."

His temper spiking, Keegan waved a fist. "Look, you nosy penguin, you bring them brats out here right now, or by damn I'll—"

"You'll what, Lieutenant?" the nun demanded icily.

Keegan seethed in helpless frustration, realizing the nun had him outfoxed. At the moment, he couldn't get to the kids.

Conceding defeat, he spat tobacco juice near her feet, growing still more enraged when she didn't even flinch. "I'll be back, you interfering biddy!" He turned on his heel and strode off.

Smiling, the nun closed the door.

Crouched at the back of the hallway, Nate watched Mother Agatha shut the door and move back inside. Heaving a huge sigh of relief, he crept back up the stairs.

Thank God for Mother Agatha! The woman was a saint to protect them from Lieutenant Keegan. But now what were they to do? Keegan would surely return, and once inside, he would likely shoot them just as he'd shot poor Paddy McIntire. He and Cathy must continue to hide until the danger was over.

He quickly climbed several flights and entered the attic. "Cathy? Are you okay?"

With Rufus in her arms, Cathy cautiously emerged from behind a scarred armoire. "I'm okay. Bessie has been keeping me company."

Nate glanced about. "Where is she?"

Cathy laughed, stepping toward him. "You know Bessie always disappears when you come around." She bit her lip. "Did you see the mean man downstairs?"

He reached out to pet the kitten. "Yeah, but he's gone now. Bless Mother Agatha, she wouldn't let old Keegan have us."

"Thank heaven." Cathy crossed herself. "But what are we to do? He'll come back and shoot us!"

Nate wrapped an arm about Cathy's shoulders and flashed her a brave smile. "We'll be safe here, goose. Later, I'll sneak downstairs and get us some food—and some milk for Rufus."

She nodded.

He slanted her a stern glance. "Cathy, you know we must stay put and be very quiet until the danger is over."

"I know," she agreed soberly.

An hour later, Mother Agatha trudged up the dusty steps to the attic. Her mind was deeply troubled, her joy over the end of war in Europe thrust aside in her concern over three of her orphans seriously ill with measles—not to mention the bizarre events regarding Cathy and Nate.

She'd left her invalids for a brief moment to come check on the children, for she'd worried about them ever since Lieutenant Keegan's strange visit. She knew they often played in the attic and that Cathy kept a kitten there. Like so many orphans at St. Christopher's, Cathy and Nate had suffered grievous losses due to the war. So far, Mother Agatha hadn't had the heart to take the children to task for breaking so many orphanage rules, including no playing in the attic and no keeping pets on the premises.

But she was certain the children weren't thieves. She wondered why Keegan wanted so badly to apprehend them.

She thrust open the creaky door, stirring up dust, and stepped inside the grimy attic. "Cathy? Nate? Are you here?"

From a far corner, she thought she heard slight shuffling sounds, followed by a kitten's whimper, and a sneeze.

Mother Agatha smiled. "Nate? Cathy?"

Silence was her only answer.

Mother Agatha glanced at the sea of clutter and sighed. She might never locate the two in such a maze of hiding places. The children were surely safe here and she hadn't the time or the will to force them out into the open now. They'd come down when they were hungry enough, and she could then question them regarding the alleged incident in town.

In the meantime, she was quite worried about a certain eight-year-old with a very high fever. . . .

When night fell, Carmichael Keegan crept back to the orphanage property. He puffed on a cigar and prowled the darkness between the residence hall and the chapel. Staring at so many orphanage windows aglow with light, Keegan was certain those whelps were inside—and they knew enough to send him to the death house.

Well, it was either them or him. Damn that nosy

nun for not cooperating! Now she would suffer. Now they would *all* suffer.

Tossing down his cigar and snuffing it out with the tip of his shoe, Keegan crossed over to a small stand of trees and picked up the can of gasoline he had hidden there. He opened the lid and slowly began circling the building. . . .

The caustic scent of smoke awakened Nate. Coughing, he jerked awake, shaking Cathy, who dozed beside him in an old armchair, the kitten in her arms.

Cathy also coughed, glancing in fear at the gray tentacles advancing toward them like evil spirits. "Nate, where is this smoke coming from?"

"I don't know," he replied anxiously. "Stay put."

Nate got up, gagging as he staggered to the door. He touched the knob and yelped in pain as hot metal seared his hand. Mother of God, the whole house must be on fire! He could hear flames licking at the opposite side of the panel, monsters eager to devour him, to devour Cathy. And smoke was pouring from the crack at the bottom, rising to smother them!

Choking, Nate hurried back across the attic and flung open a dormer window. Angry flames leaped and crackled just beneath the attic eaves, and the scene on the lawn below was terrifying. Nuns and orphans, all in night clothes, were pouring out of the building onto the lawn. He could hear their panicked cries.

Nate cupped a hand around his mouth and yelled, "Help us! Please, help us!"

Coughing violently, Cathy rushed to Nate's side, her face a picture of terror. She clutched her frightened, wailing kitten and gazed at the flames advancing toward them.

"Nate, what can we do?" she cried. "We must run."

He regarded her in helpless anguish. "No, Cathy, we can't. There are flames on the attic stairs."

She gasped, hugging her kitten. "Oh, no! We're going to die! Poor Rufus will die, too!"

Frantic for Cathy's safety, Nate turned back to the window and screamed, "Help us! Please, somebody, help us!"

Down on the ground, nuns and children were scurrying about in all directions. Near the front gate, a horrified Mother Agatha tried to count heads as she held a terrified two-year-old girl who was wailing inconsolably. Three other hysterical orphans clung to the nun's habit. Agatha cried out in fear, watching Sister Marie chase a small girl whose nightgown was on fire; she crossed herself in relief when the nun snuffed out the flames with a blanket.

A man staggered up to her, his countenance bleary and whiskered, his eyes bloodshot but filled with concern. "Sister Agatha, I called the fire department."

Mother Agatha recognized the man as Joe Morgan, a drunkard and former fireman who occasionally attended mass at St. Christopher's. Although she could smell the rank odor of whiskey on his breath, she was not about to question such a Good Samaritan. "Thank you, Mr. Morgan," she replied breathlessly. "We're trying to evacuate all the children to the church two blocks away."

"That's good—they'll be safe there." His horrified gaze returned to raging fire that had already enveloped most of the structure. "The flames are almost up to the attic."

"Oh, merciful heavens, the attic!" cried Mother Agatha in panic. "There may be two children still up there!"

As a deafening crash of collapsing timbers made all the children cry out in fear, the man uttered a gasp and crossed himself. "Holy saints, sister. You'd best take these others to the church now."

"But the children in the attic—"

"I used to be a fireman. I'll try to help them."

"Bless you, Mr. Morgan."

As the nun hurried away with her charges, Joe Morgan gazed in dread at the flaming building. He had promised the nun he'd try to help the children trapped in the attic, but he wasn't sure there was anything to be done.

Nonetheless, Morgan staggered about the perimeter of the blazing edifice, choking on acrid fumes, desperately searching for any point of entry, any door or window that was not already fully involved. There was none. Feeling keenly frustrated, he moved back to the front of the building and gazed upward. For just an instant, the flames parted, and it was then that he spotted two children framed in a high dormer window, their expressions of abject terror clawing at his heart.

He crossed himself and shuddered. Bless their sweet souls, they were doomed. . . .

"A man sees us!" cried Nate. "Look, he sees us!"

"Yes, but what can he do?" Cathy choked out. "He can't get to us and we're all going to die."

Nate saw the despair on Cathy's face and heard it in her voice. Her emotions tore at his heart. How he wished he could save her—he would eagerly give his life for her own.

"Cathy, I'm sorry," he whispered brokenly. "I'm so sorry."

The two stood staring at each other starkly, helplessly trapped between suffocating smoke and raging flames. Then all at once an eerie voice whispered, "Jump!"

Cathy gaped at Nate. "Did you hear that?"

Stunned, he nodded.

She tugged at his sleeve. "Bessie says we must jump!"

"Cathy, no," he beseeched. "We're four stories up. If we do we'll die."

"If we stay here the fire will get us!"

Nate gazed at her in terrible torment, and quickly realized she was right. The smoke would soon suffocate them, or the flames roast them alive, and surely a swift death was preferable to this. He felt intense sorrow and guilt for having let Cathy down. He had vowed to protect her—and he had failed miserably.

Blinking at tears, he touched her cheek. "Cathy, I don't want to lose you."

"We'll be together in heaven," she replied in a breaking voice.

He nodded convulsively. "I love you always."

"I love you too, Nate."

The two hugged each other for a final, desperate moment. Nate clambered out onto the edge of the roof first, taking Rufus as Cathy climbed out beside him. Then, with the whimpering kitten tucked securely beneath Cathy's arm, the two best friends stood and joined hands. Right before they made their leap, they shared a final smile of utter love. . . .

Down on the ground Joe Morgan had watched as the children emerged on the high ledge of the roof and prepared to make their suicide flight. Panic had exploded in him like a spray of sharp knives, and he'd wildly waved his arms. "No, angels, no!" he'd screamed. "Please, don't jump, I beg of you! Wait for the ladder truck!"

He knew they couldn't hear him. He knew his pleas were futile. He died a dozen agonizing deaths as he watched the two angels join hands and leap from the ledge together. In mingled horror and disbelief, he watched the children fall through the sheer bright flames . . . then disappear.

Part One

Charleston, South Carolina
August 20, 1945

Chapter One

As Vickie Cheney stood alone before the burnt-out shell of St. Christopher's Orphanage, a line from a Shakespearean sonnet penetrated the haze of pain in her mind:

Bare ruined choirs, where late the sweet birds sang . . .

Indeed, as Vickie's tormented gaze took in the charred ruins—the jagged beams left standing, the rubble strewn everywhere, the sooty chimney stretching forlornly toward the cloudless skies—a bright cardinal sang on the fire-shocked, withered limb of a crepe myrtle, its sweet song mocking her in her overwhelming grief. Across the property, a scorched foundation and altar gave grim evidence of the chapel that had once stood there, offering comfort to so many. Mother Agatha had told Vickie the fire was presumed to have been an accident, and a fund-raising campaign was underway to rebuild both edifices; but it would not be easy in the war-impoverished southern town of Charleston.

Vickie had thought she had known devastation, and anguish beyond description. She had watched young men die, had heard old men cry like babies. She had loved a man and lost him forever. In her twenty-six brief years, she had seen more suffering than most people endure in a lifetime. She had taken some fleeting comfort from knowing she must have seen the worst. . . .

She'd been so wrong. For nothing could compare with the soul-rending agony she felt at this moment, staring at the stark remains of the orphanage where her nine-year-old sister had perished.

Precious cherub, so innocent and carefree. Now her glorious spirit was lost to this world forever.

"We're so sorry," they'd just told her at the rectory two blocks away. "It was such a tragedy—such a sweet child."

The words were no comfort. There was no comfort for Vickie now—not even the comfort of tears, for she had exhausted her sobs days ago.

It had been four years since she'd seen her beloved sister, yet Cathy's memory lay fresh as a fragrant bud in Vickie's mind. Cathy had been her parents' love child, born when both were approaching their forties and Vickie was sixteen. Vickie had always thought of herself as more of a second mother to Cathy than a sister, especially after their mother passed away when

Cathy was only two. She remembered rocking the small child on the porch swing, at their family's home in Georgetown, South Carolina.

She remembered so much: Cathy's eager smile, her bright eyes, her spontaneous laughter. She remembered her tiny sister bringing her things: at three, her earthworm collection, neatly packed in dirt inside one of their father's cigar boxes; at four, a pansy bouquet; at five, a pot holder she'd woven from rags. Cathy had been so filled with zest and joie de vivre. One of Vickie's last memories was of Cathy dancing around the maypole, wearing a lacy white dress, with a garland of tea roses in her hair and eyes aglow with wonder.

Why not me? Vickie asked herself, her throat raw. She would so eagerly have given her life for Cathy's. She had come close to death so many times during the war—when shrapnel had torn through the field hospital where she had worked as a nurse; when a severely wounded, combat-crazed pilot had gone berserk and tried to strangle her—yet she had been spared time and again. After all the desolation of war, if God was still greedy for fresh souls, why not take her instead of one of this earth's few angels?

In Vickie's purse lay her last precious letter from Cathy, written in a child's cheerful scrawl, telling of her new kitten and her friend Brown Bessie. Cathy had even sent a picture of herself, a snapshot showing her sitting in a swing, grinning at the camera, a solemn older boy standing behind her. "My friend Nate," was scribbled on the back.

"Hurry home!" the letter had ended.

Vickie had received the letter in Italy just days after

she was notified that her sister had died in the fire. Such sweetness the missive had brought, yet with such cruel timing. She'd had nightmares ever since then, heart-wrenching visions in which she saw Cathy alone and terrified, trapped in the flames, choking on smoke, screaming out for help . . . with no one there to rescue her, no one to comfort her as she died.

She had failed her sister, failed her miserably. How could she describe grief and guilt that went beyond comprehension? Cathy had been all she had left, her only tie with family, with a sane world. She never should have left her sister in the first place. She had wanted to return home from her post in Tunisia three years ago, when she had been notified of her father's death in Georgetown. But getting leave then would have been next to impossible, and the wounded army soldiers needed her so desperately. At the time, Vickie had taken comfort in the reassurance she had received via the Red Cross that Cathy was being well cared for at St. Christopher's Catholic Orphanage and School in Charleston.

She had never imagined this! She should have known. She should have come running much sooner. . . . Now she was here too late, only in time for the memorial service to be held three days from now, the mass that would honor Cathy and four other orphans who had expired, either during the fire or afterward.

At last Vickie turned away from the ruins and walked back toward Meeting Street, moving past Charleston's lush lawns and ornate black iron fences that fronted the unique double and single houses facing sideways to the street. Her thoughts drifted back to the wrenching moments with Mother Agatha and Father Timothy. "You'll feel better after the memorial service," the priest had reassured her. "It will be a time of healing, you'll see."

There would be no healing for Vickie.

Mother Agatha had mostly just sobbed. "Such a dear child . . ." she'd said endlessly. When Vickie had pressed her about why Cathy's body was never recovered, the woman would not meet her eye and had only wept louder. Finally the priest had awkwardly explained, "Cathy was trapped in the attic with another child. A witness saw them in the window, just before the flames enveloped them. There was no way they could have escaped. The fire chief said . . . well, the flames would have been the most intense there."

Vickie had fled the rectory without saying another word.

On Meeting Street, Vickie joined a crowd of citizens, sailors, and soldiers trooping down the sidewalks past ancient buildings and churches, while in the street beyond, trucks, automobiles, and old mule-drawn wagons rattled past. She paused at Shaw's Market. A bell clanged as she entered the quaint little grocery, which smelled of pickles, fresh bread, flowers, and tobacco. Grabbing a basket and roving through the narrow shelves, she picked up some cans of stew and spaghetti, then moved on to grab fresh oranges, bananas, and a quart of milk. She went to the counter, setting her basket down by the cash register.

"How are you today, miss?" asked the plump grocer's wife as she began ringing up the items.

"Fine, thank you," Vickie replied, placing several dollar bills on the counter. She felt a twinge of guilt over the lie, but her grief was a very private matter. She would not share it with strangers. Indeed, only her kindly landlady, Mrs. O'Farrell, and officials at the church knew of her loss.

"Isn't it wonderful that rationing is ending?" the woman went on brightly, popping open a paper bag and putting Vickie's groceries inside. "I was just telling my Herbert that better days are here for us all."

Vickie fought a shudder, thinking of the recent unleashing of atomic bombs on Japan, the horror that had ended the war, at such cost. "It's good the suffering is over," she murmured.

"Amen," breathed the woman, handing Vickie her change.

Vickie left the market and walked several blocks to the boardinghouse where she had let a room. The old two-story frame home also sported a side entrance near the street; beyond, its three shuttered stories gleamed with fanciful iron lace balconies.

She proceeded through the gate and portico, then down the screened-in piazza to the front door. Turning inside, she heard the strains of "I'll be Seeing You" spilling out on Mrs. O'Farrell's radio. Vickie stopped in her tracks, trembling with emotion. Here she'd thought her tears were exhausted. What a fool she'd been! That song was Cathy—her joy, her laughter, the eternal youth that made her forever a spring day—and she would never see her again!

Certain she would fall apart in only seconds, Vickie rushed toward the interior stairs, clutching her bag and climbing as rapidly as her weak knees would allow. Rounding the landing, she unexpectedly slammed into a hard male body, gasped, and lost control of her bag, her groceries spilling down on the wooden planks at their feet.

"Bloody hell!" exclaimed an angry voice.

Vickie's gaze snapped up, and she found herself staring into the most vivid blue eyes she'd ever seen, eyes filled with ire and something deeper, some cloaked pain. The man she'd crashed into was tall and slender, with gray-tinged black hair; he wore the blue uniform of the RAF, an array of ribbons pinned to his jacket. His classically hewn features were gripped by a massive scowl. Even irate as he appeared, he was incredibly handsome.

"Excuse me, sir," Vickie said breathlessly.

"You should watch where you're going, miss," the man replied sharply in a deep, British-accented voice. "Have I survived the blitz only to tumble to my death at the carelessness of a clumsy girl?"

"I said I was sorry, sir," she retorted coldly.

He made a sound of contempt, hunkered down, and replaced several cans in her grocery bag. He stood and unceremoniously dumped the sack into her arms. "See that you take greater care in the future."

With mouth hanging open, Vickie watched the man turn and descend the stairs, his bearing ramrod straight. "What a beast," she muttered under her breath.

At last, safely inside her room, Vickie rushed over to the kitchenette and dumped her bag on a ladder-back chair. She gripped the edge of the oilcloth-covered table, and realized she was still shaking from her encounter with the stranger. An image of him rose to taunt her—the blue eyes blazing, the aristocratic nostrils flared in distaste, the lips thinned with anger, and the jaw clenched. Mercy! What had driven the man to such malice toward the world? Whatever demons he battled, he had no right to vent his spleen on her!

Struggling to calm herself, Vickie gazed about her room—at the sagging iron bed with chenille bedspread, the plain maple dresser with its ratty doily and crazed mirror, the scarred wardrobe, the cheap framed prints breaking the monotony of yellowed wallpaper. The desolation of the stark, anonymous room wrenched a forlorn sigh from her. . . .

Then she remembered the poignant song. And Cathy. And she fell apart. . . .

Frowning fiercely, Adrian Bennett retrieved his mail from its slot and marched back up the stairs. Only one letter today, from his cousin Ned, manager of his estate in Kent. In no hurry to read it, he shoved the envelope inside his pocket. It was likely only the usual tedious news about apple crop forecasts or a dispute with a tenant.

He decided he would forego drinks at the naval officer's club with Derrick Rand, the nice American chap he had befriended during the destroyer voyage to America. It had been good of the Yanks to give him passage to the States during his emergency leave. Derrick had rung him up an hour ago, inviting Adrian to join him and several other Yanks in a poker game. But Adrian was no longer in a social frame of mind.

Indeed, he did not much like himself following his jarring encounter with the young woman. This was the second time he'd seen her. Yesterday he had spotted her in the foyer chatting with Mrs. O'Farrell. The sight of her had sent him retreating back up the stairs, for reasons he couldn't comprehend.

Until now. Lord, he had acted a beast, upbraiding the poor girl simply for running into him. Granted, she had been heedless to go tearing up the stairs that way, and Adrian had learned much about carelessness over the past years of war—ah, yes, and he had the nightmares to prove it. He had watched dear friends make a single mistake and die for it.

Like poor Ted Peebles, the young chap from Brighton, who had perished because a careless ground crewman had improperly loaded the ammunition in his Spitfire. When his guns jammed during a dogfight, Peebles had become easy prey for the first Messerschmitt he encountered.

So many good English lads had been senselessly lost. Sometimes Adrian felt guilty for having survived it all.

Of course, none of that excused his callousness toward the young woman, and he realized the reasons for his diatribe went far beyond outrage at her negligence. When he had felt that soft body colliding with his, when her astonished gaze had riveted his, she'd awakened something long dead within him.

Passions he had no right to feel, ever again.

How lovely she was. Even now, a traitorous image of her flitted across his mind—thick red-gold hair, pulled back from an elegant widow's peak, falling in a gleaming mass to her nape; an exquisite face, long and angular, with incredibly vibrant, large light green eyes, slightly upturned nose, and full-lipped, pink mouth. A pleasing figure well displayed by a blue and white printed cotton dress that hugged her shapely bosom and trim waist, then flared nicely over the curves of her hips.

Lord help him, he could not feel these things! It was a desecration of the memory of Celeste, his dear departed wife, who lay beneath a cross on a lonely hillside in Kent. . . .

But the girl had made him dream of those days— dream of a wife's love, a child's laughter—dream of comforts he no longer deserved, of intimacy that was beyond him. The impact of the girl's sensuality had jolted him with passion and physical awareness, proving he was still alive. He had hated himself for that. Irrationally, he had hated her as well. He had lashed out in a futile attempt to deny his feelings, his own humanity.

On the upstairs landing he hesitated. Her room was next to his, he knew. Should he go apologize?

He strode down the hall, pausing by her door. That was when he heard it—the sound of her sobs, her inconsolable sorrow. She was weeping as if someone had ripped the heart out of her.

Adrian trembled, collapsing against the wall. Each breath he drew burned with self-loathing and his hands curled into fists at his sides.

Mother of God, had he caused the girl this unspeakable pain? He deserved to be shot if he had.

At last Adrian realized his brief rudeness could not possibly have caused the young woman such agonizing sorrow. Now he sensed the real reason she'd been racing up the stairs, the reason for the emotion teeming in those breathtaking eyes.

She had seen the darkness just as he had, and she knew what he knew. There was no sharing it. There was no escape.

Chapter Two

Morning found Vickie fully dressed and knocking on the door to Mrs. O'Farrell's downstairs apartment. Hearing the woman call out, "Come in!" she entered her landlady's old Victorian parlor with its faded atimaccassars, trailing ferns, bronze art nouveau lamps with trumpet shades, and framed needlepoint aphorisms on the walls.

With glasses on and silver hair in a bun, Mrs. O'Farrell sat on a rococo revival settee knitting an afghan. She greeted Vickie with a warm smile. "Well, hello, dear. May I get you some tea?"

When the woman started to rise, Vickie held up a hand. "No, please don't trouble yourself, I can only stay a moment."

"Won't you at least sit down?"

"Of course. Thank you." Vickie seated herself in

57

the armchair next to the fireplace. "I just wanted to let you know I won't be needing my room after Monday."

Mrs. O'Farrell regarded Vickie compassionately. "Ah—so you're leaving town after the memorial service, are you, dear?"

Vickie slowly nodded.

"How are you handling it all?"

"I'll muddle through, I guess," Vickie replied, feeling a lump rise in her throat.

"Such a tragedy," declared Mrs. O'Farrell, making a clucking sound. "Five dear little souls lost."

"Yes, it was devastating." Eager to change the subject, Vickie cleared her throat. "By the way, I met one of my neighbors yesterday."

"You did?"

"You might say I ran into him on the stairs," she added dryly. "A Brit in uniform."

"Ah," murmured Mrs. O'Farrell with a look of dawning recognition, "you mean Commander Bennett?"

"Yes, I suppose that must be him."

"I understand he was a wing commander in the RAF," the landlady went on. "Flew Spitfires, so he was in the thick of it."

"I would imagine."

"I'm not sure just why he's here in the States," she went on, her knitting needles clicking, "except that he's friends with some captain over at the naval base." Mrs. O'Farrell slanted Vickie a meaningful look over the rim of her glasses. "If you ask me, he's a troubled sort."

"He does have a rather abrasive personality," Vickie concurred.

Mrs. O'Farrell smoothed out the section she was knitting. "I think the poor fellow must be in a lot of pain. This war has displaced so many souls."

"Indeed, it has." Smiling, Vickie stood. "Well, I really must be going now."

"Take care, dear."

"I will." Vickie slipped from the apartment.

Emerging in the warmth of the Charleston morning, Vickie wondered why she'd been so eager to leave the boardinghouse. She really had nothing to do, yet she felt restless, unwilling just to sit in her room all day long.

She did a bit of shopping, buying new gloves and hosiery for the memorial service. She lunched on the blue plate special at a local drugstore.

That afternoon, she stopped in to watch a picture show at the Riviera, the art deco wonder that was Charleston's first air-conditioned theater. She hoped the experience might cheer her; but the newsreels from Europe proved a painful reminder of the war she'd just left behind her, and she didn't stay for the film.

Afterward, she walked aimlessly up King Street and over to Market, glancing in shop windows, feeling at loose ends. She had two more days to endure before the memorial service, two more days before she could return to her family's empty house in Georgetown. Thank God their elderly neighbor, Mr. Peavy, had watched the property while she was away. Then what would she do? During the war, she had made so many plans for afterward. Plans for herself and Cathy. Now there was no Cathy, no future. . . .

At Church Street, she paused, realizing she had ventured farther east than she had intended. She couldn't face going past the charred ruins of the orphanage again—couldn't bear it. But St. Christopher's was some distance away. She decided she would stroll down Church a few more blocks before crossing back over.

She passed the magnificent facade of St. Phillip's Church, a Charleston landmark with its soaring steeple; she marveled at the ornate spires of the Huguenot Church down from it. She paused before the quaint Dock Street Theater, where the marquee proclaimed the latest offering, underwritten by the Works Progress Administration: *A Night in August: The Story of the Great Charleston Earthquake.*

Vickie shuddered, staring at the date of the earthquake—August 31, 1886—which was emblazoned on the marquee. That particular earthquake had been the worst in Charleston history; the prominent "earthquake bolts" that still supported many structures in the city were one result. More tragic for Vickie's family, her great-great-grandmother, Sophie Davis, had been killed in the earthquake. Vickie had inherited from Sophie Davis an antique silver necklace—an amazing masterpiece of sculpted, interlocking roses—an heirloom she had unfortunately lost in Tunisia.

Well, this was one production she need not see. God knew, the newsreels, with their combat statistics and grim images of the liberation of the death camps, had depressed her enough already.

She wandered down a couple more blocks, passing the gothic marvel of St. Christopher's Church where the memorial service would be held, and the colonial rectory next door. Realizing the ruins of the orphanage were only two blocks away, Vickie was about to turn toward Meeting Street, when, all at once, she started at the sound of a child's laughter. She watched, intrigued, as a boy and a girl emerged on the corner ahead of her, the girl wearing a wide-brimmed hat and a quaint, lace-trimmed dress with long, ruffled skirt, the boy in an old-fashioned sailor suit with knickers, and a straw hat. A chill washed over Vickie as she realized the two were of approximately the same size as Cathy and the boy with her in the photo.

The girl glanced toward Vickie and smiled, then the two turned and ambled away, heading toward the orphanage property.

Vickie's heart stopped, then crashed painfully in her chest. It was Cathy! She was certain the child was Cathy.

"Cathy!"

Vickie bolted off after the two. Strangely, the youngsters gave no sign of having heard her, but just strolled on, hand in hand.

"Cathy! Stop! Please, stop!"

Ahead of her, the children passed the facade of a large antebellum home that flanked the orphanage property. Vickie watched the two cross the yard of the house and disappear behind a hedgerow, heading toward the orphanage ruins. She tore after them, passing the hedgerow, and—

Vickie gasped, stopping in her tracks. She saw only blackened timbers and piles of debris. The children were nowhere in sight.

"No!" she cried.

Vickie raced about the ruins, frantically looking behind every piece of rubble, searching everywhere. It was as if the children had vanished into thin air!

At last she paused, trembling, next to the forlorn orphanage chimney. Was her mind playing tricks on her?

No, she was certain she had seen Cathy, really seen her! Thank God, her sister must be alive, after all!

"Mother Agatha! My sister is alive!"

Rushing inside St. Christopher's Church, Vickie was heartened to spot the nun kneeling at prayer in a pew. At the sound of Vickie's loud voice, the woman flinched and struggled to her feet. As the mother superior quickly approached Vickie, several other worshipers turned to stare at the intruder with shock or annoyance.

"Miss Cheney, please, this is a house of worship," Mother Agatha implored. "I must insist you conduct yourself accordingly."

"But my sister is alive!" Vickie repeated in a charged whisper. "I just saw her near the burnt-out orphanage with an older boy!"

"An older boy?" the nun repeated in stunned tones.

"Yes. I—I think he's the lad in a picture Cathy recently sent me. She called him Nate. Do you know who he is?"

The nun blanched. "We had best speak outside, Miss Cheney."

Once the two emerged on the stone portico, Vickie retrieved the picture of Cathy from her purse and shoved it into the nun's hand. "Here, I'm almost positive this is the boy who was with Cathy. You know him, don't you?"

The nun avoided Vickie's eyes. "Why, yes. As it happens, I took that photo of Cathy. The boy is Nate, an older lad Cathy often played with. He, too, died in the fire."

"Oh, my God!" cried Vickie. "Was he the one in the attic with her?"

The nun nodded.

"But they're not dead! I just saw them!" Vickie pointed to the south. "You must come with me back to the orphanage property and help me find them!"

Handing the photo back to Vickie, the sister sighed. "Miss Cheney, I'm afraid it's quite impossible that you could have seen Cathy and Nate."

"But of course I saw them!" declared Vickie.

"Hasn't it been some years since you've actually seen your sister?"

"Yes, but I have the picture. And I know my own sister."

The nun's troubled gaze met Vickie's. "Miss Cheney, there is no way the children could have survived the fire. They were stranded in the attic—"

"Could they have jumped?" Vickie asked.

A spasm of pain crossing her features, the nun glanced away. "Not and survived a four-story fall."

Vickie clenched shut her eyes and groaned.

"If Nate and Cathy were still alive, we would have found them long before now," the sister continued gently. "After the fire, an extensive search was conducted for any children who might have strayed away, but none were found. And it's been three months."

Vickie shook her head, blinking back tears. "Then why did I just see them?"

Flashing Vickie a look of compassion, the sister squeezed her hand. "Perhaps you were mistaken. Perhaps the children you saw only resembled Nate and Cathy—"

"No, I'm sure I saw Cathy."

The nun sadly shook her head. "Sometimes, my dear, when life's pain is more than a soul can bear, we invent what we desperately hope to see rather than accept God's will with faith."

Vickie's features tightened. "Mother, I know what I just saw. And what about the other orphans, the ones who survived the fire? Perhaps I might question some of them about Cathy."

The woman stiffened. "That would be most difficult, I'm afraid. The surviving children are being housed at various other homes and orphanages throughout Charleston, until a new edifice can be built."

Vickie thought fiercely. "Cathy mentioned another friend recently—someone she called Brown Bessie."

The nun coughed. "I know of no such person."

Vickie's gaze narrowed on the woman. "Mother, I think you're hiding something from me."

"What would I hide, child?" she replied, nervously smoothing down her habit.

"I don't know, but I can't trust what you're telling me," Vickie declared bitterly. "And if you refuse to believe what I saw with my own two eyes, then I'll find someone who will!"

* * *

Vickie literally ran inside the door of the police headquarters. "Please, I need help," she cried to the
woman who sat behind the reception desk pecking at
a typewriter. "My young sister has been missing, I
just saw her over on Church Street, and I must have
help finding her!"

The startled woman asked, "Your name, miss?"

"Vickie Cheney."

Standing, she muttered, "Excuse me, I'll see what
I can do for you, Miss Cheney."

Vickie paced the small reception room until the
woman returned. "Well?"

"Lieutenant Carmichael Keegan will speak with
you. Down the hall, third door on the right."

"Thank you."

Vickie tore down the narrow corridor to the third
door and rushed inside. A surly-featured man in policeman's blues rose to his feet and regarded her suspiciously. "Miss Cheney?"

"Yes—and you're Lieutenant Keegan?"

"Yeah. Sit down." As she complied, his gaze narrowed on her. "Mildred says you're looking for a lost
sister. There was a kid named Cheney killed in the
orphanage fire. You any kin?"

"Yes! Cathy was my sister."

The man appeared stunned, blinking at her rapidly.
"B-but that's not possible! Mildred says you just seen
your sister."

"That's correct."

The man snorted a laugh. "Now tell me how you
managed to see a kid who's been dead for three
months."

Although the policeman's callous remarks appalled

Vickie and she already intensely disliked the man, she nonetheless explained about her encounter with Cathy and the older boy, how she'd followed the two to the orphanage ruins, only to find they had vanished.

Afterward Keegan appeared somewhat less cynical, his features creased in a scowl. "It's true your kid sister used to hang around with an older boy," he admitted. "One of my men knew 'em."

"Can I speak with this officer?" Vickie asked eagerly.

Keegan grunted. "I'm afraid Paddy McIntire was killed a few months back. That sometimes happens when one of us patrols the wrong part of town."

"I'm very sorry to hear that. But what about my sister?"

Keegan flung a hand outward. "Lady, your sister is dead."

"Then why did I just see her?"

He shrugged. "You tell me. I think you saw some other kid that looked like your sister. If she'd a been alive, we woulda found her by now."

"Then you won't help me?" Vickie demanded.

"Lady, if I were you, I'd go home and forget about it."

Vickie surged to her feet, her jaw clenched and eyes burning with angry tears. "I'll never forget about it. Never! And if you won't help me find Cathy, I'll find her myself!"

Carmichael Keegan watched the Cheney woman charge out of the room. Could what she had said be true? Could those two brats still be alive?

Drawing his fingers through his thinning hair, he

got up and prowled his small office. Surely it was impossible. The woman was likely delusional. Hell, the orphanage had burned down over three months ago. There was no way the brats could have survived. If they had, they surely would have come forward and cooked his goose but good by now.

Keegan lit a cigar and continued to pace. He decided he must take care, learn more about this Cheney broad. If there was any chance she was telling the truth . . . then Carmichael Keegan had a job to finish, a job he intended to do right this time. . . .

Stepping out of the police station, Vickie all but collided with the Englishman, who stood by a lamppost wearing his blue uniform and a garrison cap. She recoiled and regarded him warily. Once again his vibrant blue gaze impaled her, and she felt an almost electric jolt pass between them.

"Excuse me," she uttered.

He lifted an eyebrow and smiled faintly. "You seem to make a habit of running into me, young lady."

"I could say the same thing about you. What are you doing here?"

A mask closed over his features. "I would say that's none of your affair."

Vickie laughed ruefully. "And I should have known to expect nothing but rudeness from you."

Before he could comment, she brushed past him.

Adrian Bennett stood watching the tempting sway of the young woman's hips as she proudly retreated down the street. Today she wore another pretty dress, a green silk shirtwaist affair that nicely showcased her willowy curves, along with a sharp, wide-brimmed felt hat that bobbed saucily as she retreated. He wondered what she had been doing at the police station—and what perverse demon kept prodding him to treat her with such contempt.

He recalled the moment when she had first emerged from police headquarters, how the look in her eyes had jarred him. Such emotion had blazed there—anger, hurt, even bewilderment. Then recognition had dawned—recognition and cold fury. She had greeted him with disdain, reminding him of his own shabby conduct yesterday, and he had reacted defensively rather than making amends as any true gentleman would have done.

He couldn't deny he felt attracted to her, but he had botched his chances. At any rate, it was all for the best anyway. Pursuing the emotions the lovely girl stirred might bring him some fleeting comfort, but would do her not a spot of good.

Chapter Three

Cathy was alive . . . alive! The next day, this litany endlessly replayed itself through Vickie's mind as she roamed the Charleston Streets searching for her sister. She took a bus down to White Point Gardens, wandering through the moss-draped oaks, staring into every child's face hoping to find her sister. She strolled the palm-lined Battery beyond, scanning each bench along the boardwalk.

Afterward, she trudged up and down Meeting Street, stopping passersby, showing each person the picture of Cathy and her friend.

"Have you seen these two children?" she would ask.

"Can't help you, miss," said the businessman striding by.

"No 'um," said the kindly black man at his shoe-shine stand outside the Charleston Hotel.

"Sorry, honey," said the rag lady out scavenging for pop bottles.

As the day lengthened, Vickie began to have second thoughts about her sighting yesterday. She'd felt so certain it was Cathy she'd seen, yet she had no answers for the most obvious questions that sprang to mind: If the child was Cathy, why had she run away from her own sister? Where had she been for the past three months? Why had she and the older boy worn such antiquated clothing? How had they managed to turn a corner, then vanish into thin air?

Was Mother Agatha right that the sighting had been a trick of her own grief-crazed mind, that she had only seen what she'd desperately *wanted* to see?

No! No! her heart screamed. Cathy must be alive. She must. Perhaps she simply hadn't recognized Vickie at first, after all these years. But she had to be here in the city somewhere.

All at once Vickie paused, not realizing she had strayed so far north on Meeting Street. Her gaze was drawn to a delicate, iron-lace, slate-roofed gazebo on the corner, the small pavilion flanked on both sides by Charleston's central fire station. Moving closer, she gasped as she spotted two children inside at the drinking fountain, the boy shooting a spray of water into the air while the girl laughed and clapped her hands.

Vickie's heart lurched into a frantic rhythm. These were the same two children as yesterday, wearing the same old-fashioned clothing! And the little girl must be Cathy!

"Cathy!" Vickie yelled, racing toward the gazebo.

She watched the children nonchalantly link hands and skip away, again seeming unaware of her presence.

"Cathy, please, it's me, Vickie! Wait, I beg you!"

The children stepped between two buildings, out of view.

Vickie tore around the corner after them, only to find no trace of them in the narrow space between the buildings. She raced into an alley, and jerked about, seeing just a succession of back stoops cluttered with mops and garbage pails. Glimpsing a boulevard beyond, she ran into the street, then froze at a blaring horn.

As Vickie recoiled with a cry of fear, a black Oldsmobile Phaeton swerved past her, the male driver waving a fist and yelling, "For Pete's sake, lady, watch where you're going!"

Vickie retreated to the sidewalk, her hand on her thumping heart, her bewildered gaze darting about everywhere.

The children had disappeared once again!

Frustration churned inside Vickie. Bizarre though it seemed, it was as if Cathy and the older boy were taunting her, flitting into her life and out again, tormenting her with a promise of hope then snatching it away. The adorable younger sister Vickie remembered would never behave so cruelly.

She quickly backtracked to the fire station that had surrounded the gazebo, and found a man in dungarees hosing down a fire engine. "Sir, can you help me?" she asked. "Did you just see a boy and a girl at the gazebo?" Quickly she described the children.

The man shook his head. "No, miss, I don't recall

71

seeing them two, though the water fountain is popular with the younger ones."

She stepped closer. "Tell me, do you know anything about the fire three months ago at St. Christopher's Orphanage?"

He sighed. "No, miss, I didn't fight that fire. But you can inquire at headquarters, farther down Meeting Street."

"Thanks. I will."

Vickie walked downtown to the fire department headquarters near Meeting and Queen. She was soon shown into the office of the deputy chief, Weldon Little. Little was a jovial man with a round face and potbelly; Vickie liked him from the moment she walked inside his office and glimpsed the twinkle in his eyes. She even admired him because of the picture of FDR, draped with black, that hung above his desk.

And though she was tempted to blurt out what she'd just seen, logic argued she should take a more cautious approach this time and find out what he knew first. "Thank you for seeing me, Deputy Chief Little," she said, extending her hand.

His handshake was firm. "Won't you have a seat, Miss Cheney? The chief asked me to speak with you, since I was on duty the night the orphanage burned."

Wide-eyed, Vickie collapsed into a chair. "You were there?"

He gave a groan. "Yes, miss. A terrible tragedy. Five orphans lost, including your poor sister. Wish we could have done more."

"I'm so glad to speak with someone who actually witnessed the fire. I've been told it was an accident—is that your thinking?"

"As far as we know, it was." He flashed her an apologetic smile. "I'm afraid by the time we arrived with the ladder truck, there wasn't much left of the orphanage or chapel. But I'll be happy to answer any questions I can."

Vickie leaned toward him. "What I want to know is, could my sister Cathy have survived the fire?"

He sadly shook his head. "No, miss."

"How can you be so sure?" Vickie cried. "Cathy's body was never recovered."

"I know, miss. Neither did we recover the body of the lad who perished with her in the attic."

"But why?"

He avoided her eyes.

"*Why*, deputy?"

His miserable gaze met hers. "Miss, you must understand that at those high temperatures . . ." Heavily, he finished, "Well, it's almost like cremating a body."

"Oh, God." Vickie buried her face in her hands. "You mean there would be nothing left of them but . . . ashes?"

"I'm afraid it's possible, miss."

Vickie glanced up. "But you don't understand. I've seen my sister!"

Little's button mouth fell open. "You've actually seen her?"

"Yes, I've twice seen Cathy with an older boy. In fact, I just spotted them at the gazebo outside your central fire station."

He sat bolt upright. "Blessed saints! You're certain of this?"

She nodded. "And yesterday I spotted them near the ruined orphanage. Both times, I called out to them, but they didn't seem to hear, then mysteriously slipped away."

Now quite pale, Little crossed himself. "Then I reckon there's only one explanation, miss."

"And what's that?"

In a shaky whisper, he confided, "I reckon you seen their ghosts."

"You're joking!" cried Vickie.

"Oh, no, ma'am," he replied soberly. "Charleston's a right haunted place. Heck, we've got old Stede Bonnet prowling Hangman's Point, even Blackbeard himself strutting about the harbor. Lots of restless spirits hereabouts. Why, one of our neighbors on East Battery claims she's sharing her cottage with the ghost of an old shoemaker. The old spirit raises quite a racket with his bootmaking. And there's an ancient legend about the ghost of a female slave who sets fires, though I can't recollect her name."

"Why, forevermore," declared Vickie.

The man nodded vehemently. "Charleston is a ghost town, all right. Perhaps your baby sister—well, she might just be coming 'round to tell you good-bye."

Intensely frustrated, Vickie burst out, "But I'm so sure she's real! And the fact that I just saw her and the boy outside your fire station—doesn't that tell us something? That maybe there's more to this fire than meets the eye?"

The deputy regarded her with compassion. "Miss, do you have any idea of the search that was conducted after the orphanage fire?"

Reluctantly Vickie nodded.

"Almost three dozen of us, firemen, police, and

volunteers, scoured every inch of the Neck for days, looking for any survivors that might have wandered off. Believe me, miss, if your sister had made it, we would have found her long before now."

Vickie sat frowning a moment, then stood to leave. "Thanks again, Deputy Chief Little."

Outside the fire station, Vickie was immersed in thought. Was Deputy Chief Little right? Had she been seeing Cathy's ghost?

Her feet seemed to take her in the direction of the ruined orphanage, and she stood there watching the sun fade across the charred remains of the residence hall and chapel.

"Oh, Cathy," she murmured. "Where are you? Are you real, or a ghost? If you're here, why won't you talk to me?"

She lingered there until dusk enfolded the landscape, and finally trudged away. Several blocks later, she was about to cross over to Meeting Street when she heard a cultured voice ask, "Miss?"

Her pulse jumping, Vickie whirled to see the Englishman standing behind her, looking much too dapper in his sharp uniform and cap. He had a habit of popping up at the oddest moments, and again she felt rattled by the intensity he radiated.

"Oh—so it's you again."

He stepped closer, eyeing her sternly. "Are you sure you should be out alone this late?"

She stared at him, arrested by the unexpected question.

"You know, Charleston can be a dangerous city," he went on. "Lots of riffraff not far from here, near the harbor. You really shouldn't be out after dark unescorted."

"I shouldn't be out?" Remembering his rude comment yesterday, she lifted her chin. "I think what I do is none of your business, sir."

She turned and walked away.

After hesitating a long moment, Adrian Bennett followed.

Chapter Four

Vickie stopped in for supper at Fulton's Diner two doors down from the rooming house. She moved past sailors and stevedores eating at the long bar, and took a seat in a cozy booth with a checkered tablecloth. The strains of "I'll Remember April" spilled out from the jukebox.

Only seconds after she sat down, she was annoyed to see the Englishman enter the restaurant and head toward her booth. Tall and assured, he exuded authority. She had to admit he was a daunting, masterful presence with his finely etched features and vivid blue eyes. A slight shadow of whiskers along his strong jaw only added to his masculine appeal.

Nonetheless, she surged to her feet to confront him. "Are you following me, sir?"

Pausing before her booth, he actually smiled, removing his cap. Vickie was amazed by the change in him, the sparkle in his eyes, the flash of even white teeth, the way his thick black hair caught the light. She sensed this man might well be even more formidable when charming than when belligerent.

"I've only followed you since Church Street, miss," he admitted in his clipped British accent. "I wanted to make sure you made it safely back to the rooming house."

"Your concern is commendable," she replied coolly. "But as you can see, I'm fine, and the boardinghouse is only two doors away. So, unless there's something else—"

"Well, actually, there is."

"Yes?"

He regarded her sheepishly. "I rather think you and I got off on the wrong foot the other day."

"Yes, you might say that."

"I was rude," he went on with unexpected humility.

"I would definitely say that."

He sighed. "Look . . . Well, we both seem alone at the moment, at loose ends." He gestured toward her booth. "Might I join you for dinner?"

Vickie hesitated. She didn't like or trust this man, yet something about him strangely drew her. She regarded his face, studying his polite smile and shuttered gaze, wondering how he would feel if she rebuffed him as he had already done with her. But why reduce herself to his level?

At last she nodded. "Very well, why not?" She extended her hand. "I'm Vickie Cheney."

He shook her hand, his fingers warm and strong as they clasped hers. "Adrian Bennett."

"Yes, I know," she replied.

"You know?"

"Mrs. O'Farrell has mentioned you."

"Ah, yes, our kindly landlady."

The two sat down across from one another, each eyeing the other warily.

"Well, Commander Bennett," remarked Vickie, "so you're a wing commander in the RAF?"

He laughed. "Did Mrs. O'Farrell mention that, as well?"

Vickie nodded toward the epaulets on his shoulders. "She did, but actually, I also nursed a few of your kind in Tunisia."

He raised an eyebrow in pleasant surprise. "You don't say. In what branch of service?"

"U.S. Army. Our field hospital was in the hills not far from Tunis."

"How did you fare there?"

A bittersweet smile curved her lips. "Oh, we were safe enough with our Red Cross exemption. There were the usual tedious stretches followed by frantic activity when fresh casualties came through." She sighed. "It was hard sometimes, putting those boys on hospital ships once we'd done all we could for them. I often wondered what happened to some of the worst injuries—the basket cases, the amputees, the mentals."

He nodded. "I've seen such suffering, as well."

Vickie gazed at him, noting a flicker of pain in the depths of his eyes. "I would imagine you have."

He flashed her a smile. "What did you do for diversion?"

She grew wistful. "Some of the men went to the

79

clubs in Tunis. And there were the usual card games and picture shows on base. We didn't fraternize much with the locals—language barriers and all. There were few other pleasures, except when the shower trucks or beer rations came through."

He chuckled. "How long were you stationed in Africa?"

"Until last year, when I was transferred to Anzio."

"Then you've seen quite a bit of the war."

"I have, indeed."

They paused as a waitress came up with her order pad. "What can I get for you folks?" the woman asked. "Our special tonight is southern fried chicken with cream gravy."

"Sounds like manna from heaven after field rations," replied Adrian, winking at Vickie.

She unaccountably felt herself blushing at that wink. "Sounds fine to me, too."

After the woman moved off, Vickie asked, "Where were you stationed during the war, Commander Bennett?"

A slight frown marred his handsome brow. "At first I was based near my home, at Biggin Hill in Kent. I enlisted soon after England entered the war. I was with the first wave of RAF Spitfires that liberated our brave lads at Dunkirk." Tightly he finished, "Later I fought in the Battle of Britain."

"Mercy!" gasped Vickie, realizing that he must have endured harrowing combat experiences. "If you survived the Battle of Britain, I must say my hat's off to you."

"It was a hellish couple of months," he admitted,

"although in the end it was clear the Jerries had underestimated us."

"Absolutely." She nodded toward the red ribbon on his jacket. "Is that where you won the Victoria Cross?"

He smiled. "Smart girl. Actually, I won that later on, when I was transferred over to France. I tangled with some Jerries over the Ruhr Valley while escorting bombers." He pulled a wry face. "I took a few hits on that mission."

"I'll bet you did. Were you wounded?"

He shook his head. "My wings were pretty thoroughly peppered, although I managed to limp back to base."

For a moment, she fell thoughtfully quiet. "You know, I treated a few pilots for combat fatigue. I even wondered, I mean during our first encounter on the stairs . . ."

He laughed dryly. "You're a very perceptive young woman. Actually, over the last few years, I've not reacted well to loud noises or sudden jostlings."

"I can imagine."

In a tense voice, he admitted, "Where I fought, one tiny mistake could mean death."

"I'm sure it could."

He gazed at her thoughtfully. "Have you ever wondered why pilots wear silk scarves, Miss Cheney?"

She smiled. "To ensure the proper cavalier image?"

"Nice try," he rejoined. "When we flew our Spitfires, we could never afford to fly level for more than a few seconds, and we had to constantly cross-check for enemy aircraft. Without the scarves, our necks would have quickly been rubbed raw by our wool uniforms."

"I see."

A haunted look crossed his features. "Back when we were battling the Jerries over London, one of my dearest friends was careless for just a few seconds, and dead within a minute when a Hun shot him down." He drew a heavy breath. "I suppose after all the tension of combat, I remain somewhat . . . on edge."

Giving in to some instinct, Vickie reached across the table and touched his hand. A shiver of physical awareness passed between them as their gazes held for a charged instant. "Hey, I'll be more careful on the stairs in the future."

He grinned, displaying a hint of charming boyishness that tugged at Vickie's heart. She smiled back, withdrawing her fingers as the waitress came up with their dinners.

Once the woman left, he asked, "Are you from the city, Vickie?"

Vickie felt herself tensing at the question. She could not, of course, tell him about Cathy or her reasons for being in Charleston.

Stiffly, she replied, "No, I'm from Georgetown, farther up the coast. Actually, I don't have any family left and I'm rather at loose ends, trying to decide what to do now that I've been discharged."

A hint of sensual perception flickered in the depths of his eyes. "Do you have a beau here?"

Thrilled by his obvious interest despite herself, Vickie lowered her gaze and stirred her coffee. "I . . .

had someone during the war. An American pilot in Tunisia."

"Ah, one of our Yank flyboys."

"I lost him during the siege of the Cape Bon Peninsula."

He flashed her a look of compassion. "I'm very sorry."

"Thank you." Bravely she met his gaze. "You're still officially in the RAF?"

"Yes."

"Have you family, Commander Bennett?"

She could tell by his suddenly wary expression that her questions, too, were venturing toward forbidden territory. "I'm a widower," he said reluctantly. "I've an estate back in Kent."

She frowned, bemused. "Then what are you doing here in the States?"

Looking even more uncomfortable, he muttered, "It's a private matter."

"Ah," she murmured. Hoping to lighten his mood, she teased, "Do you have a sweetheart here?"

She could tell her attempt at humor had backfired when he glanced at his wristwatch and scowled. "No." His frown deepened. "You know, I hadn't realized the hour."

Vickie was flabbergasted. "But our meal has only just arrived. You can't mean to leave?"

"I'm afraid I must."

"Do you need to be somewhere?"

"Yes." He reached into his pocket, tossing down two dollars. "My sincere apologies, but I really must go."

Leaving her to watch in bewilderment, he got up and left the restaurant.

Vickie stared at his carelessly tossed money, anger and mortification billowing in her like black smoke. With quivering fingers, she snatched up the bills and charged toward the door, shouting to the waitress, "I'll be right back."

The woman nodded, and Vickie shot out the door. "Commander Bennett!" she called furiously.

He pivoted and frowned at her.

Vickie marched up to him, shoving the money back into his hand. "You are undoubtedly the rudest, most exasperating man I've ever met in my life!"

His cynical smile only further fueled her ire. "You're right, Miss Cheney, I'm an abrupt fellow. And you're a very nice girl. I think my staying longer with you would have been, well . . ." He drew his gaze over her slowly and finished, "not so nice."

He strode away, leaving Vickie to stare after him, trembling, her face burning. What a cad, all but admitting that only sexual interest drew him to her! For all she knew, he might well be leaving her to go to some trollop's bed.

She gritted her teeth and returned to the restaurant, determined to enjoy her meal despite his atrocious conduct. Yet as she ate she couldn't stop thinking of this strange, abrasive Englishman and the haunted look he had about him. In truth, she had seen men like him countless times before—one of the walking wounded, locked up in the prison of his own pain, bearing scars from the war that no one could see.

What demons tortured him? She knew he was hiding something, perhaps some abomination he'd seen while commanding his unit. His suffering drew her despite herself. Perhaps it was the compassionate nurse in her, the caring heart that instinctively reached out to a soul in need.

Yet he had also been so rude, so abrupt, so callous. He had no right to take out his anger on her. No right whatsoever.

Striding back toward the rooming house with hands shoved in his pockets, Adrian Bennett was filled with self-recrimination. He remembered the anger and disillusionment in Vickie Cheney's eyes, confusion he had put there. Why had he invited himself to join her for dinner, then acted the cad, leaving so abruptly?

Because she was so lovely. Because she had probed far too close to his own torment. Because, by damn, he had been celibate for too long, and just being close to her fresh beauty had put him on the rack. Because if he had stayed, he would have tried to charm her, to seduce her into his bed, his dark world, the void that would eventually consume them both.

No, better to let the poor girl be. Let her keep her youth, her beauty, her optimism, and that eager smile, until she found a man who was worthy of her.

Chapter Five

Vickie slept poorly that night. A jumble of emotions and memories raced through her mind. She would see Cathy's face, hear her laughter. She would hear the mother superior and the police lieutenant say, "The children could not have survived." She would watch the fire chief cross himself and whisper intensely, "They must be ghosts." And through it all, Adrian Bennett's face kept popping up, one moment mocking her; the next wounding her with his haunted look of pain.

When elusive slumber came at last, it brought no mercy. Nightmares of Cathy once again lashed Vickie's subconscious. Cathy, terrified as monstrous smoke curled about her, crying out hysterically: "Vickie, where are you? Save me, please!"

Well before dawn Vickie jerked awake, covered

with sweat, feeling devastated, drained, and confused. For a long moment she sat trembling in bed, her face buried in her hands. The chaos in her mind could not alter her belief that Cathy was still alive. She would find her sister—she must.

She breakfasted on coffee and a roll in her room, then left the boardinghouse early, while the streets were still deserted and the coolness of dawn lingered, her only company the hapless buzzards picking at the "rat torpedoes," bait strewn on the streets to rid the town of rodents.

She ventured over to the East Battery amid a delicate pink and gold dawn spreading across the bay. With the breeze tugging at her hair and the scent of the sea filling her lungs, she glanced ahead at the many vessels clogging the harbor on the Cooper River, craft ranging from destroyers to barges and cargo ships to fishing boats. Stevedores were already busy hefting cargo onto the vessels. She walked south, glancing at the quaint colonial homes positioned perpendicular to the shoreline, pillared old double houses still magnificent despite the fact that many of them sorely needed paint. She inhaled the crisp sea breeze and felt the spray on her face. Gulls swooped past overhead, and she could hear a mockingbird singing in a nearby magnolia tree. For an instant she could almost pretend she had never lost her life, had never seen the horrors of the past few years. It was a rare moment of solitude and peace, when the old town lay pristine and untouched, as if the great war had never ripped the fabric of the world apart.

Continuing south, she felt drawn toward White Point Gardens. She was heading toward a playground at the edge of the park when she heard the sound of a child's laughter. Intrigued, she ran through the moss-draped trees toward a swing set, where she spotted two now-familiar children. Electrified, she stopped in her tracks. In a pose quite similar to the picture Cathy had sent, the little girl sat on the swing while the boy stood behind her, pushing her to and fro. The girl held in her lap what appeared to be a kitten, a mottled blob of fur.

Oh, sweet heaven, it must be Cathy again!

Not wanting to spook the children this time, Vickie approached cautiously. Hearing the little girl's sweet laughter made her heart clench with pain and longing. But as soon as she got close enough to have a really good look, the girl hopped off the swing and the two scampered off, entering a stand of trees.

"No! No! Please wait!" called Vickie.

She rushed into the small copse, glancing about her frantically, only to stop seconds later, panting and bewildered. There was no trace of the children anywhere in the trees.

Vickie rushed off to seek answers, going first to the police station, where she questioned a new man, a Sergeant Wilkerson. Unfortunately, he gave no more credence to her claims than Lieutenant Keegan had.

"I tell you, my sister is still alive!" Vickie declared.

"Sorry, ma'am, but that just ain't possible," the man replied.

Afterward Vickie went by St. Christopher's rectory and spoke again with Father Timothy. He listened patiently to her accounts of seeing Cathy, but just as had happened with Mother Agatha, he gently suggested that she was surely seeing what she desperately wanted to see, and urged her to accept the will of God. He also invited her to come by the rectory early the next day, before the memorial service.

Vickie left, feeling despondent. Why would no one believe her? Why would no one help her?

Vickie continued searching for much of the day. She did not encounter the children, or the Englishman, again, although at times she had the funniest intuition that she was not alone. The sensation was far creepier than the shivers she'd felt when she'd spotted the children. She glanced about a time or two, but spotted nothing.

A man was stalking Vickie, skulking in and out of doorways and hiding behind parked cars, trailing her up and down Meeting Street, over to Church, and through the maze of alleyways near the docks.

Carmichael Keegan had become a very worried man. He'd been positive the brats who had eavesdropped on him had perished in the fire he'd set months ago at the orphanage. But now, the Cheney broad had come around, claiming the children were still alive and stirring up all sorts of trouble. . . .

After Sergeant Wilkerson told him she'd visited the station again this morning, insisting her sister was alive and the police must look for her, Keegan had felt alarmed enough to go searching for the nosy woman. She was easy enough to find as she aimlessly roamed the streets. Occasionally, she stopped to question a citizen or merchant.

After she spoke briefly with a black man at his fruit stand on Market Street, Keegan paused. "Hey, boy."

The old man, in apron and overalls, nodded to Keegan and stared at his feet. "Yessir, Lieutenant. What can I do for you?"

"That woman who just stopped in. You know her?"

The man shook his head. "Nossir."

"What was she doing here?"

"She be looking for her sister. Showed me her picture and as't have I seen her."

"Have you?"

"Nossir." The man smiled faintly. "But I been hearing 'bout that lady roaming the streets, askin' folks 'bout her baby sister that burned up in the orphanage fire." He tapped his head with a gnarled index finger. "Some folks think she be right touched."

Keegan spit tobacco juice on the pavement. "You keep your nose clean, boy."

"Yessir."

Brooding, Keegan strode on. Was the Cheney woman crazy? He supposed it was possible. But, considering what her sister had seen, he couldn't afford to take any chances. He would have to keep following her, make sure the brats were really dead . . . because the alternative scared the hell out of him.

He touched the revolver at his side. If those meddlesome whelps were still kicking, Mic Keegan would find them and silence them for good this time. . . .

Toward evening, Vickie returned to the boarding-house feeling exhausted, mentally and physically. She had hardly eaten all day and felt weak and light-headed, as well as devastated over finding no more clues regarding Cathy's fate. She wondered if she was losing her mind, and wasn't sure what to believe anymore.

As she trudged up the stairs, she could hear the Andrews Sisters singing "Don't Sit Under the Apple Tree" on Mrs. O'Farrell's radio, the gay tune seeming to taunt her.

In her room, she opened a can of stew, emptied it into a pan, and set the pan on the hot plate. As heat radiated outward from the gas burner, she realized the room was stifling. She opened the window and turned on the electric fan, but even the breeze it provided could not help as a wave of dizziness staggered her. Removing her shoes, she tottered over to the bed and lay down, promising herself she would get up in just a minute. . . .

Again nightmares swirled through her mind. Cathy stood in a high window, eyes wide with terror, flames licking at her as she extended her arms. *Vickie; help me, I can't breathe! Help me, please, the smoke is choking me!* Vickie tried to reach for Cathy, to find her, yet the smoke was suffocating her, too, blinding her. . . .

"Wake up, damn you! Wake up!"

The sound of the Englishman's angry voice jolted Vickie back to awareness. Coughing violently, she opened her eyes to the acrid sting of smoke, and stared into Adrian Bennett's vivid, enraged blue eyes. He loomed above her, his hands gripping her shoulders, shaking her, while smoke swirled around them and bitter fumes poisoned the atmosphere. Her throat felt raw.

Gasping, she sat up and spotted the pot with her

dinner smoking and sizzling in the sink, while water poured over it. "What happened?"

"Get up, we must get you out of here!" he ordered.

He hauled her to her feet and half-dragged her into the hallway. "Are you all right?"

Vickie sucked oxygen into her starved lungs. "Y-yes, I think so," she answered hoarsely.

"Whatever possessed you to do something so stupid?"

"Stupid?" she repeated, stunned. "I . . . fell a-sleep—"

Seizing her by the shoulders, he yelled, "Yes, you fell asleep, leaving a pot burning on your stove, and you almost set the bloody house on fire! How could you have been so careless? Don't you realize fires can hurt people? Do you know everyone in this house could have died, including yourself?"

Wounded to the core by his diatribe, Vickie couldn't even respond, but stood wilting beneath his rage and recrimination.

All at once Mrs. O'Farrell rushed up to join them, her face a picture of panic. "My god, Commander Bennett, is the house on fire?"

Adrian turned to her. "No. Miss Cheney put her supper on to cook and fell asleep, but I think I've managed to contain the damage."

Wide-eyed, Mrs. O'Farrell peered inside Vickie's room. "Well it appears no real harm has been done." She touched Vickie's arm. "Dear, you're white as a ghost. Are you all right?"

"She's damn lucky to be alive, and that she didn't kill the rest of us," put in Adrian caustically.

A cry of helpless anguish escaped Vickie at

Adrian's harsh words. She felt as if he were heaping blame for all the world's evils on her shoulders.

Features aghast, Mrs. O'Farrell whirled on Adrian. "Commander Bennett, for the love of heaven! Look at the poor girl's face and think of what you're saying to her! She's in shock, it's plain to see, and this was an accident, pure and simple."

At last gazing at Vickie's stricken face, Adrian blanched. "I—I'm sorry." Hastily he turned and stalked away.

Vickie burst into tears, falling into Mrs. O'Farrell's arms. "That monster."

"There, dear, there," soothed Mrs. O'Farrell, patting Vickie's back. "Commander Bennett didn't mean his words, I'm sure. Let's go see about your room."

Inside, Vickie collapsed into an easy chair near the window while the landlady aired the room and tidied up the kitchenette. Afterward, wiping her hands on a towel, Mrs. O'Farrell stepped forward and flashed Vickie a smile. "Dear, you're having supper downstairs with me. I made a huge pot roast yesterday, and there's plenty left in the Frigidaire for both of us."

Still feeling shaken, Vickie raised a trembling hand to her brow. "Thanks, Mrs. O'Farrell, but I really can't impose."

"In that case I'm bringing you up a tray."

"If you insist."

"I do." Moving to Vickie's side, Mrs. O'Farrell laid a hand on her shoulder and regarded her with keen sympathy. "Dear, please don't mind Commander Bennett. There's a world of hurt in that man."

Vickie glanced up into Mrs. O'Farrell's compassionate face, her own eyes stinging with bitter tears. "I'd like to give that cad a world of hurt right now."

Adrian Bennett strode into the nearest tavern, went straight up to the bar, and ordered a double scotch. With trembling fingers, he lifted the drink, downed it neatly, grimaced, and ordered another from the bartender. The balding man gave a shrug, poured Adrian's drink, and sauntered away.

Remembering the shattered look on Vickie Cheney's face, a look he had put there, Adrian felt relieved that he'd brought no weapon with him to America, or he might have shot himself. How could he have been so cruel to that poor young woman? He had behaved like a beast. He didn't deserve to be in civilized company.

It was no excuse that he knew what fires could do. Ah, yes, he'd lived through the nightmares, and had seen the worst of it. During one fierce air battle over the Channel, he had watched his wingman and dear friend Willie Watkins roast alive and go down in flames after he ignored Adrian's radioed pleas to bail out. Oh, yes, he knew what fires could do, and the image of beautiful young Vickie Cheney being hurt that way had unhinged him, although that was no excuse. . . .

He heard a cracking sound, and the bartender rushed over. "Mister, are you okay?"

Absently, Adrian glanced down to see that he had shattered the glass in his hand. His palm was streaked with blood, the wound burning from the assault of alcohol.

"Mister?"

"Nothing that won't heal," Adrian muttered.

The bartender tossed him a clean towel and ambled off.

Adrian wrapped his hand, thinking of the ironic lie he'd just told. He knew he would never be healed again.

Vickie sat trembling in her easy chair by her window, the supper Mrs. O'Farrell had brought up lying untouched nearby on the table.

How dare Adrian Bennett treat her so cruelly! The bastard! Did he assume she had no feelings? Did he presume she had decided deliberately to torment him? Did he think she didn't know what fires could do? Oh, sweet Lord, she knew! The image of Cathy suffering her horrendous death was emblazoned on her soul.

Yet despite all her outrage toward Adrian, Vickie realized she was perhaps angriest at herself because something about the Englishman still drew her. Her had lashed out at her brutally, had treated her with utter contempt.

Why, then, did she so long to comfort him?

Chapter Six

Early the next morning, Vickie stood before the mirror, preparing to leave for the memorial service. She wore a sedate black silk dress and had arranged her hair in a dignified bun. She met her own countenance in the mirror, her stark, wan face and reddened eyes giving evidence of her weeping, her lack of sleep.

Powdering her nose and putting on lipstick, she placed her small black hat on her head and lowered the veil. She sighed, wishing she still had Great-great-grandmother Davis's silver necklace to wear, but the precious heirloom was lost in Tunisia. She longed to feel some connection with family, to take some remnant of her heritage with her to the church. Instead, there was nothing, and she felt as if all her ties had been violently ripped away.

She wasn't even sure how to feel about Cathy. The

memorial service represented finality and farewell. Logic argued that Cathy was gone, yet Vickie's heart refused to give up hope. She felt deeply bereft, missing her sister to her soul.

She doubted the service today would be a comfort, but she knew she owed it to Cathy to attend. She glanced at her watch. She needed to leave, since Father Timothy had asked her to stop by the rectory prior to the service.

Proceeding downstairs, Vickie felt grateful when she did not run into anyone else—particularly the despised Englishman. As she left the boardinghouse she blinked at the bright day. How dare the sun shine, she thought bitterly; how dare the jasmine and gardenias mock her with their sweet scents?

She walked the ten or so blocks to St. Christopher's rectory, striding down a path lined with blooming roses. She climbed up to the porch and rapped on the door.

A white-haired woman in an apron, obviously a housekeeper, opened the door. "Good morning. Would you be Miss Cheney?"

"Yes."

The woman smiled. "Father Timothy is expecting you."

She ushered Vickie into the foyer and on to the parlor.

Vickie stepped inside the room only to stop in her tracks at the sight of two men rising to their feet. She glanced in horror from Father Timothy to Adrian Bennett. What on earth was *he* doing here? The Englishman was staring at her as if he'd seen a ghost!

The priest, already robed in his chasuble and raiments for the mass, stepped forward. "Miss Cheney, how good to see you. I was just telling Commander Bennett about you. I asked both of you to come early today for a reason. You see, the two of you have something in common. You both lost a child you loved in the fire."

Vickie glanced at the Englishman, feeling numb, totally unmoved by the priest's disclosure, although the pain on Adrian's face at that moment was terrible to see.

"You'll have to excuse me," she muttered.

"But, Miss Cheney," implored the astonished priest.

Ignoring his plea, Vickie turned and fled the room. She heard Adrian calling her name, too late. She was already running, running for the safety of the church next door.

Breathless and shaken, Vickie entered the church to find it already half-filled with mourners. She automatically genuflected to the altar and crossed herself, then proceeded forward, searching for a place to sit. She spotted an elderly couple sitting in a pew toward the front, with a space vacant beside them next to the aisle.

Leaning toward the woman, Vickie whispered, "Are you saving this seat for anyone?"

To Vickie's relief, the old woman smiled and whispered back, "Why, for you, dear."

Smiling back wanly and sitting down, Vickie felt grateful that the couple would act as a buffer between herself and Adrian Bennett. She would die if he joined her. Or, she would disgrace herself by fleeing the church.

The old sanctuary was beautiful, with soft light drifting though the stained glass panels, shining on the carved walnut hammer beams, on the breathtaking altar with its bronze crucifix, its urns filled with day lilies, its gleaming candles. But Vickie had no tears, no prayers. She realized if she opened that floodgate, she would be lost.

She knew she should feel something for Adrian Bennett. She knew now that he too had lost a child. Perhaps that explained why he had treated her so shabbily.

But she couldn't feel for him. She just hoped she could get through the service without falling apart, without collapsing in anguish over Cathy. She was being asked to say good-bye to her sister, and she just wasn't ready.

The sanctuary filled up, and the service began with an organ prelude of "Panis Angelicus." Father Timothy intoned the mass while nuns chanted various prayers. Vickie went through the motions of the readings and Communion. During the sermon, Father Timothy offered words of consolation to those who had lost loved ones in the fire, speaking of the joy the children had brought to so many. Yet even his words did not penetrate the fog of desolation in Vickie's mind. Not until he said, "And dear Nate Bennett and Cathy Cheney, friends in life who became inseparable in death. Now two shining cherubs sit in heaven beside the lamb of God."

That reached Vickie like a sharp lance pricking her heart, and a hoarse cry escaped her. Dear God, the

Englishman's son was the one who had been with Cathy!

She glanced almost desperately about the church, seeking out Adrian Bennett. She spotted him sitting in the pew across from her, and their stark gazes locked for a long moment. The look of misery in his eyes was unbearable to her, and for the first time she felt a soul-deep connection with his suffering.

At last Vickie felt something. At last she had tears. She buried her face in her hands and shook with helpless sobs. She felt the old lady's hand patting her heaving shoulders, comforting her.

Vickie did not remain for the reception scheduled afterward. She all but ran back to the boardinghouse, locked herself in her room, and sobbed until she had no tears left. She prayed the Englishman would not come knocking on her door. Despite their one moment of connection at the church, despite his terrible loss, she could not share her grief with him. She simply could not.

Eventually she fell into an exhausted sleep. Much later, a gentle rap awakened her. She tensed, gazing about the room to realize dusk had fallen. Sleepily, she called out, "Who is it?"

"Adrian Bennett. I must talk with you."

Vickie felt panic encroaching. "Leave me alone!"

His voice grew plaintive. "Miss Cheney—Vickie, please."

"I have nothing to say to you!"

A determined edge entered his voice. "Miss Cheney, I'm staying here until you let me in."

"Then stay there all night for all I care."

There was a moment of silence, then a deadly calm voice replied, "Open this door or I'm going to kick it in."

Outraged, Vickie shot up from her bed, not even bothering to smooth down her rumpled dress or attend to her disheveled coiffure. She charged over to the door and flung it open, heedless of the misery on Adrian's face.

"There! Are you satisfied!" she lashed out bitterly. "You've intruded on my life—must you intrude on my grief, as well? Why won't you leave me alone?"

Removing his cap, he stepped inside and shut the door. For a moment his presence staggered her—his riveting maleness and strength, the intensity of his grief-crazed eyes.

"You don't understand," he said brokenly. "I'm so damned sorry. I had no idea."

Vickie stared at him, so stunned by his humble apology that at first she couldn't respond. Then she remembered her own righteous wrath and attacked furiously. "Do you actually believe not knowing of my loss gave you the right to treat me as you did? Do you think just saying you're sorry is enough after the terrible things you said last night? Do you know no one has ever wounded me that way? I'm a nurse, for heaven's sake—I've devoted my life to helping people, not hurting them!"

"I know," he said contritely, extending his hands to her in supplication. "You're absolutely right. I behaved abominably. But you must understand, I lost my son in the fire."

"I lost my sister!" she ranted. "But I never assumed that gave me the right to hate the world!"

101

For a long moment he did not respond. Only the sounds of their labored breathing, the whistle of the wind billowing the curtains at her window, filled the void.

Adrian paced off a few steps, setting down his cap and drawing his fingers through his hair. Turning to her, he said tightly, "I'm really sorry, Vickie. I never meant to lash out at you that way. I don't hate the world, I hate myself. When the war began, I knew my child needed me, but I left him and he died. It was all entirely my fault. I don't think I'll ever be able to bear the guilt—or forgive myself."

Vickie gazed at his face, deeply affected by his suffering, which had again touched an answering chord within herself. Oh, she didn't want to feel for him, to feel *with* him, but she did, empathizing with his pain and guilt. Especially now that she knew his son had been the one with Cathy.

She sniffed, tearfully. "I left Cathy, too, and when my dad died she became an orphan. At least Nate and Cathy were friends, and had each other for comfort."

His eyes clenched shut in agony. "Oh, dear God, I know."

She stepped closer and spoke brokenly. "I . . . I thought I could make it through the service without falling apart until I realized that, until I pictured those two dear little angels together, right before . . ."

Vickie couldn't finish, for her words had already broken a dam. She stared at him, and he at her. In the next moment she was in his arms, clinging to his warmth and strength, seeking his solace like an opiate.

Adrian clutched her close and kissed her hair.

"Vickie, my dear girl, please forgive me," he begged hoarsely. "I truly didn't know. It was my fault about Nate. . . . Now I've hurt you so badly."

She lifted her brimming gaze to his. "Please, don't punish yourself. Don't you know it tortures me that I left Cathy, too? It was a war, and we both did what we felt was right. We have to learn to accept that, or neither of us will ever be able to bear it."

Her words seemed to reach him, and a long, shuddering sigh escaped him. He drew back, brushing a tear from her eyelashes, then caressing her cheek. "May I ask you something, Vickie?"

She nodded.

His voice broke as he whispered, "May I just hold you for a moment? It's been so long since I . . . since I've held anyone."

His question tore her apart, and with a low cry, she nodded. She didn't know why she instinctively trusted him. She only knew she felt a strong bond between them, a sense of communication that went beyond words.

Adrian led her to the easy chair beside the window and pulled her down onto his lap. She sighed as she felt his strength and heat envelop her, his male scent fill her senses. She shivered as his lips slowly brushed her brow, her cheek. She slipped her fingers into his; his warm hand tightly grasped hers. For long moments they just clung to each other, taking comfort from the intimacy, amid the sounds of the street drifting in—dogs barking, cars rattling past.

"How do you bear it, Vickie?" he asked at last. "How do you live from day to day?"

"I don't. I just endure somehow."

She lifted her face to his and again their gazes locked in a moment of poignant communication. Adrian leaned over and claimed Vickie's lips with unbearable tenderness. With a soft whimper she kissed him back.

Such passion, such bliss he stirred in her! The sense of connecting with another soul in need was so intense that it filled her with a keenly physical aching. Adrian's kiss was like a touch of heaven, a ray of warm, beautiful sunshine penetrating the clouds of her grief, a merciful respite for them both. She realized she had needed this desperately, had needed to feel right and sane and loved and wanted—if only for a moment.

Their lips parted on a sigh, a smile.

"This is so sweet," she murmured achingly. "I had forgotten what it's like to be held, to be comforted like this. To feel safe. It's been so long for me, too."

He nuzzled his lips against her temple and nestled her closer.

She shivered with pleasure. "It's ironic. Hours ago, I hated you. Now I feel as if I've found a kindred spirit."

"You have. Though I'm the one blessed."

His words brought a tremulous smile to her lips. He cupped her face in his strong hands and roved his lips over her cheeks, her nose, her chin, at last settling his mouth on hers with sweet, fierce ardor. Vickie moaned, welcoming the thrilling intimacy of his tongue, letting her hands wander over his sinewy shoulders and arms. But when his fingers teased the curve of her breast, she stiffened.

Adrian groaned, pressing his forehead to hers. "I

should leave," he said huskily. "I mustn't press matters when you're so vulnerable, much as I want you right now."

"You do?" she asked, heart tripping with excitement.

He kissed the tip of her nose and gazed intently into her eyes. "Vickie, dear, I've a confession to make. You've fascinated me from the moment I first laid eyes on you, and I've wanted you from that moment—probably one reason I've behaved like such a beast."

Though thrilled by his admission, Vickie was confused. "Wanting me has made you behave badly?"

He gave a harsh laugh. "What I want, dear girl, and what is best for you are quite two different matters. You've left me rather at war between my desires and my conscience."

She nodded solemnly. "I feel confused, too. But I'm glad you're here."

"As am I." He raised her hand to his lips and kissed her smooth fingers. "But I should go now, shouldn't I?"

Vickie hesitated. There was so much she yearned to share with Adrian, now that their barriers were down. Indeed, she had information that might help him, might offer him new hope. Yet if she told him what she knew, how would he react—with understanding or with ridicule?

She realized it no longer mattered. A dam truly had been burst by their intimacy, and she was beyond holding back.

Her hand clutched his. "No, don't go just yet. We must talk."

To her surprise, he replied, "Yes, I suppose we must."

Drawing a deep, bracing breath, she met his eyes. "Adrian, there's something I must tell you."

"I know."

"You do?" She eyed him questioningly, and felt encouraged when he slowly nodded back. "Adrian, I . . . I've seen Cathy."

"I know, love," he replied soberly. "You see, I've seen Nate."

Chapter Seven

Adrian's last words electrified Vickie, made her spring out of his lap and turn to face him in amazement.

"You—you've seen Nate?" she inquired in a low, hoarse whisper.

He also stood, regarding her tensely. "I've seen . . . something." He eased closer. "And you're saying you've seen Cathy?"

"Oh, yes!" Vickie cried. "Yes, I've seen her every-where—in the streets, in a gazebo, at the park. And Nate—your son—was with her!"

"Good heavens." Adrian appeared incredulous. "I've also seen a girl with Nate. I didn't know she was Cathy at time, but of course she must have been. I always saw them together, only—"

"They didn't seem to see you—and they always

ran away when you approached?" she supplied with building excitement.

"Yes. That has been my experience precisely."

Eyes rapt, Vickie grasped his hands. "Oh, Adrian, can't you see? Isn't it wonderful? We've both been seeing exactly the same things! I'm so glad to have someone with whom I can share these wondrous occurrences. I was almost afraid . . ."

"That you'd lost your mind?"

"Yes! Oh, yes! And now it's as if we're thinking as one mind. Our experiences in spotting the children have been identical. And that means they must both still be alive! Just think—Nate and Cathy are really alive! It's a miracle, Adrian, a true miracle! Now we must go find them—together!"

Saying the words, Vickie felt giddy and fully expected to see on Adrian's face the same sublime joy that she felt rushing through her. Instead, she was disappointed when he turned and strode toward the window, soberly staring down at the street.

For a moment silence thrummed in the room. Vickie approached him and touched his arm. "Adrian, what is it?"

"I'm afraid I can't agree with you there, Vickie," he admitted.

"What? Why not?"

He turned to her, his expression eloquent with longing and regret. "I wish I could share your optimistic view of things—but I just don't think that what you and I have seen is real."

She blanched. "Not real? What are you saying? That the children aren't real? But how can that—"

"I think what we've seen is not the children, but . . . their spirits."

"Spirits?" she gasped.

"Ghosts, Vickie."

Vickie stared at his earnest face, then shook her head in disbelief. "That's impossible. They seem so real."

He regarded her sadly. "Spirits of the dead have been known to linger for a time on earth, especially if the departed one was taken from this life in a sudden or violent manner."

"But—how can you know this?"

He avoided her eyes. "I just know it."

"And what proof do you have that the children aren't real?"

"I have no conclusive proof," he admitted, "but neither have you proof that they are. And let me ask you this: If the children are real as you claim, then what would make them hide out for all these months? Why would they run away from you and me—from the very people who love them the most?"

"I can't answer your questions," Vickie replied honestly. "But I have plenty of my own for you: How can you explain the children's bodies never being found? What if they're in trouble? What if the fire at the orphanage was deliberately set, and not an accident as the authorities have previously told us?"

He solemnly nodded. "Those are excellent questions, Vickie, and I can't answer them, either."

"And here's one more," she went on intently. "Why, when we spot the children, are they always wearing clothing that appears to be from an earlier time? You've noticed that, haven't you?"

109

Adrian's visage grew troubled. "Yes, I have. Nate, in his sailor suit, and Cathy in her long, lacy dress and bloomers."

Fighting a shiver, Vickie asked, "And have you also had the feeling that someone else was following you, someone besides the children?"

"Yes, I've had that sensation."

"Then don't you see?" she cried in triumph. "Our experiences have been the same. The children must be real!"

But he only shook his head. "Vickie, please don't delude yourself with false hope."

"Delude myself?" she exclaimed, wounded by his assertion. "But you've already admitted I could be right. The children could be real."

"Or, they could be visions," he added heavily. "Suffice it to say, we're both seeing the same things, but we're reaching far different conclusions."

Vickie felt her spirits sagging. For a sublime moment, she'd thought she'd found a kindred spirit in Adrian, someone with whom she could share her amazing sightings of the children, someone who *believed* as she did. Now he was claiming that what they'd both seen with their own eyes wasn't real?

"You really do think the children are gone, don't you?" she asked in a small voice.

"I do," he admitted reluctantly. "But I also think there are many unanswered questions regarding what must have happened to them."

"Then you have questions about the fire, as I do?"

"Indeed. I want to learn more about it." He stepped closer. "I've already begun to make inquiries, as I presume you have. I'd like us to look into this further—

together. Are you willing to join forces, Vickie?"

She nodded, regarding him with regret. "I suppose then that we can share this—just not in the way I'd hoped."

"You're disappointed in me," he stated.

She glanced away. "Can you blame me? Although I suppose you can't help what you feel."

He touched her cheek, compelling her to look at him. "And what about what I'm feeling for you?"

Tenderness engulfed Vickie at his touch; she did not recoil from the intensity she spotted in his dark gaze. "What is that, Adrian?"

Huskily he admitted, "I'm feeling pulled to you— drawn to you—even though I know I shouldn't."

"And why shouldn't you, Adrian? Is it because we're both still reeling with shock and grief over losing the children?"

"In part." His throat worked. "And you may recall my mentioning that I'm a widower."

"Yes, I do."

His words were forced and raspy. "I lost my Celeste to diphtheria a year before the war started. It was quite a staggering blow. Then there's Nate, all my guilt and regret over losing him, as well. All told, I doubt I shall ever completely recover—much less, love again."

Although she sympathized with his pain, Vickie was shocked at the disappointment that washed over her. She realized she cared what Adrian felt for her, even though her better judgment argued that she shouldn't become more deeply involved with a man who couldn't love in return. "I see."

He flashed her a conciliatory smile. "I felt I should

111

be honest with you, to let you know that what just happened between us, that is, our kiss—"

"Was only two people being drawn together by shared grief?"

Regret softened his countenance. "I just wanted to lay my cards on the table. I wouldn't want to take advantage of you."

Pride brought up her chin. "Take advantage of me? Don't worry yourself there. Life has made me very strong. You see, I've loved as well. I loved Cathy, the dearest sister in the world, and I lost her. I loved a fine man during the war, and he died as well. But none of that will stop me from giving my heart again. . . ." Absorbing his probing stare, she grew slightly flustered. "If conditions are right."

For a moment he continued to stare at her searchingly; she sensed that he hungered to pull her into his arms again. Then he took a step backward, as if in an effort to restrain himself. He clenched his fists at his sides. "You're a very brave woman, Vickie. Full of heart and spirit. I must say I admire that."

"I'm sure you're equally courageous in your own way," she replied awkwardly. "But I can tell already that we see life in quite different ways."

He smiled ironically. "Your optimism, my despair?"

"Something like that."

"I agree," he stated with surprising humility. "Nonetheless, I feel quite fortunate to have found you, to have someone with whom I can share my loss."

His honesty compelled a frank response. "I'm glad I've found you, too."

He cleared his throat and eyed her compassionately. "Well, I must say you look exhausted, my dear."

"I am," she admitted. "The service today and . . . well, everything else, has left me quite drained."

He reached out to touch her hand. "We'll talk more tomorrow."

She steeled herself against the excitement roused by his touch. "Yes. Tomorrow."

Retrieving his cap, he turned and quietly left her.

Long after Adrian left, Vickie mulled over their astounding conversation. At first she had been over-joyed to meet someone who shared her sightings of the children—only to realize that Adrian refused to share her hope. Where she saw life and possibilities, he saw only ghosts and gloom.

What had made him lose his faith in life? Had it been the death of his wife, Celeste? That and the loss of his son had evidently left Adrian Bennett incapable of loving, and Vickie found this very sad. Yet through it all she still sensed an affinity with him, and she felt drawn to him both physically and emotionally. In-deed, the shelter of his strong arms, the passion of his kiss, had moved her more than she should have al-lowed.

For she mustn't forget his limitations. Like so many others, something had died within him during the war. If they pursued the attraction they both felt, he'd never be able to give his heart to her. Vickie had known all the sweetness of true love—had known it and had cruelly lost it—and she would never settle for second best.

Besides, what mattered the most now was finding Cathy and Nate—and proving Adrian Bennett wrong.

Back inside his room; Adrian paused with his back against the door, feeling staggered by his moments with Vickie—the amazing revelations they'd shared, their sweet, tender kiss.

He'd been stunned to learn that Vickie had also lost a child in the fire, even more amazed to realize she'd shared his visions of the children in the Charleston streets—and, indeed, that it was Vickie's sister's spirit he had spotted roaming about with Nate. He was incredulous and humbly grateful to have found another human being with whom he could share his sightings of his son—even though he and Vickie saw those visions in starkly different terms.

His mouth twisted. How well she had stated it all. Her optimism. His despair. She had lived through the same kind of pain he had endured and yet had somehow remained untouched by it.

The trauma that had strengthened her had shattered him. For something was indeed dead in Adrian, something that refused to believe in the miracles Vickie Cheney so eagerly embraced. Miracles such as sweet, innocent children being resurrected from the dead. He knew this world as far too bleak and cruel a place to allow for such mercies. He knew himself to be one of the guilty ones who had allowed this tragedy to happen. He was now forever condemned to walk the world bereft of hope.

He was most astounded of all by Vickie's acceptance of him, her apparent forgiveness of his failings. He wasn't deserving of her trust and sweetness, her kind, loving spirit. He was a destroyer of lives—Celeste's life, his young son's life. Everything he touched seemed to crumble to dust. He mustn't destroy Vickie Cheney's life as well, shatter her bright spirit with his own dark cravings.

Yet somewhere within him, his anguished soul still cried out for the very humanity, comfort, and trust Vickie offered. Since learning they shared the same pain, those needs had only intensified. And the very demons that haunted him also impelled him to pull her into his own dark world and desperate, needy embrace.

Chapter Eight

The next morning Vickie was seated with Adrian before the desk of Lieutenant Carmichael Keegan at police headquarters. They'd already stopped by the fire department, where they'd again questioned Deputy Chief Weldon Little, asking him for more details on the fire, and whether there had been anything suspicious about it. Little had assured them the fire had been accidental, and he knew of no evidence of arson. Leaving him, Vickie and Adrian had decided it might be wise to question the police again, as well, and thus they'd ended up in Keegan's office.

The lieutenant, in his blue, brass-buttoned uniform, was sweating profusely in the midmorning heat, his pug nose an ugly red. He rapped a pencil on his desk and regarded his visitors belligerently. "So what can I do for you folks this time?"

Adrian regarded the other man coldly. "Lieutenant Keegan, as I explained during my visit the other day, I would like to know more about the fire that took my son's life and the life of Miss Cheney's sister. Have you been able to uncover any information for us?"

Keegan gave a shrug. "Why do you keep pestering me about this, instead of the Charleston fire department?"

"We've already stopped off there, and spoken with Deputy Chief Little," explained Adrian. "But if there were anything suspicious about the fire, wouldn't the police be involved in the investigation, as well?"

Keegan's gaze narrowed. "Suspicious? Who told you there's something suspicious about the fire? Did Little say that?"

"No," Adrian replied, "but Miss Cheney and I feel we'd be remiss if we didn't at least consider the possibility of arson."

"Arson!" bellowed Keegan. "You'd better watch the accusations you're tossing about, buddy."

Though a muscle jerking in his cheek betrayed his rising frustration, Adrian calmly countered, "Wouldn't it be logical to investigate the likelihood of arson, especially considering the apparent intensity of the blaze?"

"Bah!" jeered Keegan, shifting about in his chair. "Arson is about as likely as them dead children walking the streets like the broad here keeps claiming."

At Keegan's crude comment, Vickie gasped and went pale. Features livid, Adrian shot out of his chair. "Lieutenant Keegan, you will kindly keep a civil tongue in your head! I'll not hear you addressing Miss

117

Cheney in such a disrespectful and demeaning manner!"

"Ah, hold onto your stuffings, flyboy," Keegan sneered. "We don't need you Brits coming over here to Charleston to teach us how to behave."

"I disagree, sir," Adrian retorted icily. "It appears to me that a lesson in manners is quite in order for you."

At last wilting beneath Adrian's glare, Keegan turned to Vickie. "I meant no harm, ma'am," he said grudgingly.

"And you consider *that* an apology?" Adrian scoffed.

"Do you folks want my help or not?" Keegan shot back.

The two men were glaring at each other when Vickie touched Adrian's arm. "Adrian, please, sit down."

Reluctantly, he complied.

Vickie coldly regarded Keegan. "So tell me, Lieutenant, what do you think might have caused the fire?"

"Oh, some kid playing with matches or tipping over a candle."

"Brilliant deduction," mocked Adrian. "Why didn't we think of that?"

"Look, I already told you folks I ain't the everlasting fire department," Keegan grumbled back. "So is there anything else you want?" To Vickie, he added, "You still seeing your dead sister walking the streets of Charleston?"

She raised her chin. "I hardly see how that concerns

118

you, Lieutenant, since you obviously have no desire to believe me—or to help us."

"Yeah, you're right about that," he snarled. "It is none of my business. So if you'll excuse me . . ."

Keegan grabbed a stack of paperwork and buried his ugly face in it. Exchanging looks of exasperation, Vickie and Adrian took the hint and left.

"What a horrible man!" Vickie declared outside.

"I know, he's no better than a crude hooligan," Adrian concurred. "And it's strange, but I almost get the feeling that he's withholding information from us."

"You sensed that, too?" she asked. "Do you think he knows something about the fire that he's not revealing?"

Adrian stroked his jaw. "Quite possibly. We need to learn more."

"Yes. Deputy Little, though he meant well, wasn't much help, either. But you know, it's funny. When I spoke with Mother Agatha, I sensed that she might know something she wasn't letting on, just like Keegan."

Adrian raised an eyebrow. "You felt that as well?"

"We must go see her, question her further."

"I agree. Perhaps she'll be more amenable than Keegan was."

As they spoke, the two had emerged on Meeting Street. Vickie noted that shoppers and businessmen were already trooping about in the warm, humid August morning. Below them, scattered trees framed a spectacular view of the majestic pillars of Hibernian Hall and the clock tower of St. Michael's Church. The air was redolent with the scents of the sea, of greenery, mingled with the ranker odors of the grimy city streets.

She and Adrian were passing a fruit vendor's cart when all at once she stopped in her tracks as she spotted two familiar children in old-fashioned clothing standing at the window of a candy store a block away.

"Adrian, look!" she cried, grabbing his arm.

Adrian also glanced ahead, and went pale. Simultaneously, both of them began running toward the children, frantically calling their names, while the two children, seemingly oblivious to the approaching adults, laughed and danced off around the corner.

They crossed the street at a breakneck pace, Adrian clasping Vickie's hand. But when he pulled her around the corner with him, they abruptly stopped, breathing raggedly, staring ahead at nothingness. Only a stray seagull picking at crumbs on the sidewalk filled the void.

"They're gone!" Vickie cried, waving a hand. "My God, where could they be?"

Adrian appeared equally mystified. "I don't know."

"It's as if they vanished into thin air."

"I know."

Vickie felt frustrated enough to cry. "Oh, why won't they ever stay?"

Adrian pulled her close. "Easy, love. I know this is hard."

Voice thick with tears, she replied, "You'd think by now I'd be used to this. Instead I feel just as shaken as I did the first time."

He stroked her back. "I do as well."

She pulled away. "But you saw them, Adrian. You really saw them, just as I did."

"Yes, I did," he confirmed, his expression troubled.

"Adrian, they're alive! How can you believe otherwise? How can you think they're ghosts?"

He eyed her sadly. "Vickie, I'm trying to understand your perspective. Why can't you try to understand mine?"

She groaned and shut her eyes. "It's just so frustrating to have Cathy so close, so close I could touch her, to ache to hold her in my arms, and then . . . to confront empty air."

"I know, dear. I feel precisely the same way about Nate."

She sighed. "Perhaps we'll find some answers at St. Christopher's."

"Perhaps."

Vickie's spirits were sinking as they started off again. They were no longer touching, each of them locked in private torment. Glancing at Adrian, Vickie noted his face was tight with worry and pain. Obviously he was as shaken as she was. With a sigh, she realized the encounter with the children—or their ghosts—had brought them both more anguish than answers.

At St. Christopher's, they walked inside the sanctuary, their path lighted by beams of sunshine filtering in through the stained glass windows. Vickie spotted Mother Agatha at the altar with her watering can, watering the lilies in their urns. She glanced at Adrian, who nodded in deference to her, then called out, "Mother Agatha, may we have a word with you?"

The nun set down her watering can and glided toward them. "Good morning, Miss Cheney, Commander Bennett. What may I do for you today?"

"Mother Agatha," Vickie began, "I was hoping you would discuss the fire with us in greater detail."

Mingled frustration and guilt gripped the nun's features. "Forgive me, Miss Cheney, but I thought Father Timothy and I had already done that."

"There are still matters that trouble Commander Bennett and me," Vickie rushed on, "such as the children's bodies never being found. Are you certain they didn't jump?"

"Of course they didn't jump," the woman replied, fingering the crucifix hanging around her neck.

Vickie noted that the nun would not meet her eyes, and this roused her suspicions. "You're not certain, are you?"

"I—I don't know what you mean," she replied, coughing.

"Mother Agatha," put in Adrian sternly, "kindly tell us the truth."

Appearing miserable, the nun replied, "Commander Bennett, I just don't see the point—"

"The point is the fate of Miss Cheney's sister and my son," Adrian interjected in a chilling tone. "We'll not have information withheld from us."

The nun expelled a deep sigh. "Very well. I'll tell you what else I know. But I assure you it won't help matters, will likely only confuse them."

"We'll be the judge of that, madam," Adrian stated.

The nun nodded wearily. "There are a couple of details that I didn't mention before—particulars that I was certain would cause only bewilderment and pain. First, there was a witness who saw your children together in the attic window."

"A witness?" Vickie cried.

"The man's name is Joe Morgan. He's a former fireman—and now a drunkard."

"Go on," Vickie urged.

"When Joe spotted your children in the attic window, he tried to help them. When he saw that they were preparing to jump, he yelled out at them to wait for the ladder truck."

"What happened then?" demanded Adrian.

The woman grimaced. "Commander Bennett, you must understand that Mr. Morgan was intoxicated at the time, and thus anything he claimed to see—"

"Tell us what the man saw!" Adrian ordered.

"Very well," conceded the nun. "According to Morgan, the children failed to heed his warnings. He even claims he saw the children jump—and then watched them vanish into thin air before reaching the ground."

Vickie and Adrian exchanged an electrified glance.

"My God!" gasped Vickie, filled with new hope. "That must mean the children truly are alive! Why didn't you tell us this before?"

"Indeed, Mother Agatha, it seems you have some explaining to do," added Adrian.

The nun wrung her hands. "Miss Cheney, Commander Bennett, be reasonable. You must know the authorities dismissed Joe Morgan's claims as the rantings of a drunkard. The children never could have survived such a fall. Besides which, a thorough search

123

of the grounds was made, and the children's bodies were never found."

"Nevertheless, Miss Cheney and I had a right to know," put in Adrian harshly.

"Yes, especially since this proves what I've thought all along," Vickie reiterated passionately. "That the children are still alive."

The nun shook her head. "Miss Cheney, I assure you that is quite impossible."

"Don't you try to tell me what's possible!" Vickie burst out passionately. "And you still haven't answered our most important question: Why didn't you tell us this before?"

The woman sighed. "I didn't want to give either of you false hope."

Bitterly Vickie replied, "Hasn't it occurred to you that, if this drunken man was wrong about seeing the children jumping, he may have also been wrong about seeing them in the attic window in the first place?"

The nun shook her head. "Miss Cheney, I am certain the children were in the attic window. I . . . I saw them there myself."

Vickie winced.

"Had you known prior to the fire that they were in the attic?" asked Adrian.

"Well, I did go up there to check on them earlier in the day. You see, an incident had occurred, one that I believe caused the children to hide in the attic. A police lieutenant, Carmichael Keegan, stopped by and demanded to see Cathy and Nate, claiming he had just watched the two of them rob a prominent citizen."

"My God, Commander Bennett and I just met with

Lieutenant Keegan!" exclaimed Vickie. "Why did you not tell us this, either?"

"Because I thought the entire incident was just a misunderstanding," answered the nun. "When I pressed Keegan for details about the alleged robbery, he could provide none, and he soon backed down and left. I assumed it was all forgotten by now."

"But you should have told us," scolded Adrian. "Keegan might have had some part in this."

"In the fire?" cried the nun. "But it was just a tragic accident."

"Assuming that's true, it still doesn't absolve you of your obligation to be honest with us," rebuked Adrian.

Tears sprang to the nun's eyes. "You think I haven't agonized over this—over what was best to tell you and what was best left unsaid? I cannot even begin to describe my own guilt over the deaths of Nate and Cathy. I knew they were in the attic, for I had heard them there earlier that afternoon. Then I became busy caring for sick children, and forgot all about them—until it was too late, until I saw them in that window. Do you have any idea of the agonies I suffered when I viewed them there, realized it was hopeless, and that it was entirely my own fault?" She shuddered and crossed herself. "May God forgive me my terrible lapses. But you must know the children did perish in the fire. Of that I'm certain."

"We know you cared about them both, Mother Agatha," Vickie gently reassured the woman, "and we do appreciate that."

The nun nodded, wiping her tears with a handkerchief.

"Nonetheless, we'll want to question this Joe Morgan," added Adrian. "Can you tell us where to find him?"

"Yes," the nun sniffed. "The last I heard, he was living in a dilapidated rooming house over on Wragg's Lane near the harbor. The Harbor Roost, I believe it's called."

Adrian nodded. "Thank you for your help, madam."

As Vickie and Adrian left the church, Vickie felt jubilant. "I knew it!" she declared, whirling about in circles in her delight. "They're still alive! Cathy and Nate are still alive!" As she spun to a stop, she spied Adrian soberly regarding her. "My heavens! You *still* don't believe it, do you?"

He flashed her an apologetic smile. "I wish I could share your joy, my dear. You do make a pretty picture spinning about there, your cheeks all flushed and lovely."

"Adrian, this is no time to try to distract me with compliments," she chided. "Nothing that just happened has changed your mind, has it?"

He squeezed her hand. "I'm sorry, but you're right. I haven't changed my mind. Even if the children had jumped from the window as this witness claimed, Mother Agatha spoke the truth. They never could have survived a four-storey fall."

"But you do want to question Joe Morgan?" she asked.

"Of course I do."

"And what about Lieutenant Keegan's accusing the children of thievery?"

Adrian scowled. "As Mother Agatha claimed, it might have been just a misunderstanding or a case of mistaken identity."

"You can say that after the way he treated us this morning?"

"Just because the man is a jackass doesn't make him a criminal."

"True."

"But we should investigate that avenue, as well."

"I agree," Vickie replied. "There's something about Carmichael Keegan that makes my blood run cold."

The two walked back toward the boardinghouse, unaware that they were being shadowed by none other than Mic Keegan himself.

Keegan carefully trailed the couple back toward Meeting Street in the late morning warmth. After Cheney and Bennett had visited him again this morning, he had become a very worried man. He had followed them to the church—and had been eavesdropping on their conversation after they left.

Until this morning, Mic had dismissed Vickie Cheney as a crackpot. He'd been unable to unearth any proof that the two children were still alive as she'd claimed. But now, the Cheney broad had gotten the boy's father involved in the whole mess, and the two were really throwing a wrench in the works with their inquiries and investigations. Hell, Weldon Little at the fire department had already rung him up this morning, asking if he felt there was any truth in Bennett and Cheney's allegation of arson in the orphanage fire. How he would like to wring the necks of both those troublemakers!

And what about this man, Joe Morgan, that he had just heard the Cheney broad mention to the Brit? Where did Morgan fit into the puzzle? Mic Keegan was determined to find some answers . . . and to put a stop to this malarkey posthaste.

Chapter Nine

Vickie and Adrian stopped in front of the Harbor Roost, a ramshackle boardinghouse squatted on a corner in Wragg's Lane near the Charleston docks. Adrian scowled and clutched Vickie's arm as he led her through the cluttered front yard and up the sagging steps of the graying, two-story hostelry. The house emitted the stench of garbage and decay, mingled with the scents of the sea and fish emanating from the harbor beyond.

At first no one answered Adrian's sharp knock; then the panel was flung open, and a fierce-featured elderly woman appeared before them wearing a filthy dress, with a ratty kerchief binding up her hair. "Yeah? What do you folks want?"

"Does Joe Morgan live here?" Adrian inquired.

The woman sneered. "Not no more. I don't suppose

you've come to pay his back rent, have ya, sonny?"

"No—but we have some questions for him."

The woman harrumphed. "So do the police, dearie, after he stole my radio and my husband's silver beer tankard. I evicted his worthless carcass weeks ago— then he sneaked back around and robbed me and George."

"Do you have any idea of his whereabouts now?" Adrian asked.

The woman waved him off. "Ah, the no-good drunkard is likely wetting his whistle at one of the dives near the harbor."

"Thank you, madam," said Adrian.

"Yeah. Sure." The woman slammed the door in their faces.

"Nice woman," Vickie commented drolly as Adrian escorted her down the steps.

"Indeed. Why don't I escort you back to the rooming house? Then I'll go hunting for Morgan."

"No, I'm coming too," she protested.

Adrian scowled, watching two burly stevedores saunter by and leer at her. "You should not be out in this seamy part of town."

"Adrian, for heaven's sake, I just lived through a war!" Drolly she added, "Besides, I've got you to protect me."

Adrian continued to argue with Vickie, but she proved adamant. They spent several hours visiting seedy grogshops in the harbor district, pausing to question derelicts along the way. They stopped only to buy a sandwich and a drink from a street vendor. They had little luck, except for a conversation with the bum who had seen Morgan recently at a dive called the Rum Keg. Yet a visit to the squalid tavern produced no results.

The day was waning by the time Vickie and Adrian turned homeward. They stopped in again at police headquarters, hoping to question Carmichael Keegan about his run-in with the children on the day of the fire. But the receptionist informed them that Keegan had already left for the day.

Adrian offered to buy Vickie dinner, and she accepted. As they strolled up Church Street, she paused by the marquee of the Dock Street Theater, which was still offering performances of *A Night in August,* the play about the Charleston earthquake. She gazed at the sign as if mesmerized.

Adrian also eyed the marquee, then glanced curiously at her. " 'The Great Charleston Earthquake' . . . I wasn't even aware that Charleston had suffered one."

"Oh, yes, over its history the city has endured one major earthquake and a number of minor ones. Haven't you noticed all the earthquake bolts on the houses here?"

"Yes, I'd wondered what those were. Would you like to see the play, Vickie?"

She shuddered. "Actually, no, I've no desire to see it. You see, my great-great-grandmother died in that earthquake."

"You don't say? But I thought you said you weren't from Charleston."

"I'm not, but Great-great-grandmother Davis did live in Charleston and later died here, in her home, during that very earthquake. She was quite old at the time and a widow, I understand. Fortunately, by then,

131

her grown children had moved away, including my great-grandfather, who settled in Georgetown, where I was raised."

Adrian smiled sympathetically. "I'm very sorry about your great-great-grandmother, Vickie. But for my own sake, and yours, I'm glad your great-grandfather moved away."

Vickie felt herself blushing slightly at the tender look in his eyes. "Yes, so am I."

Adrian escorted Vickie into the dining room of an elegant hotel near Market Street, where the hostess settled them in at a lovely bay window with a view of a private courtyard drenched with dew and dappled by sunset. The heady scents of jasmine and roses drifted in.

As they sipped red wine and ate an excellent pot roast, Adrian remarked, "Your statements about your forebears have made me curious, Vickie. Tell me a bit more about your family."

Vickie found herself warming to the subject. "Well, as I've already mentioned, I grew up in Georgetown. It was a quiet, genteel existence. My father was a prosperous hardware merchant, and my mother did an excellent job of raising me. Cathy was born when I was sixteen and my mother almost forty. I don't think Mother ever quite recovered from Cathy's birth, and she passed away when my sister was only two."

"I'm so sorry," Adrian said feelingly.

"Thank you. Anyway, I took on much of the responsibility of raising my sister. Right about the time I graduated from nursing college, America entered the war. My father encouraged me to enlist in the Army Nurse Corps, to contribute to the war effort. I was reluctant to leave him and Cathy, especially since he had a minor heart murmur, but he insisted he'd be fine."

Adrian touched her hand. "But he wasn't?"

She shook her head. "He died three years ago, in the thick of the war, and by then it was near-impossible for me to leave Africa. I had to be content with the assurance that Cathy was being cared for here, at the orphanage."

Adrian shook his head in awe. "Why, that's so uncanny. Much the same thing happened with Nate."

She eyed him in wonder. "That's right, you mentioned that last night. Please, tell me more about your own background."

Although Adrian's fingers tensed on his fork, he complied. "As I mentioned, I'm a widower. My wife, Celeste, was from the States, and was raised on a prosperous plantation near Charleston. Her father had hailed originally from London and knew my people. We met when her parents came over to England on a visit. Celeste fell in love with the Kent countryside, and she and I spent much time together walking through our apple orchards. I was drawn to her from the outset, and managed to convince her to remain in England and become my bride."

"How romantic."

"We had six good years, the greatest joy of which was the birth of Nate. I'm afraid I was rather awkward at fatherhood, particularly when Nate was small. I kept telling myself there would be ample time when he was older." Adrian's gaze grew dark with pain. "Then I lost Celeste, and something seemed to die in me as well. I'm afraid I wasn't really there for Nate,

133

to help him through the loss that had so devastated him. Within a year the war broke out, and instead of thinking of my young, vulnerable son as I should have, I enlisted in the RAF."

She regarded him sympathetically. "Adrian, I think it was noble of you to enlist. And Nate? How exactly did he end up here in Charleston?"

"Before I reported for duty, I brought Nate here to America to ride out the war with his maternal grandmother."

"I see. But why was he sent to the orphanage?"

"His grandmother had a severe stroke nine months later and had to be confined to a rest home. She lingered until last Christmas, but of course Nate had to be cared for at the orphanage, ever since her health declined."

Noting his tense face, Vickie touched his hand. "Adrian, we both acted with the best of intentions."

"You did," he corrected, his mouth twisted with self-loathing. "You were an unattached young lady who very properly left your sister in the care of your father. I was a father who deserted his son."

She shook her head. "I think you're being too hard on yourself. I don't see such a great difference in our circumstances."

"I do. You wanted to give something to humanity, to the war effort. I wanted to escape one hell, and in doing so plunged myself—and my vulnerable young son—into another."

Vickie winced at his tone of self-recrimination. "Adrian, you need to forgive yourself."

He appeared taken aback. "Forgive?"

"Perhaps you weren't there for the boy after his

mother died, but you couldn't have predicted what happened to your son—or to Cathy—later on, at the orphanage."

"But surely I could have prevented it."

"Could you have? You're only human, Adrian. You can't know what's in the mind of God. You view yourself with such contempt, but I know better. You're a man of true courage. Only a man of exceptional valor would win the Victoria Cross. As for the hell you went through, of course you suffered. All of us did. I saw that torment in the eyes of so many soldiers I treated." She gazed at him tenderly. "You can tell me about it, Adrian. Don't be afraid you'll shock me."

He stared at her for a long, stark moment.

"You think you're the only one who has known despair?" she went on. "I've loved and lost too."

He nodded, appearing fascinated. "Just who was he, Vickie?"

"Bill Hildegard was a captain in the Army Air Corps. His people lived in Atlanta, so we had much in common, both hailing from the Old South. We met when I nursed him in Tunisia after he was wounded in a dogfight with a Messerschmitt. His leg wound wasn't life-threatening. He was sweet, kind, and had a wonderful sense of humor. A true old-fashioned southern gentleman. We went to the officer's club together, to picture shows on base, and eventually—"

"You became lovers?" Adrian's voice was charged.

Vickie blushed. "We became engaged. As for our becoming . . . well, intimate, actually, Bill wanted to wait, but under the circumstances, I didn't want to." She bravely met his eyes. "Later, after I lost him in

135

the fighting on the Cape Bon Peninsula, I . . . well, I was glad for what we'd shared."

"Were you, Vickie?" he whispered.

She nodded, even though the passion now gleaming in his eyes made her stomach clench. "Adrian, what is it?"

He gave a groan, then clutched her hand. "This is terrible of me. I know he died in combat, and yet—"

"Yes?"

His hand was now gripping her own so tightly, her fingers hurt; his gaze was burning into hers. "He made love to you."

The words, like an accusation, hung between them, explosive with meaning. "Yes, he did," she confirmed at last. "And I with him."

Adrian released her hand and glanced away. "For your own sake, my dear, I'd best not tell you what I'm thinking now."

He didn't have to. Vickie's heart was already pounding, her cheeks burning, with the impact of all he'd left unsaid. . . .

Back at the boardinghouse, Vickie thanked Adrian for dinner. "So we'll go searching for Joe Morgan again tomorrow?"

"First thing," he agreed, opening her door for her.

"Well, good night, then," she said, stepping inside.

"Just good night?" he asked, following her into the room.

Vickie turned, unnerved as she watched Adrian shut the door and steadily approach her. He was staring at her in a very intense way; the light of the fading day wafted over his striking features, making him seem all the more masculine and powerful.

"Is there something else?" she asked nervously.

Wordlessly, he drew her into his arms. Caught off guard, she gasped; then his mouth was closing over hers, his kiss demanding, passionate.

Vickie was stunned by the waves of desire that flooded her senses. Adrian crushed her body tightly against his lean, warm frame; his tongue plunged inside her mouth with fervent need. Vickie reeled giddily; had he not held her, she surely would have fainted under the rush of overwhelming excitement she felt.

Somehow, she managed to break free, staring breathlessly at his ardent face. "Adrian, what is the meaning of . . . ? I mean, just because I told you about Bill—"

"And just how do you expect a man to respond, when you tell him you've made love with another?" he rasped back. He touched her hot cheek. "Particularly a man who already very much wants you for himself."

Vickie flinched; his touch, and especially his words, seemed to scorch her. "I was just trying to be honest with you."

"As I'm trying to be with you, now. After all, you told me that you and I share a great deal."

She nodded. "Yes, we do. But that doesn't mean that you can just barge in here and try to . . ."

He stared at her for another tense moment, then gave a groan. "You're right. I'm sorry. I shouldn't be jealous of a dead man. I suppose my passions got the better of me."

She regarded him sadly. "Passions, Adrian. Not love."

"What do you mean?"

"I mean I can't expect you ever to love me, can I?"

He blanched. "Just where did that comment come from?"

She drew herself up with pride. "From what you said last night—about how you'll never love again."

He scowled fiercely. "And you think that means I'm trying to take advantage of you now?"

"I think you want to blot out the pain however you can."

He stepped closer, pressing his mouth to her cheek. "Perhaps you're right there, darling. But wouldn't you also like to forget? Would that be so awful, love?"

Reeling, blinded by tears, she broke away. "Adrian, don't do this to me. Not now."

He gazed at her with tenderness and regret. "Vickie, I know you may not be ready for more, but you must know how very drawn I feel toward you."

"I feel drawn toward you, too, Adrian," she admitted, "but I think we need to slow things down a bit. We could be only blinded by our grief."

"There's more to it than that and you know it," he countered. "There's a bond between us that few people ever share. I really want you, Vickie. Do you want me?"

She glanced away.

He moved closer again, grasping her by the shoulders. "Do you?"

Heart thundering, she replied tremulously, "Yes."

"Then why can't we take what comfort we can find

in each other's arms? Is it because I can't believe the children are still alive?"

The anguish in his gaze compelled an honest answer. "Yes, it hurts me that you won't share my faith. Sometimes, I'm not sure whether you're still alive, Adrian, or, for that matter, whether I am. I do need desperately to believe the children could still be with us. If Cathy truly is gone, I think it's going to take me a very long time to heal. As for you . . . maybe the war and what happened with Nate just took all the hope and heart out of you."

Adrian closed his eyes in silent pain. "Give it a chance, Vickie."

She sadly shook her head. "You're not ready for more, Adrian, and neither am I."

Casting her a last look of yearning and uncertainty, he turned and left.

Feeling unsettled, Adrian decided to take a walk. He left the boardinghouse and strolled down lower Meeting Street, past old double and single Charleston houses whose iron gates, moss-draped trees, and pillared facades slumbered in deep shadows softened by the misty glow of street lamps. The setting seemed so beckoning and homey, but he felt far away from home tonight. He considered the emotions that consumed him, particularly the jealousy that had spiked within him when Vickie confessed her love affair with another man.

Afterward he had tried his best to seduce her. His response had been primal and self-centered and she hadn't deserved it. Such possessiveness was beneath him. Somehow, Vickie had roused long-dead passions and tapped emotions that were better left as deeply asleep as the ancient houses he was now passing.

But, heaven help him, he wanted the girl.

No, heaven help her. He wasn't sure he could stop himself now, or resist Vickie Cheney's fresh beauty. Even from the depths of his despair, her hope and inspiration drew him. Oh, he'd be mindful of his obligations toward her. In time, he might even offer to marry her.

But she'd spoken the truth tonight. He would never love again. He would never see the world through the rose-colored glasses she wore. And even if he could somehow transcend his own grief over losing Celeste and Nate, his guilt remained insurmountable. She'd been right there, too. Never could he forgive himself for deserting his son.

Being with her tonight had brought all that pain rushing back again. He remembered how she'd questioned whether either of them was really alive. Oh, he was alive, all right. What still lived within him was his anger, a passionate rage that was almost totally self-directed.

He remembered how he'd confessed to her that he hadn't been there for Nate following Celeste's death. How could he have been so blind at the time, so consumed with his own misery? After his wife's funeral, he remembered his son coming to him, a small, shattered, six-year-old child. In tears, the boy had tugged at his dad's coat. "Dad, I want my mum!" he had sobbed. "Please, I want her!" And his own reply: "Not now, son." Over the next months those cruel words had become a litany.

In time, Nate had ceased coming to him for comfort. His formerly happy child had become cold, withdrawn, remote. And Adrian had been blind to the anger gleaming in his child's eyes, the hurt and anguish smoldering just beneath the surface.

Vickie had asked him to forgive himself for all those failings. How ironic that now that he fully realized the error of his ways, Nate was forever beyond his reach. And redemption was forever denied him.

Chapter Ten

"Is there a Mr. Joe Morgan hereabouts?" Adrian inquired.

At midafternoon the following day, Vickie stood with Adrian inside the dank, smoky interior of the Bayside Tavern in Unity Alley. It had been another frustrating day for the two of them, and the extremely humid, overcast weather had only cast a further pall on their spirits.

First, they'd again stopped by the police precinct house to question Carmichael Keegan, only to be told he was in a meeting and too busy to see them. Then they'd spent several more frustrating hours searching for Joe Morgan, until a tip from an oyster vendor had brought them here to the tavern.

The Bayside was surely the filthiest establishment they'd visited so far, Vickie mused. The hot shadowy bar teemed with sweaty roustabouts smoking, drinking, and gambling. The place reeked of garbage and liquor, and she even spotted several cockroaches and a fat rat skittering about beneath the tables.

Although Adrian had addressed the entire establishment, a large, bald man with a badly scarred cheek turned to them from his poker game at a nearby table. Jerking a thumb toward the far wall, he drawled, "That's Morgan yonder, slobbering on the bar."

"Thank God!" Vickie declared, glancing toward the man.

"Thank you, sir," Adrian added, clutching her arm.

As Adrian passed the man's table with Vickie in tow, the bald man leered at her. "May we buy your lady friend a brew?"

Adrian stiffened his spine. "Thank you, sir, but the lady and I have just concluded luncheon."

The man guffawed and turned to his cronies, lifting an eyebrow and straightening imaginary lapels. "They've just concluded luncheon—well, ain't that highfalutin?" he mocked, and all of the men fell into gales of laughter.

With a quelling glance toward the man, Adrian led Vickie on to the bar, where a gray-haired man in a filthy shirt and soiled trousers was slumped over, head resting on his folded arms, flies buzzing about his drooling face as he snored softly. Vickie sniffed in distaste at his rank smell of booze and sweat.

Adrian gently shook the man. He twitched, then jerked awake, squinting at them through bloodshot eyes. "Yeah? Whatya want?" he slurred.

Vickie struggled not to cringe at the sight of Joe Morgan's face—the puffy features and broken blood vessels giving evidence of longtime abuse of alcohol.

"Are you Joe Morgan?" Adrian inquired.

"Yeah, and what's it to you?" Morgan shot back.

"Mr. Morgan, my name is Adrian Bennett and this is Miss Vickie Cheney. My son, Nate, and Miss Cheney's sister, Cathy, were among the orphans lost in the fire at St. Christopher's."

At once the man's belligerent expression softened. He gasped, his haggard cheek twitching. "Are you two the ones—the kin of them poor little angels trapped up in the attic?"

"Yes, we are," Adrian replied heavily.

"I'm so sorry, mister, miss," Morgan said contritely. "I was there, and I tried to help your young ones."

"Yes, we know that," put in Vickie, throwing Morgan an encouraging smile. "Mother Agatha told us, and we're so grateful that you tried to rescue Cathy, Nate, and the others."

"I tried, but I couldn't help 'em," Joe admitted brokenly. Banging a fist on the bar, he repeated, "I just couldn't."

Adrian cleared his throat. "Mr. Morgan, Mother Agatha told us you saw our children jump from the attic window."

Morgan's expression grew crazed with some remembered trauma; hastily he crossed himself. "Yes, sir, I did."

"And we've been told you never saw them reach the ground," Vickie added tensely.

Morgan shuddered. "Yes, miss, that's true as well. I yelled to the mites to wait for the ladder truck, but they wouldn't listen. They joined hands, jumped, fell through the flames, and . . . and then they was gone. Nothing was there."

"Nothing?" Adrian repeated, flabbergasted. "But that's impossible. They couldn't have just vanished into thin air!"

"Ah, but they did," Morgan related, a haunted look in his eyes. "You may not believe me, but I swear to you both, as God is me witness, I saw them sweet little angels join hands, leap from the window, and then disappear before me very eyes."

Throwing Adrian a look of stark joy, Vickie clutched Morgan's arm. "Do you think the children may still be alive?"

He shivered. "Miss, I dunno know what to think."

Excitedly she pressed, "But what if I told you that Commander Bennett and I have actually seen the children in the Charleston streets?"

Morgan went pale. "Blessed saints! Then me eyes didn't deceive me? The young ones still live?"

Even as Vickie was about to reply, Adrian cut in firmly, "We're not sure, Mr. Morgan. But let's go over your story again, in detail. From the beginning . . ."

While Vickie and Adrian continued questioning Morgan, a man was hunkered down in the garbage-strewn shadows outside the tavern windows, his ear pressed to a rusty screen. Carmichael Keegan wiped sweat from his brow and kicked away a scrawny gray alley cat that tried to skitter by his feet. The scraggly varmint bounded off with a yowl of pain.

Mic Keegan was getting sick and tired of worrying about Bennett and Cheney, weary of trailing them about the city. Twice he'd managed to avoid them at police headquarters, but he knew he'd have to meet with them next time, or else risk their complaining to Captain O'Moody.

He still failed to fathom what they were doing traipsing from one grogshop to the other in this squalid part of town, hunting for the elusive Joe Morgan. Now they'd evidently found Morgan and were speaking with him at the bar. Obviously, they were questioning him about the children, for he had overheard the Cheney broad ranting that the whelps must still be alive.

Where did Morgan figure in the drama? Keegan was determined to find out. He squatted even lower as he observed Cheney and Bennett leaving the bar. He heard the Cheney broad demand, "*Now* do you believe me?" and watched Bennett shake his head and lead her away.

The couple walked out of view down the cluttered, misty lane. Keegan loosened the scratchy, confining collar of his wool jacket and pondered his next move. He needed badly to question this Morgan character, and was tempted to stride inside the tavern and collar him now. But it would be foolish to act in the presence of so many witnesses. Much as he hated crouching here in this reeking hole, he would have to wait until Morgan left the tippling house. Then he and Morgan would have a long, long chat. Mic Keegan flexed his knuckles in sadistic anticipation.

A light drizzle began to fall as Vickie and Adrian neared the center of town. She felt vastly encouraged by their meeting with Joe Morgan, although she knew

Adrian remained almost as skeptical as before. He'd already voiced several misgivings.

On Church Street, they paused by the ruins of St. Christopher's Orphanage and the burnt-out chapel next door. Both gazed starkly at the wreckage, watching several workmen gather up debris and load it onto a flatbed truck.

"There were no workmen around the other times I've walked past," Vickie remarked to Adrian. "I guess they must have collected enough money to start cleaning up the site."

"There's much that can't be rebuilt," Adrian added sadly.

"I agree."

Adrian cleared his throat. "Before the memorial service, I spoke with Father Timothy about helping to endow a memorial statue for Nate, Cathy, and the other orphans lost. They'll be including it when they rebuild, you know."

Ruefully she shook her head. "Nothing has really changed for you, has it, Adrian? Well, I don't care. What Joe Morgan told us gave me new hope."

Adrian sighed. "But what he said also made no sense. Think, Vickie. The children couldn't have jumped, then disappeared. It's impossible."

She bit her lip. "So you think he was just—"

"Hallucinating, or seeing what he desperately wanted to see." Adrian squeezed her hand. "And aren't we doing the same?"

"You mean aren't I?" she countered.

"I'm still afraid you could be deluding yourself."

Tightening her jaw, she gazed at the ruined chapel through the gathering mist. "I just can't give up hope,

Adrian. You have your way of coping. I have mine."

They fell silent, and Vickie fought the burning rush of tears. What if Adrian were right? Then all hope would be gone. But she couldn't live in a world without hope. How could he?

Watching a sparrow land on the charred altar, she murmured, "Isn't it ironic that the altar of the chapel survived? It's badly burned, but still there."

He reached out, gently stroking her cheek. "You may find this odd, my dear, but on the day when I first arrived in Charleston, I came here, saw that altar still bravely standing—and was tempted to go there and pray."

"You were?" she asked, taken aback.

"It was indeed peculiar, considering that I'm not a particularly religious chap. Losing Celeste killed much of my faith, and the loss of my son pretty much decimated the rest."

"Yet still you felt the urge to pray?"

"For Nate's sake. I wanted to pray that the soul of my son might be at rest." He tightly squeezed her hand, and his next words came thick with emotion. "That's the real reason we're seeing them, Vickie. Their souls are not at peace."

Vickie stared at him, deeply moved by his words, equally surprised that he had said them at all, a sharing of his deepest feelings that was rare for him. Then all at once she flinched as she heard the sounds of a child's laughter, a high, exultant sound, coming from a house in the residential block ahead of them. "Cathy!" she cried, tearing off down the street.

Vickie ran desperately in the direction of the sound, ignoring Adrian, who was shouting, racing along behind her. Although she couldn't see Cathy ahead of her, she recognized her familiar voice. She followed the sound past the facade of a two-story Victorian house and into the alleyway flanking it. Then she paused, seeing only parked cars and garbage cans.

"Damn!" she muttered.

Breathing hard, Adrian arrived at her side. "Vickie, what do you think you're doing?"

"Didn't you just hear that laughter?"

"Well, yes, I heard something."

"It was my sister, Cathy."

"How can you be so sure?"

"Do you think I don't know my own sister's voice?"

Adrian drew off his cap and pulled his fingers through his hair. "To be honest, I don't know what to think anymore."

Vickie glanced about, waving an arm in frustration. "It's the same every single time. Why, oh why, do they never linger? Why do they keep running from us? If this is supposed to be some sort of sign, why won't they even speak to us?"

Sadly he replied, "Because they're not real, Vickie."

"I refuse to believe that!" At her wit's end, Vickie stalked off down the alleyway, desperately searching for any clue that might explain what she'd just heard.

Adrian followed her. "What are you looking for now?"

"I don't know—something." All at once, she paused, spotting a shiny coin at her feet. "This." She leaned over, scooping it up.

"What's that? A lost nickel?"

Vickie examined the coin closely, and went wide-eyed. Immediately she knew it wasn't from this century. On one side was emblazoned the words United States of America, along with a large V surrounded by a wreath; on the reverse side was carved a Liberty head surrounded by stars, and a date. "It's a nickel, all right, a brand-new one. But it's from the year 1885!"

"What? Let me see that."

She handed him the coin. "Well?"

Adrian scowled at the coin, holding it up to the light. "Good heavens, you're right. This appears to be an 1885 Liberty head nickel."

All at once, realization dawned on Vickie, washing her with cold chills. "Oh, my God! Now I understand!"

"Understand what?"

She continued in an excited rush. "What if the children are still alive, and they somehow escaped into another time? What if they left us the coin as a sign?"

He appeared mystified. "Have you lost your mind, Vickie?"

"No, not at all. If this were true, it would explain the nickel, and why we invariably see the children wearing old-fashioned clothing."

Yet Adrian shook his head. "Vickie, we mustn't jump to bizarre conclusions simply because you found a shiny old coin."

"Then explain why Joe Morgan saw the children disappear!"

"My dear, he likely just concocted the tale to cover his own guilt for not being able to save them."

She vehemently shook her head. "I disagree. And

I think it's time we bring Joe Morgan's tale to the attention of the authorities."

"But didn't Mother Agatha tell us they had already dismissed it?"

"She also told us Keegan accused the children of thievery."

"Vickie, you're starting to see conspirators behind every tree."

She drew herself up. "Are you going to help me investigate this further or not?"

He nodded wearily. "Very well. Tomorrow we'll go back to the Bayside Tavern bright and early, and try to find Morgan before he's too far gone with grog. We'll take him to the authorities to repeat his tale. And we'll question Keegan regarding why he accused the children of theft."

"Good." She extended her hand. "May I have the coin back?"

Even as he flashed her a contrite smile and handed it back, fat raindrops splattered them both. Adrian glanced at the stormy skies and grimaced. "Oh, damn. Looks like a cloudburst is on the way, and we've no umbrella. Run with me, Vickie?"

With his arm around her, they ran off. Rain was pouring down, drenching them both by the time they reached Meeting Street. Then at the Four Corners of Law, Adrian pulled Vickie beneath the pillared portico of St. Michael's Church. Pressed safely against the front door, they stared at one another, both wet and breathless. Taking in the passionate light in Adrian's eyes, Vickie shivered.

"You look sad, darling," he murmured.

Touched by his tender tone of voice, she blinked

at unexpected tears. "I just feel so confused about everything. The children . . . and you."

"Please, don't be sad."

With a groan, Adrian drew her close. She gazed up at him helplessly; then his mouth captured hers. He kissed her again and again, hard, burning kisses, his wet body pressing hers to the door panel. Vickie felt hot and cold all at once, delirious with desire. When a whimper of longing rose in her throat, he moaned in response, seducing her with his lips and tongue until she felt desire pulsing deep inside her. Then he brushed his masterful lips over her cheek, her throat, drinking in the moisture on her face, and she struggled to catch her breath.

He regarded her ardently. "You know what I want, don't you, Vickie?"

She nodded, swallowing hard.

He pressed his lips to her temple. "Just for a moment, I want the rain in our lives to stop, to see a glimmer of hope in the black clouds of my grief. You can bring me that light, that hope, Vickie."

"Perhaps I can," she admitted. "But I still think things are going too fast. We don't know each other that well. We could end up together for all the wrong reasons."

He pulled away. "Is that the truth?"

"What do you mean?"

He scowled. "I think that's not the issue at all. You won't let yourself be intimate with me because you're obsessed with the frail hope that Cathy may still be alive. You're shutting me out because I refuse to believe the children could have survived the fire. You're punishing me for what I feel."

Stung, she whispered, "Adrian, no, I'm not trying to—"

"Aren't you? Aren't you the one throwing up barriers here?"

"I just don't think that a love affair will solve anything."

He grasped her by the shoulders. "What if I offered to take you inside this church, right this minute, and pledge myself to you as your husband? Would that make any difference to you?"

Reeling, she shook her head. "Why would you even think of marrying me? I'm a stranger whom you barely know—"

"I know you, Vickie," he cut in vehemently, "and you know me. We've shared more than most human beings ever will. I need you. We need each other. And if you still feel we aren't well enough acquainted, then I think loving each other is a pretty good place to begin. Perhaps you're a bit frightened of me—"

"Frightened?" she put in tremulously.

"Of my darker side, the part of me that may never be able to love again. I can't promise that I will." He lifted her hand, slowly, reverently kissing each finger, and spoke in a breaking voice. "But, darling, I swear I shall try to be good to you."

His words tore at her heart. Staring at his impassioned face, Vickie felt very tempted to say yes and give herself to him, especially since he was sharing more of his feelings with her. And how she would love to lose herself in the mindlessness of passion, to blot out the pain, if only for a few blissful hours. Still, in her heart she recognized that they were both merely trying to escape, and that was wrong.

Slowly she shook her head. "Adrian, I feel very drawn to you. But I think you may be right. I don't think I can give myself to you, not until we settle the issue of the children."

He fell quiet, then gave a sigh. "We'll head back, then."

With longing, Adrian eyed Vickie as she walked beside him back toward the rooming house. She appeared vulnerable, shaken by the intimacies they'd just shared. And so very appealing. Her hair hung in damp, sexy ringlets beneath her droopy little hat, her cheeks were beautifully flushed, and her blue silk shirtwaist dress clung to her lovely curves. His arms ached to reach out and hold her again, to reassure her that he would never bring her harm.

He wanted her so badly. But wasn't it more now? Almost unwittingly, he had shared himself with her today. There on the steps of the church, something sacred had passed between them. For the first time in years, a slight flicker of light had penetrated the black clouds of his soul. Vickie's light. Her warmth. Lord knows, he wasn't deserving of the joy she might bring him. The peace of mind. Indeed, it had been so long since he'd felt any emotion resembling happiness or contentment that he grew giddy at the prospect.

He wasn't worthy of her love. Logic argued that he should leave her alone.

Then he gazed at her again, and caught the slight smile hovering on her lips . . . and decided logic be damned.

Chapter Eleven

The following morning, Vickie had dressed and was fixing her hair when she heard a sharp rap at her door, followed by Adrian's frantic voice calling, "Vickie, hurry! Let me in!"

Alarmed, she rushed across the room and flung open the door. Adrian, in his dark blue bathrobe, with flecks of shaving cream still on his chin, tore in and made a beeline for her radio, quickly turning it on and flipping the dial.

Vickie was flabbergasted. "Adrian, what on earth—"

He held up a hand. "Listen, please."

Watching him turn toward her with an expression of alarm on his face, she frowned and listened to the announcer's voice with unfolding horror: "Again, to repeat, this just in. The body of a man identified as

Joe Morgan was found floating in the Charleston harbor this morning. The corpse was spotted by a roustabout and identified by the foreman of a nearby shipyard, who stated that Morgan was a drunkard who had made a nuisance of himself lately by stealing spare parts to sell for scrap metal. There was evidence of injury about the corpse's head, and it's assumed Morgan must have hit his head while prowling about the shipyard at night, and then fell into the Cooper River. Anyone having information on the next of kin of Mr. Morgan is asked to notify the Charleston police."

As Adrian snapped off the radio, Vickie gasped, "My God! How horrible!"

"Indeed," he replied grimly. "We visit with Morgan yesterday, and now he shows up dead."

"And our investigation is pretty much at a dead end as well," she stated in frustration. "Although . . . are you saying you suspect foul play in his death?"

"Frankly, Vickie, I'm pretty much at a loss, although I do find the timing of Morgan's death quite suspicious."

"Me, too."

"I think we should go by police headquarters again—and this time we must demand Keegan see us and provide some answers."

"I agree totally."

Striding back toward the door, Adrian paused in front of her. Taking in her slightly mussed hair, he reached out to straighten the collar of her green silk shirtwaist dress, then smiled sheepishly. "I must apologize for intruding on you."

"Oh, you had good reason." Feeling her body go

hot at his intimate gesture, she touched her collar and
smiled back shyly. Adrian was very close to her now.
He smelled marvelous, of shaving soap and hair po-
made, and staring at his striking face, she could see
the little dark whiskers his razor had missed, and
found this very enticing. The passionate light gleaming in his dark brown eyes made her stomach curl.
Gazing downward at the V of his robe, she caught a
glimpse of a muscled bare chest and crisp dark hair;
peeking lower, she noted his calves were bare and
realized he wore only skivvies beneath his robe, if
that. A treacherous heat began to burn deep inside
her. All at once she was very conscious of the fact
that Adrian was attired only in his bathrobe, and they
were alone in her bedroom.

He evidently recognized her discomfort, for he
smiled slightly. "My dear? Is something wrong? I realize I must seem rash to burst in on you in my bathrobe, but you're staring at me as if you've never seen
a man before."

By now Vickie's cheeks felt scalding hot. Flashing
him a guilty grin, she quipped, "Suffice it to say, I
hadn't expected a proper Brit to sleep without paja-
mas."

Instead of laughing as she would have predicted,
he grew quite solemn, slowly raking his gaze over
her. "My dear, should I linger any longer, you'd soon
discover that where you're concerned, I'm hardly a
proper Brit."

Before she could respond, he leaned over and
caught her lips in a quick, hard kiss, then turned and
strode out. Stunned and thrilled, Vickie wiped shav-

ing cream from her chin, then buried her nose in her hand, savoring his exciting scent.

When Vickie and Adrian arrived at police headquarters, the receptionist once again informed them that Carmichael Keegan was unavailable. When Adrian demanded to see someone else, the woman dashed off for a moment, then quickly returned to usher them inside the office of Keegan's boss, Captain James O'Moody. The tall, graying man with his ruddy complexion and ready smile greeted them both with friendly handshakes, then offered them chairs in front of his desk.

"I'm sorry Lieutenant Keegan is late this morning," he said. "Mildred said he was assisting you folks with a case."

" 'Assisting' may be too kind a word to describe your lieutenant's efforts," Adrian drawled.

O'Moody scowled. "What do you mean, sir? Let me assure you that it's very important to me that all my officers and beat cops give the public their utmost respect and best service."

"Good. Then you'll definitely want to hear our story."

Adrian launched into a long account, telling O'Moody all about the orphanage fire, how he and Vickie were investigating it, how they had glimpsed Nate and Cathy in the Charleston streets, and how Lieutenant Keegan had been rude to them several times when they'd made inquiries. He also mentioned learning that Keegan had accused Nate and Cathy of thievery shortly before the fire. "Now Keegan appears to be avoiding us," Adrian concluded. "At least, the last two times Miss Cheney and I have stopped in, he has been either in a meeting or otherwise unavailable."

"That is odd," O'Moody concurred with a frown. "As is the nun's account of Keegan accusing your children of theft. To be frank, this is the first I've heard of it."

Vickie and Adrian exchanged a meaningful glance, then Adrian added, "On top of that, one of the witnesses Miss Cheney and I were questioning, Joe Morgan, has turned up dead. He's the ex-fireman who saw our children jump from the orphanage window."

O'Moody had been listening with an expression of grave concern. "Ah, yes, I'm aware of Morgan, and how his body was found early today. However, you must know that we think his passing was an accident."

"Just another drunkard falling into the Cooper River?" Adrian inquired. "I must say there have been far too many deaths in this town recently. Our children lost their lives in the orphanage fire, and now the man who tried to go to their aid is dead as well."

O'Moody shifted in his chair. "You also mentioned you think you've seen the children?"

"Yes," answered Vickie. "On a number of occasions we've glimpsed them. All this leads me to believe—although Commander Bennett doesn't agree with me—that the children may still be alive."

O'Moody shuddered and crossed himself. "Miss, like anyone else, I can't claim to understand all the workings of the Almighty. But I assure you there's no way your children could still be alive."

"But don't you find the death of Morgan suspicious?"

O'Moody scratched his jaw. "Quite possibly. You know, it's odd, but there was another death on the day of the orphanage fire. One of our beat cops, Patrick McIntire, was shot earlier on."

Vickie glanced at Adrian in alarm. "Do you think it was connected with the fire?" she asked.

O'Moody hesitated. "Frankly, I think McIntire may have gotten in over his head, then stepped on the wrong toes. I have my own suspicions about the type of activities he might have been involved in. And he and Keegan were very tight."

Vickie gasped. "You mean they were corrupt?"

O'Moody appeared miserably put on the spot. "Miss, I didn't say that. As far as I know, Officer Paddy was a good sort—"

"Officer Paddy!" Vickie cried. "My God, Cathy once mentioned an Officer Paddy in a letter to me!"

O'Moody scowled. "Are you sure of that, ma'am?"

"Yes, she said Officer Paddy gave her and Nate candy money."

"Well, Paddy was quite fond of the lads and lassies," muttered O'Moody, appearing perplexed.

Adrian spoke sternly. "Captain O'Moody, I do believe we've uncovered some very serious suspicions here that deserve further investigation."

"You may be right, sir."

Vickie was about to comment further when all at once the door to the office burst open and an indignant male voice demanded, "What is going on here?"

Vickie and Adrian turned to view Carmichael Keegan looming in the doorway, fists clenched at his sides, features ugly. At once O'Moody rose from his chair. "Lieutenant, is this any way to greet your superior, not to mention members of the public whom we serve?"

At the sharp rebuke, Keegan flinched and quickly muttered, "Sorry, Captain." His shifty gaze flicked to Adrian and Vickie. "But I been helping these folks, and they should have come to me. They got no business troubling you with their petty complaints."

Adrian sprang out of his chair. "Petty complaints? My son is dead, as is Miss Cheney's sister!"

Keegan was silent, glaring at Adrian.

O'Moody strode angrily around his desk. "Keegan, I can't believe I just heard you address a citizen in such a disrespectful manner! You will apologize at once."

Grudgingly Keegan turned to Adrian. "Sorry, sir."

O'Moody contritely addressed Adrian and Vickie. "I beg your pardon, folks, but I think it's best that Lieutenant Keegan and I continue discussing this matter in private. I assure you that all of your concerns will be given our utmost attention."

"Thank you, sir," replied Adrian. Helping Vickie out of her chair, he flashed Keegan a contemptuous look and led her away.

As soon as the couple was out of the room, O'Moody advanced angrily on Keegan. "Lieutenant, you have some explaining to do."

Mic Keegan felt panic seizing him. He realized he had let his temper get the better of him, and now he was in a tight spot. "Ah, Captain, you can't be taking them two crackpots serious. Why, they're thinking they've seen the dead walking around Charleston, pretty as you please."

O'Moody charged on the other man, punching him in the chest with a forefinger. "Keegan, you've always been a marginal cop at best. In fact, if I could prove what I suspect about you . . . well, I would have drummed you off the force long ago. Know this: You make one more stupid wisecrack about Commander Bennett or Miss Cheney, or insult them again to their faces, and I'll rip off your lieutenant's stripes myself."

"Yes, sir," Keegan gritted out, despising the other man.

"Now you're going to answer my questions, Keegan. Why did you accuse Nate Bennett and Cathy Cheney of thievery? And what do you know about the deaths of Joe Morgan and Paddy McIntire?"

The panic creeping up on Mic Keegan surged into sick fear. O'Moody clearly suspected the worst, and his game might well be up. One thing was for sure: If he survived this interrogation, he was going to kill Bennett and Cheney!

"Keegan, I'm waiting!" bellowed O'Moody.

"Yes, sir." As smoothly as possible, Keegan began spilling out his lies. . . .

Vickie was walking with Adrian on Meeting Street, the two of them heading back toward the boarding-house. "Well, at least now maybe our concerns will get the proper attention," he stated.

"Yes, I think the investigation is in good hands with Captain O'Moody. But isn't it curious that the policeman Cathy knew was killed on the very day of the orphanage fire?"

"I'd call it suspicious more than curious."

"I agree."

Down the street, Carmichael Keegan had picked up the couple's trail again. The confrontation with O'Moody had been tense, even though Keegan had lied like a master. He'd claimed to know nothing about the deaths of Paddy McIntire and Joe Morgan. He'd insisted a citizen had steered him wrong about the children being thieves.

Yet still he doubted O'Moody really believed him. O'Moody remained suspicious about Paddy McIntire's death and that of Joe Morgan. He'd vowed to start up a special investigation. And Keegan had been forced to endure a severe dressing down.

Keegan was mad enough to murder Cheney and Bennett. But he couldn't risk it now. Too many witnesses here on Meeting Street.

Damn, he was thwarted at every turn!

Chapter Twelve

Near the rooming house Vickie flashed Adrian a brave smile. "Why don't we go searching a bit longer? Between us we've seen the children several times now, and we might find them again."

Slowly he shook his head. "My dear, now I think you're grasping at straws. Perhaps we've seen their ghosts revisiting old haunts, but the reason we can't actually find the children is because they're gone."

She was silent, frowning.

As they reached the boardinghouse, Adrian cleared his throat. "I need to go inside and check the post. Do you wish to come with me?"

Vickie proudly lifted her chin. "No. I'm going searching for the children again."

His jaw tightened. "Suit yourself."

His back ramrod straight, he turned and entered the

boardinghouse. Angrily, she strode away.

Once again, Vickie roamed the streets, without seeing any sign of the children. Was she unable to see the children now because her own hope was waning? Or was Adrian right in thinking that the children were truly gone?

The sun had sunk low in the sky by the time she returned to the boardinghouse. Outside her room, she was arrested by the sight of a small white box on the floor, labeled Church Street Florist. She picked up the box and opened it to the tantalizing scent of roses; inside was a lovely peach-colored corsage. Gasping in delight, she picked up the card, which read: "Vickie, I'm sorry. Will you meet me at seven at the diner? Adrian."

Vickie smiled, deeply touched by his gift as well as his obvious attempt to meet her halfway. Slipping inside her room with the box, she glanced at her watch and realized she had less than an hour to get ready. She quickly bathed, applied her makeup, and pulled back her hair, letting it fall in ringlets at her nape. Then she donned one of her favorite dresses, a peach-colored silk. Pinning on her corsage in front of the mirror, she observed the glow on her cheeks and realized she felt as giddy as a schoolgirl with her first beau.

Fifteen minutes later she slipped inside the diner to the sounds of "It's Only a Paper Moon" spilling out of the jukebox. Glancing around, she caught sight of Adrian rising to his feet at the second booth. Her heart pounded. He looked so debonair, for once out of uniform in a brown tweed sports jacket with cream-colored ascot and dark trousers. With a smile, he strode quickly to her side. Looking her over with an appreciative gleam in his eyes, he caught her hand, raised it, and kissed its back. A thrill shot through her at the touch of his lips, the scent of his aftershave.

He spoke huskily. "Thank you for coming, Vickie. You look beautiful."

"You look quite dashing yourself," she managed. "This is the first time I've seen you out of uniform. And thanks for the corsage."

"It was the least I could do. I feel I was a bit hard on you earlier." He gestured toward the booth. "Shall we sit down? I've taken the liberty of ordering us today's special, lamb with currant sauce."

She raised an eyebrow. "Confident, aren't you?"

He offered her his arm and escorted her to the booth. "Of your taste in food, or that you would dine with me tonight?"

"Of both," she answered.

He chuckled and helped her into her seat.

Their dinner was marvelous. Vickie sensed they both needed a respite from their overwhelming anxiety about the children. Adrian was charming and kept the conversation light. Each of them spoke of the happier times of youth. For a few glorious moments it was as if the tragedy of war had never touched either of them.

The lamb was also excellent, and Vickie was feeling almost content as they left the restaurant together. She didn't want her moments with Adrian to end, and when he suggested they walk along the Battery, she eagerly agreed.

The evening was balmy, a striking full moon hanging in the misty skies overhead and a salty breeze floating in off the bay. Vickie strolled along the ancient walkway with Adrian, their bodies gliding through pools of soft light cast by street lamps. To their right stretched the moonlit water, to their left, past White Point Gardens, rose majestic old colonial homes. The walkway was nearly deserted, with only a sailor passing with his girl. When Adrian slipped his arm about Vickie's waist, she didn't protest.

"It's a beautiful night," she murmured.

Adrian pressed his lips to her hair, causing shivers. "Indeed it is. A perfect night. A perfect woman by my side."

She laughed. "Now you're flattering me."

"I'm not. In fact, I was thinking that the only thing that could make this evening more perfect would be if you would dance with me."

She eyed him quizzically, touched but slightly perplexed. "Here? On the Battery? Without music?"

He nudged her to a stop. His eyes gleamed softly. "But there is music, love. You only have to listen for it."

She paused and listened; then joy lit her face as she did hear it, the poignant strains of "Smoke Gets in Your Eyes" playing on a radio in one of the houses across from them. Tenderness engulfed her. "Oh, yes, I hear it. I adore that song."

He bowed from the waist. "Dance with me, Vickie?"

"Oh, yes."

There, beneath the warm glow of the street lamp, the two danced a slow fox-trot cheek to cheek. Vickie couldn't remember when she'd felt happier. The sound of the music enchanted her, while the gentle sea breeze caressed her face. Adrian's warm body and glorious scent filled her senses. If only they could stay this way forever, clasped together, removed from all their pain.

When the dance ended, he pulled back and caressed her cheek. "That was lovely. Thank you."

"Thank you."

"This afternoon," he began awkwardly, "did you have any luck trying to find the children again?"

Taken aback, Vickie hesitated a moment. "No."

He walked off a pace or two and stared abstractedly out at the water. "Your questions, regarding why I can't believe the children are real, deserve an answer."

Pleased that he was offering to share his feelings, she answered, "Yes, I suppose they do. If you're ready."

He turned back to her and spoke fervently. "I am, darling. I want us to be close. No more secrets."

"Oh, Adrian." She touched his hand. "Okay, then."

His expression grew wistful. "You see, years ago, after I lost my dear wife, I used to see her ghost."

"Oh, my heavens!" Vickie gasped. "You really did?"

He nodded, his expression troubled. "All of the visions were quite fleeting, like our glimpses of the children, and I was never able to make . . . well, what I would call actual contact. The first time I saw her was when I was walking through the apple orchard where we used to stroll together. She floated out from behind a tree, stared at me, then slipped away. Another time I passed her in the hallway of our manor house—that image was so ethereal, I almost wondered if I were hallucinating. On a third occasion, I just heard her voice as I was drifting off to sleep."

Vickie was filled with awe. "How did you feel when this happened?"

"Sad," he answered tightly. "Unbearably sad. I saw the same sadness in her visage, and felt it to my soul. I finally discussed the sightings with the vicar of my village church, and he explained that Celeste's spirit was likely lingering near earth until she was certain Nate and I were all right. After a time . . . well, the visions stopped."

"Oh, Adrian, I had no idea," she whispered sympathetically. "No wonder you feel the same way about Nate and Cathy now."

He strode off a couple of paces, his fingers tightly clutching the railing. "But you are also right about something, Vickie. To be brutally honest, I can't believe the children are alive because I *have* lost that kind of hope in my life. If I believed Cathy and Nate were truly with us, and then it turned out I was wrong, I think it would destroy me."

Heart aching for him, she touched his shoulder. "I think I'm beginning to understand. It's not that you don't care. You care too much."

He gazed at her in anguish.

"But you must explain something to me," she went on gently. "If Nate and Cathy are indeed spirits, then why are they lingering here?"

"Because we haven't let them go," he replied passionately. "Because their souls are not at peace. They're earthbound, Vickie. They're waiting for us to release them, to let their spirits soar to heaven."

By now, Vickie was blinking at tears. Turning

away, she said brokenly, "I can't. I can't give Cathy up."

With a groan, Adrian pulled her into his arms and pressed his lips to her hair. "My darling, I'm not asking you to forget Cathy, nor shall I ever forget Nate. I'm saying we need to let them go. Vickie, I don't claim to understand everything. But we've tried it your way, and now I think it's time to try it my way for a change."

Shuddering, she turned. "What do you want me to do?"

He clutched her face in his hands. "I want you to lie with me tonight. Then tomorrow, I want us both to go back to the orphanage, to the chapel. I want us to kneel in the burned-out embers and say a prayer for the souls of Cathy and Nate, so they may be at peace. And then I want us to marry."

Both shocked and touched, Vickie pulled away. "How can you say you want to marry me, when you admit you've lost all hope in your life?"

Ardently he replied, "I may have lost hope, but knowing you has made me want to find it again. I know that as long as you cling to the belief that Nate and Cathy are still alive, you won't ever let yourself need me, and there won't be any peace in this world for either of us. Don't you know that I'm every bit as shattered by this as you are? But it's time for us to rebuild. Together, our souls can find a way out of the darkness."

Gazing at Adrian through her tears, Vickie realized he was right. He had tried everything her way, and they were still no closer to finding Cathy and Nate. It *was* his turn now.

He held out his arms and regarded her with his heart in his eyes. "Come to me, darling. Please, come to me."

Even though her own heart was breaking, Vickie couldn't resist any longer. With a sob she fell into his arms. He kissed her, wildly, hungrily, until the only reality left in her universe became *him*.

They headed back for the boardinghouse, stopping every few feet to kiss in the shadows. Inside on the second floor, when she started toward her room, he caught her arm and said firmly, "No, darling. My room."

His words washed her with chills of desire.

He pulled her inside and switched on the light. She blinked at the brightness, catching sight of his elegant four-poster. Her cheeks went hot. "That's . . . um, quite a lovely bed."

Across the room, Adrian had already removed his scarf and jacket, and was unbuttoning his fine linen shirt. Watching him step closer, she swallowed hard, catching a provocative glimpse of his dark chest hair.

At her side, he patted the mattress. "Yes, very soft. Our bed, love."

She felt herself going warm all over as he stared at her with tenderness and desire.

He reached out, pulling the pins from her hair. She panted softly, shuddering as he removed her corsage, took a whiff of the roses, then laid it on the bedside table. His gaze was intense as he began unbuttoning her dress. Startled by his boldness, she flinched slightly.

His fingers paused, and his eyes, filled with concern, shot up to hers. "Is something wrong?"

"No," she murmured. "It's just that—if you're expecting a woman of great experience, Adrian, I'm afraid you're going to be disappointed. I've only had one lover. Bill was rather shy—"

"I won't be, I'm afraid," he confessed with a guilty smile, leaning over and kissing her nose. "You're so beautiful and I want you so much. But I do want you to know this is not something I enter into recklessly. I haven't been with a woman for a long, long time— not since I lost my Celeste." He raked his gaze over her and drew a shuddering breath. "I just hope I won't be too passionate."

Tears came to her eyes again at the sweetness of his words, and her fears dissolved. How could she resist a man who wanted her so much? She thrust herself into his arms, burying her face against his warm throat. "Please, be passionate."

"Oh, darling."

He claimed her lips in a lingering kiss. Then he left her briefly, turning off the light. When he returned to her side, his features were stark with desire in the moonlight. He quickly finished unbuttoning and removing her dress, and she stepped out of her shoes. He drew her close and kissed her, while his hands raised her slip high above her waist. She felt warmth seeping deep into her belly as he gently removed her garter belt and panties. She assisted him by stepping out of her underclothes and hose, even as his hands raised her slip higher and undid her brassiere. Within seconds she stood naked before him, shivering even in the warmth of the room.

"My heaven, I can't believe you're mine," he murmured, reaching out to caress her smooth shoulder. "I never expected that I would be so blessed again."

"Nor I."

"Come here, darling."

Pulse pounding in her ears, Vickie stepped into his embrace and curled her arms around his neck. With a grunt of pleasure, he pulled open his shirt and rubbed the coarse warmth of his chest against her bare breasts. Vickie reeled and clutched him tightly. The sensation of aroused flesh touching flesh was wondrous, ecstatic. She stretched upward, eagerly kissing him. When she gently pushed her tongue inside his mouth, he made a ragged sound and ran his hands over her smooth spine and soft bottom. The sensation was so arousing that she pulled away to catch her breath.

Gently he pushed her down on the bed. Throwing off his shirt, he joined her there, pressing his lips to her breast. The rapture of his intimate kiss was shattering. Vickie called his name and raked her fingers through his hair. When he sucked on her nipple, she sobbed at the torment. Deep inside, she hurt from wanting him, ached for the intimacy that would blot out all their pain. He suckled both breasts, then slid upward, his lips burning over her throat before his mouth took hers in a devouring kiss.

The ecstasy was too much for Vickie. His masculine weight felt so marvelous against her eager body and soft, aching breasts. And she could feel his hardness pressing against her. Poignantly, she remembered how he'd said he wanted no more secrets. She wanted *nothing* between them now. She wanted him inside her, making them one, driving away all his demons, and perhaps a few of her own. When his mouth moved to kiss her cheek, she whispered an encouragement at his ear.

He uttered an agonized groan and lovingly breathed her name; then she got her wish. His deep, confident thrust left her gasping. Then his hands slid beneath her hips, lifting her to take all of him, and she passionately met him. He was vibrant and warm, filling her completely with his love. Never had she felt anything as wondrous as the tension and heat of their joining.

"Darling, darling," he murmured.

She whimpered and clung to him as he began moving with deep, consuming strokes. Her fingernails dug into his spine, only increasing his ardor. She cried out as the shattering sensations propelled them both higher; then his mouth took hers. When they climaxed together, she felt his tears mingling with her own, and for the first time in years her soul felt only joy.

Midnight found Adrian standing at the window in his robe, staring out at deserted Meeting Street. He felt deeply shaken, his emotions raw and close to the surface. He was thinking of the splendid woman who had just brought him such bliss—and remembering his dear lost son, pondering the task he had set for himself and Vickie at the ruined chapel tomorrow. Even though the lad was gone, he felt compelled to speak with him now.

"Son, it may seem strange that I would have a conversation with you tonight, when logic argues you are beyond reach. I spoke with you so little while you were here. Oh, I busied myself with matters of the estate, telling myself you were better cared for in those tender years by your mother. There would always be time when you were older, time to teach you to ride and hunt, to make a proper British gentleman out of you . . ." Hoarsely he continued, "To love you as a father should. Then before I knew it, I lost your mother, the war came, and there was no time left."

He turned to stare at Vickie on his bed. "That dear woman has given me a devotion and faith I truly don't deserve. I may never be able to love again, son, but she has made me remember the glory that love is. She has made me remember being alive—morning and rain, the smell of roses. The laughter of a child now gone. She thinks I'm deserting you now, deserting your friend Cathy, too, but she's wrong. There's so little I gave you while you were here, but there's something I can give you both now that you're gone. I can at least try. I can give you peace."

Adrian's voice broke on these last words. He stood there immersed in emotion until time grew meaningless. Later he felt a soft hand on his shoulder and turned. Vickie was there, gloriously nude in the moonlight. Had she heard? He wasn't sure, but her eyes glowed with compassion. Wordlessly she untied his robe and slid it off his shoulders. Then she stepped eagerly into his naked embrace. He clutched her close to his heart and shuddered with joy.

Chapter Thirteen

Morning found Vickie standing with Adrian in the ruined orphanage chapel, her hand tightly clasped in his. Both were in a solemn, reverent mood, as evidenced by their clothing: Vickie wore the same black silk dress and hat she'd worn to the memorial service; Adrian his blue uniform and cap.

Birds sang sweetly in the nearby trees, oblivious to the wrenching drama about to be enacted, and the skies were clear overhead. The honeyed scents of nectar and dew vied with the darker smells of ruin and decay. Vickie noted that the workmen hadn't arrived for the day, and the cleaning up they'd done so far had been at the orphanage site, not here. The chapel remained precisely as she'd seen it that first day, a "bare ruined choir." Soft morning light illuminated the charred altar and kneeling bench, as well as remnants of a few pews.

Her throat ached. She couldn't believe they were about to say a prayer that might well separate her from Cathy forever. But she felt so close to Adrian now, especially following the intimacies they'd shared the night before, and she knew that wherever they went from here, it must be together.

Nonetheless she turned to quietly beseech him with her eyes. "Are you sure we should be doing this?"

He smiled and pulled her into his arms, gazing at her tenderly. "Do you have any idea how beautiful you look right now?"

Tempted to smile, she murmured, "I must look sad."

"You look absolutely lovely. And do you have any idea of the joy you brought me last night?" He leaned over, kissing her cheek. "You made me feel reborn, love."

His words swept her with tenderness. "It meant the world to me, as well."

He drew back slightly and gazed into her eyes. "We can do this, love. Together, we can do it."

She bit her lip. "So you're really sure we should?"

"Yes, darling. We must say our prayer, that the souls of Cathy and Nate may be at rest. It's the only way to free their earthbound spirits."

"But what if we're wrong?" she asked in anguish. "What if the children are real? Or, what if they've really escaped to another time, and—"

He pressed his fingers to her mouth. "Darling,

177

they're gone. It is their souls that are not at rest. However, even if you are right and the children are real, then our prayer will do them no harm. Why are you so afraid, Vickie?"

She almost broke down then, helplessly clenching her fists at her sides. "Because it's giving up . . . it's giving up Cathy."

He squeezed her hand and implored, "Please, darling, trust me. I know we're doing the right thing."

"Adrian—"

He leaned over and gently, soulfully kissed her. "We're doing the right thing," he reiterated.

"Very well," she conceded at last.

The two walked up to the altar together. Adrian pulled a thin blue scarf from his breast pocket and laid it down flat on the charred kneeling bench. They knelt close together, and Vickie felt relieved when the bench took their weight, though it did creak a bit. When Adrian offered her his hand, she thought her heart would burst with sorrow. She joined hands with him, closed her eyes, and began her silent prayer. A strange warmth seeped through her then, almost as if somewhere in the ruins, the embers of the fire still glowed. Swallowing back tears, she prayed that the spirits of Cathy and Nate might be at rest. She sank deeper into meditation, repeating her silent litany until she felt herself slipping away. . . .

Adrian, too, was praying, beseeching the Almighty that the souls of his son and Cathy might be at peace, praying that the woman who knelt beside him might honor him with her hand and her heart, that they might go forward from this sacred place, transcend their grief, and find true peace and happiness together.

He felt oddly warmed, as if somewhere a fire still burned, and he was convinced in that moment that he and Vickie were doing the right thing. He felt himself gliding deeper into prayer, drifting away. Then stranger still, he felt the ground gently begin to shift and vibrate beneath his knees.

Vickie, too, felt the odd sensation, as if the earth were moving and trembling beneath her, and wondered what was going on. Was this a reply from the Almighty Himself? Were they truly connecting with the spirit world in a way they'd never anticipated? She sank more profoundly into her supplications, praying that God's will be done, while feeling the primal quivers to her soul. . . .

At the back of the ruined chapel stood Carmichael Keegan. He had followed Cheney and Bennett from the boardinghouse, and now he observed them praying—praying there among the ashes. What a couple of fools! Were they hoping for some kind of miracle, that the children they claimed they had spotted would magically rise from the dead?

Well, there was no more magic left for those two dimwits, for they had reached the end of the line. Mic touched the butt of his service revolver at his waist, then furtively glanced around. It was still quite early, and no one seemed to be stirring in the houses nearby. But he couldn't risk bumping off Bennett and Cheney here. No, someone might witness his crime from a window. Instead, he would pretend to arrest them for trespassing, take them to a nearby alleyway . . . and complete his dirty work there. He rubbed his hands together in vengeful pleasure at the thought.

He started toward them, only to pause, flabbergasted, as the ground began to shift beneath his feet. What in God's name was this, an earthquake? Before he could react, the shudders intensified, and he lost his balance and tumbled to his knees. Groaning in pain, he lunged and rolled about. . . .

At the altar, Vickie felt the shaking escalate. Her eyes flew open and she caught Adrian staring back, looking equally alarmed. Nearby the trees were quaking, the birds screeching and flying off. "What is going on?"

"I don't know, darling," he whispered.

She closed her eyes again and felt him squeezing her hand. The rumbles grew fiercer, and now she could hear the heave and groan of the charred boards and cracking foundation. Even as she was about to panic, all at once, everything went still. . . .

For a long moment neither of them dared to move or open their eyes. Then Vickie blinked as if coming out of a trance, and glanced around. "My God, Adrian, what has happened now?"

Both of them gazed about, stupefied. They were still in a chapel, but it was no longer the same chapel. Vickie caught sight of pristine stained-glass windows, wooden pews, soft, radiant light.

What on earth had happened to them? And what chapel was this? Not even an ash hung in the hallowed air. All traces of the fire were gone!

Part Two

Charleston, South Carolina
1886

Chapter Fourteen

Vickie blinked in disbelief. Where before there had been only ashes and debris, there now stood a lovely small chapel with vivid stained-glass windows picturing biblical scenes, a magnificent altar with brass candelabra, and a high carved pulpit, framed by a breathtaking ivory and gold-leaf shrine with a large crucifix at its center.

Even as Vickie's mind struggled to absorb and accept all these details, she realized her knees were now resting on something soft. She glanced down to see that she and Adrian knelt on a long cushion upholstered in dark red velvet.

Then she glanced up and her eyes met his. She saw in his dark gaze all the amazement and confusion she felt.

"Adrian—where are we?" she managed.

"My dear, I have no idea," he answered in a shocked voice. "One minute we were praying amid the ashes, then I felt the ground begin to shift—"

"So did I!" she cut in excitedly. "It was like an earthquake."

"—and now we find ourselves here," he finished, glancing about. "Only, where is here? And what in God's name has happened to us?"

"Well," she answered, "it looks as if the chapel has been restored. Either that, or it's a different chapel altogether."

"In either case, how is that possible?"

"I don't know!" she cried. "Perhaps we're dreaming."

"Or we've lost our minds. I never thought *this* would be the answer to my prayer."

"Nor I."

Expression troubled, he stood and offered her his hand. "I think we'd best get the lay of the land here, find out where we really are."

Fingers trembling on his, she accepted his assistance and rose to her feet. "I agree."

They proceeded down the aisle and exited the small church. Warm air wafted over Vickie, scented heavily of roses, jasmine, and gardenias—familiar Charleston summer aromas that partially reassured her. The first thing she spotted was an old, mule-drawn work wagon, laden with cotton bales, being driven down the street by a black man in a straw hat and overalls. That jarred her only slightly, since such sights were not unheard of in Charleston.

But the gentleman in old-time frock coat and top hat galloping his large bay horse past the wagon made her mouth drop open. "My heaven, Adrian, did you see that?"

"Yes," he muttered.

Then Vickie noticed three unfamiliar two-storey cottages across the street from them. All were high-Victorian in style, done in striking color schemes of beige and rust, mauve and teal, yellow and blue. Then her gaze shifted to the lot adjacent to them, and she almost fainted. St. Christopher's Orphanage, in all its Greek Revival glory, loomed there proudly, intact, its fluted columns rising three stories to the high-peaked roof with dormer windows. Off to one side of the house, a vibrant weeping willow draped its swath of splendid green branches over a gleaming fish pond.

She grasped Adrian's arm and spoke in a dazed whisper. "My God, do you see what I see?"

"Indeed—a large colonial house where the orphanage ruins used to be."

"It's not a large colonial house," she corrected him excitedly. "It's St. Christopher's Orphanage."

"You must be jesting."

But she grabbed his hand and pulled him down the chapel steps with her. "Come along, I'll show you."

Puzzled, he fell into step with her. "How can you be sure it's the orphanage? Have you seen it before?"

"No, but when my father died, our minister brought Cathy here to Charleston, since there was no suitable facility for her in Georgetown. He managed to get her a place at St. Christopher's, then sent me a picture of it, so I'd know she was living in a respectable establishment."

"I see."

As they reached the property, Adrian opened the

iron gate and gestured for Vickie to precede him inside. A few steps down the walkway, she stopped and pointed at a sign just feet away. "Look!"

He paused and read the sign aloud. "St. Christopher's Orphanage. Established 1857." He turned to her in awe. "I'll be deuced. How can this be? Moments ago, the chapel was gone, as well as the orphanage. Now they've both been resurrected!"

"Indeed," Vickie murmured. Glancing toward the next property down the street, she watched an old woman in a floor-length yellow muslin dress come out to sweep the porch of a quaint cottage. "And both buildings are on a block that looks nothing like the one where we were before. None of these houses looks familiar."

"But that's impossible, isn't it?"

Vickie thought fiercely, then snapped her fingers. "Perhaps a miracle has occurred, and we've been sent back . . . back to a time before the children were harmed."

He shook his head in consternation. "Do you have any idea how absurd that sounds?"

She waved a hand. "Then explain this!"

He groaned and took her arm. "Unfortunately, I cannot. But I think we should speak with the person in charge here posthaste."

"I agree."

They hurried up the walkway together and climbed the side steps to the pillared front piazza, complete with its ladder-back rockers and hanging baskets spilling out luxuriant ferns. Adrian rapped on the massive front door with its curtained oval glass panel. A moment later the portal swung open and a stout, stern-featured woman in a nun's habit appeared before them. She glanced irritably at Adrian, then went wide-eyed at the sight of Vickie's black silk dress with its below-the-knee hem. "May I help you folks?"

"Is this St. Christopher's Orphanage?" Vickie asked.

"Yes, it is."

"Is Mother Agatha here?"

The nun grimaced in perplexity. "There's no sister here by the name of Agatha."

"B-but she's the headmistress of this orphanage!" Vickie declared.

The woman shook her head. "Young woman, you are making no sense. I am Mother Margaret and I assure you *I* am the headmistress of this orphanage."

"You?" Vickie repeated.

Before Vickie could comment further, Adrian addressed the woman. "Mother Margaret, you must help us. I am Commander Adrian Bennett, and this is Miss Cheney. My son and Miss Cheney's sister were both sent to your establishment to live during the war, and now Miss Cheney and I have come to Charleston to retrieve the children. So you must tell us: Are Nate Bennett and Cathy Cheney still residing here?"

Now the woman appeared mystified. "Sir, I have no idea what you're talking about, and the war has been over for more than twenty years."

"Twenty years?" Adrian repeated in bewilderment.

"Furthermore, there are no orphans residing here by those names. Perhaps you have mistaken us for some other institution."

"On the contrary, we know our children were sent here," Adrian assured her.

"Well, I'm sorry, I know nothing about them."

"May we come in, have a look for ourselves?" Vickie pressed.

"Certainly not," the nun responded stoutly. "It is nap time, and the children are resting." Relenting slightly, she added, "However, if you folks are determined to see our facility, visiting hours are daily, at 10 A.M."

Sighing in frustration, Adrian said, "Thank you, madam."

He was escorting Vickie away when the nun called, "Just a moment, please."

At the edge of the piazza Vickie and Adrian turned back to Mother Margaret. "Yes?" she asked.

The nun leveled a disapproving scowl on Vickie. "I'll have you know, miss, that Charleston is a decent, God-fearing community, and garb such as you have chosen will not be tolerated."

"I beg your pardon?" Vickie gasped, glancing down at her dress.

Ignoring Vickie, the woman turned to Adrian. "As for you, sir, that is a rather strange uniform, I must say. Are you a policeman?"

"No, I'm a pilot."

The nun harrumphed. "Well, I've never seen a riverboat pilot in such ridiculous attire, either. Blue, no less. One would think you might have more respect for the feelings of this community than to wear that color."

Even as Adrian was opening his mouth to respond, the nun slammed the door.

Perplexed, Vickie turned to Adrian. "What was she

talking about?" She glanced down at herself. "Why, my dress is perfectly respectable."

Adrian removed his cap and ran his fingers through his hair. "A *riverboat* pilot?" he repeated in consternation. "What could she have meant by that?"

"What on earth is going on here?"

Adrian grimly shook his head. "I have no idea, my dear. But we're going to find out."

Next door at the chapel, Carmichael Keegan awakened with a groan, finding himself lying on a cold stone floor. Startled, he jerked upward, only to hit his head on a solid wooden object. He moaned, rubbed his head and blinked, recognizing a polished oak pew stretching over him. A pew? What the hell?

With a grunt of pain, he managed to heave himself to his feet. Wobbling, he glanced around in stupefaction. Seconds ago, he'd been standing in the pile of rubble that was once the chapel, about to go collar and kill Bennett and Cheney. And now . . . Cheney and Bennett were gone, and he'd been transported to the chapel *before* the fire. Yes, it was definitely the same orphanage chapel. At one time his wife Gladys had done charity work for St. Christopher's, and she'd dragged him here to the chapel a few times before she'd kicked the bucket.

Keegan began to tremble, his stomach roiling in disbelief. The *same* damn chapel! How could this be? Had he lost his mind? Although not an overly religious man, Mic did believe in hell and retribution. Was this his hell? Had the Almighty seen fit to send him back to a time before his foul deed had been done, in order to torment him, to drive him mad with guilt?

He must find out what was going on, before he completely lost his wits! He rushed down the aisle of the chapel, went through the doors, and burst into the bright sunshine. At the bottom of the steps he stopped in his tracks, watching an outlandish couple stride past on the flagstone walkway. The man wore an old-fashioned, striped brown suit and bowler hat, and carried an ebony walking stick. The woman was attired in an elaborate, floor-length blue suit with a huge bustle, and a large blue hat heaped with silk flowers.

The man, with his old, steel-rimmed spectacles and muttonchop whiskers, stared at Keegan in puzzlement for a moment, then murmured, "Good afternoon, officer."

Keegan made no comment. He gaped about at the unfamiliar landscape, then froze as he spotted the orphanage next door. The *orphanage* was also still here? He could hardly believe it was the same place. The trees were smaller, and the building itself appeared so much newer than it had when he'd set the fire.

Keegan began to tremble in earnest. But before he could try to gather his thoughts, the chug of a small steam engine yanked his attention back to the street. Amazed, he watched a man glide past on a high-wheeler steam velocipede; the gent wore an absurd white sack coat; green-and-white plaid trousers, and a green-banded white straw hat that he tipped at Keegan.

Feeling weak-kneed, Carmichael Keegan crossed himself, then fell back a step and collapsed onto the steps of the chapel. After a moment of fierce trembling, he turned to the orphanage next door. Mary, Joseph, and Jesus! What if the brats were still there—somehow still miraculously alive, and ready to seal his fate?

Hurriedly he walked over to the property, rushed up to the front door, and knocked. A moment later, a very irritated-looking nun flung open the panel. "Yes?"

"Are Nate Bennett and Cathy Cheney here?" he demanded.

The nun gave a cry of outrage. "What ails you people? I already told the others—the children are not here!"

She slammed the door in his face.

"What others?" Keegan muttered, going back down the steps.

"Oh, my God!" Vickie exclaimed.

She and Adrian had now emerged on Meeting Street, and the panorama that greeted them astounded her. The street was the same, yet so very different. While Vickie recognized familiar landmarks such as St. Michael's and the Hibernian Hall, so many other homes and businesses were vastly different, sporting the shutters, Palladian windows, and railed verandas of an earlier age. Telegraph wires were strung along the thoroughfare on rickety-looking poles. The paved streets and ever-present buses were gone, replaced by granite pavers and trolley tracks.

And there were no automobiles! Vickie spotted an elegant black carriage pulled by a pair of matched grays, with a young couple in historical costume inside, as well as a man riding a high-wheeler bicycle, and another gentlemen on horseback. And the people! She saw businessmen in fussy striped suits that appeared at least six decades old, women wearing ridiculous floor-length gowns with high bustles, and ludicrous large hats heaped with flowers, feathers, or fruit. She also spotted a bearded old gentleman in what appeared to be a Civil War costume reading a newspaper on a bench outside a nearby haberdashery. Spotting the two of them standing on the walkway, he frowned in fierce disapproval before returning his attention to his paper.

Vickie looked at Adrian, but he only shook his head. Before she could comment to him, he caught her arm and pulled her aside under an awning so a small troupe of elderly women could pass.

The three dowagers, in elaborate silk gowns of black and tan and lavender, and small, veiled hats, marched past, each of them giving Vickie the evil eye. The last one paused to glower at her and tap her walking stick in a clear gesture of disapproval.

"Have you no shame, you Jezebel?" she scolded.

Vickie was dumbstruck. Then another of the ladies caught the arm of the one who had spoken. "Come along, Clara. Don't waste your time dealing with such riffraff. 'Tis beneath you."

As the women trooped on with chins thrust high, Vickie turned back to Adrian in near panic. "Riffraff? Jezebel? Adrian, what has happened? Who are all these strangely dressed people, and why are they looking at us—especially at me—with such disapproval?"

"I'm at a total loss," he answered.

Vickie glanced about her, struggling for answers; then she saw that the old gentleman had left his bench and discarded his newspaper underneath. "Adrian, look!" she exclaimed, pointing.

He rushed over and retrieved the newspaper. She arrived at his side only to see all color drain from his face. "What is it?"

Stunned, he handed her the newspaper. "The date, my dear."

Vickie stared at the front page of the *News and Courier*. Colds chills washed over her as she read, "August 29, 1886."

Chapter Fifteen

Vickie and Adrian stared at one another in shock. She found what she had just read to be incredible—that the date was August 29, 1886. Yet on another level it made a bizarre kind of sense. . . .

Adrian appeared dumbfounded. "This is surely some kind of joke."

"Joke? Then how do you explain all of this? The orphanage and chapel being miraculously restored, the horses and buggies in the streets, the people dressed so strangely . . ." She paused as a peddler rattled past on the flagstone walkway, pushing a flower cart. "Sir, can you tell us the·date?"

The gray-haired gentleman, in tattered cap and dungarees, glanced askance at Vickie in her short dress. "Why, yes, ma'am. 'Tis August 29th."

"And the year?"

The man regarded her in consternation. "You don't know the year, miss?"

"Please, sir," Adrian implored. "Just tell us."

"Why, 'tis 1886, of course," the man replied, shaking his head and pushing off again.

For a moment Adrian and Vickie stood stunned. "So it's true," he managed at last. "We appear to be in another time."

"Yes, August 29, 1886." She paused, hands flying to her face. "Oh, no!"

"What, Vickie?"

Urgently she touched his sleeve. "We're living in a time three days before the great Charleston earthquake."

"Surely you jest."

"No," she continued excitedly, "I remember the date clearly. August 31, 1886. It was on the marquee at the Dock Street Theater. It was the day of my great-great-grandmother's . . . oh, good heavens! She must be here, too—somewhere!"

"She what?" Adrian's expression was half-crazed. "Slow down a bit, Vickie. You're making my head spin."

"How do you think I feel?"

Adrian could only shake his head.

Vickie glanced about her in bewilderment, her mind whirling with so much information and so many questions, she could barely think. Then her gaze fixed upon a family of six heading their way. The husband and wife were pushing an antique black baby carriage, while three older children skipped along behind them. The daughter was wearing a long, frilly gown with pantaloons; two small sons were both in sailor suits.

Cold chills streaked down Vickie's spine. "Oh, my God."

"What now?" Adrian jerked his head in the same direction.

Vickie swallowed hard, watching the group march past them. In a tense whisper, she confided, "Just look at those outfits the children are wearing. They're like the ones we saw the 'ghosts' of Nate and Cathy wearing. That must mean . . ." She grasped his arm and spoke with great animation. "Of course! The children must be here, too! It's the only explanation that makes sense!"

"Here?" Adrian repeated in perplexity. "It makes sense for the children to be here? But how? If we're now living in the year 1886, the children clearly have not even been born yet."

"Neither have we!"

He gave a groan. "Besides which, we've already checked at the orphanage and they're not there."

"They're not necessarily at the orphanage, but I just know they're here, in 1886 Charleston," she argued.

"Explain that."

"I'll try." She bit her lip and concentrated fiercely. "When the children jumped from the orphanage window, they must have landed in another time—this time."

"Forgive me, my dear, but that sounds quite insane."

"So does our being here!" She clutched his arm. "Think, Adrian. They must have left us the old coin as a clue to let us know where they are. Besides, if we could travel here to the past, to the year 1886, why couldn't they have as well?"

Adrian slowly shook his head. "I suppose you could be right, mind-boggling though the prospect is."

"I agree."

He caught her arm and pulled her aside as a couple of elderly gentlemen in well-cut suits and top hats strode past, one of them staring pointedly at Vickie's costume.

"Adrian, we must do something," she continued urgently. "I mean, if the children are really here, and Great-great-grandmother is also here—"

Adrian clasped her hand. "Just calm down, dear. We must try to think clearly."

"Clearly? When the children might at last be within our grasp?"

He escorted her into a nearby alleyway, onto the stoop of a red brick building. Gently he pulled her into his arms and stroked her back. "Easy, dear. You're trembling quite badly. We can't accomplish anything with panic."

She laughed. "You mean you're remaining calm in the face of all this?"

"Hardly," he attested ruefully. "I just think we must carefully consider what has happened to us, try to figure it out."

She stepped back, pressing her weight against the porch railing. "But there is no figuring it out. I mean, how we could have gone from 1945 Charleston to 1886 Charleston in the brief moments we prayed?"

"If this truly is 1886 Charleston."

"What else could it be, Adrian? Do you think this

is a farce someone staged for our amusement? With this kind of scope?"

He sighed, then watched a policeman in an old-fashioned uniform pass on the street flanking them, staring at them pointedly before he moved on. "Vickie, I'm as confused as you are. But we're going to have to take things one step at a time. And our first concern is that we're attracting far too much attention with our current attire."

"You mean my attire."

"Especially yours, but mine as well. If we're going to find out what's going on here, I think we must both first find more suitable clothing."

"I agree. But how?"

"We'll have to purchase it, of course." He tapped his breast pocket. "And something tells me our money won't work here."

"Probably not." She laughed dryly. "Though I still have the old nickel we found."

Adrian gave her a look of strained patience, then pointed across the street. "There's a jeweler over there. I'll try to sell my ring."

Vickie glanced at the heavily carved gold signet ring on his right hand. "That looks quite valuable."

"Well, it's more of a sentimental piece, given me by my wife."

Vickie was horrified. "Then you mustn't pawn it. And isn't it carved with your family crest?"

"It is. But we must sell it. I've nothing else of any real value on me."

Vickie snapped her fingers. "Wait a minute." She opened the clasp of her shoulder purse and dug inside, a moment later handing Adrian half a dozen gold coins. "Sell these instead."

He looked over the coins and whistled. "But these appear to be valuable gold pieces."

"They were given to me by my father."

"Then we mustn't sell them. And some of these are dated from the twentieth century."

"I doubt that will matter. Gold is gold. Besides, my father gave them to me for just this type of emergency. He once told me that if I were ever in a jam, gold could get me out of it, anywhere in the world."

"Or in another one," he added ironically.

Despite her anxious state, his quip brought a half-smile to her lips. "Please, Adrian, let's sell the coins. They can't possibly mean to me what your ring does to you."

"Very well," he wearily agreed. "And we'd best mind what we say while we're in the jewelry store. I mean, if we should mention we're from the year 1945—"

"Oh, I agree. People here already thing we're odd enough. No sense risking our being committed to an asylum."

Vickie accompanied Adrian to the jewelry store. The owner examined the gold pieces, and while he remarked on the strange dates, he didn't disagree regarding the value of the gold itself, which he weighed and priced. Ten minutes later, they emerged with fifty dollars in nineteenth-century currency tucked in Adrian's wallet.

"Well, I hope things aren't too expensive here," he remarked.

"If I remember the stories my grandparents told me, they're not. What now?"

Adrian pointed south. "The dry goods store down the street."

When they stepped inside the old-fashioned shop with its display tables crammed with period fabrics and racks hung with antique clothing, a tall, thin matron came forward wearing a white Victorian blouse and a vivid paisley skirt, a measuring tape draped around her neck. Taking in Vickie's costume, she made a clucking sound, then looked down her steel-rimmed glasses at Adrian. "Yes? May I help you?"

"The lady and I have come to purchase suitable clothing," Adrian answered.

"Well, I must say, you both appear to be in dire need of it," she answered archly.

Vickie was growing irritated by everyone's attitude toward her attire. "Would you mind explaining to me why my dress is so inappropriate?"

The woman gave a gasp. "You mean you don't know?"

Vickie glowered.

"Why, the skirt, my dear. 'Tis scandalously short, exposing your—er—your limbs. Proper folks are bound to assume you're some sort of hoyden—or even a woman of ill repute."

"What?" Vickie cried.

"You're not from here, are you?"

After glancing askance at Adrian, Vickie laughed ruefully. "Indeed I'm not."

Not commenting on Vickie's attempt at humor, the woman settled her disapproving frown on Adrian. "As for you, sir, that blue military uniform with all those ribbons—"

Realization dawning on her at last, Vickie cut in, "Don't worry, he isn't a Yankee."

The woman appeared unconvinced, raising an eyebrow. "Well, we still get our share of the varmints here, and an occasional carpetbagger as well."

Adrian cleared his throat. "Madam, I assure you, I am neither. As a matter of fact, I'm from England, and in the King's service."

The woman harrumphed. "A latter-day redcoat, are you? That's not much of an improvement."

Vickie and Adrian exchanged a look of wry amusement. "All that aside, madam, will you help us?" he asked.

She drew herself up proudly. "Why, certainly, I shall. I'm a charitable woman, after all."

Luckily, there were few customers in the store, and the saleslady quickly took Vickie in hand, finding a male clerk to assist Adrian. The next hour was fascinating for Vickie as she had a complete lesson in women's clothing of the 1880s including corsets, bloomers, bustles, silk stockings, button-top shoes, and petticoats. She actually enjoyed the brief respite from thinking about the situation she and Adrian found themselves in. And although she knew Adrian was very concerned about their limited resources, she found the prices the saleslady quoted her extremely reasonable.

But actually donning the old-fashioned garb proved challenging to say the least, and Vickie felt decidedly awkward by the time she and Adrian emerged from the shop. She wore a pink and white striped, bustled muslin gown trimmed with lace, a large straw hat heaped with silk roses, and button-top shoes that were pinching the very devil out of her toes. He wore a brown and white striped sack coat, matching trousers, and a bowler hat. Adrian carried a box for each of them with a second outfit, as well as their old clothing, tucked inside.

"I feel about as comfortable as a trussed-up turkey," he remarked.

She laughed, grimacing as she tried to navigate in the awkward shoes. "How do you think I feel? With this corset strangling the breath out of me and . . ." She rolled her eyes toward her posterior. "A wire cage on my derriere supporting this silly bustle."

He glanced in the same direction with unabashed admiration. "Oh, but I find it rather fetching."

She wrinkled her nose at him. "At least I shouldn't get as many stares now."

A hint of mischief gleamed in his eyes. "You will. But they'll be of an entirely different nature, my dear."

Vickie rolled her eyes. "I see you've not yet lost your sense of humor." She glanced at the load he was carrying. "Do you suppose we should look around for a place to stay?"

"Yes, unless we want to carry these boxes around all day. Let's head down Meeting Street and see what we can find."

Proceeding south with him, Vickie spotted the facade of a familiar house. "Hey, that's the boardinghouse!"

Adrian glanced over at the yard of the colonial home, where two small children were throwing a ball back and forth, while a woman, obviously their mother, sat in a rocking chair watching them from the piazza. "Ah, but it doesn't appear to be a boarding-house now."

"You're right. The sign is gone, and it's obviously a private residence."

"My Lord, this is so confusing." Juggling the boxes, Adrian pointed ahead. "We'll stay there."

Vickie glanced at the magnificent Greek Revival facade of the Charleston Hotel, where several styl-ishly dressed gentlemen sat reading newspapers on porch rockers. "My, it looks much newer than it did in 1945."

"Do you mind if I register us as husband and wife?" he asked.

She hesitated. "Do you really think we should?"

He tapped his breast pocket. "Well, even though the bill for our clothing was only ten dollars, our funds are quite limited."

Vickie smiled, finding herself warming to the pros-pect of being registered as Adrian's wife. "You're right there. No, I don't mind, and since we're strang-ers here, there's really no one to know the difference, is there?"

Inside the lobby of the hotel, Adrian signed them in at the front desk, and the bellhop escorted them up to a large sunny room on the second floor, with floral carpeting, a crystal chandelier, vivid blue velvet drapes, and a beautifully carved rosewood bed.

As soon as the man was out of the room, Vickie fell into Adrian's arms. "Heavens, Adrian, what a day. This is surreal."

"I know. It's taking a while for everything to sink in."

"For me, too." She drew back and regarded him earnestly. "But are you starting to believe we're really living in the year 1886 now?"

"I don't have much choice but to believe it."

"Do you suppose they miss us in the present?"

"Who knows? There might be some consternation over our departure."

"Yes, and crazy as this sounds, you might even be considered absent without leave."

He laughed wryly. "That's the least of my worries now."

"I agree."

She frowned. "Do you think . . . well, that at any moment, we might find ourselves back in the present, like in a dream or something?"

He pulled off his hat and drew his fingers through his hair. "My dear, I have no idea what to expect next. But, yes, we arrived here without warning, and I do suppose the reverse—or virtually anything else— might happen to us now."

Nodding, she began exploring the room. Glancing inside the bathroom at the old-fashioned water closet with pull chain and the bathtub with claw feet, she murmured, "They have indoor plumbing here." She flipped a switch on the wall, and a clear light bulb flickered on overhead. "As well as electricity, such as it is."

"And a telephone," Adrian added.

Vickie whirled to see him standing by the desk, touching an old-fashioned telephone on a tall stand. "My God." She started toward him. "My great-great-grandmother! Perhaps she has a telephone!"

He handed her the receiver. "Perhaps so. Be my guest."

Vickie put the old-fashioned receiver to her ear, and waited anxiously until she heard a voice say, "Operator."

"Yes, operator. I'm a guest staying at the Charleston Hotel, and I'm trying to locate my great . . ." Realizing that "great-great-grandmother" might sound ridiculous, she decided to amend her words. "That is, my *grandmother*. Can you tell me if you have a subscriber named Sophie Davis?"

"Just a moment, ma'am." After a pause, the woman replied, "Sorry, ma'am, there's no Sophie Davis."

Vickie frowned. "Do you have a William? That was her husband's name."

"Sorry, ma'am, the only Davis we have is Rodney. But this is a very small exchange. We've only been in business since seventy-nine. Most people in Charleston still don't have telephones."

"Thanks," Vickie replied. She set down the receiver.

Adrian was regarding her sympathetically. "No luck?"

She shook her head.

"Do you know where in town your great-great-grandmother lived?"

"No, just that it was somewhere in central Charleston. But I do seem to recall that she was Catholic."

"Well, there can't be that many Catholic parishes in this city."

"I agree. St. Christopher's would be one."

"Yes, we should go by the church and inquire about

her. Perhaps we can find her before it's too late."

"We'll hope so." Vickie bit her lip. "And what of the others here who might be harmed by the earthquake?"

Adrian raised an eyebrow at that. "Are you suggesting we should try to warn the general populace?"

"Don't we have an obligation to do so?"

He scowled. "Vickie, I'm as appalled about all of this as you are, but I'd suggest we take a cautious approach. If we start ranting about a coming earthquake like a couple of demented prophets, we'll only invite others to conclude we're delusional—and to treat us accordingly."

She sighed. "I suppose you're right. At any rate, we must look for Sophie Davis. Perhaps she'll know how we might warn the others. And we must hunt for the children as well, perhaps at the other local orphanages."

"You're truly convinced they're here?"

"Aren't you?"

"I just don't know, Vickie. I just don't know."

"But you'll help me look?"

He sighed heavily. "I suppose hunting for the children makes about as much sense as anything else that has happened to us."

Staring at Adrian standing across from her, his expression so skeptical, Vickie felt disappointed that he continued to doubt. Yes, it boggled the mind that they had evidently journeyed back in time to the year 1886—but why couldn't he see that they were here for a reason? To find the children, to find Sophie Davis, perhaps even to help warn others here who might be harmed by the coming calamity. Vickie was convinced of the logic of these conclusions, yet Adrian remained skeptical.

Gazing back at Vickie, Adrian realized she felt disappointed in him, disillusioned because he could not share her optimistic view of their journey back in time. First they had done the impossible, leaving the year 1945 and traveling back to the year 1886. His mind still spun each time he tried to grasp the enormity of what had happened to them. Now she expected him to believe that the children were here as well? If true, it would be wonderful beyond belief.

But sad experience had taught Adrian to take a more cautious view of life, and fate. His concept of the universe didn't allow for cosmic destinies to be wrapped up this way, in neat little packages tied with gaily gleaming ribbons.

And the fact that they were here just days before the great earthquake also hinted that there might be a darker, more sinister side to their journey through time. If their purpose in being here was to be reunited with the children, then why had destiny brought them here just as catastrophe was looming?

Across the street from the Charleston Hotel, beneath the canopy of a deep-green live oak, stood Carmichael Keegan. He lit a cigar with trembling fingers.

The last hour had been a nightmare for him. He felt as if some devious god had perversely snatched him up and hurled him through space, turning his entire world topsy-turvy. He still seemed to be in Charleston, but a vastly different Charleston it was. Crazy as it seemed, he found himself in an earlier time, a time when horses and buggies clogged the streets instead of cars, when people marched past wearing outlandish costumes.

Awakening at the chapel *before* the fire had destroyed it, and speaking with the nun next door at the orphanage, had all but unhinged him. Then he'd discovered the actual date when he'd tried to purchase some beef jerky from a street vendor, and the man had laughed at the currency he'd offered, accusing him of trying to pass counterfeit. A chill washed over him as he remembered the peddler's rebuke: "The year is 1886, not 1945, you stupid swindler."

1886 indeed! Somehow the shifting of the earth back in the chapel had landed Mic Keegan in an earlier century. And even more amazing, Cheney and Bennett were here with him. He'd spotted them standing on Meeting Street, looking as dazed as he felt. He was convinced they were the "others" the nun had referred to, the ones who had also visited the orphanage and inquired after the children there. After spotting the couple, Keegan had watched from a distance as they had visited the jeweler's and then the dry goods store, emerging in costumes that better blended with those of the citizens here. Then they'd gone into the Charleston Hotel, and so far hadn't emerged.

But he'd be here awaiting them when they left, and would discover their true purpose in being here. If they were indeed searching for the children, then he must find the brats first—that is, assuming *they* were also here. It seemed incredible that all five of them might have traveled to an earlier time, but then, little was making sense to Keegan, anyway.

He had no idea how long any of them might remain here in this fantastical purgatory, but he did know he must make the best of the opportunity the fates had offered him. He would hope this turn of events was not the devil's doing . . . unless Satan had brought him here to complete his dirty work.

In the meantime, he needed some money he could use here and some sort of disguise so he would fit in better as he stalked the couple. He prowled up and down the block, passing couples, families, and businessmen on the walkway. Damn, the streets were so crowded, and he needed a lone pigeon he could nab.

At last he spotted a gentlemen striding toward him, alone, on a side street. He was about Keegan's size, and his elegant clothing—long, tailored black coat and crisp trousers, and silk top hat—indicated that he was well fixed. He appeared the perfect victim. Decision made, Mic strode around the corner and approached the man.

Tipping his cap, he said, "Good afternoon, sir. I'm afraid I must ask you to come with me."

The man appeared astonished, nervously twirling his thin black mustache. "Is something wrong, officer?"

Quickly losing patience, Keegan whipped out his gun. "I said you'll have to come with me."

The man went bug-eyed. "What is the meaning of—"

Ignoring the man's protests, Keegan grabbed him by the arm and hauled him into a nearby alleyway. The man broke away from Keegan and whirled, shaking a gloved finger at him. "Sir, I'll have you know I'm a respectable citizen and I demand—"

The rest of the man's scolding was lost in a moan of pain as Keegan bashed him across the forehead with the butt of his revolver, knocking off his hat. After his quarry collapsed at his feet, Keegan holstered his weapon, smiled grimly, and dragged the unconscious man behind a row of garbage cans.

Ten minutes later, Keegan emerged from the alleyway whistling a jaunty tune, tipping his hat at a passing lady. He wore his victim's stylish clothing . . . and carried his fat wallet safely tucked away in his breast pocket.

Chapter Sixteen

Vickie and Adrian left the hotel and began exploring 1886 Charleston, trying to further gain their bearings while keeping an eye out for the children. They walked up and down Broad, Meeting, and Queen streets, passing citizens, sailors, and peddlers on the walkways, watching horse-down trolleys and other antique conveyances rattle past in the streets. But they spotted no signs of Cathy or Nate. They navigated through the harbor streets, awed at the sight of giant schooners, clipper ships, steamboats, and ferries docked there, watching stevedores load bales of cotton and bundles of lumber onto large cargo ships. They watched farmers hawk watermelons and butchers cut meat at their stalls on nearby Market Street.

They made inquiries everywhere they went, stopping passersby on the Battery, mothers out pushing baby carriages in White Point Gardens. At the Charleston Orphan House on Boundary Street, the headmistress informed them that no orphans by the names of Cathy Cheney and Nate Bennett were staying there. When Vickie told the woman that they had already tried St. Christopher's Orphanage without any luck, she suggested they visit two smaller local orphanages. They tried these establishments as well, but both proved to be dead ends.

Next they tried churches. At St. Christopher's Catholic Church, Vickie asked a young priest whether Sophie Davis was a member of the parish, but a search of the church rolls proved she wasn't. Then at the temporary Cathedral of St. John and St. Finbar, an older priest informed them that there was no one in his parish, either, by the name of Sophie Davis. But he did suggest they try the county courthouse, and they went there next.

Although it was nearly closing time when they arrived at the county recorder's office, a young male clerk took mercy on Vickie when she explained she was a visitor to Charleston and was hunting for her grandmother, Sophie Davis. He didn't find a birth record for Sophie, or her name on the current tax rolls or in the city directory; however, he did locate an old deed to a house on East Battery once owned by the Davis family. Showing Vickie the parchment document across the counter, he explained, "This house on East Battery was owned by a William Davis until—"

"Yes, he was my grandfather!" Vickie cut in excitedly.

"Was he? Well, in 1866, his widow, Sophie Davis, sold the property."

"And she's my grandmother. Do you know where she's living now?"

The clerk shook his head. "Sorry, ma'am. Mrs. Davis is no longer a property owner here as far as I know. Are you sure she didn't move away?"

"No, I'm sure she's still living here."

"I'd suggest you try the house on East Battery, but according to our records, that property has changed hands at least three times since the war."

Feeling discouraged, Vickie thanked the clerk and left the building with Adrian. Walking south with him in the fading light, she caught sight of an unfamiliar pillared building across the street from them, where the post office had stood in their own time. As they passed it, she read the sign.

"That is the guard house and police headquarters," she told him. "Do you think we should stop in there and inquire about Sophie and the children?"

Adrian shook his head. "Vickie, my instincts tell me we should leave the police out of this entirely."

"Why?"

"What will we tell them? That we're from the year 1945, and we're hunting for children we think died there and may have ended up here?"

"Of course not. But can't we ask if any lost children have been found?"

"If they had been found, the police would have turned them over to one of the orphanages here, and we've already visited all of them."

"So what are you saying?"

He eyed her with regret. "I'm saying I'm having

increasing doubts that the children are here—or that Sophie Davis is here."

"Then why are *we* here?"

"I wish I knew."

Vickie bit her lip. "If only we could find my great-great-grandmother. I know she could help us."

Glancing about, he replied, "We'll try again tomorrow. The sun is already sinking low, and we need to call it a day."

"Call it a day already?" she asked anxiously. "With the earthquake now less than forty-eight hours away?"

He shook his head. "What would you suggest we do, Vickie? Go from house to house in the darkness, looking for Sophie and the children?"

She fell moodily silent.

He squeezed her hand. "We'll get an early start tomorrow."

They arrived back at the hotel feeling hot, tired, and discouraged. Adrian suggested Vickie wash for dinner while he went downstairs to have a drink and perhaps mix with some of the locals, see what he could find out.

She bathed in the old claw-foot tub, and donned fresh clothing. When Adrian arrived back inside the room with a newspaper tucked beneath his arm, she was standing at the pier mirror arranging her hair. She wore a lace-trimmed, blue muslin dress, but hadn't fastened it; her corset was also untied.

Glancing at him over her shoulder, she smiled. "You're just in time to help me."

Setting down his paper, he crossed the room.

"Well, I'm hardly an expert at female rigging—"

"Rigging?" she repeated drolly.

"But I shall try my best." He pressed his mouth to her bare shoulder. "You do look—and smell—divine, darling."

Shivering at the touch of his lips, she sniffed the air. "And you smell vaguely of whiskey and cigars, sir. Now would you please tie this corset and fasten my dress?"

He chuckled. "My pleasure, dear."

Vickie grimaced as he pulled at her corset ties. "Did you learn anything helpful downstairs?"

"Oh, there were quite a few gentlemen there at the bar, talking over cigars and highballs. There was the usual polite gossip—one old gent was complaining because he'd lost his shirt on railroad bonds, while another was grousing about how uppity the 'darkies' are getting here."

Vickie ruefully shook her head. "That's right— we're not that far removed from reconstruction, and the Jim Crow laws. Old prejudices die hard here in the South."

"Indeed."

Vickie frowned a moment. "Did you ask the men about my great-great-grandmother?"

"I did mention Sophie Davis, but none had heard of her."

"Darn. And what about the newspaper you brought back? Did it offer any insights?"

"Oh, mostly more local color. An editorial complains about the smells from the phosphate and fish processing plants here. Another piece brags that the cotton warehouses at the port will receive over half a million bails of cotton this year, while a columnist begs for donations to the Ladies Fuel Society in order to help the indigent stay warm during the coming winter months. I saw nothing, however, that might help us in our search for Sophie, or the children." With a sigh, he stepped back. "There, you're all done, and you look wonderful. If you'll just give me a moment, I'll wash up."

"Of course." Fighting her own sagging spirits, Vickie crossed the room, picked up the newspaper, and sat down to read it.

The hotel's main dining room was magnificent—ninety feet long, and brilliantly lit with chandeliers. At their impeccably set, linen-draped table, Adrian ordered them glazed duck with dressing and cranberry sauce, and white wine. A waiter promptly served the mouth-watering cuisine. But Vickie was very subdued and merely picked at her food.

Adrian glanced at her with concern. "Are you still worrying, dear? There's not much else we can do tonight."

She set down her fork and regarded him soberly. "I'm just feeling so frustrated, Adrian. I'm sure Nate and Cathy are here. I *feel* it in my bones. And I can't understand why you don't share my feelings."

He offered her an apologetic smile. "I'm sorry, dear. Forgive me if I'm still a trifle confused. This morning, you and I awakened in the year 1945. We went to the ruins of the chapel, where we knelt and said a prayer. Then everything changed and we found ourselves in a totally different world. I can't claim to begin to understand anything that has happened."

216

Leaning toward him, she spoke earnestly. "But I do. We said a prayer, for the souls of the children. Then we were brought here—to them. It makes perfect sense to me."

"Then why haven't we found them?"

"We will. Surely tomorrow, we will."

He scowled. "Regarding what you said earlier . . . what if tomorrow we wake up and discover all of this has been only a dream?"

She shook her head. "Increasingly my instincts tell me that won't happen. We're here for a reason."

"So you do see a plan, some sort of cosmic order in all of this?"

"Yes. Even in the minor earthquake that brought us here."

He mulled that over. "But if you're right and the earthquake did bring us here, won't the next one take us away again?"

She blanched. "I hadn't thought of that!"

"Isn't that scenario every bit as believable as your theory that we'll find the children here?"

She considered the question, then snapped her fingers. "Perhaps we're meant to find the children and take them back with us, before the earthquake can harm them."

"Perhaps," he conceded. "Or perhaps we're meant never to really understand what's happening to us— or what happened to them."

She sighed. "So you think we're just adrift somewhere in time, at the whim of the fates?"

"Forgive me, dear, if my experiences heretofore have not prompted me to trust the fates."

She reached across the table and squeezed his hand.

"Adrian, I realize this situation is bewildering, to say the least. But I need you to believe in this with me."

His eyes were sad. "Darling, forgive me if I can't quite share your optimism. For now, all we really have is each other. Let's not lose our greatest strength by fighting between ourselves."

"We won't, Adrian."

"Do you really mean that?"

She nodded.

"You must know how much I need you," he whispered. "Especially now."

"I need you, too," she acknowledged quietly.

Once they were upstairs in their room, Adrian locked the door, removed his hat, then came to Vickie's side. The tender look in his eyes banished all her doubts. Even as he was leaning toward her, she stretched on tiptoe and kissed him. Feeling his strong arms envelop her, Vickie moaned in ecstasy—for in that moment everything seemed right again.

He drew back to gaze at her contritely. "I'm sorry I was such a skeptic at dinner. I will tell you this: Since we've been together, and since we've been here, I've felt more stirrings of hope than I have in a long time."

She hugged him. "Then you do see a logic in this—and you are sharing it with me."

"As much as my doubting Thomas nature will allow me to do." He leaned over and ran his lips over her throat. "For now, my darling, I just want to be close to you."

"And I with you," she murmured.

"Could I persuade you to forget our troubles for a

while, and just love me?" he asked poignantly.

"You've already persuaded me."

He took her hand and led her to the bed. Glancing at her elaborate dress, he quipped, "Have I any hope of getting you out of all those contraptions?"

She laughed. "Yes, indeed." She turned around, and felt his deft fingers unbuttoning the dozen or so pearl buttons stretching down her back. Then she felt his mouth on the bare flesh at her nape, and sighed in pleasure. His fingers made quick work of her corset strings, and she breathed deeply, ecstatically.

She turned, smiling. He pulled the gown up over her head, then carefully laid it across the chair. Hungrily he eyed her in her undergarments and petticoats. He reached out, pulling down one side of her chemise and freeing the tip of her breast from her corset. He leaned over and took the turgid nipple in his mouth.

She whimpered at the indescribable pleasure. He drew back and winked solemnly. "I'd best allow you to undress before I devour you."

Her sudden blush attested that the prospect pleased her immensely. With trembling fingers, she removed her corset, her petticoats, and other undergarments, while he removed his coat, suspenders, shirt, trousers, and undergarment. His gaze burned over her naked body as he drew her close. She shivered in bliss, admiring the beauty of his body, feeling the satiny warmth of his flesh against hers, the hardness of his passion pressing into her.

Turning off the lamp, he drew her down onto the bed with him. As they lay side by side in the moonlight, he took his time, drinking in her body with his eyes, running his lips over her face and mouth, and teasing all the contours of her flesh with his skilled fingers. Her skin broke out in goose bumps; she caressed his muscled body with her hands. When he pressed his fingers between her thighs, she moaned and thrust herself into his arms, kissing him hungrily, exulting in his answering sounds of pleasure.

Abruptly he rolled onto his back, pulling her into a straddle on top of him, then sinking two fingers inside her aroused womanflesh. Vickie cried out at the shattering sensations throbbing inside her so powerfully and unexpectedly. Helplessly she squirmed. "Adrian—"

His fingers sank deeper, sending hot rapture rushing through her. "Easy, darling. I intend to take my time, and to drive you quite mad."

"You—you already have." Panting for breath, she leaned over and kissed him feverishly.

He responded with a massive groan. His tongue penetrated her mouth hungrily, mimicking the plunder of his fingers. His thumb flicked against the center of her desire. Vickie could scarcely catch her breath. Then his lips moved to her breasts, sucking, nipping, delighting, even as his bold hand continued to arouse her mercilessly. The torment persisted until Vickie was gasping, until she nibbled at his ear and begged, "Please."

With his free hand, he eased her back, stroking her flushed face and gazing up into her passionate eyes. "You want me."

"Oh, yes."

"Then take me," he rasped.

Vickie greedily complied, sinking her flesh onto his, crying out when he filled her to bursting. She heard his ragged cry as he began to move.

"Oh, yes, Adrian, this is glorious," she panted. "Just loving . . . and forgetting."

He clutched her closer and poured himself into her. Vickie melted, letting his love take her, his flesh meld deeply with her own. She closed her eyes and savored the sweet oblivion of their shared passion. It would suffice, until morning came, and with it all the memories, the pain, of their desperate, confused search. . . .

Down the hallway in his own room sat Carmichael Keegan, the jacket and coat he'd stolen carelessly tossed on the bed beside him.

He'd been following Bennett and Cheney all day long, and had decided to book a room at the Charleston Hotel where they were also staying. Shaking his head, he glanced around the nicely appointed room with its oriental rug, marble-topped dresser and carved armoire. The ceiling even sported rows of gold fretwork. This same hotel had been a bit more frayed back in 1945. Nonetheless, he'd been obliged to pay only a few dollars to stay here for the night. All of which further served to convince him that he was no longer living in his own time.

He picked up the wallet of the man he'd robbed, emptied it out, and stared at the odd currency bearing dates from the 1880s. Something very strange was going on here. Something very strange indeed.

All day long, the realization that he was no longer living in 1945 had prompted thoughts of panic, had made him question his own sanity, but he'd managed to forestall his alarm in his concern over more pressing issues. Those issues concerned Cheney and Bennett—and quite possibly the brats who had started all this trouble for him in the first place.

Whatever quirk of fate had brought him and the others here, Mic was now certain that Cheney and Bennett were hunting for those same whelps who could bury him back in the present. He'd picked this up by questioning some of the same citizens they'd spoken with today. Of course, he had no way of knowing for sure that the children were here—or, for that matter, if he or any of the others would ever find their way back to the present. The prospect that he might never return to the year 1945 did hold a certain appeal for Mic, considering the trouble that likely awaited him there with Captain O'Moody. He might even be able to start a new life here, with no one the smarter.

But not while Cheney and Bennett, and possibly the brats, stood in his way. Of course he could go on the run here, try to settle somewhere else, but the possibility of leaving loose ends nagged at him.

And besides, he had a score to settle. Several scores.

Turning to the nightstand, he picked up his Smith and Wesson service revolver and checked the cylinder, finding it fully loaded with six rounds. He had another dozen rounds on his gun belt—which was fortunate, since he was sure he wouldn't be able to purchase the right ammunition here.

Part of him burned to kill Cheney and Bennett right now. But perhaps it would be best to continue following the couple around, see if they led him to the troublesome little rascals. Then he could rub out all four of them, and look forward to turning over a new leaf here, in a place where no one knew about his previous existence and his past transgressions.

He frowned. Something else about this time was nagging at him, had been pestering him all day. Hadn't there been a major earthquake in Charleston sometime in the late nineteenth century? Damn, he couldn't remember the exact year, but he well recalled how Gladys used to rant about that particular natural disaster, claiming it was God's vengeance on sinful Charleston. His wife had also repeatedly warned Mic that one day a new eruption would surely come forth, and a new demon would rise up from the bowels of hell—this time to swallow him up for his evil doings.

Mic chuckled. He was well rid of the old harridan, and he wouldn't trouble himself with her superstitious blather. Odds were, the earthquake would be no threat to him. And he had enough to be concerned about here already.

Chapter Seventeen

The next morning, Vickie and Adrian emerged early from their hotel, while the light remained soft and morning's cool fragrance hung in the air. She was dressed in her blue muslin gown, while he wore the brown suit with a fresh shirt. Although they hadn't as yet checked out of their room, Vickie hadn't been sure what to expect today, so she'd placed all of their valuables, including Adrian's Victoria Cross, in her purse.

At Vickie's suggestion, they ventured south, walking down Meeting Street and through Washington Square Park, with its statues honoring General Beauregard and the Washington Light Infantry, its old gentlemen sitting on park benches. Vickie searched through a group of children at play, while Adrian questioned a couple of the men. When neither met with success, they continued on their way along the city streets.

Although they didn't spot the children, now and then Vickie felt a funny shiver along her spine, much as she'd felt back in the present, almost as if someone were stalking them. At one point the feeling became so pronounced that she whirled to look behind her at the corner they'd just passed. As a startled businessman behind her skidded to avoid a collision, she muttered an apology and stared hard at the corner, just managing to spot a flash of dark fabric disappearing around it.

Perplexed, Adrian turned to join her. "Vickie, what do you think you're doing, freezing in your tracks like Lot's wife? You almost knocked down that poor chap."

She continued to crane her neck. "I thought I saw . . . I just get the feeling someone's following us."

"You mean the gent with whom you almost just collided?"

"No. Someone else."

"The children?"

She frowned. "I don't know."

He glanced about. "You had that same feeling back in our own time."

"Yes, I did. And so did you, remember?"

He frowned and escorted her onward.

In due course they wound up on Marion Square, where cadets from the Citadel were drilling outside the quadrangle. They continued toward the western edge of the peninsula, stopping only to buy some bread and cheese from a street vendor. At the edge of a prosperous residential area, they reached West

Point Mill Causeway, a wide dirt and gravel prome-
nade that crossed a large pond near the Ashley River.
There, several mothers were gathered outside, watching their children play in goat carts that they drove
about on the thoroughfare. The air rang with the children's laughter and the bleating of the goats. In the
distance near the river loomed the tall buildings of
the rice mill.

Adrian removed his hat as they stepped up to the
group of four women. "Good morning, ladies."

"Good morning," answered one of them, a tall,
blond matron with thin though pretty features. "May
we help you, sir? You and the lady aren't lost, are
you?"

Adrian coughed. "Actually, the lady and I are out
searching for two lost children."

"Lost children?" gasped a plump, pink-cheeked
matron. "How terrible. Who might they be?"

"Their names are Nate Bennett and Cathy Cheney.
Nate is my son and Cathy is the lady's sister. At any
rate, until recently, the two were staying at a local
orphanage, and then . . . well, they ran off and disappeared. Now Miss Cheney and I have come to
Charleston to find the children. And we were wondering if any of you ladies, or your children, might
have heard or seen anything."

The women consulted among themselves for a moment, then the tall woman shook her head. "Sorry,
sir. We've seen nothing unusual, however . . ." She
cupped a hand around her mouth and called, "Andrew, come over here, pray."

A little boy of around six wheeled his goat cart
toward the group. Vickie noted that the child was

226

quite handsome, with dark, bright eyes, and a round face; he wore a black jacket, matching short pants, and a cap.

As his billy goat stood bleating, the boy brightly inquired, "Yes, Mama?"

"Andrew, have you or your friends seen any stray children in the streets lately?"

As the boy hesitated, Adrian said, "The girl would be about nine, the boy, twelve."

"They're always together," added Vickie. "His hair is dark, and hers blond."

Andrew shook his head. "No, ma'am, we've seen nobody like that."

"You may go back to your play, then," directed his mother. She turned to Adrian. "Sorry, sir, miss."

"Thanks for trying," he said.

Vickie spoke up again. "Before we go, ladies, I'm also trying to locate my grandmother here in Charleston. Her name is Sophie Davis. Do any of you know her?"

A third woman, a petite redhead, snapped her fingers, then addressed Vickie in a thick Irish brogue. "Well, you know, missy, I'm thinkin' there's a Sophie Davis that attends our church. Would she be a widow lady?"

"Yes," Vickie answered excitely. "Do you really know her?"

"Well, just in passing, miss."

"Do you know where she lives?"

"No, but you can check at the parish office. 'Tis St. Mary's over on Hasell."

"Oh, thanks," Vickie murmured. "Thank you so much!"

They went straight to St. Mary's Catholic Church on Hasell Street. As they entered the diocese office, Vickie addressed a young priest sitting behind his desk. "Hello. We've come to inquire about Sophie Davis, whom I believe is one of your parishioners."

The priest smiled and stood. "Why, yes, Mrs. Davis is a most beloved member of this parish."

"Oh, thank heaven!" Vickie declared.

"How may I help you?"

"I'm Vickie Cheney, Mrs. Davis's great—er, her granddaughter. I'm visiting Charleston, and I was hoping you could tell me how to find her."

"Why, yes, indeed. Mrs. Davis lives not far from here, on Pinckney Street. If you'll just wait a moment, I can get you her exact address from our diocese records."

"We'd be delighted to wait," Vickie said, beaming at Adrian.

Five minutes later, they emerged from the church, Vickie clutching a precious slip of paper with her great-great-grandmother's address written on it. "Thank heaven the priest was able to help us."

"Indeed."

"And it's going to be so easy to find her," Vickie went on. "According to the priest, all we have to do is to keep walking on Hasell Street until we cross Meeting, and Pinckney will jog off just below there."

"It's certainly logical that she wouldn't live far from her church."

"The best part is that we may be able to save her life, to get her out of harm's way before the earthquake strikes tomorrow."

"I hope you're right."

Adrian had no sooner spoken than Vickie was distracted by another flash of motion in her peripheral vision, and a sense of impending danger washed a chill over her. She glanced behind her and was horrified to see a man quickly approaching them with a pistol in hand. Panic seized her, along with the sharp suspicion that she knew this man—even though his old-fashioned clothing seemed odd, out of place.

"Adrian, look—"

"My God!" Seizing her arm, he cried, "Run, Vickie!"

Even as they raced off, Vickie heard a shot scream over their heads. Shock and disbelief jolted her. She heard Adrian curse; then he hauled her with him into an alleyway. They tore off down the narrow, cluttered lane, dodging debris and garbage cans.

They were halfway down the squalid passage when all at once a young black woman loomed ahead in their path. She materialized so suddenly that Vickie gasped, half afraid she was seeing a ghost. There was a spooky, almost luminous quality about her. The girl wore a long, plain blue cotton skirt and shirt, a matching turban binding up her hair. Two thin gold bracelets dangled from one of her wrists; a small burlap sack was attached to a rope encircling her waist.

Adrian, too, saw the girl. "Miss, get out of our way!" he shouted, frantically waving his arms. "You're blocking our path—and we're all in danger!"

Yet the girl stood her ground even as the two skidded to a halt before her. Then, in a low voice with a soft Negro inflection, she intoned, "Master, mistress, come with me."

Even as Vickie and Adrian stared mystified at the

girl, she reached out and tugged at Vickie's sleeve. "Come with me, master, mistress," she repeated urgently.

Breathlessly Vickie gazed into the girl's honey-gold eyes and was amazed to spot an age-old wisdom there. Though she wasn't quite sure why, she instinctively trusted this girl.

Then another shot rang out, and Vickie whirled to see the gunman running toward them down the alleyway—and preparing to shoot a third time!

"Come!" the girl shouted.

Vickie and Adrian needed no further prompting. With the girl in the lead, they began blindly running again. . . .

Chapter Eighteen

With the young black woman leading them, Vickie and Adrian raced for their lives. The girl guided them on a zigzag course out of the alleyway, across a street, and into another dank passageway cluttered with discarded crates and barrels. Avoiding hazards as she ran, Vickie glanced behind her and was relieved to note that the gunman was no longer on their heels. She remembered how familiar he had seemed. Was he truly who she thought he was? That seemed impossible, yet . . .

Outside a decaying brownstone building, the black girl stopped, pointing at a yawning doorway where a scarred door hung askew. "Come. We hide there."

Adrian hurried over to the door and struggled to pull it open. With a protesting squeal, it gave way, and Adrian held it open so the women could pass.

After they were inside, he forced the door shut behind them.

Coughing at rising dust, Vickie glanced around. She found herself in a dank-smelling, dark building. Crumbling stone steps rose before them, with a shaft of light spilling over the landing at the top.

"Come," the girl said softly, preceding them up the stairs. "You best watch your step, folks."

Adrian took Vickie's arm and the two climbed the deteriorating steps as best they could. They entered a large room with high ceilings, tall, grimy windows, and a scarred pine floor covered with saw horses, lumber, discarded cans of paint, and other refuse. Vickie surmised the place must be some sort of abandoned store or office.

Adrian turned to the girl. "Who are you, young woman?"

The girl fixed them with her solemn, radiant smile. "I be Brown Bessie."

A shiver washed over Vickie at the girl's words, her serene expression. This astounding young woman who called herself Brown Bessie radiated a presence that was keenly spiritual, almost spooky.

"My heavens, are you the friend Cathy mentioned in her letters?" Vickie asked.

"Aye, mistress. I be the one that save your children from the fire."

Bessie's last calm words staggered Vickie and she hastened closer to the girl. "Oh, my God. You're saying you actually saved Cathy and Nate? That they're really still alive?"

"Yes'um," the girl answered simply.

Overwhelmed with joy, Vickie turned to thrust herself into Adrian's arms. "My heavens, Adrian, they're alive!"

Appearing stunned, Adrian pulled Vickie close for a moment, then turned to the girl. "Young woman, are you really telling us our children are alive?"

Bessie nodded. "Yessir, they be fine. They with Grandma Davis now."

"They're with my great-great-grandmother?" Vickie whispered.

"Yes, mistress. They safe."

Tears in her eyes, Vickie gazed at Adrian. "Adrian, do you hear her?"

Though he appeared troubled, he nodded. "Yes, dear, I do."

Vickie turned back to Bessie. "Oh, thank God. All of you are safe. But . . . but how did you and the children end up here—in nineteenth-century Charleston?"

The girl lowered her gaze. "Bessie explain later. Right now, you jes' trust Bessie. The Evil One, he near."

"Evil one?" Vickie repeated.

Bessie inclined her head toward the window. Vickie walked over, with Adrian close on her heels. She gazed out into the cluttered alleyway, then recoiled slightly as she spotted a man in a frock coat and top hat pacing about with a gun in his hand.

"That's the same man who was chasing us, and firing at us," Adrian whispered urgently.

Vickie turned to face him. "It's Carmichael Keegan."

"What? Are you sure?"

She nodded grimly. "I saw his face when he fired

233

at us the first time. He's also here in 1886 Charleston, bizarre as it seems."

"Well, I'll be deuced."

Bessie moved toward them. "He the Evil One. He try to hurt your children."

"He did? But how? And why?" demanded Adrian.

Bessie paused a moment, cautiously eyeing Keegan, who was still prowling the alleyway. "I take you to the children. They explain. But first we wait till the Evil One go away."

"Perhaps I should sneak down there and try to get the drop on him," Adrian suggested.

"Adrian, no," Vickie protested. "He has a gun and you have nothing with which to defend yourself."

"I could still have the element of surprise."

"Adrian, he's a trained policeman. What if he kills you? Where will Bessie and I—and the children—be then?"

Expression torn but contrite, he reached out to stroke her cheek. "You're right, of course, dear. We'll take a more cautious approach. I just feel so frustrated, and I'm itching to throttle that blackguard."

She squeezed his hand. "Don't worry, you don't have to convince me of your bravery."

Bessie spoke up again. "You two wait now. The Evil One, he leave soon."

While Bessie continued to keep watch over Keegan, Adrian took Vickie aside. "My dear, you're still trembling. Are you all right?"

Vickie was staring mesmerized at Bessie at the window. Was she hallucinating, or did the light seem almost to be passing through the young black woman?

"Vickie?" Adrian nudged.

Nodding tremulously, she embraced him. "Oh, yes, I'm fine. Now that we know Cathy and Nate are safe, we can face anything. Oh, Adrian, isn't it wonderful? The children are still alive!"

He drew back and frowned skeptically. "Well, yes, what the young woman has told us does sound very encouraging."

Vickie was taken aback. *"Encouraging?* You don't believe her?"

Lowering his voice, he argued, "A young woman, a complete stranger, comes to us with the most outlandish tale—"

"You left out that she's Cathy's friend, and she just saved our lives."

He smiled apologetically. "Vickie, I'm sorry. Things still aren't making that much sense to me. There's something strange about the girl. She seems—"

"Luminous?" Vickie supplied.

With a scowl, he studied Bessie. "I'm not sure. But there's something odd and eerie about her. And what if she's conspiring with the man who just tried to kill us—"

"That man is Carmichael Keegan," Vickie cut in.

"So you say."

"So I know," she stated adamantly. "And if Bessie were in cahoots with him, we'd already be dead, wouldn't we?"

"Yes, that's an apt point," he conceded.

Vickie gripped his arm. "Don't you understand, Adrian? Keegan somehow came here across time. We came here across time. For a reason. To find Nate and Cathy. And Bessie will lead us to them. I know this—

and I trust her. When will you begin to accept things on faith?"

He smiled sheepishly. "I suppose I'm still one of those doubting Thomases who must see to believe."

Vickie was about to reply when all at once she flinched, and realized that Bessie now stood next to them. Mercy! She hadn't even heard—or seen—the young woman approaching. "Yes?" she inquired.

"He gone now. We safe."

Vickie nodded to Bessie, then turned proudly to Adrian. "Well, my darling, you're about to see for yourself." To Bessie, she added simply, "Please, take us to our children."

With Bessie in the lead, they were off again, walking quickly east, then turning down Pinckney Street. Vickie could hardly contain her sense of breathless anticipation. Was Cathy truly alive? If so, this was an answer to her prayers, and beyond her wildest dreams. If her sister and Nate still lived, then everything would be right and sane again. Her sense of joy and relief was overwhelming. Glancing at Adrian walking beside her, she noted his preoccupied mien and only wished he could share her hope.

Adrian was indeed feeling quite tense and worried. First a stranger whom Vickie claimed was Carmichael Keegan had fired at them and chased them into an alleyway. If he truly was Keegan, then how on earth had he gotten here to nineteenth-century Charleston? And how had he found them?

Then, this extraordinary young woman who called herself Brown Bessie had materialized in their path like a ghost, and had led them away to safety. Most astounding of all, Bessie had claimed the children were still alive, that they were safe in the care of Vickie's great-great-grandmother. Now she claimed to be taking them there.

Adrian prayed that Bessie had spoken the truth. He hardly dared hope that his dear son might still live, that darling Cathy might be alive as well. That his dark world, into which Vickie had brought the first bright beams of happiness, might at last be flooded with the full light of day.

But Adrian had suffered too much in this life to accept everything so readily, on faith. And what of dear Vickie? He glanced at her beside him, saw the sublime bliss and expectation on her face. What if this were all simply a cruel joke and her hopes were dashed? He wanted so badly to protect her, to save her from any more hurts and disappointments. But could he save her from herself, from being devastated again if Bessie had steered them wrong?

Next to Adrian, Vickie was hardly sharing his sense of caution. Her heart lurched into a wildly expectant rhythm as they proceeded down a row of charming single houses. Then she recognized a cottage that stood apart from the rest—a white, two-story frame house that, unlike most other Charleston homes, squarely faced the street. In the yard a tall oak tree beckoned; on the porch a cozy swing invited leisure moments.

Within a few feet of the property, she asked, "Is that where my great-great-grandmother lives?"

Bessie turned. "How you know that, mistress?"

Vickie shook her head. "It's funny, but I don't know how I know. I've never seen her house, not even a picture. I just always imagined her living in a two-story white frame house, with a railed porch across the front and a large bay window on one end."

"Well, we be here," Bessie agreed matter-of-factly, opening the white picket gate.

Going up the sidewalk with Adrian, Vickie glanced at him. He appeared as uneasy as before. Surely he must share a bit of her hope, even though he wouldn't admit it. Surely he was thinking what she was thinking, wondering if the children were really there, hoping against hope that it was true, that their long search was finally over. . . .

Without knocking, Bessie opened the front door, then gestured for the two of them to precede her inside. "Miss Sophie, we be home," she called softly.

Vickie stepped into the entryway, eagerly drinking in the smells of freshly cut flowers and furniture polish. She found the flowers in a crystal bowl on the nearby pier table, then noted the gleam of the polish on the oak staircase bannister curving to their left. She glanced to her right at a homey parlor with carved rosewood furniture upholstered in burgundy-colored velvet, a rich burgundy and blue oriental rug, gold flocked wallpaper, and drapes of burgundy velvet. Her attention was particularly drawn to a beautifully carved mahogany piano occupying one corner.

Then she glanced ahead as a hunched little woman appeared at the back of the hallway and started toward them. Her hair was silvery gray and caught in a bun, her face thin and lined, but still quite lovely. She walked with a cane and wore a floor-length gown of emerald green silk.

She smiled in greeting, and her fine gray eyes sparkled. "Bessie, dear, who have you here?"

"They be the ones I tell you about, Miss Sophie."

The old woman gasped, her visage a mixture of surprise and joy. "You mean . . . you don't mean they're Cathy's sister and Nate's father?"

"Yes, ma'am," Bessie replied. "They come here, just like Bessie tell you."

The woman drew closer, gazing intently at Vickie. "Forevermore! Bessie told me you might come, but this is simply incredible! Tell me, are you really Vickie Cheney?"

In a voice choked with emotion, Vickie replied, "Yes, I am."

The old woman hugged her, and Vickie could feel her frail arms trembling about her as she whispered, "Oh, my dear, my dear. I'm so pleased to meet you. I'm your great-great-grandmother, Sophie Davis."

Vickie drew back, wiping away tears. "Yes, I know. I'm so glad to meet you!"

Sophie turned to Adrian and extended a thin hand. "And you must be Commander Bennett. Oh, I simply cannot believe you're both actually here!"

Adrian solemnly shook her hand. "Yes, madam, I am Commander Bennett, and it is a pleasure to meet you. Now, kindly forgive our impatience, but you must tell us: Are Nate and Cathy really here?"

Surprisingly, Sophie laughed, a sound of pure joy. "Why, I think they should answer that for themselves." She turned and hobbled toward the stairway. "Oh, Nate! Cathy! Come down here, pray. You have visitors."

Adrian glanced at Vickie with wild hope. She smiled through her tears and reached out to squeeze

239

his hand. His obvious emotion made her heart fill with tenderness toward him.

Then both turned toward the staircase and stood mesmerized, their gazes riveted to the landing above. They waited in agony as the seconds ticked past. . . . At last at the head of the stairs, there appeared a boy and girl, holding hands. Slowly, the two started down the steps together.

Chapter Nineteen

As the children continued moving tentatively down the stairs, Vickie almost couldn't believe her own eyes . . . but yes, Cathy was there! She recognized her sister, with her golden pineapple curls and bright blue eyes. To Vickie, the child seemed an angel in human form, dressed in a floor-length, lace-trimmed pink cotton gown, and carrying a blob of orange and brown fur in her arms. Vickie's heart seemed to burst with the joy she felt.

"Cathy!" she cried.

The little girl gazed down at Vickie, her eyes going wide with recognition and joy. "Vickie! Is it truly you?"

Leaving the boy behind, Cathy raced down the stairs, almost tripping in her haste. Vickie reached out and grabbed Cathy, enfolding the child in her arms, kitten and all. "Oh, Cathy, Cathy darling," she murmured, clutching her sister close, inhaling the well remembered scent of her hair. Tears streamed down her cheeks and she trembled with emotion. Never in her life had she felt such overwhelming happiness and relief. To think that the dear child she had thought dead was now alive and well, warm and breathing, in her arms!

Then a piteous "meow" made Vickie realize she must be squeezing the kitten, and she quickly put Cathy down. The two sisters laughed, while the kitten stared from one to the other with his dark-gold eyes.

Vickie hugged her sister again and kissed Cathy's soft cheek, this time taking care not to squash the kitten. "Cathy, I'm so thrilled you're alive!"

"And I'm so glad to see you, Vickie!" Cathy replied brightly. "How was the war? Did you nurse all those poor sick soldiers until there were none left?"

"Something like that, darling," Vickie replied, wiping away tears. "But, you must tell me, dear—how did you end up here?"

"Why, Bessie brought us, of course," Cathy declared. "Me and Nate'll tell you all about it." With a perturbed look, Cathy turned back toward the stairs. "Nate, what are you doing up there all alone? Come on down and say hello to my sister Vickie."

Vickie also turned. She'd been so preoccupied with finding Cathy that she hadn't noticed the drama still unfolding back at the stairs. Nate stood halfway up, staring down warily at his father, who entreated his son with a trembling hand. . . .

Adrian almost couldn't believe his own eyes as he recognized his dear son, in the flesh, there on the stairs. To think that Nate was alive! Really alive and well! Emotions staggered him—shock and disbelief, relief and joy, longing, awe, and the overwhelming desire to crush his dear child in his arms. Guilt also assailed him as he realized Vickie had been right—right about everything—and he had put her through utter hell with his doubts. And even greater remorse plagued him because he did not deserve to be reunited with this darling boy he had abandoned, this dear lad who regarded him now with such anger and mistrust.

How the boy had grown! Since he'd last seen him, Nate had surely shot up a foot, his frame tall and slender, his face revealing the stronger, more angular lines of pending adolescence. He looked almost like a lad from another time, dressed in his knickers, boots, and a long-sleeved blue broadcloth shirt, his long hair sadly in need of a haircut. But this was his Nate, all right; there was no mistaking those dark brown eyes and the proud tilt of his chin. Nor was there any confusing the boy's distance and reserve—a gap Adrian was determined to bridge.

"Nate, it's your dad," he greeted the boy hoarsely. "I'm so very glad to see you. Won't you please come down, son?"

Nate swallowed hard, his eyes flashing with turbulent emotion. Then he started down the steps. But at the bottom, even as Adrian reached out, Nate quickly sped past his father and rushed to Cathy's side, turning to eye Adrian in defiance.

The boy's snub brought a gasp from Sophie. Adrian stood stunned, crushed by his son's rejection. Not that he didn't deserve it. . . .

Watching the emotional scene unfold, Vickie found

243

her heart going out to Adrian. She yearned to help both father and son, to try to bring them together, but didn't know what she could say or do to improve matters.

Sophie stepped in, speaking firmly to Nate. "Now Nate, dear, this is no way to treat your father. Why, he's come a very long way, with Cathy's sister, to be with you."

Nate hurled a belligerent glance at his father. "I don't want him here."

Vickie watched Adrian grimace at his son's harsh tone, and again she keenly sympathized. Cathy, however, was not the least bit daunted by Nate's hostility. Aghast, she turned to him and scolded him with a wagging finger. "Nate, how dare you act that way! Your dad is here to see you, after all these years. You go over and say hello, right now."

"No, I don't want him here!" Nate reiterated, his angry voice causing the kitten to squeal.

"Now look what you've done," Cathy chided, petting the tense animal. "You've upset Rufus. You go say hello to your dad right this minute or neither of us will speak to you again. *Ever*."

Evidently Nate recognized that Cathy meant business, for even though his expression seethed with resentment, he strode over to Adrian and stiffly extended his hand. "Hello, sir."

Vickie thought her heart might break at this cold formality between father and son; indeed, the shattered look on Adrian's face made her hurt for him all the more. Nonetheless, he was a trooper to the end, forcing a smile and bravely shaking his son's hand, when Vickie knew he must be dying inside, aching to wrap his lost, alienated son in his arms.

"Hello, son," he said awkwardly. "I'm so very glad to see you, to know you're alive and well. Vickie and I have been desperately worried about you. . . ." His gaze flicked to Cathy, and he smiled tenderly. "And about Cathy, too, of course."

Nate was unmoved. "If you were so worried about me, sir, then you might not have deserted me in the first place."

"Son, I'm sorry," Adrian replied earnestly. "I deeply regret that I wasn't there for you when you needed me."

"Well, maybe it's too late for your regrets," Nate shot back.

"Nate!" exclaimed Cathy. "You mustn't act so mean to your dad!"

Nate clenched his jaw and didn't reply.

"Nate, that is enough," seconded Sophie. "You are a guest in my home, as is your father. Here my guests treat each other with courtesy and respect."

Nate remained silent, his visage rebellious.

Sophie forced a pleasant expression. "Now come along, everyone. Let's go inside the parlor and become acquainted—or reacquainted, as the case may be." She trilled a laugh. "We have so much to discuss—and isn't *that* an understatement?"

The group of six took seats in the parlor, Adrian and Vickie occupying the settee, with Cathy between them, Sophie and Nate on the loveseat, and Bessie seated on a stool near the hearth. For a moment an awkward silence fell.

Clearing her throat, Sophie again assumed the role of leadership. "I must say this is quite an occasion. I can't remember a happier day since before I lost my husband. Not only have I been visited by Bessie, Nate, and now his father, Commander Bennett"—she paused to smile at each of them in turn—"but also by my own, as yet unborn, great-great-granddaughters."

"That's right," Vickie put in with amazement. "From your perspective, Great-great-grandmother, Cathy and I *are* as yet unborn. Yet here we are—staggering though it seems."

"Indeed," agreed Sophie. "My mind has been spinning ever since the day Bessie and the children arrived here. And now, the two of you . . . why, I can't even comprehend it all. Though I suppose sometimes 'tis best to try to accept matters on faith and be grateful to the Almighty for the miracles he has granted us."

"All of this is certainly miraculous, Great-great-grandmother," Vickie concurred.

"And please, dear Vickie, just call me Grandmother. Cathy already does, and it's so much easier, much less confusing." Sophie pressed a hand to her breast. "And at my age, dear, I'm all too easily confused."

Vickie nodded. "Very well. I'm honored to call you Grandmother."

"There's so much I want to ask you and Commander Bennett," Sophie continued, "such as how you were able to follow the children, when from what they've told me, you're also from the year 1945, just as they are. But first, I sense there is much the two of you need to ask the children. They and Bessie have already filled me in on how they came to be here, but surely you want to hear the story for yourselves."

"Oh, yes, we're dying to know," Vickie replied.

"Nate'll tell you!" Cathy exclaimed.

"Can you do that, son?" Adrian asked. "Can you tell me and Vickie how you and Cathy came to be here?"

Nate stared at his father with barely disguised antagonism and did not reply.

Cathy glowered at the boy. "Nate, you tell them, right now!"

Nate hesitated, then eyed Vickie. "I'll tell the lady."

"You'll tell them both!" Cathy insisted.

After balking for another moment, Nate sighed. "Very well." But he stared straight at Vickie as he began telling of the murder he and Cathy had witnessed.

When Nate concluded his story, explaining that when they had jumped from the burning attic they'd landed in a fish pond outside the 1886 orphanage, the adults were silent for several moments.

"How extraordinary!" Vickie said at last, turning to Bessie with an expression of awe. "So it's just like what you told us. You saved the children, and brought them here, to another time."

"Yes 'um," Bessie concurred with a quiet smile.

"But *how* did you do it?" Adrian asked.

The black girl gave a shrug. "Bessie jes' do what she need to do. Not ask how, or why. Jes' believe, and do."

"Well, thank heaven for you!" Vickie declared.

"Yes, Bessie saved us," Cathy declared excitedly. "Then she brought us to Grandma Davis's house, and we've been here ever since."

"My gracious—how long has that been?" Vickie asked.

Cathy glanced at Sophie. "How long, Grandma?"

"Why, for the summer."

Vickie could only shake her head.

"We've had fun, too," Cathy went on gaily. "Grandma bought us new clothes—people dress funny here, you know!—and she took us to church, to the library, to concerts at the park, and swimming at the Battery."

"Madam, thank you so much for taking such good care of the children," Adrian put in sincerely to Sophie.

"Amen," seconded Vickie.

"You're both most welcome," Sophie replied. "Having the children here has been one of the greatest pleasures of my life—not to mention, the most extraordinary experience I've ever known."

"I'll say," agreed Vickie. She patted Cathy's hand. "And that's an amazing story, honey. We're so grateful that you and Nate are okay."

"We're glad you're okay, too!"

Vickie turned to Bessie. "I don't know how you pulled off the miracle you did, but Commander Bennett and I thank you from the bottom of our hearts."

Bessie smiled shyly. "Bessie glad to help."

"We'll be grateful to you for the rest of our lives," Adrian added humbly. "And we owe you the lives of our children."

"I take care of them, master," Bessie told him quietly. "That my job."

"Well, you do it magnificently," Adrian praised.

Vickie glanced quizzically at Bessie. "But I do have a question for you."

"Bessie try to answer."

"If you and the children have been here ever since the fire, then why did Commander Bennett and I keep seeing Nate and Cathy in the Charleston streets back in the present?"

"You saw us, Vickie?" whispered Cathy.

"I sure did, honey. At various times, Commander Bennett and I saw you and Nate all over Charleston— at the orphanage, on Meeting Street, at the Battery. Why one time, you even left us a Liberty head nickel."

Cathy clapped her hands. "I bet that's the nickel Grandma gave me! I lost it on the way to the candy store!"

Vickie smiled wonderingly. "How incredible. Well, we found it, honey. Our sightings of you were always brief, and they rattled us quite badly, since we'd been told . . ."

"What, Vickie?" Cathy prompted.

Vickie hesitated a moment, then admitted, "Well, that you and Nate had both died in the fire."

Cathy giggled. "How silly. We aren't dead. We're here!"

"We know that now, honey," Vickie answered tactfully. "But you see, back in the present, you disappeared during the fire, and the authorities assumed . . . well, that you were gone."

Cathy chortled. "We were gone, all right. Gone *here*."

"Yes, honey." Vickie squeezed Cathy's hand, then addressed Bessie. "Can you tell us why Commander

Bennett and I saw Cathy and Nate back in the present, when they were actually here with you?"

"Yes' um. It their spirits come to beckon you," the girl answered simply.

"My heaven—how astonishing," Vickie murmured.

"Indeed," remarked Sophie. "Every aspect of the children's journey here has been utterly miraculous. Bessie has explained it to me several times now, and so has Nate. But I still can't claim to understand it."

"Perhaps we never will," said Vickie. She gave Cathy a quick hug. "But I'm so glad."

"Me, too!" cried Cathy, grinning at her sister.

Turning to Adrian, Sophie asked, "So, Commander Bennett, how did you and Vickie come to journey back here? Was your experience as remarkable as that of Cathy and Nate?"

"It was remarkable all right, if not nearly as dramatic," Adrian replied. "You see, Vickie and I met in Charleston when we both went there for a memorial service for the children. At first, neither of us knew that the other had also lost a child in the fire. In due course, we compared notes, and that's when we realized we'd both been seeing Nate and Cathy—or their ghosts—in the Charleston streets. But every time we would spot the children, they would run away, and we never could get really close. I felt we were seeing the children's spirits, while Vickie insisted they were real."

"And you know, Adrian, it seems we both were right," Vickie commented with awe.

He smiled in pleasant surprise. "That's quite true, my dear. We *were* both right."

250

"What happened then, Commander Bennett?" Sophie asked.

Turning back to Sophie, he continued. "Vickie and I searched and searched for the children, without success. Then I talked her into accompanying me to the burnt-out chapel so that we could say a prayer together, that the children's spirits might be at peace. We did say our prayer, and both slipped into an almost trancelike state. That's when the ground began to move, like a small earthquake . . . and then we ended up here, in the year 1886, with the chapel fully restored."

"Forevermore," Sophie breathed. "Some mystical power must have brought you here, where you needed to be, to be reunited with your children. Oh, I never thought I'd be blessed with seeing such a marvel. And now I suppose you can all remain here, and live 'happily ever after,' as the fairy tale goes?"

Vickie and Adrian exchanged a tense look. "I'm afraid it's not quite that simple, madam," he replied. "You see, the man who threatened the children, Carmichael Keegan, remains a menace. Now that Nate has told us what really happened to him and Cathy back in the present, I feel it's quite possible that Keegan actually set the fire at St. Christopher's Orphanage, to ensure that the children could never testify against him for murdering the other officer."

Vickie snapped her fingers. "Adrian, I bet you're right! Why, it's all finally making sense to me! Keegan must have set that fire in the hope of eliminating the children as witnesses!"

"And now . . . well, now it seems Keegan has followed us here to the past," Adrian finished grimly.

"Here?" Sophie repeated in shock.

"Did you bring him here with you?" Nate accused his father.

Adrian flinched at the boy's sharp tone. "No, son, we're not sure just how Keegan got here."

"But he's been following us around, and actually fired two shots at us earlier," Vickie added. "That's when Bessie appeared to rescue us."

"My kingdom!" exclaimed Sophie. "You two are lucky to be alive. And once again we have Bessie to thank."

"Yes, we do," agreed Adrian. "And now, perhaps the best thing for us to do would be to take Cathy and Nate back to the orphanage chapel. Perhaps if we said our prayer again, we might all be transported back to the present, away from Keegan."

Vickie stared at Adrian, impressed by his logic, which did make a certain sense. But before anyone could comment on his astounding suggestion, Nate leaped to his feet. "No, I'm not going anywhere with you!" he declared to his father.

Instead of scolding Nate, Cathy turned fretfully to Vickie. "Do we have to, Vickie? I want to stay here with Bessie and Nate, and with Grandma Davis. I've had lots of fun this summer, and I don't want to leave."

Vickie nodded sympathetically to her sister. In truth, the situation they found themselves in was so mind-boggling, she had no real idea what they should do.

Then, surprising everyone, Bessie stood and walked to the center of the room, and turned to Adrian. "No, master, you not leave."

"I beg your pardon?" Adrian asked.

An almost surreal glow came over Bessie's countenance. "That other world, it not your time. The Evil One, he be here. You fight him here. If you go back, you all die."

Chapter Twenty

Vickie felt stunned by Bessie's calm words. If they returned to the present, they would all die? What on earth did this mean? That they should all remain here, subject to the whims of the madman who was stalking them, and the certainty of the earthquake tomorrow? She glanced at Adrian, only to see that he looked equally baffled.

Then Sophie spoke up. "Commander Bennett, I'm quite a foolish old woman, given to flights of fancy, willing to believe much that defies comprehension. But I believe Bessie has spoken the truth, and we must trust her. You and Vickie need to stay here with the children."

Adrian shook his head. "You fail to understand, madam. I hate to alarm you, but Vickie and I happen to know that a terrible earthquake will strike Charleston tomorrow."

Sophie uttered a cry of dismay. "An earthquake? Merciful heavens! Charleston has been hit by some minor quakes before, but nothing major."

"Well, this is going to be major, madam—trust me on that point," Adrian replied grimly. "All of our lives will be in jeopardy if we remain here. You, the children, and Bessie should all try to accompany us back to the present. At the very least, we should all leave Charleston."

Even as the children would have protested again, Sophie held up a hand. "Commander Bennett, I still think you're wrong."

"Yes, we want to stay here!" seconded Cathy.

Vickie wondered if she should tell Sophie the truth about the dire fate awaiting her tomorrow in this very house. But her instincts urged her not to divulge this as yet. Instead, she asked Sophie, "But what about Carmichael Keegan, and the threat he poses to the children?"

Sophie rose, went to a Queen Anne desk, and opened a drawer, pulling out a Colt revolver and a small box of bullets. She walked over to Adrian and handed him both.

"Commander Bennett, this is the pistol my beloved William carried during the Civil War. I want you to have it now to protect us all."

Although Adrian accepted the weapon and bullets, tucking the pistol at his waist and placing the box of ammunition in his pocket, he appeared quite troubled. Vickie felt concerned as well. She watched Sophie hobble around the room, drawing down the shades. . . .

A moment later, Adrian asked Sophie to excuse

him and Vickie so the two of them could talk, and Sophie suggested the couple might adjourn to the courtyard at the back of her house.

As Adrian escorted Vickie down the back steps, she marveled at the beauty of the blooming crepe myrtles and roses, the high brick walls covered with Carolina jasmine. The air was warm, thick with the scent of nectar, and Vickie could hear a cardinal singing in a nearby pear tree. Sunlight dappled the mossy ground and the stone bench at the center of the charming little garden. A breeze rustled leaves and made shifting patterns of light about them.

Wordlessly Adrian led Vickie to the bench. They sat down and fell reverently quiet.

Vickie was relieved to have these few moments to consider her turbulent emotions. She felt an overwhelming confluence of feelings—sheer joy over having found Cathy, relief that Adrian had found his son, all mingled with confusion and concern over their current plight, worry about their uncertain future.

She squeezed Adrian's hand and forced a smile. "It's lovely here, so quiet and pristine."

"Indeed, yes," he murmured, getting to his feet. "I just wish our situation were as simple and lovely."

"But, Adrian, aren't you ecstatic to have found your son?"

"Of course I am," he replied earnestly. "My joy at finding Nate knows no bounds. And I owe you an apology, darling. You were right. About everything."

She stood. "You give me too much credit. I didn't figure everything out. Far from it."

"Who could have figured out all of this? But my point is, you were always ready to move forward on faith, while I discouraged you every step of the way."

"You can't help what you felt. But I just had a strong intuition all along that Nate and Cathy were still alive, and that if we kept on trying, we'd surely find them."

"Well, you were absolutely correct." He eyed her tenderly. "Forgive me for not having more faith in you?"

She slipped into his arms. "Of course. There's nothing to forgive."

He hugged her tightly. "I can't believe we've really found them."

"I know. I'm still pinching myself, afraid they may disappear again at any moment."

He drew back and smiled. "We won't let them. Not now. I'm so happy for you, my love. Cathy is just darling."

"So is Nate. Although I know he didn't greet you warmly."

"I can't blame the lad there," Adrian said heavily. "But he'll come around in time."

"Time," Adrian repeated, glancing about him almost helplessly. "Time seems to be the one commodity we have very little of."

She nodded. "I know, we do seem to be in great danger here. I agree with your suggestion that all of us try to return to the present. There may well be some type of time portal there at the chapel. Only . . ." She paused, biting her lip.

"Yes?" he prompted.

She regarded him soberly. "Perhaps we should stay here. Bessie could be right about that."

"Bessie," he repeated, shaking his head. "Much as

I feel grateful toward her, what do we really know about her?"

"We know that she has been Cathy's friend. We know she saved the children's lives, as well as our own."

"That doesn't mean she has all the right answers, Vickie."

"Adrian, I trust her. And I think you should, too." As he would have protested, she rushed on. "Think about it, Adrian. There's been a plan, a purpose, in everything that has happened to us. First, Bessie rescued the children from the fire and whisked them off here, to safety. Then the two of us met in Charleston, and fell—well, we became close, sharing our need and our grief. All the while the children were drawing us here, and then at last we too were brought here as well, to find them. Don't you see, Adrian? It all makes sense, and there's clearly some sort of divine purpose at work. It all seems to center on Bessie somehow. I think we should believe her, and let her continue leading us, as she has already done so well."

"What about Keegan?" Adrian put in darkly. "We're only just beginning to understand the true depths of his depravity, and that he may even have deliberately set the fire that initiated this entire tragic chain of events. So, tell me, did Bessie lead that miscreant to us as well?"

Vickie waved a hand. "Adrian, you're trying to apply strict logic to a situation that must be viewed in broader, more mystical terms. When will you learn to accept things on faith, as I do, as the children do, as Sophie does?"

"So you can't explain Keegan's being here?"

She sighed. "Well, I do remember that we both felt we were being followed back in 1945 Charleston. What if Keegan were the one trailing us there, just as he later did here?"

"That makes sense," he agreed.

"And what if he happened into the ruined orphanage chapel, right as we were saying our prayer, right as we were being transported here?"

Adrian scowled. "I suppose that's possible, as well. So you're thinking he became caught up in our journey here more or less by accident?"

"Yes." She frowned. "Or maybe it wasn't just a quirk of fate."

"What do you mean?"

"Again, Adrian, I must go back to the overall plan I see in everything. Maybe we *are* meant to deal with Keegan's treachery here. Perhaps that was part of the reason he was brought here as well, to force him to face up to those he has harmed and make him accept some sort of judgment for his sins. And I think we should stay and see this through."

"My dear, I still can't agree."

"Why not?"

"Why, the danger Keegan poses, for starters. We know now that he has tried to murder the children as well as ourselves. We know he's been following us around here. He will surely think to question the same priest we spoke with earlier—if he hasn't already—and he will soon doubtless learn of our whereabouts. Your great-great-grandmother has no telephone, which puts us all in grave danger. Indeed, much as I've resisted our contacting the authorities, I'm wondering if I shouldn't leave now and summon the police."

"But wouldn't your leaving place the rest of us in danger?"

With rising frustration, he asked, "Should I take you, Nate, and Cathy along, and risk Keegan's taking potshots at all of you out in the streets? Don't you think it's better that I go alone to seek help?"

She released a heavy breath. "But as you pointed out earlier, how can we enlist the aid of the police without telling them our entire, bizarre story? You didn't even want us to warn folks about the earthquake. And I must admit, that makes sense. Can we risk being detained by the authorities, with the earthquake to occur tomorrow?"

Adrian pulled his fingers through his hair. "Vickie, I don't claim to have all the answers. I'm just trying to protect us all as best I can."

"Well, what if Keegan is lurking somewhere outside this house, even now, lying in wait for us? If you leave, you could be killed. Besides, Keegan strikes me as the kind of coward who likes to shoot people in the back. I doubt he'll try to invade a house filled with six people."

Adrian nodded. "You may be right, but I'll be keeping this gun with me at all times and will hold vigil over the household tonight."

"Good."

He sighed. "But unfortunately, Vickie, we will have to take some sort of action soon, since the earthquake will hit tomorrow."

"I know."

"Do you remember what time the strike will come?"

She struggled to remember. "I'm not certain, but it will definitely be after dark, since the play that we saw running about the earthquake was entitled *A Night in August* . . ." Her voice trailed off, and she bit her lip.

He touched her cheek. "What is it, dear?"

"Do you think I should tell Grandmother Davis she will die if she remains in the house tomorrow?"

Adrian shook his head. "No, dear. Not yet. After all, we do have at least one night to try to decide on the best course of action for everyone."

"Including the town itself," Vickie added grimly. "It still bothers me that we're keeping this to ourselves. There's bound to be loss of life tomorrow."

"Can we help the townsfolk if they lock us up as lunatics?" he demanded.

She groaned. "Oh, Adrian, I just feel so helpless, so scared and confused."

He pulled her close and pressed his lips to her temple. "Me, too, darling. I'd suggest that for now, we just try to cherish this evening with the children, since God only knows what tomorrow may bring for us all. . . ."

Vickie clutched him tightly. "I know. Be my strength, Adrian."

"I will, darling."

"We need each other so badly, especially now."

"I know."

As the breeze stirred the foliage again, Adrian leaned over and tenderly kissed Vickie. Joy welled in

261

him. It felt so wondrous holding her close, so glorious to know the children were safe inside.

Yet he felt such anxiety for them all. Was Vickie right? Should they all remain here, and face whatever tomorrow held in store for them? Should they confront Keegan, try to withstand the earthquake? Or should they at least try to return to the present? Logic argued they would be safer there—yet Bessie claimed if they went, they would all die.

Adrian wasn't sure which way to turn. But he did know one thing with absolute certainty: He was determined to protect those he loved from all harm, no matter what the cost, even if that meant his own life.

Inside the house, Nate stood at the back window, grimly watching his dad kiss Cathy's sister. Just as he'd done earlier, he hardened his heart against his father.

As for Cathy's sister, Nate liked her okay. But he remained furious that his dad had come here, threatening the secure world he'd found for Cathy and himself, trying to destroy the miracle Brown Bessie had brought to them.

He had no love left for his father. He told himself this fiercely, even as hot emotion welled up in his chest to belie the claim that he didn't care.

He chided himself for his weakness. He was far too old, and had too many adult responsibilities, to wallow in the anguish of a lost, wounded child.

He'd turned to his father after his mum had died, and his dad had spurned him, heartlessly shunning him again and again, as if the sight of Nate were abhorrent to him. He'd made his contempt for his child obvious. Then the final blow had come when his dad had enlisted in the air force and deserted him.

Now he'd come around again, six years too late, begging for Nate's forgiveness.

Well, Nate wouldn't give it. He was much older and wiser now. He was determined to remain right here with Cathy. And to heck with the others.

Feeling a hand on his shoulder, he flinched, then turned to see Cathy regarding him with concern.

Cathy was indeed feeling very worried about her best friend. When Adrian and Vickie had first arrived, she'd felt only joy at seeing her sister again. Adrian had seemed real nice, too. But now that things had settled down a bit, she realized that Nate was still acting tense and withdrawn.

"Nate, are you okay?" she asked.

Nate jerked his head toward the window. "I'd be better if those two had never come around."

Cathy sucked in a horrified breath. "Nate, how can you say that about Vickie and your dad? Aren't you glad they're here?"

"No, I wish they would go away. And they brought with them the bad man who tried to hurt us."

"Nate, it isn't their fault that he's here."

"I think it is." Nate tightened his jaw. "Besides, they're going to try to pull us apart, Cathy, and take us away from Grandma Sophie. You know how much we both like staying with her."

Cathy cast him a pleading look. "No, Nate, they won't tear us apart. Your dad seems very kind—"

"Don't you dare be fooled by him!"

Cathy gasped, feeling bewildered by Nate's hostility. "But, Nate, they know how much we love each other. They'll keep us together."

Nate swallowed hard. "They won't. Just you watch. I don't trust them."

"But Bessie told us they would be coming for us."

"I don't trust her, either."

Hurt and confused, Cathy touched his arm. "Nate, don't you even trust *me* anymore? Why are you so mad?"

At once contrite, he gave her a quick hug. "Of course I trust you, goose, and how could I be mad at you? You are my sweetheart, forever."

"You're just angry because I'm happy to see Vickie," she accused with a wounded air. "You're jealous, aren't you?"

Blinking rapidly, Nate didn't answer.

"Well, I won't be sorry. I won't!" Cathy burst out.

Stung by her words, Nate clenched his fists. "See, they're already tearing us apart. Already!"

Cathy felt miserably torn. "Nate, no . . ." She reached for him, but he had already turned and stalked away.

Outside, across the street from the Davis home, Carmichael Keegan lurked behind the large trunk of an oak tree. He stared at the white frame house across from him, where someone had just drawn all the blinds. Cheney and Bennett were inside there now, he was sure. He was almost glad his earlier bullets had missed their mark. It was just as well the two were still alive, for they might well have led him to his ultimate targets.

Keegan had followed Bennett and Cheney again,

all day, with growing frustration. He'd become sick and tired of traipsing after them all over the city. They'd seemed to be wandering aimlessly, questioning folks at random and accomplishing nothing. He'd lost his patience, and had fired at them after they'd left St. Mary's Church.

Then he'd lost them, and had backtracked to the church. There, he had questioned the same priest who had spoken to them. That was how he had learned that the two were bound for this house—Sophie Davis's place. The priest had even told him the Cheney woman was related to Sophie Davis.

Could it be that the brats he was seeking were also inside?

He rubbed his hands together in anticipation. All four of the people he wanted to kill might well be within his grasp.

The only problem was, he had foolishly tipped his hand to Cheney and Bennett when he had fired at them, alerting them to his presence. Hell, he had always been too much the hothead for his own good, too damn quick on the draw, like that day when he'd impulsively killed Paddy McIntire. By now, Cheney and Bennett would surely be expecting him and be prepared to defend themselves.

How could he get to them?

He would simply bide his time. Then, once all of them were asleep, he would deal with them, and begin his new life here, without anyone knowing about his misdeeds.

Chapter Twenty-one

When Adrian and Vickie went back inside, she could smell the succulent aroma of food coming from the kitchen, and figured her great-great-grandmother must be cooking. She smiled at the sight of her sister, seated on the living room floor next to Bessie. Both were watching the kitten cavort, batting its paws at some curious small stones Bessie was spinning about. Moving closer, Vickie noted that the objects were gold or brownish, crystalline in appearance, and none was perfectly round. Some were ovals, some squarish, while others were shaped like pyramids or octahedrons. Yet Bessie spun them all with amazing skill, while the kitten danced about and Cathy laughed and clapped her hands.

"What are you two doing?" she asked.

Cathy beamed up at her older sister. "Rufus is playing with Bessie's marbles. You want to play, too?"

Vickie sank down beside the girls. "Looks like fun. Bessie, those are very interesting stones you're whirling about."

"They're *marbles*," Cathy solemnly corrected.

"Ah, marbles."

Bessie glanced up at Vickie and shyly smiled. "They from Africa, like Bessie."

"Africa?" Vickie repeated, rather bemused. Bessie was from Africa? She was certainly a creature of mystery.

"Bessie's the best marble player ever!" Cathy declared.

Vickie hugged her sister and fondly tousled her blond curls.

As the girls continued to play, Vickie glanced over to see Adrian approaching his son. Nate stood apart from the others in a corner, arms akimbo and jaw set belligerently. Vickie's heart went out to the boy as she considered the pain he must be in, not just feeling rejected by his father, but also resenting Adrian's coming here. Evidently Adrian could do nothing right in Nate's eyes. . . .

Adrian was trying as hard as he could to communicate with his alienated son. Despite the boy's look of antagonism, Adrian flashed him an encouraging smile. "Son, Vickie and I just want you to know that we aren't going to try to separate you and Cathy. And we're not taking the two of you anywhere—at least, not yet."

Nate was silent, warily regarding his dad.

"Son, I know you must be angry at me, and I don't blame you at all," Adrian went on. "But right now,

267

you and I, as the men of the household, have a much more pressing problem at hand."

Pausing, Adrian observed the struggle on Nate's young, vulnerable face. Obviously he was intrigued by his father's comments.

"You mean the man who tried to hurt me and Cathy?" the boy at last replied. "The evil policeman you brought here with you?"

Adrian blanched. "Son, we didn't bring Carmichael Keegan here with us. He must have somehow followed us."

"And now, thanks to you, he wants to kill us all, right?"

Adrian sighed. "Nate, I'm perfectly willing to accept blame for Keegan's being here, if that's the way you're determined to see it. But that doesn't absolve either of us from our responsibilities. We must protect the women—Cathy, Vickie, Bessie, and of course, Mrs. Davis—from Keegan."

Evidently that comment reached Nate, for his expression softened slightly. He shifted from foot to foot, then inclined his head toward the revolver Adrian carried, the butt of which was just visible inside his jacket. "Will you let me shoot him?"

A half-smile pulled at Adrian's mouth. "Nate, guns are very dangerous—"

"I know that!" Nate retorted. "But you could still show me how to use it."

"I'll be happy to remove the bullets and show you the gun," Adrian replied diplomatically, "and to demonstrate how it must be safely handled. However, as far as teaching you how to shoot is concerned, I'm sure you'll agree that there simply isn't time for such lessons right now. But later, say, when you're sixteen or so, I'd be honored to teach you."

Nate hesitated. "You had a revolver during the war, didn't you?"

"Yes, although I didn't shoot it. I did fire my machine guns when I tangled with Jerries in the skies over Europe."

Again Adrian could see the conflict on Nate's face—his natural male curiosity over his father's combat experiences warring with the resentment and wounded pride that forbade him from asking for more details.

When the boy remained silent, Adrian cleared his throat. "Anyway, son, when I was facing combat, we had strategy sessions before each mission—you know, sizing up the enemy's strengths, his location, and so forth, looking at maps and charts, planning battle tactics."

"So you think we should do that to guard against Keegan?"

Adrian grinned, taking pride in the boy's quick mind. "Yes. Excellent deduction, son. I think we should do precisely that."

Nate frowned for a long moment, then drew himself up. "Okay, I agree that we have to protect the women from Keegan. I'll help you with that, for now—but that doesn't mean I'll forgive you."

Though his heart was aching, Adrian maintained a stoic facade. "I understand, son. I accept your help on whatever terms you're willing to give it."

Nate pointed at a desk in the corner. "Grandma Sophie told Cathy and me we may borrow her paper and pencils. So we can use them now—that is, if we need to do maps and strategy."

"Great idea, son. Let's do just that." Adrian was reaching out to touch Nate's arm when the boy ducked away and hurried toward the desk. With a sigh, he followed.

Across the room, Vickie had been eavesdropping on the touchingly awkward conversation between father and son. Her heart had welled with pride when she'd heard Adrian asking his son for help—for what better way to try to reach him. Nonetheless, she had felt twinges of sadness for Adrian due to Nate's bristly attitude. But now, watching father and son pull up chairs together at the desk, she was encouraged. It would take some time and some patience, but surely Adrian would be able to win Nate's trust.

Then Vickie was distracted by the sound of Cathy squealing, and turned to watch her sister whirl Bessie's marbles for Rufus.

"Hey, you're good at that," she told Cathy, giving her a fond squeeze.

Cathy held up a handful of marbles. "Now you try."

Vickie laughed ruefully. "Sure, though I won't be as good at it as you or Bessie."

"We'll teach you," Cathy assured her. "I'm so glad you're here, Vickie."

Vickie kissed Cathy's hair. "I am, too, sweetheart."

Over the next moments, both Cathy and Bessie laughed as Vickie tried unsuccessfully to spin the odd-shaped marbles. Even lessons from Cathy did not help, and the poor kitten was left to look on in bewilderment as Vickie continued to fumble with the stones.

Vickie felt almost relieved when Sophie emerged from the kitchen in her apron. "How are you folks doing?"

"Oh, I'm about ready to be rescued, as I'm a disaster at playing marbles," Vickie cheerfully replied. "What are those divine smells coming from the kitchen?"

"Chicken and dumplings, biscuits, green beans, and pecan pie. And don't worry, there's plenty for all."

Vickie stood. "It's so very kind of you to cook for us all, Grandmother. May I help you?"

"You may come keep me company." Sophie winked at Cathy. "Actually, I was hoping for a volunteer to set the table."

Cathy popped up. "Bessie and me will help. But what will Rufus do?"

"Oh, I think I've a saucer of milk and some chicken scraps that will keep him plenty busy," Sophie replied.

"Yippee!" Cathy cried, jumping up and down. "Come on, Bessie."

Out in Sophie's large, homey kitchen, Vickie talked with her great-great-grandmother by the iron stove while Bessie and Cathy set the table in the adjacent dining room. "Well, I see you're overjoyed to be with your sister again," Sophie remarked, rolling dumplings and putting them in a pot of simmering chicken and sauce.

"Oh, you have no idea," Vickie replied feelingly. "I don't know if Cathy told you, but I was an army nurse. I hadn't seen her in over three years."

"Oh, I understand. Cathy told me all about your separation and the letters you two used to exchange. She missed you terribly."

"As I missed her. And of course after the orphanage fire, the authorities in Charleston told Adrian and me that she and Nate were dead." She ended her words with a shiver.

Clucking sympathetically, Sophie patted Vickie's shoulder. "Yes, my dear. I just don't see how you could have borne that."

"It was devastating." Vickie braved a smile. "But now we know the wonderful truth, that Bessie brought the children here, and the two of you have kept them safe from harm. I am so grateful you were here for Nate and Cathy."

Sophie pressed a hand to her breast. "Oh, my dear, you have no idea how delighted I was to see them. Indeed, I shudder to think of what might have happened to the poor mites had I not been around. Our Mayor Courtenay is the darling of the Broad Street bankers, and hardly sympathetic to the plight of the poor and indigent. Why, he cut the budget of the almshouse and declared the city should no longer feel obliged to support foundlings."

"But that's awful." Vickie glanced around the kitchen at the old-fashioned sideboard with iron sink, the pie safe, the huge iron pots hanging from their pegs on the walls. "It's so mind-boggling for me to realize you live in a time totally different from my own. I mean, intellectually I realize it, but it's taking some time to sink in."

"You live here, too, now, dear, astounding though that might be to you."

"Amen." Thoughtfully Vickie frowned. "Guess it must have been some shock for you when Bessie first brought the children here."

Sophie laughed. "My kingdom, I just about swooned."

"How did you react? Did you believe Cathy was really your own great-great-grandchild, and from almost sixty years in the future?"

Sophie mulled over the question. "Well, it did take some getting used to, although I wouldn't have turned away those darling children and Bessie for all of Mr. Blackbeard's gold."

"But did you understand what had happened to the children—and how they came to be here, in another time?"

Sophie chuckled. "Oh, they all tried to explain it. Cathy just about gave me fits, babbling on about how they had jumped from a fire to a fish pond and found themselves in a new century. Bessie made things so much easier to understand, stating it in her own, simple way, that the children had been threatened by the Evil One before, and were meant to be here with me now, safe from harm—and that in due course you would come for them."

Vickie shook her head. "Yes, Bessie is truly amazing. And mysterious. Adrian and I were just discussing the fact that we know so little about her."

Sophie smiled in pleasant surprise. "You mean you've never heard of the legend of Brown Bessie?"

"Legend?"

"It's quite an old tale here in Charleston."

"Ah—but I wasn't raised in Charleston."

Sophie grew pensive. "Perhaps it's more a story for

my time—you know, with all the problems the city has had with fires."

"Fires?" Vaguely, Vickie could remember Weldon Little mentioning some legend regarding a female slave and fires.

Sophie touched Vickie's arm. "I really think Bessie should tell you about her legend herself. She explains it so much better than I can, and has taught her tale to the children by heart. They love to hear it."

"It must be fascinating. Indeed, she was just telling me about her marbles, and how they—and she—came from Africa, of all places."

"Yes, Bessie's not from here."

Absently Vickie began tidying up the countertop. "You know, it's funny, but I hadn't even thought that much about where Bessie must have come from. In her letters to me, Cathy once described Bessie as a friend. But she hardly dresses like someone from the 1940s."

Sophie stirred a pot of green beans. "She's an odd one, all right. I've had the summer to observe her. Never seems to eat or sleep, and comes and goes quite mysteriously. Have you noticed how she makes no sound when she approaches?"

Vickie's eyes lit with wonderment. "Yes, and when I first watched her stand at a window, I thought— well, I know this sounds absurd—"

"That you saw the light pass through her?" Sophie finished.

Vickie nodded solemnly.

Sophie's visage grew wistful. "When the three of them first arrived here, the children were in their nightclothes—and all drenched, the poor darlings. But

Bessie wore the very costume of blue cotton, and the turban, that she wears now. When I bought new clothing for the children, I offered to get her something as well. But she refuses to wear anything but that one outfit."

"It does appear to be from another time," Vickie remarked.

Sophie's lined face tightened. "My dear, I don't want to give away too much, but I will tell you this: I've been around long enough to know that what Bessie is wearing is authentic slave cottonades."

"My gracious," Vickie murmured.

"I haven't seen them since the war, but I also haven't forgotten." Sophie gave a shudder. "I well recall those days, when Negroes were sold like so much cattle at auctions on the streets near the harbor. Of course, Will and I never owned any blacks, and we were opposed to the institution of slavery for moral reasons. Nonetheless, he enlisted with the Confederacy soon after South Carolina seceded. He saw it as an issue of states' rights, rather than a question of slavery." She paused, crossing herself.

"Grandmother, I'm so sorry," Vickie put in, patting Sophie's shoulder. "I mean, I know you lost him in the war."

"At the first battle of Manassas, along with so many other brave Charlestonian men, may God rest their souls," she confided heavily. "But, thank heaven, we didn't lose our son. Will Junior was only eighteen when he enlisted."

"That's right. He lives up in Georgetown now, doesn't he?"

Sophie shook her head in awe. "My, I can't get

used to the fact that you know so much about our family. Yes, Will Junior fell in love with a lovely young lady, Mary Alice Mills from Georgetown, and he moved up there to start his own hardware business."

"And by now, my grandfather, Will the Third, will have been born," Vickie mused.

Sophie flashed Vickie a startled smile. "Not just born, but he's now twenty years old, and will soon graduate from college in Chapel Hill, North Carolina."

"How amazing!" Vickie declared. "But of course you're right. Grandfather would be grown by now, since my mother was—that is, will be—born in 1896." She paused, noting that Sophie's face had paled. "Is it bothering you that I'm telling you all about our family? Things that have yet to happen in your life?"

"My dear, I want you to feel free to speak your mind," Sophie replied wisely. "However, I do think there are some things that perhaps . . . well, perhaps we shouldn't know."

Vickie wondered if Sophie were referring to her own death—an event that, unbeknownst to her, was imminent. Tactfully she asked, "You mean, like about the future?"

Sophie nodded. "And don't think that your sister hasn't already given me a healthy dose of talk about the future. My stars, when Cathy starts chattering about the time from which she and Nate hail—about flying machines, automobiles, moving pictures—it all but gives me the vapors."

Vickie chuckled. Then she sobered, remembering

the earthquake tomorrow. "And what about your own future? What if we could tell you about that?"

"Are you referring to my own death, dear?"

Caught off guard, Vickie stammered, "Well . . ."

Sophie reached out to touch Vickie's hand. "My feelings are the same there. Perhaps I'm being foolish and superstitious, but I think I'm better off not knowing."

Vickie bit her lip. Much as she wanted to respect Sophie's wishes, she desired much more to shield her from harm. Perhaps she could find a way to protect Sophie from the earthquake tomorrow without specifically telling her that the coming natural disaster would claim her life.

"I respect your feelings, Grandmother," she replied. "However, you do need be prepared for the earthquake. It's going to be quite a bad one, the worst in all of Charleston history. It won't hit until sometime tomorrow night, of that I'm sure. But we will need to make preparations."

Sophie nodded. "You'll need to protect the children and Bessie."

"We'll need to protect *everyone*. I think we should all evacuate."

But Sophie shook her head. "You and Commander Bennett evacuate with the others. But I shall remain here."

"But you can't—it will be too dangerous!"

Sophie spoke with strained patience. "Vickie, this is my home. I won't argue the point. You just keep those children safe."

Although frustrated, Vickie felt it might be best to wait and broach the subject with Sophie again later.

Instead, she asked, "What about the general population? Should we try to warn them?"

Sophie scowled. "I can try to spread the word through a few friends and neighbors, suggest it may be better that they go elsewhere tomorrow night, though they'll all assume I'm daft. I wish we could go to the police with this, and also tell them about the man who has threatened you."

"Carmichael Keegan."

Sophie added pepper to the pot. "But I'm afraid if the officials here heard our entire story, they'd only consign us all to the Maniac Department—if that's what they still call it."

"No doubt they would," Vickie ruefully agreed. "Adrian and I haven't approached the authorities out of that same fear."

Sophie wiped her hands on her apron. "Well, it looks as if the food will be ready before much longer, and I note the rest of the house has grown quiet. Would you go find the others and suggest they start washing up for dinner?"

"I'd be delighted. Thanks, Grandmother."

Giving Sophie a fond hug, Vickie stepped into the dining room, where the large Queen Anne table had been beautifully set, though Cathy and Bessie were nowhere in sight. She ventured back inside the parlor to see Adrian standing at the back window, gazing out at the courtyard. She could hear the sound of Cathy's laughter drifting in the back window, and her heart warmed as she noted the wistful expression on his face.

"Sophie says it's about time to call Bessie and the

children for dinner," she remarked, moving toward him. "Are they outside?"

He turned. "Bessie took them out to play with the kitten in the courtyard."

She smiled warmly. "I saw you and Nate talking— you were so smart to ask for his help in protecting all of us from Keegan. How did it go?"

Adrian sighed. "About as well as could be expected. Nate is very concerned about you, Cathy, and Sophie, but he's still furious at me, and deeply alienated."

She squeezed his hand. "Give it some more time, Adrian. You've already made a good beginning."

He nodded, then his expression shone with pride. "He's so bright, Vickie." He tugged on her hand. "Come with me a moment."

"Of course."

He led her to the desk and handed her several drawings. "Nate did these. He sketched out all stories of this house for me, as well as the surrounding property, and pointed out every spot where he thought we might be vulnerable from an attack by Keegan."

Vickie studied the meticulous drawings, which showed a skill well beyond Nate's twelve years. "These are remarkable."

"He was also right in all his deductions," Adrian went on. "And actually, I think he'll be an able assistant in helping to defend us all."

"That shows real maturity on his part."

Sadly he added, "But he made it clear that, while he would work with me to protect the rest of you, I wasn't to assume he would forgive me."

With a surge of compassion, Vickie put down the

drawings and embraced him. "Darling, he won't be able to keep up this pretense for long. He's hurt, of course, but deep inside, he's still a little boy who loves and needs his father. He can't keep hating you. It's not possible. Why, think of how I despised you at first, and now—"

"Yes?" Adrian gazed searchingly into his eyes.

Seeing the need and vulnerability on his face, Vickie realized that she loved Adrian Bennett, loved him with all her heart. The knowledge jarred her deeply, delighted her, made her want to laugh and cry all at the same time. She desperately wanted to tell him of her newly discovered feelings, but wasn't sure he was quite ready to hear about them as yet. The memory of his declaring that he'd never love again still troubled her.

Instead she stretched upward and tenderly kissed him. "Now I want nothing more than to be with you and the children, every minute."

With a moan, he kissed her back. "Oh, Vickie, Vickie darling . . ."

"Are you happy?"

"As happy as I can be, knowing the threat that still exists. And desperately hoping I can close the distance between myself and my son."

"You will," she whispered. "I have every faith in you."

"You always did, didn't you, darling?"

Vickie thought her heart might burst at the expression of joy she spotted in his eyes as he leaned over to kiss her again, and crushed her close.

After a long, poignant moment, he drew back to

smile at her. "How did your conversation go with Sophie?"

Vickie expelled a heavy breath. "Adrian, it was wonderful, but I couldn't convince her that we should all evacuate. I'm still wondering if I shouldn't tell her the truth about her coming fate."

He frowned. "Well, we won't have to face that obstacle until tomorrow. In the meantime, I'll check Sophie's supply of food and water, and make sure all the doors are locked, as well as any windows that seem vulnerable. And it wouldn't hurt to get the others to pack some bags."

"You're afraid Keegan will find us here, aren't you?" she asked.

"We certainly can't afford to ignore the possibility."

"I agree, and I'll help you."

After Adrian called out to the children and Bessie to come wash up for dinner, he and Vickie went out to the kitchen together to begin seeing to their other tasks.

Chapter Twenty-two

Dinner proved a festive occasion. Sophie and Adrian sat at opposite ends of the dining table, with Vickie and Cathy occupying one side, Nate and Bessie the other. Eating the excellent chicken and dumplings and vegetables and drinking Sophie's fine fruit wine, Vickie delighted in her great-great-grandmother's warm hospitality, Cathy's happy chatter, and Bessie's wise, reassuring presence. Vickie was pleased to note that Sophie had insisted Bessie join them, like a cherished member of the family—even though, just as Sophie had indicated, the girl did not eat but sat solemnly spinning one of her odd-shaped stones on her plate.

The occasion was somewhat dampened by Nate's stubborn silence, his hostile mien. And Adrian seemed only a wan reflection of a joyous father just reunited with his son, although he tried to maintain a brave facade. He also seemed on edge, excusing himself several times during the meal to check the doors and windows, or to peer outside. She knew he remained worried about Keegan possibly discovering them here.

Over dessert and coffee, Vickie flashed Sophie a warm smile. "Grandmother, this is the best meal I've had in ages. And I've never tasted a better pecan pie."

"It's an old southern family recipe passed on to me by my neighbor, Mrs. Ashburn," Sophie confided.

"Well, it's divine, madam," said Adrian.

"Thank you, Commander Bennett." Sophie lifted a steaming porcelain coffeepot. "More coffee?"

"I should be delighted," he replied, passing her his cup.

After pouring Adrian more coffee and handing it back, Sophie mused, "I have a suggestion, everyone. Usually at this point I like to adjourn to the parlor, but tonight I suggest we stay here at the table and talk. There's something so intimate about a family sharing experiences around a supper table, don't you think?"

Vickie at once picked up on the spirit of her suggestion. "Yes, I agree. Completely."

"We all face grave challenges," Sophie went on. "Especially tomorrow. Tonight may in fact be the only night we'll all be together as a family, and have a bit of time for sharing."

Silence greeted Sophie's statement, for no comment was needed.

Softly, Sophie continued, "When I was a child, we would offtimes follow our supper with storytelling around the table. Each of us would tell the best story we knew to entertain the others. I'd like to suggest we do that tonight. But I think each of us should tell our *own* stories instead."

While Adrian and Nate appeared taken aback, Cathy burst out, "Oh, goody! I love stories, Grandma! Why don't you tell yours first?"

"Well, if it's acceptable to the others, I should be happy to begin," Sophie replied modestly.

"Of course, we'd love to hear about your life," Vickie encouraged.

"Very well," Sophie agreed. "I was the daughter of Irish immigrants who moved to Charleston in the early 1820s, back when I was still a small child. My father, Matthew McBride, quickly became a successful hardware merchant, a deacon at St. Mary's Catholic Church, and a member of the Hibernian Society. He saw to it that my brother and I had the finest education and lacked for nothing. Unfortunately, yellow fever took the life of my brother Patrick at the age of ten, and that left Father pinning all his hopes on me. He wanted me to become a debutante, even though Irish Catholics tended to be poorly received by the Episcopalian elite here. At any rate, Father had business dealings with William's father, a prominent landowner and businessman here, and the two men became friends. As a consequence, at seventeen, I was invited to the Davis family's annual harvest ball, at their plantation on the Ashley. That was back in 1835."

"Did you have fun, Grandma?" Cathy asked.

Sophie nodded. "Oh, yes, and you can imagine my mother's joy at my being invited to such a prestigious occasion. Why, all of Charleston's elite was present. Only the St. Cecilia Society ball could have surpassed it."

"The St. Cecilia's Society," Vickie murmured. "I believe I heard my mother mention them back in Georgetown. Isn't that an association of the city's aristocracy?"

"Indeed, and many members were in attendance that night. When I arrived, there was Will in his beautiful tailcoat, and he couldn't take his eyes off me. Charleston's fair-haired son, who hobnobbed with the Rhetts, the Pinckneys, and the Middletons, had eyes only for little Sophie McBride. Why, he filled up every dance on my dance card."

"How romantic," Vickie breathed.

"Will hailed from one of the most wealthy and influential families in the state, with investments in shipping, the railroads, cotton, and rice mills. His people received me, though I know they were less than pleased that their darling son had chosen as his bride a socially inferior Irish Catholic. Nevertheless, we married the following year, at St. Michael's. You see, I converted to the Episcopal faith for Will. Of course he had insisted he would become Catholic for me, but I just couldn't ask him to turn his back on everything his family had built. We had a wonderful life together—we attended all the cotillions and balls, the theater, the horse races out at the Washington Race Course. We heard Jenny Lind sing when she came through on her American tour. But of course our greatest joy was the birth of our two children, our daughter, Meryl, and our son, Will Junior, who will one day become your great-grandfather, Vickie."

"Yes, I know," she put in with awe.

"In fact, on the day Will got married in 1860, I gave his bride a silver necklace of beautiful carved roses that I expect may be yours one day. I'm certainly hoping it will become a family heirloom."

Vickie gave a frozen smile, not having the heart to tell Sophie that she had lost the precious heirloom in Tunisia, back in another century.

"Our lives were so perfect," Sophie went on. "Then the war came . . . and everything ended."

Vickie reached out to squeeze Sophie's hand. "I know, Grandmother."

Sophie braved a smile. "Will and I never quite understood why folks here were so giddy over the prospect of civil war. Of course passions ran very high in this state, and the clash between the old guard and the abolitionists, the unionists and the nullifiers, goes way back. But people had no idea what the conflict truly meant. Will enlisted as soon as South Carolina seceded, and his brigade was called up long before the first shots were fired here. But I was there, standing on the piazza of our East Battery home, when Beauregard's cannon opened fire on Fort Sumter." She paused to cross herself. "I'll never forget that awful night, the scream of the mortar, the flashes of light across the harbor, the explosions as the rounds met their mark. The Battery teemed with citizens celebrating the start of the war, but the sounds of their cheers left me cold. From the outset, I feared the worst. I was here on the day in November when Lee arrived, and nearly lost my house in the horrible fire that swept our city the following month. I was here during the siege and had to evacuate right before

Charleston fell. I witnessed all the horrors—but none was worse than receiving the telegraph informing me of my husband's death."

She paused, wiping away tears, and Vickie patted her shoulder. "We're so sorry, Grandmother."

Sophie nodded convulsively. "At least the Confederacy brought my Will home. I still decorate his grave, every Memorial Day, at Magnolia Cemetery. Nothing was the same after the conflict. Oh, the old guard carried on with pride, but this time without me. Will's enterprises had suffered heavily during the conflict, but thank heaven, he had the foresight to leave me an emergency account in a Boston bank. That, and the monies I received from selling our East Battery home, have sustained me over the years. I rented this house from my neighbor, Eliza Ashburn, and went back to my Catholic roots, spending my free time doing charity work for the Ladies Mutual Aid Society and volunteering at the Confederate Home and Roper Hospital. It's been a simple, quiet life." She forced a brighter expression. "There, I've said enough."

"No, Grandmother, it was a wonderful account," said Vickie. "And so moving."

"Indeed, madam," Adrian concurred.

"Thank you, but now it's time for someone else to speak." Sophie turned to smile at Nate. "How about you, son?"

Nate blinked rapidly. "I have nothing to say."

"Nate!" exclaimed Cathy with an expression of dismay.

"Then you talk." Tossing down his napkin, the boy stood. "Besides, I'm going to go check around the house while the rest of you jabber, and make sure we're all safe from Keegan."

Adrian rose. "Son, stay put. I was just about to make another round myself."

"I said I'll do it, sir," Nate gritted out.

Adrian sighed. "Very well, son. But stay inside, and call if you need us."

Wordlessly Nate turned and left the room.

Watching Adrian slump back into his chair, Sophie murmured, "I'm sorry, Commander Bennett."

"Thank you, madam."

Cathy tightened her jaw. "That's okay, Grandma, just let Nate sulk. I'll tell a story for both of us."

"You do that, honey," Vickie encouraged, patting her hand.

Cathy beamed at her sister, then began in a child's burst of enthusiasm. "Well, me and Vickie were born in Georgetown, you see, and then when I was still a baby, Mama went to be with Jesus, so it was only me, Vickie, and Papa. Then that mean old war came along—not Grandma Sophie's war, of course, but the one in 1941—and Vickie had to leave to go nurse people far way across the ocean. Then Papa went to heaven to be with Mama and Jesus, and I was sent to the orphanage." She paused, breathless, then blurted out, "And that's where I met my three best friends, Nate, Bessie, and Rufus. And we all spent hours and hours playing together. The best part was in the attic, when Rufus and I would play with Bessie's marbles. Even though Nate didn't believe in Bessie then." In a more sober vein, she continued. "Then one day the bad man shot our friend Officer Paddy dead, and chased Nate and me back to the orphanage. We hid in the attic with Bessie and Rufus. Then the fire came . . . and Bessie saved us and brought us here. So now Nate *really* believes in Bessie—even though he still acts likes a grump sometimes." Appearing relieved, she grinned at Vickie. "There, is that a good story?"

Vickie hugged Cathy's neck. "It's a wonderful story, darling."

"Well, then, who shall be next?" prompted Sophie. "Bessie, dear, how about you?"

Bessie gazed shyly at Sophie. "You want for Bessie to tell her story?"

Before Sophie could reply, Cathy burst out, "Oh, yes, Bessie, we love to hear your story. Oh, do tell it! It's the best!"

While the others laughed, Bessie seemed puzzled. "Where I begin, Miss Cathy?"

"Why, with where you were born, silly goose," Cathy replied.

Bessie gravely nodded. "All right, Miss Cathy. I tell where Bessie born. I not from here."

"*Tell us*, Bessie," Cathy implored.

"I tell." Turning to the others, Bessie said solemnly, "Bessie from Africa. I be born there, in the year 1802."

A gasp shook the room, and Vickie and Adrian exchanged looks of mystification.

"My heaven, young woman," Adrian declared. "You can't be saying you were actually born in the year 1802. You're so young. Do you perhaps mean 1872?"

But Bessie vehemently shook her head. "Nossir. Bessie born in the year 1802."

"But—"

"Let her tell her story, Adrian," Cathy cut in imperiously.

Adrian grinned. "Yes, my dear. I stand corrected."

"Cathy, you must call him Commander Bennett," Vickie admonished.

But Adrian held up a hand. "No, Vickie, it's fine for Cathy to call me Adrian if she likes." He winked at the girl, then nodded to Bessie. "Please continue with your tale, Bessie. It promises to be fascinating, and we've interrupted you quite enough."

"Yessir." Bessie paused a moment, watching Nate saunter back into the room and sullenly take his place, fixing his gaze possessively on Cathy. "Bessie was a baby back in Africa. I remember my mama, she good to me and keep me safe and fed. My papa, he hunt for us. I remember we sleep in our hut and eat fruit we pick from trees, meat we cook on the fire. And these." She pulled out her small sack of marbles. "These I gather on the banks of the River Limpopo."

"May we see those, Bessie?" Adrian inquired.

Bessie solemnly handed him the sack. Adrian pulled out a couple of the crystalline stones and stared at them, then replaced them in the sack and handed it to Nate. Despite his taciturn demeanor, the boy spilled out several of the pebbles on the tabletop, and studied them more closely.

Bessie went on speaking, her expression growing turbulent. "In Africa, we all be happy, till the slavers come. That when Bessie still be a small child. The slavers, they big and mean, with dogs and whips. They chase us with sticks of fire."

"Do you mean muskets?" Adrian asked.

Bessie nodded. "They kill with sticks of fire, and

what they don't kill, they put in chains." Her gaze darkened. "Me, my mama. My papa—we don't know what happen to him. A mean slaver chase him, then he gone and we never see him again. They put Bessie and Mama in chains and shove us in a big hole at the bottom of a ship, with lots of other folks. It filthy and it stink there. They take us to America, only many die in the voyage. Die for the fever and the shaking. My mama and me, we live, though we be weak and sick."

"Bless your hearts," put in Vickie.

"Then we come to Charleston," Bessie continued in an ominous voice. "We sold at the slave market. Bessie and Mama be bought by Crazy Cal. He be the innkeeper at the harbor. He work us both hard, in his kitchen, and scrubbing the floors, making the beds. He be mean and a drunkard. He thrash us with his whip. He hurt my mama."

"Bessie, how awful," said Vickie.

"Many years pass, then my mama, she die of the ague, and Cal, he start hurting me. He force himself on me when I be only fourteen."

"The monster," declared Adrian.

Curiously, Bessie's expression lightened then, growing almost radiant. "Then, everything change for Bessie. When Bessie be sixteen, she fall in love. His name be Josiah. He seventeen year old. He bound out by his master to work at the stables near the inn. Josiah and Bessie, we meet at the harbor—Josiah, he take me out in this old rowboat don't nobody miss. We row up the Cooper River where nobody see us, and we walk in the woods. Talk, laugh, and sing together. Bessie teach Josiah the old songs from Africa.

291

Josiah, he teach Bessie the spirituals. 'Swing Low, Sweet Chariot' and 'Deep River.' He promise one day he marry Bessie."

"Oh, Bessie, that's so romantic!" interjected Cathy.

Bessie frowned. "Only Crazy Cal, he mad at me 'cause I be away so long. When I come back, he call me a whore and he beat me, but this time Bessie fight back. Bessie hit Cal with the iron candle mold, and he be in a fury, whip me even worse."

Bessie paused for a moment, shuddering, as everyone waited in mesmerized silence.

"That be a bad, bad summer," she continued. "1818. They be fires—many fires in Charleston. Folks blame the slaves. People mean all over. After the fires, several black man got lynched at old Hangman's Point by the vengeance crowds."

Amid shocked murmurs, Sophie gazed at Bessie compassionately. "My dear, I'm well aware of all the fires in the history of Charleston, and it's truly a scandal that Negro insurrectionists were so often blamed, when wooden buildings and poor fire-fighting resources were the real problems."

"Yes 'um," Bessie agreed. "Sometimes many blocks burn down, and then more black men, they swing. All that summer, me and Cal, we still fight. Me and Josiah, we more in love. I don't tell Josiah about Cal. If I do, Josiah try to kill Cal, maybe. Then Bessie gone with Josiah all night one time. Josiah and me, we sit high in a tree together, talk and sing all night, watch the moon rise and the stars come out. When I go home, Cal be in a fury. He punish Bessie by selling her for a whore at the inn."

"What a beast!" exclaimed Vickie. "He's the one who should have been lynched!"

Bessie's chin proudly came up. "But Bessie still fight Cal. My love for Josiah so strong. The first man Cal put me with be Dastardly Dirk. He a pirate. When Dirk take Bessie upstairs, I pull a knife on him. Dirk take the knife away from Bessie, but he not punish me like Cal. He listen to Bessie's story, hear how I love Josiah, how Cal beat me, how he beat my mama till she dead. Dirk, he promise he make Cal stop, and then he talk to Cal. Only Cal angry at Dirk. Dirk and Cal, they fight. Cal scream at Dirk, say leave the inn and never come back, or he turn him over to the guard house, see him hanged. Dirk, he afraid of Cal. They hang pirates in those days. Old Stede Bonnet, he gasp and dangle forever on the hangin' tree. Dirk remember this and say he ain't gonna help Bessie no more. After Dirk leave, Cal, he come at me with his whip, say he going to kill Bessie this time."

"How did you survive?" asked Vickie.

"They be another fire then," stated Bessie. "This time it be at St. Christopher's Orphanage."

"Good Lord, do you mean there was actually a St. Christopher's Orphanage back in the year 1818?" Vickie asked in a shocked whisper.

"Yes 'um. That be the first St. Christopher's."

"And it burned down, too, like the one in 1945?" Vickie pursued.

"Yes 'um," Bessie answered. "And six children die in that first fire. Worse than the other. Folks go crazy afterwards. A mob run through the streets a-screamin', folks lookin' for a black man to punish. Crazy Cal, he hear 'em. That when Cal haul Bessie out in the streets and yell out that she be the wench that start the fires. Folks start howlin' then, and carry Bessie off to Hangman's Point."

"You don't mean to tell us you were hanged, Bessie?" put in Adrian, aghast.

"Bessie not sure," she answered matter-of-factly. "By then the sky is black and the rain is coming down. They put the noose around my neck. Then when I start to swing, lightning, it strike the gallows . . . and then Bessie disappear."

"Tell them what happened to you then, Bessie!" Cathy ordered.

Bessie smiled. "Folks ain't sure what really happen to Brown Bessie then. Some say I die, some say lightning done broke the rope, Bessie fell in the river and swum away."

"Which was it?" asked Vickie.

Bessie gave a shrug. "Folks don't know, but they fear Brown Bessie from then on. Whenever a fire start, folks blame Bessie, say she did it, she start the fire for vengeance on the white folks that done her wrong."

Vickie snapped her fingers. "My gracious, I heard about that legend—although it can't be true."

"Of course it's a mean old lie," declared Cathy. "You would never hurt folks, would you, Bessie? Tell them what *really* happened at Hangman's Point!"

"Bessie not sure," the girl repeated with a soulful frown. "Bessie go to the spirit world then. Bessie watch over the orphanage and all the city. Warn people of fire."

"And that's how Bessie became a legend in Charleston," Sophie added proudly to Vickie.

"How amazing," she breathed.

"And how absurd that anyone was ever afraid of you," added Adrian. "Why, you're like a guardian angel. And I can't begin to tell you how awed we are to be in the presence of a true legend."

Bessie lowered her gaze. "Bessie be just folks."

"Hardly," he stated with a low laugh. "You, young lady, are positively amazing. Now tell us what happened when you rescued Cathy and Nate."

"Jes' like I tell you, Bessie knew she be needed when the fire come. I get the children and carry them away here, to be safe at Miss Sophie's house."

"But how did you know to come *here*, to this very house?" Vickie inquired.

Bessie smiled enigmatically. "Bessie see things others don't see. I know the children, they safe here with Miss Sophie."

"Then you're a prophet, and a seer, as well as a guardian spirit," commented Adrian with wonder. "Can you tell us what will happen to all of us tomorrow?"

Bessie hesitated. "You must destroy the Evil One and find your rightful place. That all I know."

"You said our place is not back in 1945," Vickie remarked. "Are you trying to tell us it's not here, either?"

"You will find your place," replied Bessie, "and one day, there be a sign you meant to be there."

An awed silence fell, then Sophie spoke up. "My dear, I know I speak for us all in telling you how moved we are by your account, and how grateful we all are for what you've done for this family, and especially the children."

"Amen," seconded Vickie.

"Bessie glad to help," the girl said modestly.

"And now, I suppose we should move on to Commander Bennett," Sophie added.

Adrian spoke briefly and awkwardly of his life history in England: the birth of Nate; the loss of his wife; and his years away at war. He surprised Vickie when he described meeting her in Charleston. "When I came to Charleston, I was a broken man, devastated by the war, by the loss of my wife, and most of all by what I thought was the death of my son." He paused to glance at Nate, but the boy was stubbornly staring at the tabletop. "I thought my life was over, not realizing that I was about to be reborn." Gazing at Vickie with devotion in his eyes, he went on in an emotional voice, "Then I met Vickie, and my entire life began to turn around. She has brought me a joy and optimism I was convinced I'd never know again. Through her hope and inspiration, I now have my son back, my life back, a future for us all to look forward to, a future that I trust will bring all of us together. I've been blessed far more than I deserve."

His words left Vickie deeply moved. "Oh, Adrian. I think that's the sweetest thing I've ever heard."

Reaching out, he caught Vickie's hand and smiled at her tenderly. She smiled back tremulously, as Sophie, Cathy, and Bessie looked on with pride. Nate, however, appeared more suspicious and resentful than ever, still refusing even to look at his father.

"Thank you, Commander Bennett," Sophie commented. "Vickie? Would you like to speak?"

Vickie told the others of her upbringing, the birth of her sister and loss of her mother, how she'd become a second mother to Cathy. She spoke of her years at war, how much she'd missed Cathy, how saddened she'd been to hear of her father's death, and later, how devastated she'd been when she'd thought Cathy had perished in the fire. She described coming to Charleston and meeting Adrian. "Commander Bennett spoke of how I've brought new hope to his life," she admitted hoarsely. "But he has also brought hope to mine. I remember once how he told me that we needed each other to find our way out of the darkness." She gazed at him tenderly. "And I think that together, we're managing to do that."

"Indeed," he whispered ardently.

"Do you love him, Vickie?" Cathy asked.

At first Vickie felt herself blushing at Cathy's typically brash curiosity. But as she looked at Adrian and saw the desperate hope on his face, she was glad, fiercely glad, that her sister had asked the question. She knew the time had come for her to be completely honest with him—even if he wasn't entirely ready.

Looking at him with her heart in her eyes, she admitted, "Yes, Cathy, I love him dearly."

The child yelled out "Yippee!" and clapped her hands. Vickie's gaze remained riveted to Adrian's face. When she saw the naked joy reflected there, she knew her instincts had been right, and ecstasy flooded her own heart. His hand tightly clasped her own, and their gazes held for a poignant moment.

At last she continued speaking. "I hope that, when all of this is over, Adrian and I can marry, and all of us can become a family together."

Delight lit Adrian's face. "Darling, that is my most

fervent desire, too." He glanced at Nate and Cathy. "What do you say, children?"

"I say yes!" Cathy cried, clapping her hands. "Let's all get married and become a family."

The others chuckled at the child's exuberance. Then the happy atmosphere was shattered as Nate lunged to his feet and angrily spoke. "And I say Cathy and me want nothing to do with either of you! You're both a couple of traitors who deserted us during the war. Cathy and I will be just fine all by ourselves. I'm going to marry her when she's old enough."

Vickie flinched at the boy's diatribe, and one look at Adrian's face confirmed that he, too, was stricken. But before either of them could respond, Cathy surged to her feet and charged around the table to confront Nate. "Nate, how dare you say such cruel things! Vickie is my sister and Adrian is your father, and you know they both had no choice but to do their part in the war."

But Nate proved unyielding. "Well, your sister is welcome to come live with us." He glared at Adrian. "But my father can rot in hell."

"Nate!" scolded Sophie, horrified.

Vickie felt heartsick for Adrian, who was staring, white-faced, at his angry son. But Cathy again took charge. With tears shining in her blue eyes, she bravely faced him. "I want Vickie and Adrian to marry and I want to go live with them. You just don't understand, Nate. You think I'm all grown up like you, but you're wrong. I'm still a child, and I can't be yours yet. I need a family. I'm going to live with Vickie and Adrian, and you can do whatever you please."

As Nate trembled, devastated by Cathy's apparent rejection, the girl went to Adrian, threw her arms around his neck, and kissed his cheek. She drew back to smile at his starkly emotional face. "I don't care what Nate says. I love you because Vickie loves you. And I always will."

Vickie could have sworn she saw tears in Adrian's eyes then as he clutched the child to his heart and kissed her back.

The sight made Vickie's eyes burn with emotion. Then she glanced at Nate and almost flinched at the rage and hurt she saw reflected on his young face as he watched his father with Cathy.

"Damn you all to hell!" he cried.

Nate fled the room.

Chapter Twenty-three

"Adrian, go get him!" Vickie cried.

He was already on his feet, hurrying out of the room. Then Sophie called after him, "Oh, Commander Bennett! Nate's room is up on the third floor."

At the archway, he turned. "Thank you, madam. All of you, please excuse me."

He rushed off, and Vickie glanced helplessly at Sophie.

"Perhaps you should go, too, dear," she wisely suggested.

Vickie stood, but Cathy tugged at her skirts. "I think you should leave Nate alone. He's being a brat."

"Honey, he just feels hurt and left out."

But Cathy vehemently shook her head. "He said awful things to you and Adrian."

Vickie leaned over and kissed Cathy's soft cheek.

"Sweetheart, I'm sure he didn't mean them. Look, I must go now, and try to help Adrian."

"You tell Nate to quit acting so mean," Cathy ordered.

"I'll see what I can do, honey."

Vickie rushed out of the room and up two flights of stairs to the house's third story, a small attic converted into a bedroom wing. By the wan light of a naked light bulb in the corridor, she found Adrian, standing outside a closed door, pounding on the panel and calling Nate's name. "Nate! Son, please unlock the door and let me in. We must talk."

From the depths of the room beyond, she heard Nate yell back, "Go away! Leave me alone!"

Arriving at Adrian's side, Vickie touched his rigid shoulder. "Adrian, give it a little more time."

She glimpsed the look of crazed pain in his eyes; then he turned and crushed her in his arms. His body trembled against hers, and she was shocked to feel the wetness of his tears on her own face.

"Adrian?" she queried softly.

"God, Vickie, I've ruined everything," he said hoarsely. "I've been a wretched father to Nate."

"No, you haven't."

"But I have."

She drew back and gazed into his anguished eyes. "Then you must reach deep into your own soul, Adrian, and forgive yourself."

Myriad emotions crossed over his face then—despair, hope, sadness, yearning. "I can't, Vickie."

"You *must*."

He pulled her close again and pressed his lips to her hair. "Oh, Vickie. I'm not worthy of you, either."

"You are." She took his hand. "Come on, now. Let's give Nate some time to cool off."

She led him over to the stairs, and the two sat down on the top step together. She watched him wipe away his tears and stare off at some point in space.

"Adrian, why were you weeping just now? Was it because of Nate?"

His gaze met hers. "It's not just Nate. It's everything that's happened tonight, all of the incredible things we shared as a family."

"Oh, I know," Vickie whispered. "Tonight was so special. In fact, it was truly mystical. When I heard Bessie's story, all those incredible details she told us . . . Well, I'm still struggling to digest it all."

"Believe me, I am as well."

"But when you really think about it, it does make a certain kind of sense. Bessie being a guardian spirit, and saving the children from the fire."

"Indeed. But to tell you the truth, love, I was even more moved by Cathy. When she asked you if you loved me and you said yes, I can't even begin to describe my emotions. I felt so humble, so joyous, so blessed . . . and so undeserving."

"Adrian, you're *not* undeserving," Vickie reiterated.

He smiled tenderly. "I think Cathy tried her best to communicate that to me, too. When that dear child hugged me and told me she loved me, I felt I held in my arms everything our world—the world we left behind—has lost. You have given me that same hope, Vickie, but it took a child's love to break through my barriers."

"Oh, Adrian," she cried, throwing her arms around his neck. "I love you so much."

He pressed his lips to her cheek. "I love you too, darling."

She drew back, amazed and overjoyed at his admission. "You do?"

Reverently he kissed her hand. "I was an idiot not to see it before now, but I think I must have loved you from the moment we first met, when you collided with me on those stairs. You have shaken up my life and my emotions every minute since then. I've been foolishly fighting my feelings, but thank God you never gave up on me."

Ecstatic, she hugged him close. "I couldn't, Adrian. You maddened me, but you drew me. I was falling in love with you, too."

He groaned with pleasure. "Now I can say I love you, without reservation, and feel it to my soul. If only I could have Nate's love, too."

"You will," Vickie promised. "There's just so much hurt in that boy."

"I know, but with everything that has happened, all the dangers we face, I'm afraid I won't be able to reach him before it's too late."

"You'll have time," she reassured him.

"Will I?" he asked poignantly. "What about tomorrow, Vickie, what about the earthquake? And all our lives being threatened by Keegan? What if he tries to harm us or the children again?"

His questions were quite sobering. But before Vickie could respond, that fear was reinforced as she heard the sounds of screams coming from downstairs. "Oh, my God, Adrian!"

Adrian shot to his feet, pulling the pistol from his waist. "Good Lord! I never should have left the others alone!"

Adrian tore off down the stairs, with Vickie close on his heels. They arrived in the entryway to view a scene of horror in the living room beyond. Shards of glass were scattered about, and smoke was billowing from the center of the room, where a small fire was blazing on the rug. Sophie and Bessie were already trying to beat out the flames with brooms, while Cathy stood in the background clutching her wailing kitten.

Both Vickie and Adrian sprang into action. Shoving the pistol into his waistband, Adrian grabbed the rug from the entryway floor and rushed into the parlor, helping Sophie and Bessie beat out the flames. Vickie dashed after him, grabbing Cathy and pulling her back out into the entryway.

Coughing from the smoke, Vickie ran her hands over Cathy's clothing, searching for any cinders. The child appeared dazed—no wonder, considering the awful fire she'd experienced at the orphanage. "Darling, are you all right?"

Convulsively, Cathy nodded. "Somebody threw a bomb through the window."

"My God! A bomb?"

"What about Nate?" Cathy asked anxiously. "Is he all right?"

Vickie glanced toward the stairs. "My heaven, he probably is, though he's still locked in his room up in the attic. We must check on him. You stay here, and—"

"No, I want to go," wailed Cathy.

Bessie came forward from the parlor. "I go with Miss Cathy. The fire out now."

Vickie glanced inside the room to see that only smoke lingered; Sophie was sweeping up glass, while Adrian was opening windows. "Very well."

"Come on, Bessie!" Cathy cried, grabbing Bessie's hand and hurrying off.

Blinking at the acrid smoke, Vickie went back inside the living room. She approached Sophie, who appeared pale and shaken, and touched her arm. "Grandmother, are you all right?"

Slightly breathless, Sophie paused with her broom. "Yes, dear. And what about Nate?"

"I assume he's okay, but Bessie and Cathy went to check on him, anyway." Glancing about, she shook her head. "How did the fire start? Cathy said it was a bomb."

Sophie gave a shudder. "Why, yes, I suppose it was. You see, someone threw a burning bottle of kerosene in through our front window. Bessie and I both witnessed it."

Adrian stepped forward. "How horrible. I don't suppose you caught any glimpse of the perpetrator, Mrs. Davis?"

Sophie shook her head.

"It the Evil One," Bessie said ominously.

Vickie gave a gasp and turned to the entryway to see Bessie looming there. She wondered how the girl had gotten back down the stairs so quickly. "Is Nate all right?"

"Yes 'um. Miss Cathy with him."

Adrian stepped toward the girl. "You said the Evil One did this. You mean Keegan?"

"Yessir."

"Is he still around?"

Bessie nodded.

Tensely Adrian turned to Vickie and Sophie. "You ladies remain here, and stay away from the windows. I'm going to go do some checking outside."

"But Adrian, you could get hurt," Vickie protested.

"We could all get hurt if I don't take steps to protect us. Stay put, ladies."

He rushed outside, and Vickie waited in terrible anxiety. Then she heard the sounds of two shots being fired! Crying out, she went running out the front door, and spotted Adrian standing out in the yard, the smoking pistol in his hand.

"What happened?" she cried, hurrying down the steps. By now she could hear dogs barking nearby, and lights were going on in the adjacent houses.

He eyed her approach in horror. "Damn it, Vickie, I told you to stay inside!"

Ignoring him, she demanded, "Was it Keegan? Did he fire at you? Are you hurt?"

"No, Keegan didn't fire at me," Adrian answered, shoving the revolver in his waistband. "But I just spotted him lurking behind the neighbor's tree, and I fired two shots. I missed him, but he ran like the devil. I doubt he'll be bothering us again tonight."

Now Sophie hobbled out onto the porch with her cane, followed by Bessie and Cathy. "Commander Bennett, are you all right?" Sophie called.

"Yes, madam. I just scared Keegan away."

"Oh, good heavens!" declared Sophie. "Then Bessie was right."

Adrian nodded grimly.

Now a woman in a housecap and robe emerged on the porch across the street. "Sophie Davis, what is going on over there?" she shouted. "I thought I heard shots being fired."

Sophie faltered her way down the steps. "It's quite all right, Eliza. My guest, Commander Bennett, just scared away a prowler."

"My stars, Sophie, should I telephone the police?" the woman asked.

"Thanks, but I think not. We have things in hand now."

Though the woman across the street shook her head, she didn't protest further and reentered her house.

Adrian ushered the women back toward the house. "Come on, ladies, let's get you back inside."

Vickie turned to Cathy. "Is Nate okay?"

She nodded morosely. "Yes, but he wouldn't come out of his room. He said he didn't care about the fire, or even the shots we heard. He said it was all Adrian's fault anyway for bringing Keegan here."

Seeing Adrian wince, Vickie wished there were something she could do. It was going to take a lot of patience to get through to that boy. "I'm sorry, honey."

Cathy bit her lip. "I'll try again."

"You do that."

Cathy ran off ahead of them. Once the rest of them were back inside the front door, Adrian said briskly, "Ladies, I'd suggest we all evacuate immediately, but I'm afraid we might be easy marks for Keegan. Therefore, I advise you to pack a few things for yourselves and the children, so we can leave at any time if need be, then get some sleep. I'll tidy up the parlor and keep watch there for the rest of the night in case Keegan should return."

"I'll help you," Vickie volunteered.

Adrian shook his head. "That won't be necessary, dear."

"I didn't ask whether you thought it was necessary," she firmly replied, then turned to Sophie. "You and Bessie should do as Adrian says."

"Bessie and I will be happy to pack some things for the children," Sophie replied. "But what about the two of you? When will you rest?"

"Not before first light," Adrian replied. "Please, madam, Bessie, go on upstairs. And Vickie, you really should join them."

"I said I was staying with you." Her words were adamant.

"Very well," he conceded, though she could see the relief in his eyes.

Sophie and Bessie went up the stairs. Vickie and Adrian cleaned the living room as best they could, and he set the ruined rugs out back. He returned just as she finished the sweeping.

"Well, at least her wood floor appears to be unharmed," Vickie remarked. "Though it will be some time before the smells of kerosene and smoke leave this house."

"I know. That miscreant could have killed us all."

Vickie set aside her broom and dustpan. "I agree. But I think you've put the fear of God in him for now."

"Let's hope so. But we must keep watch nonetheless."

"Of course."

The two settled in on the settee. After reloading the revolver, Adrian set it on the tea table in front of them and wrapped his arm about Vickie's shoulders. Though his eyes remained troubled, he forced a smile. "Are you planning to keep me awake now, love?"

She smiled at him tenderly. "I'll try my best. I loved how we all talked tonight."

"Except for Nate."

"In time your love will bring him around."

Adrian raised himself and kissed her hand. "Our love, darling."

"Our love," she repeated almost reverently. "I love the sound of that, though I must admit it will take some getting used to."

He kissed her chin. "It's for real, I promise you."

"I believe you. And I know Nate will respond to you, before long. After all, you're much alike."

"What do you mean?"

"You've both suffered so much, Adrian."

"Ah, yes. My son has lost just as much as I have."

"And some of your pain is still there, isn't it?" she added wisely. "I mean, there are some things you've never spoken of."

He sighed deeply. "Yes. You know, sometimes it's hard for me even to remember a life without pain. It was losing Celeste, sitting there helplessly by her bed while she slipped away from me. You know in some ways you remind me of her."

"Really?"

"She was such a good person, so kind and self-sacrificing. Yet she died and I was spared. I never could understand that. Afterward, it was knowing that my son needed me, but being too locked up in my own despair to reach out to him." He groaned. "In the war, it was watching my friends suffer terrible deaths in combat. During one fierce battle over the Channel, one of my best chums was roasted alive right before my very eyes, and I was powerless to help him, to do anything but watch helplessly and listen to his screams on my radio. You see, he had ignored my pleas that he bail out."

"Oh, Adrian."

Adrian's gaze darkened with remembered pain. "So many good lads were needlessly lost, and their fates seemed so random and cruel. Just like with Celeste. I felt such guilt because I should have stopped the deaths, should have saved them all, guilt because *I* was spared, when so many others, so much more deserving, weren't."

"Oh, Adrian, don't say that," she pleaded. "I know you did all you could. You are very deserving of life. A good, long life." She tapped her purse, which sat on the floor nearby. "I've got your Victoria Cross here to prove it. Besides, Nate needs you so, even though he won't admit it yet. Cathy and I need you as well."

He clutched her close. "Darling, I'm so fortunate to have found you all. And you've given me a second chance at happiness, something I never thought I'd have. I do hope we can all have a life together—if only we can survive the present crisis."

She regarded him wistfully. "What type of life would you want us to have—I mean, assuming we can all survive the next twenty-four hours?"

He smiled, obviously savoring the subject. "First, I want to marry you, and make a home for us all. Of course there's my estate in Kent, back in the twentieth century. I did enjoy our simple life in the country. But who knows if we'll ever make it back there? Besides, that time has become so complicated, with all the horrors of the war—"

"And the dropping of the atomic bombs," she put in with a shiver.

Thoughtfully he nodded. "Perhaps Bessie is right that we don't belong there." He sighed deeply. "Truth to tell, love, I think I'd like to become a farmer or planter, in a simpler time. A time in which the most important thing is not war or earthquake, but our being together as a family."

"Oh, Adrian, what beautiful sentiments," Vickie breathed. "And you're right. We need a time when we can all thrive together. I think I'd like to be a planter's wife, in a simpler time. But will this be our time, Adrian? Bessie doesn't seem to think this world is right for us, either."

"I agree with Bessie. Something about this age doesn't feel quite right to me. I suppose it's just too close to the twentieth century and our lives back there."

Vickie was puzzled. "Then what will we do? When we all get through this, will we try to go back to 1945? Bessie said we would all be doomed there."

"I wish I knew the answers," Adrian replied heavily. "However, I suspect what Bessie is really trying to tell us is that our course may already be set, and we likely won't have a great deal to say about it."

"Bessie knows, but she's not going to tell us," Vickie added perceptively.

Adrian pulled her close again, tucking her head beneath his chin. "Perhaps, my darling, that is for the best."

"Nate! Nate, please let me in!"

Upstairs in his attic room, Nate was pacing, his jaw clenched and unshed tears gleaming in his eyes. He could hear Cathy pounding on his door, along with her plaintive pleas and the whimpering of her kitten.

Much as he loved her, anger and pride kept him from going to her.

Let them all wait until hell froze over, he thought fiercely. As far as he was concerned, Cathy had betrayed him by giving her allegiance to Vickie and his father—and so quickly! Her haste in forsaking him made his head spin. Just hours after his dad had come here, Cathy had embraced him, and told him she loved him, and kissed his cheek! The memory of it ate at him like bile. Cathy was his world, and tonight his dad had taken his world away from him.

Now Cathy wanted all of them to live together as a cozy little family. The very prospect made him ill. Cathy saw this move as bringing them closer together—but Nate well knew that he and Cathy would be torn asunder instead. Much as he loved her, he recognized that she was still a naive child, so innocently trusting. Why couldn't she believe him when he told her that Adrian Bennett was a man neither of them could trust?

Not that his father wasn't clever and cunning. Nate remembered how his dad had slyly asked for his help today. Nate had felt something treacherous stealing inside his heart then, some primal pull that scared him more than his dad did. It had been the raw desire to reconnect with his father, to surrender his anger and be held close, bringing with it a strange burning in his throat, and dim memories of rare, happier times back in England when he'd sat on his dad's knee by the fire. . . .

Home. Love. Warmth. Belonging. He and Cathy had suffered without such solace from their elders for so long. But how could he want such comfort from the man who had abandoned him? He had to steel himself against such traitorous yearnings. He didn't want his father's love, didn't need it. Cathy's love would more than suffice, if only his dad would just leave them alone.

Why couldn't Cathy see that his father and Vickie had already brought disaster to their door? For they had allowed Keegan to follow them across time, and now the monster had tried to set fire to dear Miss Sophie's house.

Again, he heard Cathy's plaintive voice. "Nate, please. Please, I must speak with you."

Something seemed to burst in Nate then—a conflagration of pride, anger, love, and pain. Even though he hadn't intended to, he spun on his heel, crossed the room, turned the key, then threw open the door. Cathy stood there clutching her kitten, shivering even in the warmth, her expression stark and vulnerable. Fighting the softer emotions that tugged at his heart, he demanded, "What do you want?"

"I want you to come out and talk to me."

"We'll talk here."

Cathy sighed. "Nate, Grandma says we must pack. We may have to leave with your dad and Vickie."

"Leave?" he retorted furiously. "I'll leave with

them when hell freezes over. But you can't wait, can you, Cathy?"

She beseeched him an outstretched hand. "Nate, you know I love you. But I love Vickie and Adrian, too."

"Yes, you've made that very clear," he shot back. "How can you love my dad? How could you *tell* him you love him? And—and kiss his face! You've only just met him."

"Well, I do love him. I need you, Nate, but I need your dad and Vickie, too. And it's not fair for you to ask me to choose between them and you."

Nate laughed scornfully. "You've already made your choice. It took you all of ten minutes."

"Is it so wrong of me to want us all to be a family?"

"Yes, because I'll die before I go to live with my father again."

"But what else can we do?" she asked plaintively.

"You can trust me to take care of you."

"Nate, I can't. You're still a boy."

"I am not! I'm almost a man, and plenty old enough to take care of you. I can hire out as a silversmith and support us." He touched her arm and entreated her with desperate eyes. "Run away with me, Cathy. Before the others make us go. *Please*. Maybe Bessie will come with us. You'd like that, wouldn't you?"

"But what about tomorrow? The earthquake? And Keegan. We'll need Adrian and Vickie to protect us."

Nate blinked rapidly. "*You* need them. It's them or me, Cathy."

"Nate, please."

Nate's mouth curled bitterly. "Go back to your sister, Cathy. And my father."

Before she could protest, he slammed the door in her face.

Then he heard Cathy scream, "I hate you!" He heard the sounds of her heartbroken sobs and retreating footsteps, and a low cry of anguish escaped him. Suddenly Nate detested himself even more than he hated his father. So overpowering was his self-loathing that he almost ran after Cathy to beg her forgiveness. Yet again pride held him back. He stood beating his fists against the door panel, helplessly calling her name, heedless of the tears now streaming down his face.

Chapter Twenty-four

Toward dawn, when grayish light was drifting through the front windows, Vickie and Adrian were about to nod off when Sophie stepped inside the parlor, trailed by Bessie. Vickie managed to lift her heavy eyelids and murmur, "Good morning."

Adrian, too, sat up and shook his head. "Madam. Bessie."

Sophie gasped in dismay. "Why, just look at the two of you, all but dead from exhaustion. I want both of you to go upstairs and get some rest, right now. Bessie and I will keep watch."

"But madam, I'm fine," protested Adrian, picking up his revolver, then unsteadily getting to his feet.

"You're about to keel over onto the floor, young man."

"But who will watch out for Keegan?"

Using her cane, Sophie limped over and held out her free hand. "Give me that revolver, Commander Bennett. Believe it or not, I know how to fire it. Will taught me before the war."

Adrian scowled. "Madam, I don't mean to be critical, but at your advanced age—"

"At my advanced age, I'm still perfectly capable of sending Bessie to fetch you—or firing the weapon myself if need be," Sophie cut in sternly. "I do have a bad knee from taking a fall several years ago, but these old hands work as well as ever—and my mind is perfectly sound." Insistently she stretched out her hand. "The weapon, Commander Bennett."

Though Adrian appeared doubtful, he handed over the Colt.

Sophie held the pistol barrel-down. "Now you two go on upstairs. There are two empty bedrooms at the end of the hallway on the second floor. I promise I'll send Bessie up for you at any sign of danger."

"You do that," Adrian replied.

He pulled Vickie to her feet, led her out of her room and up the stairs. Once they reached the last two doors at the end of the second-story hallway, he pulled her close and tenderly kissed her. "Darling, we must both try to grab a bit of rest, and then . . ."

"I know," she whispered, hugging him back. "This promises to be a most dramatic and challenging day. We'll need whatever rest we can get."

"Don't let me sleep too long," he advised.

"Or me. If you wake up first, come get me."

He kissed her brow. "I shall, my love."

Giving each other a last look of longing, they departed to their separate rooms. But inside her small

317

room, Vickie felt bereft as she stared at the cold, empty cot. Much as she knew Adrian was right that they both must rest now, she couldn't bear the thought of being apart from him, especially after all they had shared last night. She hungered to be in his arms again, if only for a few more brief moments.

Quietly she crossed the hallway, tiptoed into his room, and shut the door behind her. He was already asleep on the single bed near the wall. Unshaven, his hair rumpled, he slept on his side, facing her with one arm outstretched, and with such an expression of innocence on his handsome face that it tore at her heart. She stripped off all of her clothing, then went over and slipped under the covers with him. She shivered in delight as her body contacted his warm frame, and realized he was naked, too.

She heard him moan. He stirred, opened his eyes, gazed at her in surprise and delight, and drew her into his arms. "What is this?" he managed sleepily. "A naked nymph in my bed?"

She snuggled against him, kissing his stubbly chin and inhaling his male scent. "I couldn't sleep without you."

"Oh, darling. I'm so glad you're here. Though we're committing a scandal."

"I won't stay long," she murmured.

"That remains to be seen." He kissed her cheek, the corner of her mouth.

The touch of his lips excited her deeply, and she kissed him back almost feverishly, and felt him responding with equal ardor. She pressed her hand to his chest and felt his heart hammering beneath her fingertips. "And I was thinking—who knows what

318

this day will bring? Or if we'll even have a tomorrow."

He nestled her closer. "You mustn't think that, darling."

She pulled back and gazed up into his beautiful
dark eyes. "But we have now, this moment. Make
love to me, Adrian."

"Now?" he murmured. Even as he spoke the word,
she saw the naked joy in his eyes and felt his manhood stirring against her.

Moaning in delight, she buried her face in his neck.
"Yes, now. Now that we know we love each other. I
can't bear it if we don't."

"Oh, my sweet, darling Vickie. I can't bear it either."

She heard him groan; then he rolled, covering her
body with his own. The weight of his warm, naked
flesh felt marvelous on hers. He stared down intently
into her eyes. "You know, love, you are absolutely
right. When I made love with you before, it was out
of need. Now I want to join my body with yours for
love."

"Give me your love," she whispered.

He brushed her hair away from her forehead and
kissed her brow. "I shall, my darling. I shall give you
all my love for the rest of our lives. And I'd like to
give you even more."

She looked up at him, bemused and intrigued.

Caressing her breast, he whispered, "I'd like us to
have a child together, Vickie. Before, when I pointed
out that there might be a child, when I offered to
marry you, I did so more out of respect and concern
for your reputation. Now I want to marry you because

I love you, and I want us to have a child as an expression of that love, to bring our worlds even closer together."

"Oh, Adrian. Nothing would make me happier than to have your child," she replied joyously. "But what of Nate? Wouldn't this make him feel even more threatened and left out?"

Adrian sighed. "I would never try to replace Nate, or even want to. But our having a child together would also let him know that we're in this together, forever, as a real family. Perhaps he would choose to become a part of that family in time. And we mustn't forget how much loss that boy has already suffered. His mother's death devastated him. Now I'm the only family he has left." In a breaking voice he finished, "A little brother or sister would give him another family member to love, even if he can't ever love me."

Tears sprang to Vickie's eyes, for his last words were tearing her apart. She clutched him close and planted ardent kisses all over his face. "Oh, Adrian, he'll love you. He *will*. As I do."

"Come here, darling."

With these words Adrian threw off the covers, sat up on the side of the bed, and pulled Vickie onto his lap. Riveted by the fervor burning in his eyes, she straddled him without shame. Sunshine poured down upon their bodies and she could see every part of him—his beautifully chiseled face, muscled chest with crisp dark hair, sinewy thighs, and his wondrous manhood, so swollen and hard with love for her. She touched it, caressing him with her fingers, and heard his answering sound of pleasure.

He raked his gaze over her, too, reaching out to

caress her face, her breasts, her belly, to stroke her between her thighs. He spoke with infinite love and caring. "It's morning, now, love, the beginning of our lives together. No more shadows, no more pain. I want to see you, to see our love."

"Oh, Adrian." She hugged his neck, shivering against him.

Adrian caught her face in his hands and kissed her passionately. He slid his lips down her throat, then suckled at her breasts. By now Vickie was in agony, trying to sink her body onto him.

"No, darling, not yet," he murmured.

They kissed and caressed for what seemed an eternity, until both were ravenous, breathing raggedly. Then Adrian drew back slightly and smiled. When he finally thrust upward, deeply joining their bodies, Vickie cried out in exquisite, shattering ecstasy. Adrian clenched his arms about her waist and rocked her to and fro, heightening the intense, delirious sensations inside her. Sobs shook Vickie, cries she knew Adrian recognized as sounds of rapture.

As his hands roved her body, caressing her spine, her breasts, she began to move, arching upward then sinking deeply onto his lap. Their lips joined passionately as both began losing control. The heat and tension built until neither of them could bear it. At last Adrian caught Vickie close and took them to rapture, drowning her mouth with his kiss as their love found completion there in the light.

Afterward, as Vickie lay sleeping, Adrian remained awake, staring at her beloved face with great tenderness. She'd brought him such beauty, such exquisite love, that his chest ached with the intensity of it.

Never had he expected to be so blessed, to feel such bliss! To love an incredible woman for one more time in his life. His life was complete now, complete and whole again, except for two more major hurdles he had to withstand: regaining his son's love and trust, and getting them all through the next twenty-four hours.

Adrian felt the need to pray. He slipped out of bed, onto his knees in the sunlight. "Dear God, thank you for the miracle you have brought me in the form of this dear woman. Thank you for the incredible blessing of our children, whom you have kept safe from harm. Now all of us need you even more. Give me the strength I need to get through the next hours, to defeat Keegan, and keep all of my loved ones safe from harm."

After another long moment spent silently meditating, Adrian slipped back into bed and drew Vickie close.

Moments later, Vickie awakened in Adrian's arms. She slipped out of bed, feeling exhilarated, satiated, a bit tender from the wondrous lovemaking the two of them had just shared. She put on her clothes and for a moment just watched him sleeping. Then she kissed his noble mouth, tucked the covers around his neck, and tiptoed out of his room, returning to her own.

She was so exhausted that she tumbled onto her cot still fully clothed, and immediately fell into a deep slumber. . . .

It seemed only a moment later when Cathy burst

inside her room, frantic, with Sophie and Bessie following close behind. As Vickie blinked at the glaring sunshine, her sister cried, "Vickie, you must come help us! Nate is gone!"

Chapter Twenty-five

Vickie jerked awake, sitting up in bed. "Nate is missing?" she queried, still half-dazed.

"He is, indeed," replied Sophie.

Vickie turned to Cathy. "What happened?"

Cathy sniffed at tears. "I think it may be my fault. I went to Nate's room last night and tried to make up with him. I told him I love him, too, but it's not fair, he can't make me choose between him and you and Adrian. But he wouldn't even listen, and when I went back this morning, he wouldn't let me in. Now I just went back to his room and he's gone."

"We've searched the rest of the house, and the yard, and he's nowhere about," put in Sophie worriedly.

Vickie struggled to her feet. "Oh, my heavens, we must go wake Adrian, and . . . What time is it?"

"Just after two o'clock," Sophie replied.

"Two in the *afternoon*?" Vickie gasped, horrified. "Why didn't you wake us up?"

"We didn't have the heart to," Sophie replied. "Besides, I remembered your saying that the earthquake won't come until nightfall."

"Yes, but that could be within hours now," Vickie fretted. "Come on, let's hurry over to Adrian's room."

The four females rushed into the hallway, only to find Adrian emerging from his room, pulling on his jacket, appearing sleepy and unshaven. "I heard the commotion you ladies were making and it woke me up. Good Lord, what time is it?"

Vickie answered, "It's two o'clock."

"Two?" he cried.

"But I'm afraid I've got worse news for you," she went on. "Nate has run away."

"What?"

"Cathy just noticed him missing."

"Damn!" he exclaimed, tearing his fingers through his rumpled hair. "I must go search for him immediately."

"I want to hunt for Nate, too," Cathy declared.

"As do I," Vickie added. "Besides, it's getting so late now that we must all evacuate the house."

"You're right. Very well, we'll all leave, but I shall hunt for Nate myself. We'll go back into town, to St. Christopher's Orphanage, and you ladies can stay there. With all the nuns and children around, you should be safe until I can find Nate. And there's always a chance he may have instinctively gone back there. If not, I'll still try to return with him and we can all go to the chapel before the earthquake commences."

"Why the chapel?" Vickie asked.

"It's where we were when we came here, and I sense it's the place where we'll all be safest now."

"Are you thinking we might still make our way back to 1945?" she asked.

"I don't know, Vickie. I just know we were in the chapel before when we felt the earth move and were sent here. I sense that's where we should all be when the earth moves again tonight."

Vickie turned to Bessie. "What do you think?"

Bessie solemnly nodded. "I think he be right. The chapel, we all be safest there when the earthquake come."

"Very well," Vickie agreed. "Now everyone, get your things and let's go."

The group dispersed to their respective rooms. Moments later when Vickie came downstairs, she was puzzled to see her great-great-grandmother rocking in the parlor, holding a rosary and reading her prayer book. "Grandmother, why aren't you packed and ready to leave?"

Sophie looked up, smiling serenely at Vickie. "I'm not leaving with you."

Alarmed, Vickie crossed the room. "What? But you must. You won't be safe here alone. There's Keegan, and the earthquake."

But Sophie only shook her head. "This is my home. I'll not abandon it. And besides, after you go, perhaps I'll still have time to warn a few neighbors and friends."

Sophie's calm statement left Vickie immersed in

terrible turmoil. Should she tell her grandmother the truth, even though Sophie had expressed wishes to the contrary?

She moved closer and clasped Sophie's frail hands with her own. "Grandmother, I didn't want to tell you this before, but you've left me no choice. If you stay here tonight . . . you're going to die in the earthquake."

Surprisingly, Sophie only smiled. "Then it is simply my time to go."

"No," Vickie replied, fighting a building sense of panic. "Please listen to me. I'm trying to tell you that you're in grave danger, that you won't survive if you remain in this house, and you must come with us now."

Sophie only shook her head. "Don't worry about me, dear. I've had a good, long life, and I want to be with my Will. But I shall try to alert my neighbors."

Vickie was about to protest further when a calm voice behind her stated, "It be her time. She stay here."

Vickie whirled to see Brown Bessie standing nearby carrying a small carpetbag, while Cathy was coming down the stairs with Rufus in her arms, Adrian close behind her. Absorbing the profound wisdom and compassion in Bessie's eyes, Vickie realized Bessie was right and there was nothing more she could do.

She turned to hug Sophie, her arms trembling about the old woman's frail body. Committing the feel, the scent of her to memory, she whispered, "This is so hard. I've only just found you, Grandmother. I can't give you up."

As Vickie drew back, Sophie gazed up at her great-great-granddaughter with sadness and love. "Oh, we'll meet again, my dear. I firmly believe that some of us are meant to go on ahead to prepare the way for the rest of us. Will and I shall be there to greet you and the others when you join us in heaven."

Vickie wiped away tears with her sleeve. "Goodbye, Great-great-grandmother. Godspeed."

"And you, my dear."

Cathy rushed up to tug at Vickie's skirts, her face stricken. "Isn't Grandma coming with us?"

Before Vickie could speak, Sophie replied, "I'm sorry, dear, but I can't. I'm staying here in my home."

"No!" Cathy wailed. "Vickie, make her come."

Even as Vickie struggled, feeling very torn, Bessie crossed the room and calmly took Cathy's hand. "No, Miss Cathy. Miss Sophie not come. Her place here. We go now."

Though Cathy's underlip trembled, she bravely nodded to Bessie. Then she broke away to give Sophie a last hug. "If you change your mind, we'll be at St. Christopher's Orphanage. We love you."

Sophie patted Cathy's back. "I know, dear. I love all of you, too. Now, go."

The child clung to Sophie another moment, until Bessie caught her hand and led her away. Throwing her great-great-grandmother one last, bittersweet smile, Vickie turned away and went over to the stairs, where Adrian waited for her, his expression filled with compassion.

The group of four walked briskly toward town, Vickie and Adrian in the lead, Cathy and Bessie following.

"I think it's a good idea to leave Cathy and Bessie at the orphanage," Vickie told him, "but I want to help you find Nate."

"I want to help, too!" added Cathy from behind them.

Adrian shook his head. "I'm afraid that's quite impossible. I can't subject the rest of you to the danger Keegan poses."

"What about the danger Nate is in?" Lowering her voice, Vickie asked, "What if Keegan has kidnapped him? What if he was lurking around the house again when Nate left, and . . ."

"Perish the thought," Adrian replied vehemently. "However, I don't suppose we can afford to ignore the possibility."

"I just wish we knew more about where . . ." All at once Vickie snapped her fingers and turned. "Bessie, do you know anything about Nate's disappearance, and where he is now?"

"No, 'um," Bessie answered. "But I know he in trouble bad."

Vickie grew even more concerned, while Cathy turned to Bessie. "Oh, no! Does that mean the bad man has Nate?"

Bessie didn't reply. Vickie turned to squeeze Cathy's hand. "Don't worry, honey. We'll find him."

"But how can I stop worrying, Vickie? You said a big, mean earthquake is coming. What if it catches Nate before we do?"

The thought was frightening, Vickie had to admit. Turning to Adrian, she insisted, "I'm coming with you to hunt for Nate, whether you like it or not."

329

"Vickie—"

"I'm coming with you."

"Is this the orphanage?" Cathy asked with a frown.

On the path leading to the steps of the orphanage, Vickie noted that her sister was gazing about them in puzzlement. "Yes, dear, it's where you lived. But in 1945. It's also the place where you and Nate came back in time, remember?"

"Yes, but that was at night, in the fish pond," Cathy replied. "It doesn't really look like the place I remember from before."

"I know, dear."

"Is Mother Agatha here, or somewhere else?"

Vickie had to smile, musing that, although Cathy had seemed to understand her and Nate's time-travel experience, sometimes all the implications must be too much for a nine-year-old mind to comprehend. "No, dear, Mother Agatha is back in 1945. Look, Cathy, let's not worry about that now, okay?"

"Okay," Cathy replied, though she still appeared confused.

The group hurried up the steps of the Greek Revival mansion, and Adrian knocked firmly on the door. A moment later the stern-featured nun Vickie remembered as Mother Margaret opened the door and frowned at the newcomers.

"Yes?" she inquired. "Haven't we met before?"

Adrian removed his hat. "Yes, Mother Margaret. Miss Cheney and I were here two days ago, searching for our children."

"Ah, yes. So you found them?"

"Well, yes and no. We did find Miss Cheney's sister, Cathy"—he paused to gesture at the child—"as well as my son, Nate. However, Nate somehow slipped away from us a little while ago and now we're out searching for him. I don't suppose he came here?"

"Certainly not," the woman answered coldly. "And I must say you people are rather careless with your offspring."

Adrian grimaced. "We were wondering if Cathy and her companion, Bessie, might stay here while Miss Cheney and I search for my son."

The nun appeared taken aback. "Well, this request is most unusual."

"Just for a few hours," Vickie put in with a look of supplication. "We wouldn't want to lose Cathy and Bessie while we're hunting for Nate."

"Indeed." The woman hesitated, and Rufus let out a wail. "But what about that creature? We don't allow pets here."

Vickie reached out to touch the woman's arm. "Please, sister, I know you're a God-fearing woman, and it won't be for long."

At last the nun relented with a sigh. "Very well, I suppose it will be all right. Just for a few hours. That is, if you promise to be back before nightfall."

"Oh, we promise," Adrian vowed.

"All right, then." The nun gestured to Cathy and Bessie. "Come along, girls."

"Thank you, sister," Adrian said.

Beseechingly, Cathy turned to Vickie. "I still want to go with you."

"No, honey. You and Bessie must stay here where it's safe."

Steeling herself against the look of pitiful pleading on Cathy's face, Vickie turned and left with Adrian.

"Step lively, now, girls," Mother Margaret ordered. "If you'll just follow me, we'll get you settled."

Inside St. Christopher's, Cathy glanced at her friend Bessie as the two followed the mother superior down the long central corridor just inside the front door. Cathy remained puzzled by their surroundings, and Vickie's attempt at explanation hadn't really helped.

Even though Cathy had tried her best to understand the remarkable journey through time that she and Nate had taken, she felt very strange now to be walking through the halls of St. Christopher's again—for this orphanage was quite different from the one she remembered in 1945. Indeed, as they strolled past an ornate black table that served as a shrine to the Holy Virgin, with a central statue surrounded by numerous lighted candles, Cathy paused to gasp.

The mother superior turned sharply to Cathy. "Is something wrong, young lady?"

Cathy pointed at the table. "Where did that come from? It wasn't here before."

The nun's eyebrows shot up. "And just when were *you* here, young lady?"

Cathy frowned. "I'm not sure, but the last time I was here, your name was Agatha and the orphanage was on fire."

The nun sucked in a horrified breath and turned to Bessie. "What ails the child? Is she simple?"

"No, 'um," Bessie quickly answered. "She jes' running on at the mouth." Turning sternly to Cathy, Bessie scolded, "You hush up now."

Wide-eyed, Cathy nodded, realizing she'd said far more than she should have.

The sister led them to the back of the building, where a staircase curved to their right, and a door loomed on the left. She opened the door and ducked her head inside. "Oh, Sister Gertrude? Are you in there?"

After a moment, the nun turned back to Cathy and Bessie with an annoyed frown. "Don't know what happened to the sister. She was supposed to be on duty in the office." The nun indicated a bench near the staircase. "You two sit down right there, and I'll go find her so she may watch you."

"Yes, ma'am," Cathy said respectfully. She took a seat, and Bessie followed suit.

The nun lingered a moment, wagging a finger at the two girls. "Now you two wouldn't run off, would you?"

"Oh, no, ma'am," Cathy replied solemnly.

The sister cast a stern glance at Bessie. "I'm making you responsible for the child. See that she does not indulge in any further flights—of fancy, or otherwise."

"Yes 'um."

The woman pointed at Rufus. "And see that the varmint doesn't get into any mischief, either."

"Yes 'um."

Lifting an eyebrow in final warning, the sister went off up the stairs. At once Bessie turned to Cathy. "Miss Cathy, you gettin' us in trouble with your mouth."

"I'm sorry, Bessie," Cathy replied contritely. "I know I should have watched what I was saying. Only I'm so confused by everything, and it feels so weird to be in the orphanage again. Besides, I'm very worried about Nate, and the earthquake."

"Bessie worried, too."

Cathy grabbed her friend's arm. "Let's go follow Adrian and Vickie! Quick, while the sister is still gone. If we hurry we can still catch them."

Bessie hesitated a moment, then nodded solemnly. "Yes. We go help them, help find Nate."

The two girls all but ran for the front door.

Vickie and Adrian were in a race against time. They walked all over central Charleston—past the banks on Broad Street, the taverns on Queen, the business and homes on Meeting—desperately hoping for some sign of Nate. So preoccupied were they with their search that they were unaware that a half a block behind them, two smaller figures shadowed their every step.

"Come along, Bessie, we don't want to lose them!" Cathy whispered anxiously, pulling her friend along as she scanned the street ahead and watched Vickie and Adrian turn a corner.

"Miss Cathy, if we too close, they see us," Bessie warned.

Cathy gave a sigh, realizing Bessie was right. "I know. I just want to find Nate so bad."

"We find him, Miss Cathy. We find him."

Cathy nodded, while saying a desperate prayer that Vickie and Adrian would soon lead them to Nate. She was worried sick about him. Maybe she'd been too hard on him back at Grandma Sophie's house, but her words had given him no cause to run away and put everyone to all this worry and trouble. She must give him a sound scolding once they found him.

As the hours trickled past and dusk began to fall, Vickie fought a building sense of doom. Hardest of all was to stare into the faces of the townspeople of Charleston and to know she was powerless to save them from the coming earthquake. When she passed the vegetable lady out chanting for customers with a basket on her head, when she watched a young family troop into the drug emporium, when she spied a sailor romancing his sweetheart in Washington Square, she was tempted to call out, "Please, leave Charleston at once! Go to a place of safety! A disaster is looming!"

But she knew no one would believe her. Worse yet, she and Adrian couldn't afford to call such attention to themselves while Nate was still missing and possibly in Keegan's clutches.

After scouring the town and unsuccessfully questioning countless passerby regarding whether or not they'd seen the boy, Vickie and Adrian paused just outside St. Michael's Church. By now the skies were quite dark.

"I'm so frustrated," she told him. "We haven't found the slightest clue about Nate, and night is here. We must go get Cathy and Bessie."

Adrian nodded. "You're right. With the earthquake imminent, we can't just leave them at the orphanage. They should be with us now."

They quickly walked back to the institution. When Adrian knocked on the door, Mother Margaret opened it and lifted an eyebrow. "Oh. You two again."

335

"We've come to get Cathy and Bessie," Adrian said.

"Really?" the nun mocked. "I had thought the girls were with you."

"You mean they're not here?" Vickie exclaimed.

The nun shook her head. "You people are clearly the grossest incompetents I have ever met. As for those incorrigible girls, they sneaked out right after you left. Why, I only turned my back for a moment, and they were gone. I assumed they had rejoined you."

"Well, they haven't, madam, and now they're lost as well," Adrian retorted.

Irate, the nun drew herself up. "Don't you take that tone of voice with me, sir. Why, I did you two a great favor out of the kindness of my heart. I cannot be held responsible for the mischief of that—that child and her servant."

Before either of them could respond, the woman slammed the door in their faces.

Vickie gestured in exasperation. "Wonderful. Now all three of them are missing."

"Easy, dear, we'll find them," Adrian replied, though he, too, appeared quite worried.

He led her down the steps. Then, near the gate, Vickie spotted a flash of motion in the nearby trees. Heart hammering with fresh hope, she ran toward the source. "Cathy, are you there? Or is it you, Nate?"

A shame-faced Cathy stepped out of the foliage with her kitten in her arms; she was followed by an equally solemn Bessie. "No, Vickie, it's me."

Vickie ran to her sister's side, taking Cathy by the shoulders. "Cathy, what are you and Bessie doing

336

here? Why did you run away from the orphanage?"

Cathy's underlip trembled. "Bessie and me wanted to help find Nate. We've been following you all afternoon."

"Cathy!" Vickie scolded. "You gave us such a scare."

Adrian strode up to join them. "I'm appalled at both of you. You should have remained at the orphanage as you were instructed to do."

"But we're here with you, now," Cathy argued. "Please don't make us go back. Can't we help?"

Vickie and Adrian exchanged a questioning look, then he nodded wearily. "Very well, you two may as well help. With the earthquake so close at hand, we can't risk leaving you again, anyway. But stay close."

"Yes, sir." Cathy turned to her sister. "Where should we go now?"

Vickie concentrated fiercely. "Well, we haven't tried the Battery as yet."

"That's right, White Point Gardens," agreed Adrian.

The group started off briskly for the Battery.

At White Point Gardens, Carmichael Keegan lounged against an oak tree, smoking a cigar. With nightfall the park was deserted, the mothers having long since taken their children home. An odd stillness hung in the air, an almost unnatural quiet. The trees and shrubs seemed frozen in place, strangely lifeless, and not even a whisper of a breeze flowed off the bay.

Keegan was not concerned. He had no argument with the elements as long as they cooperated and didn't disrupt his plans.

In the clearing beyond, the boy was handcuffed to the merry-go-round, staring murder at him, and yelling out threats. Not that Keegan cared. Indeed, he laughed as he remembered how the stupid brat had walked straight into his trap.

He'd been lurking outside the Davis home when the boy had left the house earlier this afternoon. He'd trailed the lad for a block or so, then grabbed him at gunpoint and pulled him into an alleyway. He had handcuffed him and threatened to shoot him if he tried to resist or called out for help. He'd kept the child his prisoner in an abandoned warehouse near the docks until darkness came . . . and with it, the best time to complete his dirty work.

Now he was holding the boy here at the park to draw in the others. He knew it would be only a matter of time before they searched for him here, before they, too, would be snared in his net. Then he would kill them all.

Not a moment too soon, either. The boy had been a pain in the neck all day. Heedless of his own safety, he had struggled and screamed. The brazen lad had demanded to be freed, had insisted his father would be along at any moment to rescue him. Even now the boy was behaving no differently, still hurling insults.

"You let me go, you snake," the boy shouted, waving his free fist. "My dad will be along any moment now. He's a decorated war veteran, and he'll kill you, squash you like the snake you are!"

"Ah, shut up, you little brat, or I'll come over there and gag you!" Keegan yelled back.

"You're a filthy stinking murderer, a coward who

tries to hurt children, and I'll see you rotting in hell," the boy taunted.

Enraged, Keegan raised his weapon. "You shut up, or I swear I'll shoot you."

Nate fell silent, though his eyes seethed with hatred.

Keegan chuckled to himself. It would do the boy no good whatsoever to resist. There was no one in the park to hear him.

Across from Keegan, Nate was feeling desperate and very, very foolish. Here he had bragged to Cathy that he could take care of them both, when clearly he couldn't even take care of himself. He had insisted the two of them didn't need anyone else, especially not her sister and his dad.

He couldn't have been more wrong on either count. He remembered how Mother Agatha had often scolded that pride was the deadliest of sins, and the most destructive. Nate had allowed his own wounded pride to endanger all of their lives. Cathy had been right all along that the two of them were still children, that they still needed adult guidance. He had just abundantly proven her point.

When he had childishly run away from Sophie Davis's house, Keegan had quickly captured him. Never had Nate felt so stupid. Now Keegan was using him as bait to pull in the others—and to kill his beloved Cathy. The very thought of his darling Cathy suffering the horrendous fate Keegan had in mind for her made Nate's throat burn. He didn't care that much about himself, but he was so scared for her, terrified he would be responsible for her death. Even if Keegan didn't kill them, his dad and Vickie had warned about a coming earthquake that might claim all their lives.

Nothing in Nate's life had ever mattered more to him than Cathy's love—that, and making his dear mother proud of him. What would his mum think now if she could see how he had botched up everything through his own stupid anger and pride? How would she feel if she knew he had placed his wounded ego and fear of loss above Cathy's welfare?

And what of his father? Nate remembered the message Cathy had tried to drill into his head: "He did the best he could, Nate." Had Cathy been right all along? Could his dad have felt as devastated by his mum's death as he had? Could it be that his dad had gone off to the war because it was the only way he could deal with his own grief?

And hadn't his dad done everything in his power to try to find Nate, even crossing time with Vickie to be with him? Hadn't he apologized again and again and vowed that he cared, that he would be a good father in the future, if only Nate would give him another chance? Hadn't he promised he would not try to pull Nate and Cathy apart?

In his hurt, rage, and fear, Nate had been blind to the olive branch his dad had extended, though he could see the truth clearly now. Yet he had come to his senses too late.

Was there any hope left? It had been so many years since Nate had prayed, but he did so now. Fiercely, reverently. "Dear God," he whispered, "please forgive my pride and my fear, and help me in my hour of need. If only you'll save Cathy, I promise I shall never again behave so foolishly. I'll be good, I'll go to church, and I'll never allow my temper to get the better of me. And I promise . . ." Even though bitter tears welled in his eyes, Nate forged on. "I promise I shall forgive my dad . . . really, I will, if only you'll save Cathy." In a breaking voice, he finished, "And maybe in time, I'll even be able to forgive myself."

Chapter Twenty-six

Vickie noted a strange quiet in the air as she, Adrian and the girls hurried past old colonial homes while approaching White Point Gardens. Although the park was flanked by gaslights on the street above and the Battery below, the gardens themselves were shrouded in darkness, save for a patina of moonlight.

They entered the shadowy expanse and walked through the moss-draped trees, catching no glimpse of Nate. Together the group combed the rest of the park, calling out for him. All of them grew frustrated as no trace of the boy was found, and the darkness grew deeper and more ominous.

Cathy began racing around almost aimlessly, yelling, "Nate, what are you? Where *are* you, please?"

Vickie watched Cathy run alone into some darkened trees. Fear quickened her pulse. "Cathy, you must stay with the rest of us!"

She ran after Cathy, with Adrian and Bessie close on her heels. By now the darkness was so profound that at times she couldn't even see Cathy, though she could hear the kitten mewling somewhere ahead of her. She stumbled over roots and plants, avoiding the ghostly shapes of trees. The air was thick with the smell of earth, plants, and the scent of the sea.

At last she watched her sister emerge ahead in a pool of gaslight, and wended her way toward it. She entered a clearing and could finally see Cathy running ahead of her. Looking around, she realized her sister had led them all into the playground at the edge of the park. A single gas lamp on the street beyond illuminated a merry-go-round, which was slowly turning, squeaking. A dark shape was crouched on the platform. Vickie squinted, then her heart pounded with relief and fear as she recognized Nate. He appeared to be handcuffed to a large bracket and was twisting his wrist, trying to yank free.

Cathy had also spotted him. "Nate!" she screamed, running toward him.

"Cathy, wait!" Vickie cried. "It could be a trap!"

She tore after the child, at last grabbing Cathy by the arm, only to see a dark figure lunge out from a tree just to the left of the merry-go-round. "Not so fast, folks," drawled Carmichael Keegan, leveling a gun at them.

Vickie skidded to a halt with Cathy, then turned as Adrian arrived at their side. Grim-faced, he hauled out his own revolver and shouted, "Keegan, you let my son go! Now!"

Quickly Keegan ducked down behind Nate on the merry-go-round, shielding himself with the boy's body, and aiming his gun at Nate's head. "You drop your gun, Bennett, or I'll blow the brat's head off!"

Adrian hesitated, his face stark with fear and desperation. Vickie burned with helpless frustration, hurting for him, and for Nate.

"Don't do it, Dad!" shouted Nate. "Don't let this fool bluff you."

"I ain't bluffing, kid," Keegan growled to the boy. "Now shut up."

"You let Nate go!" shouted Cathy, waving her fist at Keegan.

Keegan cocked his revolver. "Drop your weapon *now*, Bennett!"

Even as Adrian reluctantly laid his gun on the ground, Vickie realized Bessie was no longer with them. Had she moved back into the trees?

Suddenly Vickie heard a blood-curdling scream, the primal yell of a mother animal protecting its young. Then in wonder she watched Brown Bessie leap from the trees near the merry-go-round and fling herself on Keegan.

Vickie gasped, watching the two grapple on the merry-go-round. Meanwhile, Adrian was running toward them. Right before he arrived, a shot rang out, and Keegan thrust Bessie away.

Everything happened at once then. Cathy screamed and ran for Bessie. With a roar of rage, Adrian fell on Keegan and yanked the gun from his fingers. The two struggling men tumbled off the merry-go-round

344

and rolled about on the ground, kicking and cursing. Keegan managed to break free from Adrian, to stagger to his feet and run. Adrian sprang up after him, firing a shot into the air and shouting, "Stop, you miserable coward!"

Then, amazingly, the earth began to move! Vickie could hear the horrible keening and groaning of the ground, and felt the grassy terrain undulating beneath her feet. She heard the screams of people and animals rise up from the houses beyond, the rattle, roar, and crash of buildings being shaken off their foundations in Charleston proper.

"Oh, my God, it's the earthquake!" Swaying as the ground shook and tipped beneath her, she tried to stagger her way toward Cathy and Bessie. "Cathy! Dear heaven, Cathy!" She caught a glimpse of Adrian, white-faced, clutching his son on the wildly tilting merry-go-round. Reeling crazily, she struggled her way toward the girls. . . .

Mic Keegan ran for his life, wincing at the sound of the shot Bennett fired after him. Damn the Brit for disarming him! He vowed he would still kill the bastard, still murder them all, but not now. For now he must get away, make good his escape before Bennett shot him.

He had almost reached the street when a great trembling, an earsplitting rumble, shook the Battery. Mother of God, was this the earthquake? The ground began violently shuddering, rolling beneath his feet. He rocked precariously, almost falling down. Then a huge explosion in the distance spewed a fireball into the sky, and Keegan watched the earth begin opening up just beyond his feet.

It *was* the earthquake! Bitter smoke assaulted his nostrils, and cinders burned his eyes. Heaven help him, he must turn around at once or be sucked under!

But changing directions proved impossible. Even as Keegan tilted wildly, trying desperately to steady his tottering body, he began to lose his balance. Terror shaking him to the core, he helplessly watched the jaws of the growling monster open wider beneath him. A horrendous bang sounded as the nearby gas lamp popped and toppled over into the abyss; then flames spewed from the widening chasm beneath his feet.

Keegan screamed, staggering violently. Blessed Saints, Gladys had been right—he *was* bound for hell! Howling like an animal in torment, Keegan tumbled into the blazing inferno and disappeared.

Chapter Twenty-seven

Back in the park, Vickie saw Keegan run, heard him scream, watched the jaws of hell open to snatch him up as cinders, ashes, and smoke spewed into the air. She had no real time to contemplate the poetic justice of this arsonist and murderer being claimed by earthquake and fire. Coughing and staggering to keep her footing on the rolling ground, she fought her way toward Cathy and Bessie, who were clinging together a few feet from the merry-go-round. She tumbled down beside them and clutched Cathy close for the final seconds until the horrible heaving stopped. Cathy was shaking, crying, the kitten yowling in fear.

At last Vickie raised her head. "Cathy, are you all right?"

"Yes," Cathy sobbed, sitting up. "But Bessie is hurt. The bad man shot her!"

Quickly Vickie glanced down at Bessie, who lay flat on her back, staring vacantly into space. Though Vickie could spot no obvious wound or sign of blood in the darkness, the girl did appear quite pale, in obvious distress. She patted Bessie's hand and found it limp and cold. "Bessie, hold on!" She turned back to Cathy. "I'm going to check on Adrian and Nate. Stay here—I'll be right back."

"Okay, Vickie," Cathy replied, hiccuping.

Vickie rushed over to the merry-go-round, which was now tilted askew, slanting downward into a narrow fissure in the earth. By the light of the flames still spewing out on the street beyond, she saw father and son huddled together on the sloping turntable. "Adrian, Nate, are you okay?"

"Yes," Adrian replied, coughing, "we're both fine." He gestured toward the flames beyond them. "And I see the devil has reclaimed his spawn."

"And good riddance to him," Vickie agreed. Blinking at the smoke stinging her eyes, she leaned toward Nate. "Are you all right? Did Keegan hurt you?"

"No, I'm fine." Nate pulled at the handcuff still binding his wrist to the bracket. "But I can't get out of these handcuffs." Turning to his dad, he swallowed hard. "Sir, can you help me?"

"Of course, son." Standing, Adrian drew out Keegan's revolver. "I'm afraid I'll have to shoot off the handcuffs, though."

"Are you sure you should do that?" Vickie asked skeptically.

"Vickie, we must free Nate. There are bound to be aftershocks, and this merry-go-round might—"

Vickie heard a frightening squeal and watched the

merry-go-round slide a bit further into the fissure, while Nate stoically held on and his father grasped the tilted platform to steady it. She in turn grabbed Nate and held him fast. "Please, I understand."

Once the platform was stationary again, Adrian straightened. "Son, stand up. Vickie, please hold him as far away from the merry-go-round as you can while I shoot through the chain."

"Of course." Vickie helped Nate stand, wrapped her arms around him and held him away from the turntable. "Go ahead and shoot."

Both Vickie and Nate flinched as the shot rang out. Nate held up his freed arm and regarded his father in awe. "Dad, you did it."

"Thank God." His face stark with emotion, Adrian embraced his son and spoke in an unsteady voice. "I'm so glad you're okay, Nate. And so sorry for anything I've done to hurt you. I love you, son. Please forgive me."

Adrian's heartfelt pleas touched Vickie deeply. She watched Adrian move back and wait for Nate to respond—and didn't think she could bear it if the boy rejected his dad yet again.

Then joy lit her heart as Nate hugged his father back, blinking at tears himself. "I'm sorry, too, Dad. I put everyone's life in danger and that was wrong."

With an expression of sublime relief, Adrian tousled the boy's hair. "Don't worry about that now, son. What matters is that everyone is safe."

Vickie was nodding in heartfelt agreement when she heard Cathy yell, "Everyone, come quick! Bessie is fading!"

Vickie glanced wildly at Adrian. "Oh, poor Bessie! I think Keegan must have shot her."

The three rushed over to join Cathy and Bessie. Vickie sank to her knees and went wide-eyed. Although the light was dim, the fire from the broken gas line providing the only illumination, she could tell Bessie had gone even more limp and pale was beginning to fade before their eyes. The girl gazed almost unseeingly into space.

Vickie shook her. "Bessie! Bessie, say something!"

Bessie was silent, still staring.

Cathy clutched her friend's arm. "Bessie, please don't go!"

Then something amazing happened. Bessie blinked slowly, then turned to smile luminously at Cathy, and reached out to squeeze her hand. Weakly she spoke. "It be all right, Miss Cathy. Time for Bessie to go now. We meet again some time, but not here. My work here done."

"Bessie, no!" Cathy wailed.

"You hush now, Miss Cathy, and listen to Bessie." The Negress handed Cathy the small sack from her waist. "Bessie go now. You keep my marbles."

"But, Bessie—"

Insistently, Bessie pressed the sack into Cathy's hand. "You keep." Turning to the others, she said solemnly, "You folks best be on your way now. It not over for you. Go to the orphanage chapel, and pray together. You ain't where you meant to be. Not yet."

Adrian and Vickie glanced at each other in confusion and concern.

Then Cathy screamed as a new tremor shook them. By now cinders were flying everywhere and the atmosphere was acrid. Vickie hugged Cathy tight and pleaded, "Hold on, darling. It's likely only an after-shock."

The shaking lasted for several frightening seconds as the sisters huddled together. Then Vickie heard Cathy cry, "Oh, no!"

Vickie opened her eyes, blinking as a cloud of smoke rolled over them. "Darling, what is it?"

Cathy's face had paled with shock. "Bessie is gone! Look, she's really gone! All I have left now are her marbles."

Vickie ran her hands over the grassy ground, squinting to see. Then, as the smoke cleared, she gazed downward in stupefaction. Where Bessie's body had lain, there was only emptiness and a slight, lingering warmth.

Vickie was amazed. "My God, you're right. She was here a second ago, and now she's gone."

"We must go find her," Cathy implored, beseeching Vickie with her eyes.

Now Adrian spoke up. "No, Cathy, Bessie isn't here any more. We must follow her directions and go to the chapel."

"Will she be there?" Cathy asked forlornly.

Adrian shook his head. "Honey, all we can do is what she asked."

"No, we can't leave her!"

Nate stepped forward, pulling Cathy to her feet, then retrieved the kitten and Bessie's marbles. "Come along, Cathy, we must do what Bessie said."

"Nate is right," added Adrian. "We must hurry to the chapel, and we've no time to waste. Come along now, everyone."

Cathy hiccuped. "Okay, then."

As the four started off, Vickie blanched, then clutched Adrian's hand. "Oh, my God, I almost forgot. First we must go check on Grandmother Davis."

He hesitated a moment, then soberly nodded.

Huddled together, the group of four made their way out of White Point Gardens, dodging fissures in the earth and large geysers of fire and water. Adrian pulled Cathy out of the way as a giant column of mud spurted into the air just inches from her feet. The child cringed at the sight and clung to him.

A nightmare awaited them on the Battery. All around them, Charleston's beautiful old mansions were collapsing, pillars falling, timbers groaning and heaving. People, dogs, horses, and livestock ran everywhere in the streets, crying, moaning, the humans as confused and helpless as the beasts.

"My God, it's like the end of the world," Adrian murmured as they started up Meeting Street. Ahead of them, stately stone facades were cracking, sirens wailing, gas pockets exploding and shooting out flames. Utility poles tottered at crazy angles and broken lines spewed out sparks. A team of horses, minus their carriage, raced down the street, both screaming as they dodged fissures, debris, and broken trolley tracks. A goat with a bell around its neck scampered along behind them, bleating plaintively.

As they arrived at the center of town, Vickie declared, "Look, St. Michael's appears pretty much intact, though there does appear to be some cracking."

Adrian pointed at a huge Georgian building across

the street, with crumbling pediment and pillars. "The old guard house wasn't as fortunate."

They made their way to Church Street, passing St. Philip's, which had sustained some heavy damage to its tower. They hurried north, to Pinckney Street, and proceeded west.

Within yards of the house, Cathy shouted, "Look, Grandmother's house is okay!"

The four rushed through the yard, up the steps and inside, to find the woman Vickie recognized as Sophie's neighbor seated in the parlor. "May I help you folks?" she asked, getting to her feet.

Vickie stepped forward. "I'm Sophie Davis's granddaughter, Vickie Cheney. Is she all right? Was she hurt in the earthquake?"

A pained look crossed the elderly woman's face. "I'm Mrs. Ashburn, Sophie's friend and neighbor. You know, I thought Sophie had lost her mind when she warned me about an earthquake hitting Charleston tonight, but it seems she was right, bless her heart. Fortunately the tremor did not harm our block. But when I came over to check on her. . . ."

"Yes?" Vickie inquired anxiously.

Glancing at the children with their worried faces, the woman whispered to Vickie, "I think you'd better come with me, miss."

Even as Vickie started to follow the woman toward the stairs, Cathy tugged at her skirts. "Is Grandma okay?"

Vickie turned, touching Cathy's cheek. "Honey, stay here with Adrian and Nate. I'll be right back."

Vickie followed Mrs. Ashburn upstairs, to Sophie's bedroom. By the light of a single candle on the nightstand, Vickie made out her great-great-grandmother's form on the bed, and a sound of anguish escaped her. Although Sophie was in her nightgown under the covers, she was much too still, her face gray. At once she knew Sophie was gone.

Tears spilled from Vickie's eyes. "What happened?"

Mrs. Ashburn sniffed at her own tears. "The poor dear must have passed away in her sleep, possibly during the earthquake. I just found her like this, a few moments ago. And . . . and she was still warm."

"Oh, my God," Vickie whispered. "She said it was her time."

Looking on compassionately, Mrs. Ashburn touched Vickie's shoulder. "Perhaps it was, dear."

Vickie gave the woman an apologetic look. "I hate to impose on you, but I'm afraid we can't stay. We must get the children to safety."

Mrs. Ashburn nodded. "You just go on. Sophie and I have been close friends for years, and I'll take care of her now. Don't you worry about her. Her priest and I will handle the arrangements."

"Bless you." Vickie hugged the woman, then leaned over and kissed Sophie's cool brow. "It's all right, great-great-grandmother. You're with your Will now. Good-bye."

With heavy heart, Vickie went down the stairs to see the troubled faces of the others. She fell into Adrian's arms.

"I'm sorry, darling," he murmured, kissing her hair. "Is she—"

"Yes. But she didn't feel any pain." Bravely Vickie turned to the children. "Let's go now."

"But can't Grandma come?" asked Cathy.

Gently Vickie replied, "Grandma is where she needs to be, honey. We must go on."

Cathy sniffled. "But I just lost Bessie—I can't lose Grandma, too!"

Vickie pulled the child close. "Honey, listen to me, please. You haven't really lost either of them."

Cathy gazed up at her sister with forlorn hope. "What do you mean?"

"You'll see them again one day, I promise. I'll explain more later. But for now, you must trust me—and we must go."

"Okay, Vickie," Cathy said heavily.

The group departed, hurrying toward the orphanage property. Approaching the chapel with the others, Vickie noted that the orphanage next door appeared largely intact, although she couldn't see too much through the acrid haze that now hung everywhere. She could, however, hear the excited cries of nuns and children drifting over from the piazza and yard.

They rushed inside the chapel, which was deserted and lit by only a few candles. "Everyone hurry, to the altar," Adrian directed.

The four knelt at the altar and joined hands. "Now all of us must close our eyes and pray to the Almighty to take us where we're meant to be," Vickie directed.

Silence fell as they all shut their eyes and began making their entreaty. Vickie prayed for her grandmother's soul, and for the safety of them all. Then she was amazed to feel the prayer bench begin to tremble beneath her knees, and she realized they were being hit by yet another aftershock. Heavens, this was just like what had happened when they'd traveled through time in the first place! She closed her eyes more tightly, clutched Adrian's hand, and slipped deeper into her trance. . . .

Moments later, Vickie awakened, choking on smoke. Gasping for air, she recognized the shadowy shapes of Adrian and the children kneeling beside her, but could see little else through the blinding smoke now surrounding them. Hearing a crackling noise coming from above, she gazed overhead to see horrifying flashes of red.

Merciful heavens, was the chapel on fire now?

She felt Adrian squeezing her hand, and heard him yell, "Outside, everyone, now! The building is on fire! Keep your hands joined!"

With him in the lead, the four stumbled down the aisle of the chapel. Coughing furiously, they staggered out the door and into the smoke-filled churchyard. Ashes and cinders hung in the pink-gray haze.

Vickie and the others stood stunned, gazing about them in mystification. Where had happened to them now? It was no longer night, but dawn, over a very different Charleston.

All around her Vickie could hear shouting, along with the howling of dogs and the distant pealing of a bell. Flames were spewing from the roof of the chapel they had just left, and next door another structure was fully ablaze. That fire was being attended by a bucket brigade of townsfolk dressed in absurdly antiquated clothing; Vickie could hear them yelling to one another as they passed the buckets. Other citizens in bizarre garb and strange hats were running about, shouting orders at one another and gesturing wildly.

Most distressing of all, on the walkway not far from the bucket brigade lay a half-dozen small human forms shrouded with blankets, obviously the bodies of dead children. Nuns wept over the corpses, while a priest with a prayer book stood intoning last rites.

Vickie was about to say something when she heard the thud of approaching footsteps, and someone shouted, "Stand aside, woman!"

Vickie turned to see a man running toward them. He wore a bicorne hat, a jacket with tails, and breeches. Carrying a full bucket, he shoved his way past her, sloshing water on her skirt.

"Woman, give way!" he bellowed. "Can you not see there is a fire here?"

Vickie glanced at Adrian in bewilderment. "Where are we now?"

Part Three

Charleston, South Carolina
1818

Chapter Twenty-eight

Before Adrian could respond, another man marched past Vickie, distracting her. Obviously the newcomer was a city guardsman; he wore a blue and yellow uniform, and carried both a musket with a bayonet and a blazing torch.

She touched his arm. "Sir, can you tell us what year it is?"

The soldier swung about. "Are you daft, missy, that you do not know the date?"

Adrian stepped forward. "Please, sir. The lady, the children and I were—well, we were praying in the chapel and got caught in the fire. I guess you might say we became confused."

The man gaped at the group of four in their late-nineteenth-century attire, then snorted a laugh. "From the look of your dress, sir, I should say all of you are addlepated." Evidently taking mercy on them, he added, " 'Tis the year of our Lord 1818."

"Did you say 1818?" Vickie cried.

"Aye. Now stand aside, citizens, and allow the bucket brigade to be about their work. I must go help the others douse the flames. No doubt the Negro insurrectionists have been at their dirty work again." Grimly he nodded toward the corpses on the walkway beyond. "And this time heads will roll, let me assure you."

Watching the man march off, Vickie turned to Adrian. "My God, it's now 1818. That must mean—"

"That we've all traveled back in time again, and we're now standing before the very blazing orphanage that Brown Bessie will shortly be accused of torching," Adrian finished.

"My heavens, that is amazing!" Vickie exclaimed.

"Oh, no!" wailed Cathy. "Are we really back in the year 1818, Adrian?"

"That's how it looks, honey," he gently replied.

She tugged at his coat. "That means the vengeance crowd will soon hang Bessie. We mustn't allow her to die! We must go find her and save her, now!"

As yet another citizen rushed past, almost colliding with the group, Adrian took charge. "Come on, everyone. First we must move out of harm's way."

Adrian ushered them away from the fire toward a nearby blacksmith's shop, where they took shelter in the doorway. Cathy grabbed his hand. "Adrian, can we go save Bessie now?"

Distractedly he glanced about them. "Love, I think we must first try to gain our bearings."

"But we know where we are, and Bessie's gonna

hang real soon! Why aren't we doing something?"

Nate spoke up earnestly. "Cathy, I'm not sure we can save Bessie. If we save her now and change history, then maybe she won't be able to come forward in time and save us from the fire in the year 1945. I don't care that much for myself, but I must protect you."

"You know, Nate has a point," commented Adrian. "That's pretty inspired logic, son—and a downright mind-boggling prospect."

"Yes, Nate does raise a disturbing possibility," Vickie agreed.

"But he's wrong!" Cathy protested. "You don't understand at all! None of you do. Even though she appeared real to us, it was always Bessie's spirit— not her body—that was with us before. But now she *is* real and she could die!"

Cathy's words dashed them all with fear.

Vickie concentrated fiercely, then snapped her fingers. "You know, I think Cathy may be right. We must have been thrust back to the year 1818 for a reason—just as we were sent to the year 1886 for a reason—and the only plausible explanation is that we are indeed meant to save Bessie's life and to help her at last fulfill her destiny of being with the man she loves, Josiah."

"Yes!" Cathy concurred, clapping her hands.

"Vickie, I'm not so sure," Adrian cautioned. "What Cathy wants may mean we will all shortly have to confront a lynch mob, which could place our lives in jeopardy."

Turning to him, Cathy pleaded, "But Bessie saved us! We have to help her now."

Adrian sighed. "I know, dear, but we must make this decision together, as the family I want us all to become." He turned to Nate. "What do you say, son?"

Nate mulled it over a moment, staring at Cathy's stricken face. "I think Cathy is right. I think we must try to save Bessie."

Cathy beamed and hugged Nate. "Oh, thank you, Nate!"

"Very well, son," Adrian agreed. "That's just what we'll do then."

Glancing back toward the burning buildings, Vickie mused that they were making their decision not a moment too soon. Both structures were now fully involved; huge flames billowed out the windows and black smoke filled the atmosphere. The townspeople had backed away with their buckets, evidently recognizing the futility of further attempts to fight the fire.

Then a fierce-looking, unshaven man jumped up on a wagon parked in the middle of the street. "Citizens, hear me now!" he yelled.

As a crowd began to form around the wagon, Vickie glanced at Adrian to see that he, too, had noticed the speaker. "Adrian, do you think—"

"That it's already beginning?" he grimly supplied. "Indeed, love, I think we had best listen."

Vickie, Adrian and the children moved toward the gathering crowd. The speaker was waving his fist and shouting. " 'Tis clear what has transpired here, citizens. These fires were clearly set by Negro traitors who wanted to vent their spleen on their white masters."

"Hear! Hear!" shouted a man in the crowd.

"Death to the insurrectionists!" yelled another.

Vickie fought a building sense of alarm as around them, the anger of the crowd escalated.

Holding up a hand to quiet the mob, the speaker then pointed to the small, lifeless forms on the walkway. "And this time six innocent babes have lost their lives due to the treachery of the black devils. Well, an eye for an eye is what I say!"

"Kill the bastards!" roared a guardsman.

"String them up on the hangman's tree!" exclaimed another.

Vickie had been listening in rising horror. "Heavens, we need to so something," she muttered to Adrian.

"I'll take care of this," he replied. "You and the children stay here."

"But, do you really think you should—"

"Just stay put."

Sick with worry, Vickie watched him work his way through the mob toward the wagon. Then he cupped a hand around his mouth and yelled, "Sir, what proof do you have of your claim?"

At once an ominous silence fell, broken only by the snapping of the fire, the breaking of timbers, and the yowling of Cathy's kitten. Several men in the crowd turned to cast Adrian angry looks. Vickie's heart burned with pride at his courage.

One of the irate citizens shouted to Adrian, "Who are you, sir, a Negro lover?"

Contemptuous laughter erupted. Bravely waiting until the mirth died down, Adrian calmly stated, "I'm simply a citizen trying to point out that we should not condemn any person without proof."

"But Negroes ain't people!" declared another. "They're no better than animals!" He pointed toward the corpses. "Just look what them vipers done, roasting innocents alive!"

Screams of bloodlust welled from the crowd. Vickie listened and tried to comfort Cathy, who kept whispering anxiously at her side.

Then the priest who had been performing extreme unction stepped forward to join Adrian. "The gentleman here is right, citizens. 'Tis wrong to seek revenge in this manner. 'Vengeance is mine, saith the Lord.' "

"Then we'll just give him a helping hand," shouted a city guardsman, raising his musket.

The throng went wild then, stamping and cheering, and the rabble-rouser on the wagon waved his hat to get everyone's attention. "Enough debate, citizens. 'Tis time to make a door-to-door search and question both masters and slaves until the perpetrators are found."

Howls of approval poured from the crowd.

"I call on every able-bodied man here to form a posse with me and help me find and apprehend the culprits."

At least a dozen men, several of them guardsmen with muskets, stormed the wagon and climbed on board. The leader jumped onto the driver's bench and snapped the reins.

Watching the vengeance wagon rumble off, Vickie felt awash with sick fear. "This is like a nightmare—and one we've already seen once, through Bessie's eyes," she murmured, watching Adrian rejoin them.

Cathy was bounding up and down, tugging at his sleeve. "Adrian, those mean men are going after Bessie! We must go find her now! Remember what she said in her story? When the fire broke out, she was in Crazy Cal's Inn, with Dastardly Dirk."

"I remember, honey. You stay here with Vickie and Nate. I'll go find her."

"No, we must all go," Cathy insisted.

"She's right, Adrian," said Vickie.

"But, Vickie, the danger—"

"We must all go," Vickie repeated.

"We're not afraid, Dad," Nate added firmly. "And didn't you just say we must do this together, as a family?"

Adrian glanced at his son with love and concern, then nodded. "Very well, son. You're right. We'll see if we can't find Bessie before the mob does."

Their decision made, the small group headed toward the harbor area. By now an overcast dawn shrouded the landscape, with occasional booms of thunder and flashes of lightning. Vickie noticed again what a different Charleston they had come to. Gone were the Victorian buildings, utility poles, and granite streets of 1886 Charleston, replaced by colonial and Georgian buildings and dirt thoroughfares. Gone were the women in bustled gowns, the men in frock coats and top hats, and in their stead Vickie saw ladies in simple calico frocks and mobcaps, gentlemen in bicorne hats, jackets, and breeches.

As they combed through the area searching for Crazy Cal's Inn, they questioned citizens they met: the housewife out emptying her slops; the scavenger driving by in his smelly oxcart; the baker setting out rolls on a stand outside his bakery.

Although the citizens seemed taken aback by the

group's strange clothing, the inhabitants answered their queries politely enough. However, they had no luck at all finding the inn until they turned onto a narrow lane not far from the harbor. As fat raindrops began to fall, Vickie spied a long line of brothels and tippling houses. And the lynch mob was already gathered there! The men were thronged about their wagon at the end of the street, yelling and waving fists.

"They might already have Bessie!" Cathy cried, pointing ahead.

The four ran down the street. At the edge of the crowd, a couple of the men moved aside to let them pass. Breaking through the circle with the others, Vickie was startled at what she saw.

Outside a shabby inn with a sign that read Crazy Cal's, she spotted Brown Bessie standing amid the mob, looking younger, more vulnerable, and much more human than Vickie remembered. Her skin was deeply flushed, her eyes darting about wildly, her damp cottonades clinging to her slender body. She was cringing in horror while a bearded giant wearing a filthy apron held her by the hair and yelled at the men.

"I tell you, gentlemen, you have come to the right establishment! This here is the wench who started the fires! She's the insurrectionist, I tell you! She just confessed her crimes to me!"

Vickie glanced at the enraged faces of the mobsters, as cries of "Kill the wench!" and "Hang her!" filled the air. Screaming out Bessie's name, Cathy tried to lunge inside the circle, but Vickie managed to restrain her. Nonetheless, the child shrieked out,

"Bessie did not start the fires! You're a liar, Crazy Cal! You let her go right now!"

Cathy's words sent a ripple of shock over the mob. Crazy Cal glared at Cathy, while Bessie regarded the child in wide-eyed awe.

The leader of the mob marched over to confront Cathy and the others. "So it's you folks again. I tell you, you had best mind your own affairs. This wench started the fires, and we're going to string her up."

"No!" Cathy screamed.

The man shook a finger at her. "We're hanging the wench, and if you troublemakers don't want to be publicly flogged and placed in the stocks, I'd suggest you let us be."

He stormed off. Several men grabbed Bessie and began dragging her toward the wagon. Crazy Cal marched away with them, shouting, "On to Hangman's Point, men!"

Adrian was lurching after the crowd when Vickie grabbed his arm. "Adrian, no!"

He touched the pistol at his waist. "Vickie, let me try to save her."

"You against two dozen men, a number of whom are armed with muskets?" she countered. "No, Adrian, you mustn't take them on alone. They'll only shoot you, and maybe the rest of us, too."

Adrian groaned, obviously torn.

Cathy tugged at Adrian's coat. "Can't we go get the sheriff or something?"

Adrian shook his head. "Honey, there is no sheriff now, and several members of the lynch mob are obviously city guardsmen. I don't know what we can do."

"I do," Nate stated quietly.

As the others turned to him, he spoke to his father. "Dad, don't you remember the rest of Bessie's story? We must find Dastardly Dirk to prove Bessie was with him when the fire started. That is her only hope."

Adrian smiled and patted the boy on the shoulder. "Son, your thinking is brilliant, and of course you're exactly right."

Cathy jumped up and down. "Yes, Dirk will help us save Bessie! Let's go find him!"

Adrian glanced at the inn to their right. "We'll start here."

The four rushed inside the establishment, which Vickie noted was filthy and reeked of liquor and garbage. A young, plump bar maid with a pock-marked face stepped forward and spoke with a pronounced Cockney accent. "May I help you folks?"

"We're looking for Dastardly Dirk," Nate informed her. "Is he here?"

The barmaid shook her head. "Nay, young master, he departed just moments ago, right before the mob come here. Truth to tell, I was hoping he might stay and kill that bastard Cal. I can't believe Cal just told them brawlers Bessie started the fire."

"I take it you're not fond of your master?" Adrian asked.

The girl spat on the floor—luckily, away from the others. "I hate the blackguard! He beats poor Bessie, as well as the rest of us. I was hoping Dirk might save us all—but no such luck. The coward slinked away after Cal threatened to turn him in."

"Yes, we know Cal's story," Nate interrupted impatiently. "Where is Dirk now?"

Though the woman appeared taken aback, she replied, "Likely at the harbor, young master, about to set sail in his sloop."

"Thank you, miss," Nate said.

Just as the group emerged from the inn, a handsome young black man, in drenched white shirt, dungarees, and straw hat, ran toward them from a stable down the street. His face a picture of anxiety, he skidded to a halt before them. "Pardon me, folks. Have you seen Bessie?"

Cathy rushed forward. "Are you Josiah?"

"Yes, young miss, I be Josiah."

Cathy turned to the others and spoke in a conspiratorial whisper. "It's Bessie's sweetheart!"

Vickie smiled indulgently. "Yes, honey, we know."

Appearing perplexed, Josiah explained, "I be cleaning the horse stalls for Master Bailey when I hear shouting in the street, and I be fearful for Bessie. I come as soon as master let me."

Cathy spoke in a rush. "We already know all about you, Josiah. We're Bessie's friends. The bad people just took her away to Hangman's Point to lynch her. We're on our way to get Dastardly Dirk to help us save her. Want to come?"

As Cathy spoke, shock and bewilderment appeared on Josiah's face. Now he could only stare at her.

Nate walked over to touch Josiah's arm. "Don't worry, Josiah, you can trust us. We just want you to come with us now."

The young man gulped. "They's gonna hang Bessie? But why, young master?"

"It's too complicated to explain now," Nate said. "We must hurry."

371

Josiah glanced fearfully back toward the stable, then stammered, "B-but master won't—"

"Young man, do not concern yourself with your master," Adrian put in sternly. "If you want to help us save Bessie, we must all leave now."

Josiah nodded, and the five literally ran the final block to the harbor, where dozens of masted ships were lined up against the rainy skies. Quickly Vickie scanned a large contingent of great square-masted merchant ships, large frigates and Baltimore clippers bobbing about in the choppy waters. But she saw no sign of a smaller vessel about to set sail.

"Look!" Nate yelled at last, pointing south.

Wiping rain from her brow, Vickie glanced down the docks, and spotted a small, single-masted sloop that evidently was about to get underway. Several mates in striped shirts and colorful turbans were stowing cargo and tack, while another sailor was untying the vessel from the wharves.

The group ran for the sloop, Nate yelling, "Dirk! Dastardly Dirk, are you there?"

As they arrived at the small ship, half a dozen sailors turned to regard them curiously. Then a tall, slender man wearing a drenched, long-sleeved white shirt, black leather pants, and jackboots jumped down to greet them. His shoulder-length hair shone raven black and dripped with rain; he sported a mustache and a twinkle in his dark brown eyes.

"Good morrow, young master," he greeted Nate, executing a courtly bow. "I cannot remember when a man has called me 'dastardly' to my face and lived to see another day. You are a brave lad indeed."

"Are you really Dirk?" Nate asked anxiously.

"Aye, Dastardly Dirk in the flesh."

Cathy drew closer to Dirk and scowled suspiciously. "You can't be a pirate. You don't have an eye patch."

Laughing, Dirk touched the weapon at his waist. "Ah, but I have a cutlass, young miss."

Cathy went wide-eyed at the sight of it.

Tensely Nate implored, "Dirk, you must help us."

Dirk gestured toward his sloop. "I apologize, young gentleman, but as you can see I'm about to set sail—"

"And Bessie is about to be hanged!" Cathy burst out.

The pirate's dark brows shot up. "Bessie? Do you mean the young woman who is Crazy Cal's slave, the one I just left?"

"Yes!" Nate exclaimed. "That very one. Right after you left, Cal turned her over to a vengeance mob. He lied and said she started the fire at the orphanage."

"There was a fire at the orphanage?"

"Yes, sir," answered Adrian, stepping toward Dirk. "Indeed, a fire is still blazing at St. Christopher's Orphanage and chapel. We were just there. Six orphans perished, and now a mob is seeking retribution, and preparing to lynch Bessie, thanks to Cal."

Thunderstruck, Dirk regarded the newcomers. "*Sacre bleu!* The blackguard! That Cal is a liar, for Bessie could not possibly have started the fire. She was with me all last night. We had a long talk, and she told me all about Crazy Cal's numerous cruelties toward her and the other women working at the inn. Afterward, I tried to intercede with Bessie's master—without success, I'm afraid."

"We already know all about that," Cathy interrupted. "Now you must help us."

"How?"

"By furnishing Bessie with an alibi," Adrian said.

"A what?"

"Will you help us by telling the lynch mob what you just told us?" Adrian explained. "Will you come with us to Hangman's Point to save Bessie?"

Dirk hesitated.

"Please, man, there isn't much time," Adrian implored. "We need you to tell the crowd that Bessie was with you when the fire broke out."

Frowning, Dirk remained silent.

"Please, will you help us free Bessie?" Cathy pleaded.

Dirk considered this for a long moment, then shook his head. "I'm sorry, young lady. I would like to help you, but Cal threatened to turn me in for piracy, and that is why I am taking my leave from Charleston so hastily. I don't want Bessie to hang—but neither do I want to dangle from the tree myself."

"So you'll let Bessie die?" Cathy wailed.

Dirk grimaced.

Josiah edged closer and shyly spoke. "Please, master, will you help save my Bessie?"

"Who are you?" Dirk asked.

"I be Josiah."

"Ah, yes—Bessie's young man. She told me about you."

Cathy tugged on Dirk's sleeve. "Please, there's no more time."

Dirk scratched his jaw. "You say they took your friend Bessie to Hangman's Point?"

374

Cathy nodded vigorously.

"That is on the water near White Point," Dirk mused aloud. He turned toward his boat. "If we all sail down there in my sloop, then my men and I can take our leave quickly if need be."

"Then you'll help us?" Cathy asked raptly.

Abruptly Dirk grinned and tugged on one of Cathy's blond curls. "Ah, what can I say? I cannot resist a damsel in distress. I shall try my best, young lady."

"Yippee!" Cathy yelled.

Dirk gestured to the others. "Come along, everyone. Time to set sail."

The five quickly boarded, and Dirk's men cast off. While Adrian lingered at the wheel with Dirk, and the mates worked the halyards and raised the main and top sails, Vickie stood with the children and Josiah at the bow, all of them gazing ahead as the vessel bobbed through the rough waters of the Cooper River, sailing south.

"Vickie, do you think we'll get there in time?" Cathy fretted.

"Darling, we'll try our best." She gazed back at Adrian to see that he was now engaged in what appeared to be an intense conversation with Dirk.

Then the vessel tacked starboard, and Vickie watched them round the point. She winced; on the embankment above them, she could see the crowd with their torches, gathered about the wagon.

"There they are!" yelled Cathy, pointing.

"I know, honey."

Adrian returned to Vickie's side, flashing her a brave smile. "We're almost there, love. And not a minute too soon, I see."

375

"Indeed. What were you and Dirk talking about?"

He only winked. "Oh, strategies."

Vickie would have questioned him more, but Dirk and his men were already anchoring the craft. A mate lowered the gangplank. Adrian, Dirk, and Josiah helped Vickie and the children disembark and climb the slippery embankment toward the Point.

A scene of horror awaited them. At the center of a grove of oaks, the vengeance crowd was gathered about the parked wagon. A drenched and shivering Bessie stood on the wagon bed with a noose around her neck, the rope attached to a tree limb overhead; next to her stood the instigator. Vickie's heart went out to Bessie, though she noted that the girl's expression was stoic—until she glimpsed Josiah approaching. At once her face was filled with love, desperation—and fear for him.

As soon as he spotted her, Josiah surged forward. "Bessie!"

But Adrian grabbed his arm. "Stand back, young man, or they'll hang you both."

"Please, master," Josiah pleaded.

"I mean it."

Though his expression seethed with frustration, Josiah nodded and stepped back.

Dirk burst through the crowd, with Adrian following. "Wait, gentlemen, I beseech you!" Dirk yelled. "Do not lynch this woman! I know she is innocent."

Grumbling, the men warily eyed Dirk. "State your business, citizen," one of them ordered.

Dirk strode over to the wagon, and pointed at Bessie. "This woman is innocent. Brown Bessie was with

376

me, at Crazy Cal's Inn, when the fire broke out. I swear it on my mother's grave."

The men exchanged looks of uncertainty. "Then why did Cal testify that she started the fire at the orphanage?" another called out.

Dirk gazed at Cal with loathing. "Because he's a vicious, cruel liar who beat this girl—and also attacked me."

"That's a damn lie!" bellowed Cal, lunging forward to confront Dirk.

"It's the God's truth!" Dirk roared back.

As Cal and Dirk faced each other in fury, Vickie heard skeptical comments from the crowd. "Is what the man says true, Cal?" one called. "Are you steering us false just to vent your spleen on an innocent wench?"

Cal turned on the man. "No, I did not steer you false about the wench! She's an insurrectionist, I tell you! She started the fire." Cal swung back to Dirk. "And you're a pirate and a fraud."

Dirk faced him down. "I'm telling the truth and you damn well know it! This wench has done no wrong. She was with me."

By now several members of the mob were backing away, muttering to one another in obvious misgiving. Then all grew hushed as Nate stepped forward with three of Bessie's marbles in his hand, and addressed Cal, a slender boy bravely facing an enraged giant. "Please, Cal, my father and I wish to buy this slave from you. We offer you these—three uncut diamonds from Africa. They're worth a small fortune."

Cal stared insolently at the boy, like a confident Goliath sizing up David. He waved a huge hand in dismissal. "Be gone, lad, and quit interfering in the business of men. Why, you're as big a swindler as Dirk!"

Adrian was about to step forward to help his son when Vickie caught his arm. "No, give Nate a chance first."

With a groan, Adrian backed away.

Nate continued to stand his ground before Cal. "Please, sir, I swear, these are priceless stones which will make you a wealthy man. Please accept them in payment for this slave. I vow to you, if I have lied and the diamonds aren't real, my father and I will return the woman to you."

Cal glanced around, absorbing the now hostile looks of many of the men. At last he snapped up the rocks and snarled, "Ah, take the worthless chit. It's glad I am to be rid of the uppity baggage."

Cal stormed away with his stones. The remaining members of the mob mumbled among themselves, then retreated. Josiah hopped up onto the wagon, removed the noose from around Bessie's neck and threw his arms around her. For a poignant moment, the two clung together. That was when Vickie noticed that the rain had stopped, and a beautiful pink dawn was breaking through the trees, painting the verdant, lush landscape around them.

Josiah helped Bessie down to the ground. The two held hands and shyly faced the others.

"Thank you, folks," Josiah said humbly. "Thank you for my Bessie."

"You're most welcome, young man," Adrian replied.

Cathy ran to Bessie's side and hugged her. "Bessie,

darling, it's me, Cathy! Are you all right?"

Bessie stared at Cathy in puzzlement. "I be all right, young miss."

Cathy's eyes went wide and she moved back a step. "Don't you know us, Bessie?"

Bessie seemed baffled as she glanced about the small group gathered around her and Josiah. "I not sure, young miss."

Adrian took a step toward Bessie. "We're so glad we were able to save you—that is, thanks to Dirk and . . ." He gazed about in puzzlement. "Where is Dirk?"

Vickie noticed Dirk's sloop shoving off. "Look, he's already sailing away!"

Adrian stared at the departing sloop. "Well, I'll be deuced. The rascal didn't stick around long enough for us to express our gratitude." He turned back to Nate. "Anyway, son, I was about to say that we were able to save Bessie thanks to Dirk and you. Nate, what you did just now was very brave—but you shouldn't have lied to Cal about those stones."

Nate only grinned as he held up the sack with Bessie's marbles. "Dad, I didn't lie. You see, Mr. Graves, the jeweler who trained me back in 1945, used to let me watch him cut and polish rough diamonds from Africa. That's exactly what Bessie's marbles are. I recognized them as soon as I studied them closely at Grandmother's house last night." He extended the bag with the rest of the marbles to Bessie. "And they belong to you."

Bessie merely stared at the bag. "Where you get my marbles, young master?"

"Why, you gave them to me, silly!" declared Cathy.

But Bessie shook her head. "I never give them to you, young miss. Bessie find her marbles on the banks of the River Limpopo in Africa, when I still be a baby. I bring them with me to America. Then one time, when Cal beat me, I throw my sack of marbles at him, and he take them away and throw 'em down a well. I ain't seen 'em since."

Cathy appeared flabbergasted. "You mean you really don't remember giving me your marbles, Bessie?"

"No, young miss."

Cathy frowned for a moment, then broke into a grin. "Now I understand. That is in the future. I guess you wouldn't remember that now, or remember us, would you?"

Bessie only shook her head.

"You know us but you don't *really* know us," Cathy explained.

Bessie was bemused. "I know someone come for Bessie one day. I see it in a dream."

"Really?" Cathy asked in awe. "Then you *do* know us—sort of." She took the sack from Nate's hand and extended it toward Bessie. "Do you want your marbles now?"

Bessie shyly smiled. "No, you keep them, young miss. You keep them as thanks for saving Bessie."

Cathy hugged her friend again. "Oh, Bessie, isn't it wonderful? We're all here now, and we're going to take care of you. And don't worry if you're confused. We'll teach you all about your legend."

Bessie frowned. "If you say so, young miss."

"We'll teach you *everything*," Cathy went on. "And the best part is, now you can be with your Josiah."

At this, Bessie beamed at her sweetheart, and he grinned back. "Yes, we all be happy now."

"Is this where we're meant to be—here with you and Josiah?" the child questioned.

Bessie hesitated a moment, then nodded. "Yes, young miss. Maybe this where you belong, with Bessie and Josiah."

As Bessie and Cathy continued to chatter, Vickie glanced at Adrian. "Well, my darling, what do you think?"

Placing his arm around her, Adrian gazed about them at the incredible golden dawn, at green trees dripping with golden sparkles of rain, at birds sweetly singing, at a ripe, beautiful land filled with promise. Leaning over, he kissed her cheek. "You know, I think Bessie may be right. This may be our time, love. It's uncomplicated, and far removed from the world we knew. I think I could be a planter here."

Clutching his hand, Vickie replied, "And I think I could be a planter's wife."

The two were tenderly kissing when Cathy cried, "Hey, are you two going to get married now?"

Laughing, Adrian and Vickie pulled apart. "That's how it appears, honey," he replied.

"Yippee!" she shouted. Beaming, she stepped toward them and placed the bag of uncut diamonds in Adrian's hands. "I want you and Vickie to have these as Bessie's and my wedding present—and to pay for Josiah's freedom."

"But Cathy, these are yours," protested Adrian.

Cathy raised her chin. "You don't understand," she

said imperiously. "I'm still a child, and I already have a kitten to care for, as well as Nate, who can be really contrary at times."

"Now, Cathy, wait a minute," scolded Nate.

Cathy pressed the sack into Adrian's hands. "I can't be responsible for these, too."

"Very well, sweetheart." Looking about them, he sighed. "What a glorious morning—the dawn of our lives together. Now let's all go find a home."

A true family at last, the six left Hangman's Point and turned toward Charleston proper, toward their bright and happy future together.

Epilogue

1827

Excitement thrummed in the air that April morning at the Bennett family plantation north of Charleston, where a garden wedding was about to be performed. Nate Bennett, a handsome young man of twenty-one dressed in formal black, rushed up the stairs of the beautiful Georgian mansion, raced down the second-floor hallway, and banged on the door of his fiancée's room.

"Cathy, you come out right this minute," he demanded. "Everyone is ready for you outside by the river. I've waited nine long years to marry you, and I'm not going to wait one minute longer!"

Laughing, Cathy called out, "Nate, hold onto your

horses. Vickie and I will be down in a moment. She just needs to finish my coiffure."

"Cathy, please—"

"Nate, you heard me. Go away! It's bad luck for you to be talking to the bride on her wedding day, anyway."

Nate stood burning with frustration. This was the happiest day of his life, and he couldn't wait to proceed. Just as he'd shouted to Cathy, this moment was the culmination of nine long years of waiting, and he was most impatient to claim the woman he loved.

Not that those years hadn't been wonderful for him. So much had happened to them all since they'd taken their last journey through time and saved dear Bessie, but Nate felt particularly blessed. Here in early nineteenth-century Charleston, he'd found a caring stepmother in Vickie, and he and his dad had completely mended their fences. Nate knew now that his dad had never intended to reject him after his mother's death. The years had brought new understanding, forgiveness, and trust to both men. Now they were as close as any father and son could be.

Over those same years, Nate's friendship with Cathy had deepened as they lived first on the family's farm, then on this plantation. When Cathy had turned sixteen, Nate had begun formally courting her, and their friendship had blossomed fully into love. Now at last Cathy would become Nate's cherished bride.

If she *ever* came out of her room!

At the sound of approaching footsteps, Nate turned to watch his father stride up to join him in the corridor. He felt calmer in his dad's reassuring presence.

A handsome man dressed in a black cutaway that

matched his son's, Adrian Bennett fondly laid a hand on Nate's shoulder. "She still isn't ready, eh, son?"

"No, and she's giving me fits."

Adrian chuckled. "Come back downstairs, Nate. Women are always skittish on their wedding day."

"I just can't wait until she is truly mine, Dad."

"She will be, quite shortly," Adrian assured his son. "You must simply show her a lot of patience."

Nate broke into a grin. "Very well, Dad. You and Vickie have certainly been plenty patient with me."

Laughing and talking, father and son strode off toward the stairs together.

Back inside the bedroom, Cathy sat on a stool before the pier mirror. Now a beautiful young woman of eighteen, she wore a pearl-trimmed white satin wedding gown. Vickie, ensconced in a gown of lavender silk, stood behind her sister, putting the finishing touches on Cathy's coiffure, arranging blond ringlets about her lovely round face. Pinning on Cathy's veil, she gazed at her younger sister in the mirror and wiped away tears. "Oh, Cathy, you look so beautiful."

Cathy stood and moved around the stool, embracing her older sister. "Thank you, Vickie. You look wonderful, too, and you've been such a help with the wedding, why, with everything."

"My pleasure, darling. It means so much to me and Adrian to see you and Nate marry." She brightened. "Well, shall we go on down to the bower before your bridegroom truly pops his cork?"

Cathy laughed. "Yes, let's do."

Vickie handed her younger sister a nosegay of violets, and the two women left the room together. Presently they emerged on the front porch of the pillared mansion, went down the steps, and strolled toward the bower just beyond the house.

The setting for the ceremony could not have been more romantic, Vickie mused. Created by a vast dome of oak branches, the river bower was flanked by rows of blooming roses and azaleas. Beneath the arc of greenery, many of the Bennett family's friends sat in several rows of chairs. At the edge of the arbor near the river, an archway festooned with white roses stretched over the heads of Nate and the Episcopalian priest from Charleston.

Nate's handsome face lit up with joy at the sight of his bride approaching, and he reminded Vickie poignantly of Adrian. Beyond the two men at bankside, a string quartet played "Greensleeves."

At the woman's approach, Adrian got up from his chair and strode over. Regarding both fondly, he reached out to squeeze their hands. Emotion shook his voice as he murmured, "Ladies, I can't decide which of you looks more beautiful."

Vickie laughed. "Why, Cathy does, of course."

"No, you do, Vickie!" Cathy insisted.

"We'll not argue on such a joyous day." Vickie turned to hug her sister. "Good luck, darling."

"Thanks, Vickie."

The two women moved apart, and Adrian took Vickie's arm. "Cathy, dear, I'll just show your sister to her seat, then I'll be back to escort you down the aisle."

"I'll be waiting," Cathy replied gaily.

Moving down the aisle on her husband's arm, Vickie glanced at him, noting the streaks of gray around his temples, the lines around his mouth, and mused that time had only enhanced his handsomeness. She loved him more than ever.

Seeming to note her perusal, he winked tenderly. "Happy, darling?"

"I think this is the happiest day of my entire life," she whispered back.

"And mine," he reverently agreed.

Adrian helped Vickie into her chair in the front row just as the string quartet began playing the "Ave Maria." As he left to rejoin Cathy, Vickie heard a young voice whisper, "Is Cathy ready, Mama?"

Vickie turned to smile at her son, eight-year-old David, who was seated beside her in his dark jacket, short pants, and round hat. Like Nate, the boy was the spitting image of his handsome father. Next to him sat their other two children: five-year-old Amy, a young beauty with the hair and eyes of her mother; and two-year-old Jeremy, a dark-haired cherub who also resembled his dad. Beyond Jeremy sat the family's best friends, Bessie and Josiah, who had come from their neighboring farm with their own four children. Bessie had bloomed into a beautiful young matron, dressed today in a dark blue silk dress, with her ebony hair bound up in braids beneath a stylish ribboned bonnet. Josiah was a handsome man of thirty, wearing a brown striped suit and a bowler hat. Their children, three boys and a girl, ranged in age from three to seven and were all attired in their best "go to meeting" clothes.

Vickie turned back to her son. "Yes, darling, Cathy is ready. Look, Daddy is bringing her up the aisle even now."

All watched as a radiant Cathy glided up the aisle on Adrian's arm. Then the guests began to chuckle as Cathy's huge calico tomcat trailed down the aisle behind her, meowing plaintively. Vickie nodded to David, who dashed out and grabbed Rufus as Vickie and Adrian passed, prompting more laughter from the guests.

Adrian smiled at Vickie before moving on with Cathy. She smiled back, thinking poignantly of all the love they'd known over the past nine years. Of course they'd also been required to work hard, but they hadn't minded that.

They'd gotten their start when they had bought a small cotton farm, which they'd worked side by side with Bessie and Josiah. Later they had given that farm to the Negro couple and had bought this larger plantation, hiring on free blacks to work it. Those years had been filled with love and joy, and Vickie felt especially proud of how close Nate and Adrian had grown as father and son.

It had been a good life for them all, although they'd faced a few stumbling blocks. They'd raised more than a few eyebrows in Charleston proper by not only manumitting Josiah and Bessie, but by regarding them as cherished family. But they'd also chosen their circle of friends carefully, from among those in the Charleston community who, like them, were opposed to the institution of slavery.

Of course they had not been able to tell any of their new friends or acquaintances about their remarkable adventures in time, or about the legend of Brown Bessie, Guardian Spirit of Charleston, who had figured so prominently in all of their journeys. Those subjects were reserved for late-night family gatherings around the supper table, when all of them—including Bessie, Josiah, and their children—were present. During such sessions, Bessie had learned all about her legend, and Adrian had taken out his Victoria Cross and educated their children about the coming "great war" in the future, and how its aftermath had brought him and Vickie together.

Thus the tradition begun by dear Sophie remained dear to the hearts of the entire extended family. There at the dining table they would all relive those amazing stories, and share many new ones.

Vickie now listened as the Episcopalian priest began intoning the marriage mass. Her heart felt full as she listened to Nate and Cathy exchanging their vows. Soon Adrian returned to her side, sat down and clutched her hand; she knew he had bought Cathy and Nate a house in town as a wedding present. For Nate had already established his reputation in Charleston as a fine silversmith.

A sigh rose from the crowd as the ceremony was concluded and Nate tenderly kissed his bride. When the couple turned to the crowd, the priest announced, "Ladies and gentlemen, I present to you Mr. and Mrs. Nate Bennett."

The guests erupted in applause and cheers.

Both bride and groom were beaming, Vickie noted. With Cathy on his arm, Nate stepped forward and humbly spoke. "Friends and neighbors, my bride and I would like to thank you, from the bottom of our hearts, for being here today to share our joy. I'd especially like to thank our family—and there, I include Bessie, Josiah, and their children. And Vickie." Clearing his throat, he turned to her. "Mother, would you come forward, please?"

As always, Vickie was touched to hear Nate call her "mother." Wondering what he intended, she glanced at Adrian in bemusement, but he only nodded and nudged her to her feet. She went to stand before Nate, who leaned over and kissed her cheek.

As Cathy smiled at her sister, Nate held Vickie's hand and spoke with heartfelt emotion. "Vickie, you are the one who has kept this family together over the years through your love, strength, and support. You have made my father—and all of us—so very happy." Nate dug in his jacket pocket, then pulled out a glittering chain and handed it to her. "Thank you for being such a wonderful mother to us all."

With a gasp, Vickie gazed down at an intricate silver necklace of interlocking leaves and roses, with a small diamond at the center of each bloom. Tears burned her eyes, and poignant emotion clutched at her heart. "My God, Nate, you made this?"

He nodded.

She hugged him tightly. "Nate, it's magnificent beyond words, but I can't believe what I'm seeing! This is the necklace—the one I lost in Tunisia!"

Now Nate seemed baffled. "I—I don't understand, Mother."

But Vickie did. She was electrified and deeply moved to find herself holding in her hand the very antique necklace that she had lost back in the present—Great-great-grandmother Davis's heirloom! It was almost as if Sophie's gentle spirit were joining them at the celebration today and bringing her own timeless gift.

With tears in her voice, Vickie patted Nate's hand. "Never mind now, darling. I adore the necklace, and I'll explain more about its significance some evening soon when we're all gathered around the supper table." She embraced both bride and groom. "Thank you both so much."

Cathy beamed. "May I put it on you?"

"Oh, yes."

Vickie turned, and Cathy slid the necklace around her neck and fastened it. Again she trembled with emotion, realizing that they had come full circle.

As the guests came forward to congratulate the couple, Adrian joined Vickie, and she threw herself into his arms. "Oh, Adrian, I'm so happy!"

Pulling back, he gazed at the necklace. "Darling, the necklace is beautiful. I had no idea Nate was making it for you."

"Nor did I." Vickie glanced toward the front row. "Bessie, Josiah, won't you and the children come up and join us?"

Bessie and Josiah gathered their children and all moved forward to join the others.

Vickie wrapped an arm around Bessie's waist. "Bessie, dear, remember when you said that one day we would be shown a sign that we had found our rightful place?"

Bessie frowned. "Yes, Miss Vickie, I remember how you and Miss Cathy tell me 'bout it."

Vickie touched the necklace. "Well, this is the sign. It's the necklace passed down to me by Great-great-grandmother Davis, the one I lost in Tunisia."

"Great Scot," cried Adrian. "You mean this is actually the necklace you lost in the 1940s?"

"It is indeed," she declared ecstatically.

"Then the necklace started out here?"

Vickie gazed at him through happy tears. "Yes, it did. It's the sign. We *are* meant to be here, Adrian!"

Adrian pulled her close. "Oh, my darling, I think you are right. This is so wonderful. And I've a surprise of my own to present."

"By all means," Vickie encouraged.

Adrian went over to the bride and groom. "Congratulations, you two," he said, kissing Cathy's cheek and hugging Nate. "Son, the necklace you made for Vickie is fabulous. Now I have something for the bride." He pulled a small bag from his breast pocket and handed it to Cathy. "I think it's about time to return these to you, young lady."

Gazing at the sack, Cathy cried out in joy. "Bessie's marbles! Bessie, look, it's your marbles!"

Staring at the small burlap sack, Bessie nodded. "I see, Miss Cathy."

"I can't believe you still have them!" Cathy said to Adrian. She turned to Bessie. "Would you like them back now?"

Bessie broke into a rare grin. "Miss Cathy, you know they be yours now."

"Are you sure?"

"Yes, Miss Cathy."

Cathy faced Adrian with a puzzled frown. "But didn't you sell these to buy Josiah's freedom and our family's first farm?"

Adrian shook his head. "Remember when Dastardly Dirk sailed us all down to Hangman's Point? Well, Dirk stuffed my pockets with Spanish doubloons so I could buy Bessie's freedom. But Nate rescued Bessie before I could offer them, then Dirk and his crew sailed off before I could return the gold to him. We bought Josiah's freedom, as well as our first farm, with Dirk's gold, and we've been saving Bessie's marbles for you all this time."

"Oh, thank you, Adrian!" Cathy turned to clutch Bessie's hand. "Oh, Bessie, we have your marbles, and Vickie has her necklace." She smiled lovingly at her bridegroom. "Best of all, we have each other, and all of us are together. Our lives are complete now."

"Amen," agreed Adrian, pulling Vickie close.

As Nate leaned over to kiss his bride, the extended family continued to celebrate, their hearts warmed by the knowledge that the brightest diamond they'd been given was the legacy of their shared joy and love.

AUTHOR'S NOTE

Although every attempt has been made to accurately depict historical Charleston in the writing of this novel, a few minor liberties have been taken with the setting for dramatic purposes. It should be noted that the major earthquake depicted in this story did actually hit Charleston on August 31, 1886.

Dear Reader:

Ever since I wrote my first time-travel romance, *A Tryst in Time,* for Leisure Books in 1992, readers have been begging me to write another story with those same emotional, mystical and unique qualities. I do hope you'll agree that *Embers of Time* is that story. It's a time-travel romance that's very close to my heart, and I welcome your questions and comments regarding it.

If you enjoyed the post-World War II setting in *Embers of Time*, I do hope you'll read *Strangers in the Night* (Leisure Books, September 2000), a collection of nostalgic love stories set in the glamorous 1940s. *Strangers in the Night* features my novella, "Night and Day," a romantic tale about a beautiful heroine who gets in trouble with gangsters during Galveston's "Open Era"—and the dashing hero who comes home from the war to rescue her.

I also have several other titles still available from Dorchester under the Love Spell imprint: *Lovers and Other Lunatics,* a zany and adventurous contemporary romance set in Galveston; *Bushwhacked Bride*, a fun, sexy time-travel romance set in the Old West; and *New Year's Babies*, an anthology that includes my Victorian time-travel novella, "The Confused Stork."

Hope you'll order these titles from Leisure Books or your local bookseller. And please watch for my future releases from Leisure Books and Love Spell, including *A Tryst in Time*, to be reissued by Love Spell in January 2001.

Thanks, as always, for all your support and encouragement. I welcome your feedback on all my projects. You can reach me via e-mail at eugenia@eugeniariley.com, visit my website at http://www.eugeniariley.com, or you can write to me at the address listed below (SASE appreciated for a reply; free bookmark and newsletter available):

Eugenia Riley
P.O. Box 840526
Houston, TX 77284-0526

Bushwhacked Bride

Eugenia Riley

"JUMPING JEHOSHAPHAT! YOU'VE SHANGHAIED THE NEW SCHOOLMARM!"

Ma Reklaw bellows at her sons and wields her broom with a fierceness that has all five outlaw brothers running for cover; it doesn't take a Ph.D. to realize that in the Reklaw household, Ma is the law. Professor Jessica Garret watches dumbstruck as the members of the feared Reklaw Gang turn tail—one up a tree, another under the hay wagon, and one in a barrel. Having been unceremoniously kidnapped by the rowdy brothers, the green-eyed beauty takes great pleasure in their discomfort until Ma Reklaw finds a new way to sweep clean her sons' disreputable behavior—by offering Jessica's hand in marriage to the best behaved. Jessie has heard of shotgun weddings, but a broomstick betrothal is ridiculous! As the dashing but dangerous desperadoes start the wooing there is no telling what will happen with one bride for five brothers.

___52320-5 $5.99 US/$6.99 CAN

Get Ready for . . . The Time of Your Life!

Teresa Phelps has heard of being crazy in love. But Charles Everett seems just plain mad. Her handsome kidnapper unnerves her with his charm and flabbergasts her with his accusations. He acts under the misguided belief that she holds the key to finding buried treasure. But all Tess feels she can unearth is one oddball after another.

While Charles' actions resemble those of a lunatic, his body arouses thoughts of a lover. And while Charles helps to fend off her dastardly and dangerous pursuers, Tess wonders if he has her best interests at heart—or is she just a pawn in his quest for riches? As the madcap misadventures ensue, Tess strives to dig up the truth. Who is the enigmatic Englishman? What is he after? And most important, in the hunt for hidden riches is the ultimate prize true love?

___52371-X $5.99 US/$6.99 CAN

Dorchester Publishing Co., Inc.
P.O. Box 6640
Wayne, PA 19087-8640

Please add $1.75 for shipping and handling for the first book and $.50 for each book thereafter. NY, NYC, and PA residents, please add appropriate sales tax. No cash, stamps, or C.O.D.s All orders shipped within 6 weeks via postal service book rate. Canadian orders require $2.00 extra postage and must be paid in U.S. dollars through a U.S. banking facility.

Name_____
Address_____
City_____State_____Zip_____
I have enclosed $_____ in payment for the checked book(s).
Payment <u>must</u> accompany all orders. ❏ Please send a free catalog.

ENCHANTED TIME
Amy Elizabeth Saunders

With an antique store to run, Ivy Raymond has an eye for members of the opposite sex, as long as they are named Shakespeare, Rembrandt, or Louis XVI. But she is too busy to look at men from her own century. Then a kooky old lady sells her a book of spells, and before Ivy can say abracadabra, she is living in a crumbling castle with a far-from-decayed knight. Stripped of his land, wealth, and title, Julian Ramsden is still arrogant enough to lord it over Ivy. But the saucy wench has powers over him that he cannot deny. Whether the flame haired stranger is a thief, a spy, or a witch, Julian is ready to steal a love that is unquestionably magic.

___52313-2 $5.50 US/$6.50 CAN